PRAISE FOR NERO WOLFE

"It is always a treat to read a Nero Wolfe mystery. The man has entered our folklore. . . . Like Sherlock Holmes . . . he looms larger than life and, in some ways, is much more satisfactory."
—*New York Times Book Review*

"Nero Wolfe towers over his rivals . . . he is an exceptional character creation." —*New Yorker*

"The most interesting great detective of them all."
—Kingsley Amis, author of *Lucky Jim*

"Nero Wolfe is one of the master creations." —James M. Cain, author of *The Postman Always Rings Twice*

AND FOR REX STOUT

"Rex Stout is one of the half-dozen major figures in the development of the American detective novel." —Ross Macdonald

"I've found Rex Stout's books about Nero Wolfe endlessly readable. . . . I sometimes have to remind myself that Wolfe and Goodwin are the creations of a writer's mind, that no matter how many doorbells I ring in the West Thirties, I'll never find the right house." —Lawrence Block

"Fair warning: It is safe to read one Nero Wolfe novel, because you will surely like it. It is extremely unsafe to read three, because you will forever be hooked on the delightful characters who populate these perfect books." —Otto Penzler

AND FOR ARCHIE GOODWIN

"Archie is a splendid character." —Dame Agatha Christie

"Stout's supreme triumph was the creation of Archie Goodwin."
—P. G. Wodehouse

"If he had done nothing more than to create Archie Goodwin, Rex Stout would deserve the gratitude of whatever assessors watch over the prosperity of American literature. . . . Archie is the lineal descendant of Huck Finn." —Jacques Barzun

PRAISE FOR *THE RUBBER BAND* AND *THE RED BOX*

"[*The Rubber Band*] is among the best Wolfe–Archie Goodwin tales; the whole gang makes an appearance—Inspector Cramer, Saul Panzer, etc.—and the writing crackles." —*Washington Post*

"[*The Red Box*] has practically everything the seasoned addict demands in the way of characters and action; you may guess the motive, but the mechanism is properly obscure." —*New Yorker*

The Rex Stout Library

The Rubber Band

• • • • 1 • • • •

I THREW down the magazine section of the Sunday *Times*
and yawned. I looked at Nero Wolfe and yawned again. "Is
this bird, S. J. Woolf, any relation of yours?"

Wolfe, letting fly with a dart and getting a king of clubs,
paid no attention to me. I went on:

"I suppose not, since he spells it different. The reason I
ask, an idea just raced madly into my bean. Why wouldn't
it be good for business if this S. J. Woolf did a picture of you
and an article for the *Times?* God knows you're full of material." I took time out to grin, considering Wolfe's size in the
gross or physical aspect, and left the grin on as Wolfe grunted,
stooping to pick up a dart he had dropped.

I resumed. "You couldn't beat it for publicity, and as for
class it's Mount Everest. This guy Woolf only hits the high
spots. I've been reading his pieces for years, and there's been
Einstein and the Prince of Wales and Babe Ruth and three
Presidents of the United States (O say, can you see very
little in the White House) and the King of Siam and similar
grandeur. His idea seems to be, champions only. That seems
to let you in, and strange as it may appear, I'm not kidding,
I really mean it. Among our extended circle there must be a
couple of eminent gazabos that know him and would slip
him the notion."

Wolfe still paid no attention to me. As a matter of fact,
I didn't expect him to, since he was busy taking exercise.
He had recently got the impression that he weighed too
much—which was about the same as if the Atlantic Ocean
formed the opinion that it was too wet—and so had added
a new item to his daily routine. Since he only went outdoors
for things like earthquakes and holocausts, he was rarely
guilty of movement except when he was up on the roof with

Horstmann and the orchids, from nine to eleven in the morning and four to six in the afternoon, and there was no provision there for pole vaulting. Hence the new apparatus for a daily workout, which was a beaut. It was scheduled from 3:45 to 4:00 P. M. There was a board about two feet square, faced with cork, with a large circle marked on it, and 26 radii and a smaller inner circle, outlined with fine wire, divided the circle's area into 52 sections. Each section had its symbol painted on it, and together they made up a deck of cards; the bull's-eye, a small disk in the corner, was the Joker. There was also a supply of darts, cute little things about four inches long and weighing a couple of ounces, made of wood and feathers with a metal needle-point. The idea was to hang the board up on the wall, stand off 10 or 15 feet, hurl five darts at it and make a poker hand, with the Joker wild. Then you went and pulled the darts out, and hurled them over again. Then you went and pulled . . .

Obviously, it was pretty darned exciting. What I mean to convey is, it would have been a swell game for a little girls' kindergarten class; no self-respecting boy over six months of age would have wasted much time with it. Since my only excuse for writing this is to relate the facts of one of Nero Wolfe's cases, and since I take that trouble only where murder was involved, it may be supposed that I tell about that poker-dart game because later on one of the darts was dipped in poison and used to pink a guy with. Nothing doing. No one ever suffered any injury from those darts that I know of, except me. Over a period of two months Nero Wolfe nicked me for a little worse than eighty-five bucks, playing draw with the Joker and deuces wild, at two bits a go. There was no chance of getting any real accuracy with it, it was mostly luck.

Anyhow, when Wolfe decided he weighed too much, that was what he got. He called the darts javelins. When I found my losses were approaching the century point I decided to stop humoring him, and quit the thing cold, telling him that my doctor had warned me against athlete's heart. Wolfe kept on with his exercise, and by now, this Sunday I'm telling about, he had got so he could stick the Joker twice out of five shots.

I said, "It would be a good number. You rate it. You admit yourself that you're a genius. It would get us a lot of new clients. We could take on a permanent staff—"

One of the darts slipped out of Wolfe's handful, dropped to the floor, and rolled to my feet. Wolfe stood and looked at me. I knew what he wanted, I knew he hated to stoop, but stooping was the only really violent part of that game and I figured he needed the exercise. I sat tight. Wolfe opened his eyes at me:

"I have noticed Mr. Woolf's drawings. They are technically excellent."

The son of a gun was trying to bribe me to pick up his dart by pretending to be interested in what I had said. I thought to myself, all right, but you'll pay for it, let's just see how long you'll stand there and stay interested. I picked up the magazine section and opened it to the article, and observed briskly:

"This is one of his best. Have you seen it? It's about some Englishman that's over here on a government mission—wait—it tells here—"

I found it and read aloud: *"It is not known whether the Marquis of Clivers is empowered to discuss military and naval arrangements in the Far East; all that has been disclosed is his intention to make a final disposition of the question of spheres of economic influence. That is why, after a week of conferences in Washington with the Departments of State and Commerce, he has come to New York for an indefinite stay to consult with financial and industrial leaders. More and more clearly it is being realized in government circles that the only satisfactory and permanent basis for peace in the Orient is the removal of the present causes of economic friction."*

I nodded at Wolfe. "You get it? Spheres of economic influence. The same thing that bothered Al Capone and Dutch Schultz. Look where economic friction landed them."

Wolfe nodded back. "Thank you, Archie. Thank you very much for explaining it to me. Now if you—"

I hurried in: "Wait, it gets lots more interesting than that." I glanced down the page. "In the picture he looks like a ruler of men—you know, like a master barber or a head waiter, you know the type. It goes on to tell how much he knows about spheres and influences, and his record in the war—he commanded a brigade and he got decorated four times—a noble lord and all prettied up with decorations like a store front—I say three cheers and let us drink to the King, gentlemen! You understand, sir, I'm just summarizing."

"Yes, Archie. Thank you."

Wolfe sounded grim. I took a breath. "Don't mention it. But the really interesting part is where it tells about his character and his private life. He's a great gardener. He prunes

7

his own roses! At least it says so, but it's almost too much to swallow. Then it goes on, new paragraph: *While it would be an exaggeration to call the marquis an eccentric, in many ways he fails to conform to the conventional conception of a British peer, probably due in some measure to the fact that in his younger days—he is now 64—he spent many years, in various activities, in Australia, South America, and the western part of the United States. He is a nephew of the ninth marquis, and succeeded to the title in 1905, when his uncle and two cousins perished in the sinking of the* Rotania *off the African coast. But under any circumstances he would be an extraordinary person, and his idiosyncrasies, as he is pleased to call them, are definitely his own.*

"He never shoots animals or birds, though he owns some of the best shooting in Scotland—yet he is a famous expert with a pistol and always carries one. Owning a fine stable, he has not been on a horse for fifteen years. He never eats anything between luncheon and dinner, which in England barely misses the aspect of treason. He has never seen a cricket match. Possessing more than a dozen automobiles, he does not know how to drive one. He is an excellent poker player and has popularized the game among a circle of his friends. He is passionately fond of croquet, derides golf as a 'corrupter of social decency,' and keeps an American cook at the manor of Pokendam for the purpose of making pumpkin pie. On his frequent trips to the Continent he never fails to take with him—"

There was no point in going on, so I stopped. I had lost my audience. As he stood facing me Wolfe's eyes had gradually narrowed into slits; and of a sudden he opened his hand and turned it palm down to let the remaining darts fall to the floor, where they rolled in all directions; and Wolfe walked from the room without a word. I heard him in the hall, in the elevator, getting in and banging the door to. Of course he had the excuse that it was four o'clock, his regular time for going to the plant-rooms.

I could have left the darts for Fritz to pick up later, but there was no sense in me getting childish just because Wolfe did. So I tore off the sheet of the magazine section I had been reading from, with the picture of the Marquis of Clivers in the center, fastened it to the corkboard with a couple of thumbtacks, gathered up the darts, stood off 15 feet and let fly. One of the darts got the marquis in the nose, another in his left eye, two of them in his neck, and the last one missed him by an inch. He was well pinned. Pretty good shooting,

8

I thought, as I went for my hat to venture out to a movie, not knowing then that before he left our city the marquis would treat us to an exhibition of much better shooting with a quite different weapon, nor that on that sheet of newspaper which I had pinned to the corkboard was a bit of information that would prove to be fairly useful in Nero Wolfe's professional consideration of a sudden and violent death.

• • • • 2 • • • •

FOR THE next day, Monday, October 7th, my memo pad showed two appointments. Neither displayed any promise of being either lucrative or exciting. The first one, down for 3:30 in the afternoon, was with a guy named Anthony D. Perry. He was a tycoon, a director of the Metropolitan Trust Company, the bank we did business with, and president of the Seaboard Products Corporation—one of those vague firms occupying six floors of a big skyscraper and selling annually a billion dollars' worth of something nobody ever actually saw, like soy beans or powdered cocoanut shells or dried llama's hoofs. As I say, Perry was a tycoon; he presided at meetings and was appointed on Mayor's Committees and that kind of hooey. Wolfe had handled a couple of investigations for him in previous years—nothing of any importance. We didn't know what was on his mind this time; he had telephoned for an appointment.

The second appointment was for 6:00 P. M. It was a funny one, but we often had funny ones. Saturday morning, October 5th, a female voice had phoned that she wanted to see Nero Wolfe. I said okay. She said, yes, but she wanted to bring someone with her who would not arrive in New York until Monday morning, and she would be busy all day, so could they come at 5:30. I said, no, but they could come at six, picking up a pencil to put down her name. But she wasn't divulging it; she said she would bring her name along with her, and they would arrive at six sharp, and it was very important. It wasn't much of a date, but I put it on the memo pad and hoped she would turn up, for she had the kind of voice that makes you want to observe it in the flesh.

Anthony D. Perry was there on the dot at three-thirty. Fritz answered the door and brought him to the office. Wolfe was

10

at his desk drinking beer. I sat in my corner and scowled at the probability that Perry was going to ask us to follow the scent of some competitor suspected of unfair trade practices, as he had before, and I did not regard that as a treat. But this time he had a different kind of difficulty, though it was nothing to make your blood run cold. He asked after our health, including me because he was democratic, inquired politely regarding the orchids, and then hitched his chair up and smiled at Wolfe as one man of affairs to another.

"I came to see you, Mr. Wolfe, instead of asking you to call on me, for two reasons. First, because I know you refuse to leave your home to call on anyone whatever, and, second, because the errand I want you to undertake is private and confidential."

Wolfe nodded. "Either would have sufficed, sir. And the errand?"

"Is, as I say, confidential." Perry cleared his throat, glancing at me as I opened up my notebook. "I suppose Mr. . . ."

"Goodwin." Wolfe poured a glass of beer. "Mr. Goodwin's discretion reaches to infinity. Anything too confidential for him would find me deaf."

"Very well. I want to engage you for a delicate investigation, one that will require most careful handling. It is in connection with an unfortunate situation that has arisen in our executive offices." Perry cleared his throat again. "I fear that a young woman, one of our employees, is going to suffer an injustice—a victim of circumstances—unless something is done about it."

He paused. Wolfe said, "But, Mr. Perry. Surely, as the directing head of your corporation, you are its fount of justice —or its opposite?"

Perry smiled. "Not absolutely. At best, a constitutional monarch. Let me explain. Our executive offices are on the thirty-second floor of our building—the Seaboard Building. We have some thirty private offices on that floor, officers of the corporation, department heads and so on. Last Friday one of the officers had in his desk a sum of money in currency, a fairly large sum, which disappeared under circumstances which led him to suspect that it had been taken by—by the employee I spoke of. It was not reported to me until Saturday morning. The officer requested immediate action, but I could not bring myself to believe the employee guilty. She has been —that is, she has always seemed to merit the most complete confidence. In spite of appearances . . ."

11

He halted. Wolfe asked, "And you wish us to learn the truth of the matter?"

"Yes. Of course. That's what I want." Perry cleared his throat. "But I also want you to consider her record of probity and faithful service. And I would like to ask you, in discussing the affair with Mr. Muir, to give him to understand that you have been engaged to handle it as you would any investigation of a similar nature. In addition, I wish your reports to be made to me personally."

"I see." Wolfe's eyes were half closed. "It seems a little complex. I would like to avoid any possibility of misunderstanding. Let us make it clear. You are not asking us to discover an arrangement of evidence that will demonstrate the employee's guilt. Nor are you engaging us to devise satisfactory proof of her innocence. You merely want us to find the truth."

"Yes," Perry smiled. "But I hope and believe that the truth will be her innocence."

"As it may be. And who is to be our client, you or the Seaboard Products Corporation?"

"Why . . . that hadn't occurred to me. The corporation, I should think. That would be best."

"Good." Wolfe looked at me. "If you please, Archie." He leaned back in his chair, twined his fingers at the peak of his middle mound, and closed his eyes.

I whirled on my swivel, with my notebook. "First the money, Mr. Perry. How much?"

"Thirty thousand dollars. In hundred-dollar bills."

"Egad. Payroll?"

"No." He hesitated. "Well, yes, call it payroll."

"It would be better if we knew about it."

"Is it necessary?"

"Not necessary. Just better. The more we know the less we have to find out."

"Well . . . since it is understood this is strictly confidential . . . you know of course that in connection with our business we need certain privileges in certain foreign countries. In our dealings with the representatives of those countries we sometimes need to employ cash sums."

"Okay. This Mr. Muir you mentioned, he's the paymaster?"

"Mr. Ramsey Muir is the senior vice-president of the corporation. He usually handles such contacts. On this occasion, last Friday, he had a luncheon appointment with a gentleman from Washington. The gentleman missed his train and telephoned that he would come on a later one, arriving at

12

our office at five-thirty. He did so. When the moment arrived for Mr. Muir to open the drawer of his desk, the money was gone. He was of course greatly embarrassed."

"Yeah. When had he put it there?"

An interruption came from Wolfe. He moved to get upright in his chair, then to arise from it. He looked down at Perry:

"You will excuse me, sir. It is the hour for my prescribed exercise and, following that, attention to my plants. If it would amuse you, when you have finished with Mr. Goodwin, to come to the roof and look at them, I would be pleased to have you." He moved halfway to the door, and turned. "It would be advisable, I think, for Mr. Goodwin to make a preliminary investigation before we definitely undertake the commission you offer us. It appears to present complexities. Good day, sir." He went on out. The poker-dart board had been moved to his bedroom that morning, it being a business day with appointments.

"A cautious man." Perry smiled at me. "Of course his exceptional ability permits him to afford it."

I saw Perry was sore by the color above his cheekbones. I said, "Yeah. When had he put it there?"

"What? Oh, to be sure. The money had been brought from the bank and placed in Mr. Muir's desk that morning, but he had looked in the drawer when he returned from lunch, around three o'clock, and saw it intact. At five-thirty it was gone."

"Was he there all the time?"

"Oh, no. He was in and out. He was with me in my office for twenty minutes or so. He went once to the toilet. For over half an hour, from four to until about four-forty, he was in the directors' room, conferring with other officers and Mr. Savage, our public relations counsel."

"Was the drawer locked?"

"No."

"Then anyone might have lifted it."

Perry shook his head. "The executive reception clerk is at a desk with a view of the entire corridor; that's her job, to know where everyone is all the time, to facilitate interviews. She knows who went in Muir's room, and when."

"Who did?"

"Five people. An office boy with correspondence, another vice-president of the company, Muir's stenographer, Clara Fox, and myself."

"Let's eliminate. I suppose you didn't take it?"

"No. I almost wish I had. When the office boy was there,

13

Muir was there too. The vice-president, Mr. Arbuthnot, is out of the question. As for Muir's stenographer, she was still there when the loss was discovered—most of the others had gone home—and she insisted that Muir search her belongings. She has a little room next to Muir's, and had not been out of it except to enter his room. Besides, he has had her for eleven years, and trusts her."

"Which leaves Clara Fox."

"Yes." Perry cleared his throat. "Clara Fox is our cable clerk—a most responsible position. She translates and decodes all cables and telegrams. She went to Muir's office around a quarter after four, during his absence, with a decoded message, and waited there while Muir's stenographer went to her own room to type a copy of it."

"Has she been with you long?"

"Three years. A little over."

"Did she know the money was there?"

"She probably knew it was in Muir's office. Two days previously she had handled a cablegram giving instructions for the payment."

"But you think she didn't take it."

Perry opened his mouth and closed it again. I put the eye on him. He didn't look as if he was really undecided; it seemed rather that he was hunting for the right words. I waited and looked him over. He had clever, careful, blue-gray eyes, a good jaw but a little too square for comfort, hair no grayer than it should be considering he must have been over sixty, a high forehead with a mole on the right temple, and a well-kept healthy skin. Not a layout that you would ordinarily regard as hideous, but at that moment I wasn't observing it with great favor, because it seemed likely that there was something phony about the pie he was inviting me to stick my finger into; and I give low marks to a guy that asks you to help him work a puzzle and then holds out one of the pieces on you. I don't mind looking for the fly in a client's ointment, but why throw in a bunch of hornets?

Perry finally spoke. "In spite of appearances, I am personally of the opinion that Clara Fox did not take that money. It would be a great shock to me to know that she did, and the proof would have to be unassailable."

"What does she say about it?"

"She hasn't been asked. Nothing has been said, except to Arbuthnot, Miss Vawter—the executive reception clerk—and Muir's stenographer. I may as well tell you, Muir wanted to send for the police this morning, and I restrained him."

14

"Maybe Miss Vawter took it."

"She has been with us eighteen years. I would sooner suspect myself. Besides, someone is constantly passing in the corridor. If she left her desk even for a minute it would be noticed."

"How old is Clara Fox?"

"Twenty-six."

"Oh. A bit junior, huh? For such a responsible position. Married?"

"No. She is a remarkably competent person."

"Do you know anything of her habits? Does she collect diamonds or frolic with the geegees?"

Perry stared at me. I said, "Does she bet on horse races?"

He frowned. "Not that I know of. I am not personally intimate with her, and I have not had her spied on."

"How much does she get and how do you suppose she spends it?"

"Her salary is thirty-six hundred. So far as I know, she lives sensibly and respectably. She has a small flat somewhere, I believe, and she has a little car—I have seen her driving it. She—I understand she enjoys the theater."

"Uh-huh." I flipped back a page of my notebook and ran my eye over it. "And this Mr. Muir who leaves his drawer unlocked with thirty grand inside—might he have been caught personally with his financial pants down and made use of the money himself?"

Perry smiled and shook his head. "Muir owns some twenty-eight thousand shares of the stock of our corporation, worth over two million dollars at the present market, besides other properties. It was quite usual for him to leave the drawer unlocked under those circumstances."

I glanced at my notebook again, and lifted my shoulders a shade and let them drop negligently, which meant that I was mildly provoked. The thing looked like a mess, possibly a little nasty, with nothing much to be expected in the way of action or profit. The first step, of course, after what Wolfe had said, was for me to go take a look at the 32nd floor of the Seaboard Building and enter into conversation. But the clock on the wall said 4:20. At six the attractive telephone voice with her out-of-town friend was expected to arrive; I wanted to be there, and I probably wouldn't be if I once got started chasing that thirty grand. I said to Perry:

"Okay. I suppose you'll be at your office in the morning? I'll be there at nine sharp to look things over. I'll want to see most of—"

"Tomorrow morning?" Perry was frowning. "Why not now?"

"I have another appointment."

"Cancel it." The color topped his cheekbones again. "This is urgent. I am one of Wolfe's oldest clients. I took the trouble to come here personally . . ."

"Sorry, Mr. Perry. Won't tomorrow do? My appointment can't very well be postponed."

"Send someone else."

"There's no one available who could handle it."

"This is outrageous!" Perry jerked up in his chair. "I insist on seeing Wolfe!"

I shook my head. "You know you can't. You know darned well he's eccentric." But then I thought, after all, I've seen worse guys, and he's a client, and maybe he can't help it if he gets on Mayor's Committees, perhaps they nag him. So I got out of my chair and said, "I'll go upstairs and put it up to Wolfe, he's the boss. If he says—"

The door of the office opened. I turned. Fritz came in, walking formal as he always did to announce a caller. But he didn't get to announce this one. The caller came right along, two steps behind Fritz, and I grinned when I saw he was stepping so soft that Fritz didn't know he was there.

Fritz started, "A gentleman to—"

"Yeah, I see him. Okay."

Fritz turned and saw he had been stalked, blinked, and beat it. I went on observing the caller, because he was a specimen. He was about six feet three inches tall, wearing an old blue serge suit with no vest and the sleeves a mile short, carrying a cream-colored ten-gallon hat, with a face that looked as if it had been left out on the fire escape for over half a century, and walking like a combination of a rodeo cowboy and a panther in the zoo.

He announced in a smooth low voice, "My name's Harlan Scovil." He went up to Anthony D. Perry and stared at him with half-shut eyes. Perry moved in his chair and looked annoyed. The caller said, "Are you Mr. Nero Wolfe?"

I butted in, suavely. "Mr. Wolfe is not here. I'm his assistant. I'm engaged with this gentleman. If you'll excuse us . . ."

The caller nodded, and turned to stare again at Perry. "Then who—you ain't Mike Walsh? Hell no, Mike was a runt." He gave Perry up, and glanced around the room, then looked at me. "What do I do now, sit down and hang my hat on my ear?"

I grinned. "Yeah. Try that leather one over there." He

16

panthered for it, and I started for the door, throwing over my shoulder to Perry, "I won't keep you waiting long."

Upstairs, in the plant-rooms on the roof, glazed-in, where Wolfe kept his ten thousand orchids, I found him in the middle room turning some off-season Oncidiums that were about to bud, while Horstmann fussed around with a pot of charcoal and osmundine. Wolfe, of course, didn't look at me or halt operations; whenever I interrupted him in the plant-rooms he pretended he was Joe Louis in his training camp and I was a boy peeking through the fence.

I said, loud so he couldn't also pretend he didn't hear me, "That millionaire downstairs says I've got to go to his office right now and begin looking under the rugs for his thirty grand, and there's an appointment here for six o'clock. I expressed a preference to go tomorrow morning."

Wolfe said, "And if your pencil fell to the floor and you were presented with the alternative of either picking it up or leaving it there, would you also need to consult me about that?"

"He's exasperated."

"So am I."

"He says it's urgent, I'm outrageous, and he's an old client."

"He is probably correct all around. I like particularly the second of his conclusions. Leave me."

"Very well. Another caller just arrived. Name of Harlan Scovil. A weather-beaten plainsman who stared at Anthony D. Perry and said he wasn't Mike Walsh."

Wolfe looked at me. "You expect, I presume, to draw your salary at the end of the month."

"Okay." I wanted to reach out and tip over one of the Oncidiums, but decided it wouldn't be diplomatic, so I faded.

When I got back downstairs Perry was standing in the door of the office with his hat on and his stick in his hand. I told him, "Sorry to keep you waiting."

"Well?"

"It'll have to be tomorrow, Mr. Perry. The appointment can't be postponed. Anyhow, the day's nearly gone, and I couldn't do much. Mr. Wolfe sincerely regrets—"

"All right," Perry snapped. "At nine o'clock, you said?"

"I'll be there on the dot."

"Come to my office."

"Right."

I went and opened the front door for him.

In the office Harlan Scovil sat in the leather chair over by the bookshelves. As, entering, I lamped him from the door,

17

I saw that his head was drooping and he looked tired and old and all in; but at the sound of me he jerked up and I caught the bright points of his eyes. I went over and wheeled my chair around to face him.

"You want to see Nero Wolfe?"

He nodded. "That was my idea. Yes, sir."

"Mr. Wolfe will be engaged until six o'clock, and at that time he has another appointment. My name's Archie Goodwin. I'm Mr. Wolfe's confidential assistant. Maybe I could help you?"

"The hell you are." He certainly had a smooth soft voice for his age and bulk and his used-up face. He had his half-shut eyes on me. "Listen, sonny. What sort of a man is this Nero Wolfe?"

I grinned. "A fat man."

He shook his head in slow impatience. "It ain't to the point to tease a steer. You see the kind of man I am. I'm out of my country." His eyes twinkled a little. "Hell, I'm clear over the mountains. Who was that man that was in here when I came?"

"Just a man. A client of Mr. Wolfe's."

"What kind of a client? Anybody ever give him a name?"

"I expect so. Next time you see him, ask him. Is there anything I can do for you?"

"All right, sonny." He nodded. "Naturally I had my suspicions up, seeing any kind of a man here at this time, but you heard me remark that he wasn't Mike Walsh. And God knows he wasn't Vic Lindquist's daughter. Thanks for leaving my ideas free. Could I have a piece of paper? Any kind."

I handed him a sheet of typewriter bond from my desk. He took it and held it in front of him spread on the palms of his hands, bent his head over it and opened his mouth, and out popped a chew of tobacco the size of a hen's egg. I'm fairly observant, but I hadn't suspected its existence. He wrapped the paper around it, clumsily but thoroughly, got up and took it to the wastebasket, and came back and sat down again. His eyes twinkled at me.

"There seems to be very little spittin' done east of the Mississippi. A swallower like me don't mind, but if John Orcutt was here he wouldn't tolerate it. But you was asking me if there's anything you can do for me. I wish to God I knew. I wish to God there was a man in this town you could let put your saddle on."

I grinned at him. "If you mean an honest man, Mr. Scovil, you must have got an idea from a movie or something. There's

18

just as many honest men here as the other side of the mountains. And just as few. I'm one. I'm so damn honest I often double-cross myself. Nero Wolfe is almost as bad. Go ahead. You must have come here to spill something besides that chew."

With his eyes still on me, he lifted his right hand and drew the back of it slowly across his nostrils from left to right, and then, after a pause, from right to left. He nodded. "I've traveled over two thousand miles, from Hiller County, Wyoming, to come here on an off chance. I sold thirty calves to get the money to come on, and for me nowadays that's a lot of calves. I didn't know till this morning I was going to see any kind of a man called Nero Wolfe. All that is to me is just a name and address on a piece of paper I've got in my pocket. All I knew was I was going to see Mike Walsh and Vic's daughter and Gil's daughter, and I was supposed to be going to see George Rowley, and by God if I see him and what they say is true I'll be able to fix up some fences this winter and get something besides lizards and coyotes inside of 'em. One thing you can tell me anyhow, did you ever hear of any kind of a man called a Marquis of Clivers?"

I nodded. "I've read in the paper about that kind of a man."

"Good for you. I don't read much. One reason, I'm so damn suspicious I don't believe it even if I do read it, so it don't seem worth the trouble. I'm here now because I'm suspicious. I was supposed to come here at six o'clock with the rest of those others, but I had my time on my hands anyhow, so I thought I might as well ride out and take a look. I want to see this Nero Wolfe man. You don't look to me like a man that goes out at night after lambs, but I want to see him. What really made me suspicious was the two daughters. God knows a man is bad enough when you don't know him, but I doubt if you ever could get to know a woman well enough to leave her loose around you. I never really tried, because it didn't ever seem to be worth the trouble." He stopped, and drew the back of his hand across his nostrils again, back and forth, slowly. His eyes twinkled at me. "Naturally, your opinion is that I talk a good deal. That's the truth. It won't hurt you any, and it may even do you good. Out in Wyoming I've been talking to myself like this for thirty years, and by God if I can stand it you can."

It appeared to me that I was going to stand it whether I wanted to or not, but something interfered. The phone rang. I turned to my desk and plucked the receiver, a female voice asked me to hold the wire, and then another voice came at me:

19

"Goodwin? Anthony D. Perry. I just got back to my office, and you must come here at once. Any appointments you have, cancel them, if there's any damage I'll pay it. The situation here has developed. A taxi will get you here in five minutes."

I love these guys that think the clock stops every time they sneeze. But by the tone of his voice it was a case either of aye, aye, sir, or a plain go to hell, and by nature I'm a courteous man. So I told him okay.

"You'll come at once?"

"I said okay."

I shoved the phone back and turned to the caller.

"I've got to leave you, Mr. Scovil. Urgent business. But if I heard you right, you've been invited here to the six o'clock party, so I'll see you again. Correct?"

He nodded. "But look here, sonny, I wanted to ask you—"

"Sorry, I've got to run." I was on my way. I looked back from the door. "Don't nurse any suspicions about any kind of a man named Nero Wolfe. He's as straight as he is fat. So-long."

I went to the kitchen, where Fritz had about nine kinds of herbs spread out on the shredding board all at once, and told him:

"I'm going out. Back at six. Leave the door open so you can see the hall. There's an object in the office waiting for a six o'clock appointment, and if you have any good deeds to spare like offering a man a drink and a plate of cookies, I assure you he is worthy. If Wolfe comes down before I get back, tell him he's there."

Fritz, nibbling a morsel of tarragon, nodded. I went to the hall and snared my hat and beat it.

• • • • 3 • • • •

I DIDN'T fool with a taxi, and it wasn't worth while to take the roadster, which as usual was at the curb, and fight to park it. From Wolfe's house in West 35th Street, not far from the Hudson, where he had lived for over twenty years, and I had slept on the same floor with him for eight, it was only a hop, skip and jump to the new Seaboard Building, in the twenties, also near the river. I hoofed it, considering meanwhile the oddities of my errand. Why had Anthony D. Perry, president of the Seaboard Products Corporation, taken the trouble to come to our office to tell us about an ordinary good clean theft? As the Tel & Tel say in their ads, why not telephone? And if he felt so confident that Clara Fox hadn't done it, did he suspect she was being framed or what? And so on.

Having been in the Seaboard Building before, and even, if you would believe it, in the office of the president himself, I knew my way around. I remembered what the executive reception clerk on the 32nd floor looked like, and so was expecting no treat in that quarter, and got none. I now knew also that she was called Miss Vawter, and so addressed her, noting that her ears stuck out at about the same angle as three years previously. She was expecting me, and without bothering to pry her thin lips open she waved me to the end of the corridor.

In Perry's office, which was an enormous room furnished in The Office Beautiful style with four big windows giving a sweeping view of the river, there was a gathering waiting for me. I went in and shut the door behind me and looked them over. Perry was seated at his desk with his back to the windows, frowning at his cigar smoke. A bony-looking medium-sized man, with hair somewhat grayer than Perry's, brown eyes too close together, and pointed ears, sat near-by.

21

A woman something over thirty, with a flat nose, who could have got a job as schoolteacher just on her looks, stood at a corner of Perry's desk. She looked as if she might have been doing some crying. In another chair, out a little, another woman sat with her back to me as I entered. On my way approaching Perry I caught a glimpse of her face as I went by, and saw that additional glimpses probably wouldn't hurt me any.

Perry grunted at me. He spoke to the others: "This is the man. Mr. Goodwin, from Nero Wolfe's office." He indicated with nods, in succession, the woman sitting, the one standing, and the man. "Miss Fox. Miss Barish. Mr. Muir."

I nodded around, and looked at Perry. "You said you've got some developments?"

"Yes." He knocked ashes from his cigar, looked at Muir, and then at me. "You know most of the facts, Goodwin. Let's come to the point. When I returned I found that Mr. Muir had called Miss Fox to his office, had accused her of stealing the money, and was questioning her in the presence of Miss Barish. This was contrary to the instructions I had given. He now insists on calling in the police."

Muir spoke to me, smoothly. "You're in on a family quarrel, Mr. Goodwin." He leveled his eyes at Perry. "As I've said, Perry, I accept your instructions on all business matters. This is more personal than business. The money was taken from my desk. I was responsible for it. I know who stole it, I am prepared to swear out a warrant, and I intend to do so."

Perry stared back at him. "Nonsense. I've told you that my authority extends to all the affairs of this office." His tone could have been used to ice a highball. "You may be ready to swear out a warrant and expose yourself to the risk of being sued for false arrest, but I will not permit a vice-president of this corporation to take that risk. I went to the trouble of engaging the best man in New York City, Nero Wolfe, to investigate this. I even took pains that Miss Fox should not know she was suspected before the investigation. I admit that I do not believe she is a thief. That is my opinion. If evidence is uncovered to prove me wrong, then I'm wrong."

"Evidence?" Muir's jaw had tightened. "Uncovered? A clever man like Nero Wolfe might either cover or uncover. No? Depending on what you paid him for."

Perry smiled a controlled smile. "You're an ass, Muir, to say a thing like that. I'm the president of this company, and you're an ass to suggest I might betray its interests, either the most important or the most trivial. Mr. Goodwin heard my conversation with his employer. He can tell you what I engaged him to do."

"No doubt he could tell me what he has been instructed to tell me."

"I'd go easy, Muir." Perry was still smiling. "The kind of insinuations you're making might run into something serious. You shouldn't bark around without considering the chances of starting a real dogfight, and I shouldn't think you'd want a fight over a triviality like this."

"Triviality?" Muir started to tremble. I saw his hand on the chair-arm begin to shake, and he gripped the wood. He turned his eyes from Perry onto Clara Fox, sitting a few feet away, and the look in them made it plain why trivialities were out. Of course I didn't know whether he was hating her because she had lifted the thirty grand or because she had stepped on his toe, but from where I stood it looked like something much fancier than either of those. If looks could kill she would have been at least a darned sick woman.

Then he shifted from her to me, and he had to pinch his voice. "I won't ask you to report the conversation you heard, Mr. Goodwin. But of course you've had instructions and hints from Mr. Perry, so you might as well have some from me." He got up, walked around the desk, and stood in front of me. "I presume that an important part of your investigation will be to follow Miss Fox's movements, to learn if possible what she has done with the money. When you see her entering a theater or an expensive restaurant with Mr. Perry, don't suppose she is squandering the money that way. Mr. Perry will be paying. Or if you see Mr. Perry entering her apartment of an evening, it will not be to help her dispose of the evidence. His visit will be for another purpose."

He turned and left the room, neither slow nor fast. He shut the door behind him, softly. I didn't see him, I heard him; I was looking at the others. Miss Barish stared at Miss Fox and turned pale. Perry's only visible reaction was to drop his dead cigar into the ash tray and push the tray away. The first move came from Miss Fox. She stood up.

The idea occurred to me that on account of active emotions she was probably better looking at that moment than she ordinarily was, but even discounting for that there was plenty to go on. In my detached impersonal way, I warmed to her completely at exactly that moment, when she stood up and looked at Anthony D. Perry. She had brown hair, neither long nor boyish bob, just a swell lot of careless hair, and her eyes were brown too and you could see at a glance that they would never tell you anything except what she wanted them to.

She spoke. "May I go now, Mr. Perry? It's past five o'clock, and I have an appointment."

Perry looked at her with no surprise. Evidently he knew her. He said, "Mr. Goodwin will want to talk with you."

"I know he will. Will the morning do? Am I to come to work tomorrow?"

"Of course. I refer you to Goodwin. He has charge of this now, and the responsibility is his."

I shook my head. "Excuse me, Mr. Perry. Mr. Wolfe said he would decide whether he'd handle this or not after my preliminary investigation. As far as Miss Fox is concerned, tomorrow will suit me fine." I looked at her. "Nine o'clock?"

She nodded. "Not that I have anything to tell you about that money, except that I didn't take it and never saw it. I have told Mr. Perry and Mr. Muir that. I may go then? Good night."

She was perfectly cool and sweet. From the way she was handling herself, no one would have supposed she had any notion that she was standing on a hot spot. She included all of us in her good-night glance, and turned and walked out as self-possessed as a young doe not knowing that there's a gun pointed at it and a finger on the trigger.

When the door was shut Perry turned to me briskly. "Where do you want to start, Goodwin? Would fingerprints around the drawer of Muir's desk do any good?"

I grinned at him and shook my head. "Only for practice, and I don't need any. I'd like to have a chat with Muir. He must know it won't do to have Miss Fox arrested just because she was in his room. Maybe he thinks he knows where the money is."

Perry said, "Miss Barish is Mr. Muir's secretary."

"Oh." I looked at the woman with the flat nose still standing there. I said to her, "It was you that typed the cablegram while Miss Fox waited in Muir's room. Did you notice—"

Perry horned in. "You can talk with Miss Barish later." He glanced at the clock on the wall, which said 5:20. "Or, if you prefer, you can talk with her here, now." He shoved his chair back and got up. "If you need me, I'll be in the directors' room, at the other end. I'm late now, for a conference. It won't take long. I'll ask Muir to stay, and Miss Vawter also, in case you want to see her." He had moved around to the front of his desk, and halted there. "One thing, Goodwin, about Muir. I advise you to forget his ridiculous outburst. He's jerky and nervous, and the truth is he's too old for the strain

24

business puts on a man nowadays. Disregard his nonsense. Well?"

"Sure." I waved a hand. "Let him rave."

Perry frowned at me, nodded, and left the room.

The best chair in sight was the one Perry had just vacated, so I went around and took it. Miss Barish stood with her shoulders hanging, squeezing her handkerchief and looking straight at me. I said, friendly, "Move around and sit down—there, where Muir was. So you're Muir's secretary."

"Yes, sir." She got onto the edge of the chair.

"Been his secretary eleven years."

"Yes, sir."

"Cut out the sir. Okay? I'm not gray-headed. So Muir looked through your belongings last Friday and didn't find the money?"

Her eyes darkened. "Certainly he didn't find it."

"Right. Did he make a thorough search of your room?"

"I don't know. I don't care if he did."

"Now don't get sore. I don't care either. After you copied the cablegram and took the original back to Miss Fox in Muir's room, what was she carrying when she left there?"

"She was carrying the cablegram."

"But where did she have the thirty grand, down her sock? Didn't it show?"

Miss Barish compressed her lips to show that she was putting up with me. "I did not see Miss Fox carrying anything except the cablegram. I have told Mr. Muir and Mr. Perry that I did not see Miss Fox carrying anything except the cablegram."

I grinned at her. "And you are now telling Mr. Goodwin that you did not see Miss Fox carrying anything except the cablegram. Check. Are you a friend of Miss Fox's?"

"No. Not a real friend. I don't like her."

"Egad. Why don't you like her?"

"Because she is extremely attractive, and I am homely. Because she has been here only three years and she could be Mr. Perry's private secretary tomorrow if she wanted to, and that is the job I have wanted ever since I came here. Also because she is cleverer than I am."

I looked at Miss Barish, more interested at all the frankness. Deciding to see how far down the frankness went, I popped at her, "How long has Miss Fox been Perry's mistress?"

She went red as a beet. Her eyes dropped, and she shook her head. Finally she looked up at me again, but didn't say anything. I tried another one:

25

"Then tell me this. How long has Muir been trying to get her away from Perry?"

Her eyes got dark again, and the color stayed. She stared at me a minute, then all at once rose to her feet and stood there squeezing her handkerchief. Her voice trembled a little, but it didn't seem to bother her.

"I don't know whether that's any of your business, Mr. Goodwin, but it's none of mine. Don't you see . . . don't you see how this is a temptation to me? Couldn't I have said I saw her carrying something out of that room?" She squeezed the handkerchief harder. "Well . . . I didn't say it. Don't I have to keep my self-respect? I'll go out of my way too, I don't know anything about it, but I don't believe Clara Fox has ever been anybody's mistress. She wouldn't have to be, she's too clever. I don't know anything about that money either, but if you want to ask me questions to see if I do, go ahead."

I said, "School's out. Go on home. I may want you again in the morning, but I doubt it."

She turned pale as fast as she had turned red. She certainly was a creature of moods. I got up from Perry's chair and walked all the way across the room to open the door and stand and hold it. She went past, still squeezing the handkerchief and mumbling good night to me, and I shut the door.

Feeling for a cigarette and finding I didn't have any, I went back to the windows and stood surveying the view. As I had suspected, the thing wasn't a good clear theft at all, it was some kind of a mess. From the business standpoint, it was obvious that the thing to do was go back and tell Nero Wolfe it was a case of refusing to let the administrative heads of the Seaboard Products Corporation use our office for a washtub to dump their dirty linen in. But what reined me up on that was my professional curiosity about Clara Fox. If sneak thieves came as cool and sweet as that, it was about time I found it out. And if she wasn't one, my instinctive dislike of a frame-up made me hesitate about leaving her parked against a fireplug. I was fairly well disgusted, and got more disgusted, after gazing out of the window for a while, when I felt in my pockets again for a cigarette with no results.

I wandered around The Office Beautiful a little, sightseeing and cogitating, and then went out to the corridor. It was empty. Of course, it was after office hours. All its spacious width and length, there was no traffic, and it was dimmer than it had been when I entered, for no more lights were turned on and it was getting dark outdoors. There were doors along one side, and at the further end the double doors, closed, of

26

the directors' room. I heard a cough, and turned, and saw Miss Vawter, the executive reception clerk, sitting in the corner under a light with a magazine.

She said in a vinegar voice, "I'm remaining after hours because Mr. Perry said you might want to speak to me."

She was a pain all around. I said, "Please continue remaining. Which is Muir's room?"

She pointed to one of the doors, and I headed for it. I was reaching out for the knob when she screeched at me, "You can't go in there like that! Mr. Muir is out."

I called to her, "Do tell. If you want to interrupt Mr. Perry in his conference, go to the directors' room and give the alarm. I'm investigating."

I went on in, shut the door, found the wall switch and turned on the lights. As I did so, a door in another wall opened, and Miss Barish appeared. She stood and looked without saying anything.

I observed, "I thought I told you to go home."

"I can't." Her color wasn't working either way. "When Mr. Muir is here I'm not supposed to go until he dismisses me. He is in conference."

"I see. That your room? May I come in?"

She stepped back and I entered. It was a small neat room with one window and the usual stenographic and filing equipment. I let the eyes rove, and then asked her, "Would you mind leaving me here for a minute with the door shut, while you go to Muir's desk and open and close a couple of the drawers? I'd like to see how much din it makes."

She said, "I was typing."

"So you were. All right, forget it. Come and show me which drawer the money was in."

She moved ahead of me, led the way to Muir's desk, and pulled open one of the drawers, the second one from the top on the right. There was nothing in it but a stack of envelopes. I reached out and closed it, then opened and closed it again, grinning as I remembered Perry's suggestion about fingerprints. Then I left the desk and strolled around a little. It was a vice-president's office, smaller and modester than Perry's but still by no means a pigpen. I noticed one detail, or rather three, a little out of the ordinary. There was no portrait of Abraham Lincoln nor replica of the Declaration of Independence on the walls, but there were three different good-sized photographs of three different good-looking women, hanging framed. I turned to Miss Barish, who was still standing by the desk:

27

"Who are all the handsome ladies?"

"They are Mr. Muir's wives."

"No! Honest to God? Mostly dead?"

"I don't know. None of them is with him now."

"Too bad. It looks like he's sentimental."

She shook her head. "Mr. Muir is a sensual man."

She was having another frank spell. I glanced at my watch. It was a quarter to six, giving me another five minutes, so I thought I might as well use them on her. I opened up, friendly, but although she seemed to be willing to risk a little more chat with me, I didn't really get any facts. All I learned was what I already knew, that she had no reason to suppose that Clara Fox had lifted the jack, and that if there was a frame-up she wasn't in on it. When the five minutes was up I turned to go, and at that moment the door opened and Muir came in.

Seeing us, he stopped, then came on again, to his desk. "You may go, Miss Barish. If you want to talk with me, Goodwin, sit down."

Miss Barish disappeared into her room. I said, "I won't keep you now, Mr. Muir. I suppose you'll be here in the morning?"

"Where else would I be?"

That kind of childishness never riles me. I grinned at the old goat, said, "Okay," and left him.

Outside in the corridor, down a few paces towards the directors' room, a group of four or five men stood talking. I saw Perry was among them, and approached. He saw me, and came to meet me.

I said, "Nothing more tonight, Mr. Perry. Let's let Mr. Muir have a chance to cool off. I'll report to Nero Wolfe."

Perry frowned. "He can phone me at my home any time this evening. It's in the book."

"Thanks. I'll tell him."

As I passed Miss Vawter on my way out, still sitting in the corner with her magazine, I said to her out of the side of my mouth, "See you at the Rainbow Room."

28

• • • • 4 • • • •

DOWN ON the sidewalk the shades of night were not keeping the metropolitan bipeds from the swift completion of their appointed rounds. Striding north toward 35th Street, I let the brain skip from this to that and back again, and decided that the spot Clara Fox was standing on was probably worse than hot, it was sizzling. Had she lit the fire herself? I left that in unfinished business.

I got home just at six o'clock and, knowing that Wolfe wouldn't be down for a few minutes yet, I went to the office to see if the Wyoming wonder had thought of any new suspicions and if his colleagues had shown up. The office was empty. I went through to the front room to see if he had moved his base there, but it was empty too. I beat it to the kitchen. Fritz was there, sitting with his slippers off, reading that newspaper in French. I asked him:

"What did you do with him?"

"*Qui?* Ah, *le monsieur*—" Fritz giggled. "Excuse me, Archie. You mean the gentleman who was waiting."

"Yeah, him."

"He received a telephone call," Fritz leaned over and began pulling on his slippers. "Time already for Mr. Wolfe!"

"He got a phone call here?"

Fritz nodded. "About half an hour after you left. More maybe. Wait till I look." He went to the stand where the kitchen phone extension was kept, and glanced at his memo pad. "That's right. 5:26. Twenty-six minutes past five."

"Who was it?"

Fritz's brows went up. "Should I know, Archie?" He thought he was using slang. "A gentleman said he wished to speak to Mr. Scovil in case he was here, and I went to the office and

29

asked if it was Mr. Scovil, and he talked from your desk, and then he got up and put on his hat and went out."

"Leave any message?"

"No. I had come back to the kitchen, closing the office door for his privacy but leaving this one open as you said, and he came out and went in a hurry. He said nothing at all."

I lifted the shoulders and let them drop. "He'll be back. He wants to see a kind of a man named Nero Wolfe. What's on the menu?"

Fritz told me, and let me take a sniff at the sauce steaming on the simmer-plate; then I heard the elevator and went back to the office. Wolfe entered, crossed to his chair and got himself lowered, rang for beer and took the opener out of the drawer, and then vouchsafed me a glance.

"Pleasant afternoon, Archie?"

"No, sir. Putrid. I went around to Perry's office."

"Indeed. A man of action must expect such vexations. Tell me about it."

"Well, Perry left here just after I came down, but about eight minutes after that he phoned and instructed me to come galloping. Having the best interests of my employer in mind I went."

"Notwithstanding the physical law that the contents can be no larger than the container." Fritz arrived with two bottles of beer, Wolfe opened and poured one, and drank. "Go on."

"Yes, sir. I disregard your wit, because I'd like to show you this picture before the company arrives, and they're already ten minutes late. By the way, the company we already had has departed. He claimed to be part of the six o'clock appointment and said he would wait, but Fritz says he got a phone call and went in a hurry. Maybe the appointment is off. Anyhow, here's the Perry puzzle. . . ."

I laid it out for him, in the way that he always liked to get a crop of facts, no matter how trivial or how crucial. I told him what everybody looked like, and what they did, and what they said fairly verbatim. He finished the first bottle of beer meanwhile, and had the second well on its way when I got through. I rattled it off and then leaned back and took a sip from a glass of milk I had brought from the kitchen.

Wolfe pinched his nose. "Pfui! Hyenas. And your conclusions?"

"Maybe hyenas. Yeah." I took another sip. "On principle I don't like Perry, but it's possible he's just using all the decency he has left after a life of evil. You have forbidden me to use the word louse, so I would say that Muir is an insect.

30

Clara Fox is the ideal of my dreams, but it wouldn't stun me to know that she lifted the roll, though I'd be surprised."

Wolfe nodded. "You may remember that four years ago Mr. Perry objected to our bill for an investigation of his competitors' trade practices. I presume that now he would like us to shovel the mud from his executive offices for twelve dollars a day. It is not practicable always to sneer at mud; there's too much of it. So it gives the greater pleasure to do so when we can afford it. At present our bank balance is agreeable to contemplate. Pfui!" He lifted his glass and emptied it and wiped his lips with his handkerchief.

"Okay," I agreed. "But there's something else to consider. Perry wants you to phone him this evening. If you take the case on we'll at least get expenses, and if you don't take it on Clara Fox may get five years for grand larceny and I'll have to move to Ossining so as to be near her and take her tidbits on visiting day. Balance the mud-shoveling against the loss of my services—but that sounds like visitors. I'll finish my appeal later."

I had heard the doorbell sending Fritz into the hall and down it to the door. I glanced at the clock: 6:30; they were half an hour late. I remembered the attractive telephone voice, and wondered if we were going to have another nymph, cool and sweet in distress, on our hands.

Fritz came in and shut the door behind him, and announced callers. Wolfe nodded. Fritz went out, and after a second in came a man and two women. The man and the second woman I was barely aware of, because I was busy looking at the one in front. It certainly was a nymph cool and sweet in distress. Evidently she knew enough about Nero Wolfe to recognize him, for with only a swift glance at me she came forward to Wolfe's desk and spoke.

"Mr. Wolfe? I telephoned on Saturday. I'm sorry to be late for the appointment. My name is Clara Fox." She turned. "This is Miss Hilda Lindquist and Mr. Michael Walsh."

Wolfe nodded at her and at them. "It is bulk, not boorishness, that keeps me in my chair." He wiggled a finger at me. "Mr. Archie Goodwin. Chairs, Archie?"

I obliged, while Clara Fox was saying, "I met Mr. Goodwin this afternoon, in Mr. Perry's office." I thought to myself, you did indeed, and for not recognizing your voice I'll let them lock me in the cell next to yours when you go up the river.

"Indeed." Wolfe had his eyes half closed, which meant he

31

was missing nothing. "Mr. Walsh's chair to the right, please. Thank you."

Miss Fox was taking off her gloves. "First I'd like to explain why we're late. I said on the telephone that I couldn't make the appointment before Monday because I was expecting someone from out of town who had to be here. It was a man from out west named Harlan Scovil. He arrived this morning, and I saw him during the lunch hour, and arranged to meet him at a quarter past five, at his hotel, to bring him here. I went for him, but he wasn't there. I waited and . . . well, I tried to make some inquiries. Then I met Miss Lindquist and Mr. Walsh, as agreed, and we went back to Mr. Scovil's hotel again. We waited until a quarter past six, and decided it would be better to come on without him."

"Is his presence essential?"

"I wouldn't say essential. At least not at this moment. We left word, and he may join us here any second. He must see you too, before we can do anything. I should warn you, Mr. Wolfe, I have a very long story to tell."

She hadn't looked at me once. I decided to quit looking at her, and tried her companions. They were just barely people. Of course I remembered Harlan Scovil telling Anthony D. Perry that he wasn't Mike Walsh. Apparently this bird was. He was a scrawny little mick, built wiry, over sixty and maybe even seventy, dressed cheap but clean, sitting only half in his chair and keeping an ear palmed with his right hand. The Lindquist dame, with a good square face and wearing a good brown dress, had size, though I wouldn't have called her massive, first because it would have been only a half-truth, and second because she might have socked me. I guess she was a fine woman, of the kind that would be more apt to be snapping a coffee cup in her fingers than a champagne glass. Remembering Harlan Scovil to boot, it looked to me as if, whatever game Miss Fox was training for, she was picking some odd numbers for her team.

Wolfe had told her that the longer the story the sooner it ought to begin, and she was saying:

"It began forty years ago, in Silver City, Nevada. But before I start it, Mr. Wolfe, I ought to tell you something that I hope will make you interested. I've found out all I could about you, and I understand that you have remarkable abilities and an equally remarkable opinion of their cash value to people you do things for."

Wolfe sighed. "Each of us must choose his own brand of banditry, Miss Fox."

32

"Certainly. That is what I have done. If you agree to help us, and if we are successful, your fee will be one hundred thousand dollars."

Mike Walsh leaned forward and blurted, "Ten per cent! Fair enough?"

Hilda Lindquist frowned at him. Clara Fox paid no attention. Wolfe said, "The fee always depends. You couldn't hire me to hand you the moon."

She laughed at him, and although I had my notebook out I decided to look at her in the pauses. She said, "I won't need it. Is Mr. Goodwin going to take down everything? With the understanding that if you decide not to help us his notes are to be given to me?"

Cagey Clara. The creases of Wolfe's cheeks unfolded a little. "By all means."

"All right." She brushed her hair back. "I said it began forty years ago, but I won't start there. I'll start when I was nine years old, in 1918, the year my father was killed in the war, in France. I don't remember my father much. He was killed in 1918, and he sent my mother a letter which she didn't get until nearly a year later, because instead of trusting it to the army mail he gave it to another soldier to bring home. My mother read it then, but I never knew of it until seven years later, in 1926, when my mother gave it to me on her deathbed. I was seventeen years old. I loved my mother very dearly."

She stopped. It would have been a good spot for a moist film over her eyes or a catch in her voice, but apparently she had just stopped to swallow. She swallowed twice. In the pause I was looking at her. She went on:

"I didn't read the letter until a month later. I knew it was a letter father had written to mother eight years before, and with mother gone it didn't seem to be of any importance to me. But on account of what mother had said, about a month after she died I read it. I have it with me. I'll have to read it to you."

She opened her alligator-skin handbag and took out a folded paper. She jerked it open and glanced at it, and back at Wolfe. "May I?"

"Do I see typewriting?"

She nodded. "This is a copy. The original is put away." She brushed her hair back with a hand up and dipping swift like a bird. "This isn't a complete copy. There is—this is—just the part to read.

"*So, dearest Lola, since a man can't tell what is going to*

33

happen to him here, or when, I've decided to write you about a little incident that occurred last week, and make arrangements to be sure it gets to you, in case I never get home to tell you about it. I'll have to begin away back.

"I've told you a lot of wild tales about the old days in Nevada. I've told you this one too, but I'll repeat it here briefly. It was at Silver City, in 1895. I was 25 years old, so it was 10 years before I met you. I was broke, and so was the gang of youngsters I'm telling about. They were all youngsters but one. We weren't friends, there was no such thing as a friend around there. Most of the bunch of 2000 or so that inhabited Silver City camp at that time were a good deal older than us, which was how we happened to get together—temporarily. Everything was temporary!

"The ringleader of our gang was a kid we called Rubber on account of the way he bounced back up when he got knocked down. His name was Coleman, but I never knew his first name, or if I did I can't remember it, though I've often tried. Because Rubber was our leader, someone cracked a joke one day that we should call ourselves The Rubber Band, and we did. Pretty soon most of Silver City was calling us that.

"One of the gang, a kid named George Rowley, shot a man and killed him. From what I heard—I didn't see it—he had as good a right to shoot as was usually needed around there, but the trouble was that the one he killed happened to be a member of the Vigilance Committee. It was at night, 24 hours after the shooting, that they decided to hang him. Rowley hadn't had sense enough to make a getaway, so they took him and shut him up in a shanty until daylight, with one of their number for a guard, an Irishman. As Harlan Scovil would say—I'll never forget Harlan—he was a kind of a man named Mike Walsh.

"Rowley went after his guard, Mike Walsh. I mean talking to him. Finally, around midnight, he persuaded Mike to send for Rubber Coleman. Rubber had a talk with him and Mike. Then there was a lot of conspiring, and Rubber did a lot of dickering with Rowley. We were gathered in the dark in the sagebrush out back of John's Palace, a shack out at the edge of the city—"

Clara Fox looked up. "My father underscored the word city."

Wolfe nodded. "Properly, no doubt."

She went on: "—and we had been drinking some and were having a swell time. Around two o'clock Rubber showed up again and lit matches to show us a paper George Rowley had

34

signed, with him and Mike Walsh as witnesses. I've told you about it. I can't give it to you word for word, but this is exactly what it said. It said that his real name wasn't George Rowley, and that he wasn't giving his real name in writing, but that he had told it to Rubber Coleman. It said that he was from a wealthy family in England, and that if he got out of Silver City alive he would go back there, and some day he would get a share of the family pile. It said it wouldn't be a major share because he wasn't an oldest son. Then it hereby agreed that whenever and whatever he got out of his family connections, he would give us half of it, provided we got him safe out of Silver City and safe from pursuit, before the time came to hang him.

"We were young, and thought we were adventurers, and we were half drunk or maybe more. I doubt if any of us had any idea that we would ever get hold of any of the noble English wealth, except possibly Rubber Coleman, but the idea of the night rescue of a member of our gang was all to the good. Rubber had another paper ready too, all written up. It was headed, PLEDGE OF THE RUBBER BAND, and we all signed it. It had already been signed by Mike Walsh. In it we agreed to an equal division of anything coming from George Rowley, no matter who got it or when.

"We were all broke except Vic Lindquist, who had a bag of gold dust. It was Rubber's suggestion that we get Turtle-back in. Turtle-back was an old-timer who owned the fastest horse in Silver City. He had no use for that kind of a horse; he only happened to own it because he had won it in a poker game a few days before. I went with Rubber down to Turtle-back's shanty. We offered him Vic Lindquist's dust for the horse, but he said it wasn't enough. We had expected that. Then Rubber explained to him what was up, told him the whole story, and offered him an equal share with the rest of us, for the horse, and the dust to boot. Turtle-back was still half asleep. Finally, when he got the idea, he blinked at us, and then all of a sudden he slapped his knee and began to guffaw. He said that by God he always had wanted to own a part of England, and anyway he would probably lose the horse before he got a chance to ride it much. Rubber got out the PLEDGE OF THE RUBBER BAND, but Turtle-back wouldn't have his name added to it, saying he didn't like to have his name written down anywhere. He would trust us to see that he got his share. Rubber scribbled out a bill of sale for the horse, but Turtle-back wouldn't sign that either; he said I was there as a witness, the horse was ours, and that *was enough. He put on his boots and took us over to Johnson's corral, and we saddled the horse, a palamino with a white face, and led it around the long way, back of the shacks and tents and along a gully, to where the gang was.*

"We rescued George Rowley all right. You've heard me tell about it, how we loosened a couple of boards and then set fire to the shanty where they had him, and how he busted out of the loose place in the excitement, and how Mike Walsh, who was known to be a dead shot, emptied two guns at him without hitting him. Rowley was in the saddle and away before anyone else realized it, and nobody bothered to chase him because they were too busy putting out the fire.

"The story came out later about our buying Turtle-back's horse, but by that time people's minds were on something else, and anyway our chief offense was that we had started the fire and it couldn't be proved we had done that. It might have been different if the man we helped to escape had done something really criminal, like cheating at cards or stealing somebody's dust.

"So far as I know, none of us ever saw Rowley or heard of him since that night. You've heard me mention twenty times, when you and I were having hard going, that I'd like to find him and learn if he owed me anything, but you know I never did and of course I meant it more or less as a joke anyhow. But recently, here in France, two things have come up about it. The first one is a thought that's in my mind all the time, what if I do get mine over here, what kind of a fix am I leaving you and the kid in? My little daughter Clara—God how I'd love to see her. And you. To hell with that stuff when it's no use, but I'd gladly stand up and let the damn Germans shoot me tomorrow morning if I could see you two right this minute. The answer to my question is, a hell of a fix. My life would end more useless than it started, leaving my wife and daughter without a single solitary damn thing.

"The other thing that's come up is that I've seen George Rowley. It was one day last week. I may have told you that the lobe of his right ear was gone—he said he had it hacked off in Australia—but I don't think I really knew him by that. There probably is a mighty good print of his mug in my mind somewhere, and I just simply knew it was him. After twenty-three years! I was out with a survey detail about a mile back of the front trenches, laying out new communication lines, and a big car came along. British. The car stopped. It had four British officers in it, and one of them called to me and I went over and he asked for directions to our division headquarters.

36

I gave them to him, and he looked at my insignia and asked if we Americans let our captains dig ditches. I had seen by his insignia that he was a brigade commander. I grinned at him and said that in our army everybody worked but the privates. He looked at me closer and said, 'By Gad, it's Gil Fox!' I said, 'Yes, sir. General Rowley?' He shook his head and laughed and told the driver to go on, and the car jumped forward, and he turned to wave his hand at me.

"So he's alive, or he was last week, and not in the poorhouse, or whatever they call it in England. I've made various efforts to find out who he was, but without success. Maybe I will soon. In the meantime, I'm writing this down and disposing of it, because although it may sound far-fetched and even a little batty, the fact is that this is the only thing resembling a legacy that I can leave to you and Clara. After all, I did risk my life that night in Silver City, on the strength of a bargain understood and recorded, and if that Englishman is rolling in it there's no reason why he shouldn't pay up. It is my hope and wish that you will make every effort to see that he does, not only for your sake but for our daughter's sake. That may sound melodramatic, but the things that are going on over here get you that way. As soon as I find out who he is I'll get this back and add that to it.

"Another thing. If you do find him and get a grubstake out of it, you must not use it to pay that $26,000 I owe those people out in California. You must promise me this. You must, dearest Lola. I'm bestowing this legacy on you and Clara, not them! I say this because I know that you know how much that debt has worried me for ten years. Though I wasn't really responsible for that tangle, it's true that it would give me more pleasure to straighten that out than anything in the world except to see you and Clara, but if I die that business can die with me. Of course, if you should get such a big pile of dough that you're embarrassed—but miracles like that don't happen.

"If something should come out of it, it must be split with the rest of the gang if you can find them. I don't know a thing about any of them except Harlan Scovil, and I haven't heard from him for several years. The last address I had for him is in the little red book in the drawer of my desk. One of the difficulties is that you haven't got the paper that George Rowley signed. Rubber Coleman, by agreement, kept both that and the PLEDGE OF THE RUBBER BAND. Maybe you can find Coleman. Or maybe Rowley is a decent guy and will pay without any paper. Either sounds highly improbable. Hell, it's all a daydream. Anyhow, I have every intention of getting

37

back to you safe and sound, and if I do you'll never see this unless I bring it along as a souvenir.

"Here are the names of everybody that was in on it: George Rowley. Rubber Coleman (don't know his first name). Victor Lindquist. Harlan Scovil (you've met him, go after him first). Mike Walsh (he was a little older, maybe 32 at the time, not one of the Rubber Band). Turtle-back was a good deal older, probably dead now, and that's all the name I knew for him. And last but by no means least, yours truly, and how truly it would take a year to tell, Gilbert Fox, the writer of these presents."

Clara Fox stopped. She ran her eyes over the last sentence again, then placed that sheet at the back, folded them up, and returned them to her handbag. She put her hand up and brushed back her hair, and sat and looked at Wolfe. No one said anything.

Finally Wolfe sighed. He opened his eyes at her. "Well, Miss Fox. It appears to be the moon that you want after all."

She shook her head. "I know who George Rowley is. He is now in New York."

"And this, I presume—" Wolfe nodded—"is Mr. Victor Lindquist's daughter." He nodded again. "And this gentleman is the Mr. Walsh who emptied two guns at Mr. Rowley without hitting him."

Mike Walsh blurted, "I could have hit him!"

"Granted, sir. And you, Miss Fox, would very much like to have $26,000, no doubt with accrued interest, to discharge debts of your dead father. In other words, you need something a little less than $30,000."

She stared at him. She glanced at me, then back at him, and asked coolly, "Am I here as your client, Mr. Wolfe, or as a suspected thief?"

He wiggled a finger at her. "Neither as yet. Please do not be so foolish as to be offended. If I show you my mind, it is only to save time and avoid irrelevancies. Haven't I sat and listened patiently for ten minutes although I dislike being read aloud to?"

"That's irrelevant."

"Indeed. I believe it is. Let us proceed. Tell me about Mr. George Rowley."

But that had to be postponed. I had heard the doorbell, and Fritz going down the hall, and a murmur from outside. Now I shook my head at Clara Fox and showed her my palm to stop her, as the office door opened and Fritz came in and closed it behind him.

38

"A man to see you, sir. I told him you were engaged."

I bounced up. There were only two kinds of men Fritz didn't announce as gentlemen: one he suspected of wanting to sell something, and a policeman, uniform or not. He could smell one a mile off. So I bounced up and demanded:

"A cop?"

"Yes, sir."

I whirled to Wolfe. "Ever since I saw Muir looking at Miss Fox today I've been thinking she ought to have a lightning rod. Would you like to have her pinched in here, or out in the hall?"

Wolfe nodded and snapped, "Very well, Archie."

I crossed quick and got myself against the closed office door, and spoke not too loud to Fritz, pointing to the door that opened into the front room: "Go through that way and lock the door from the front room to the hall." He moved. I turned to the others: "Go in there and sit down, and if you don't talk any it won't disturb us." Walsh and Miss Lindquist stared at me. Clara Fox said to Wolfe:

"I'm not your client yet."

He said, "Nor yet a suspect. Here. Please humor Mr. Goodwin."

She got up and went and the others followed her, Fritz came back and I told him to shut that door and lock it and give me the key. Then I went back to my desk and sat down, while Fritz, at a nod from Wolfe, went to the hall for the visitor.

The cop came in, and I was surprised to see that it was a guy I knew. Surprised, because the last time I had heard of Slim Foltz he had been on the Homicide Squad, detailed to the District Attorney's office.

"Hello, Slim."

"Hi, Goodwin." He had his own clothes on. He came on across with his hat in his hand. "Hello, Mr. Wolfe. I'm Foltz, Homicide Squad."

"Good evening, sir. Be seated."

The dick put his hat on the desk and sat down, and reached in his pocket and pulled out a piece of paper. "There was a man shot down the street an hour or so ago. Shot plenty, five bullets in him. Killed. This piece of paper was in his pocket, with your name and address on it. Along with other names. Do you know anything about him?"

Wolfe shook his head. "Except that he's dead. Not, that is, at this moment. If I knew his name, perhaps . . ."

39

"Yeah. His name was on a hunting license, also in his pocket. State of Wyoming. Harlan Scovil."

"Indeed. It is possible Mr. Goodwin can help you out. Archie?"

I was thinking to myself, hell, he didn't come for her after all. But I was just as well pleased she wasn't in the room.

• • • • 5 • • • •

SLIM FOLTZ was looking at me.

I said, "Harlan Scovil? Sure. He was here this afternoon."

Foltz got in his pocket again and fished out a little black memo book and a pencil stub. "What time?"

"He got here around 4:30, a little before maybe, and left at 5:26."

"What did he want?"

"He wanted to see Nero Wolfe."

"What about?"

I shook my head regretfully. "There you've got me, mister. I told him he'd have to wait until six o'clock, so he was waiting."

"He must have said something."

"Certainly he said something. He said he wanted to see Nero Wolfe."

"What else did he say?"

"He said there seemed to be very little spittin' done east of the Mississippi River, and he wanted to know if there were any honest men this side of the mountains. He didn't say specifically what he wanted to see Mr. Wolfe about. We'd never seen him or heard of him before. Oh yes, he said he just got to New York this morning, from Wyoming. By the way, just because that license was in his pocket—was he over six feet, around sixty, blue serge suit with sleeves too short and the lapel torn a little on the right side, with a leathery red face and a cowboy hat—"

"That's him," the dick grunted. "What did he come to New York for?"

"To see Nero Wolfe I guess." I grinned. "That's the kind of a rep we've got. If you mean, did he give any hint as to who might want to bump him off, he didn't."

41

"Did he see Wolfe?"

"No. I told you, he left at 5:26. Mr. Wolfe never comes down until six o'clock."

"Why didn't he wait?"

"Because he got a phone call."

"He got a phone call here?"

"Right here in this room. I wasn't here. I had gone out, leaving this bird here waiting for six o'clock. The phone was answered by Fritz Brenner, Mr. Wolfe's chef and household pride. Want to see him?"

"Yeah. If you don't mind."

Wolfe rang. Fritz came. Wolfe told him he was to answer the gentleman's questions, and Fritz said "Yes, sir" and stood up straight.

All Foltz got out of Fritz was the same as I had got. He had put down the time of the phone call, 5:26, in accordance with Wolfe's standing instructions for exactness in all details of the household and office. It was a man phoning, and he had not given his name and Fritz had not recognized his voice. Fritz had not overheard any of the conversation. Harlan Scovil had immediately left, without saying anything.

Fritz went back to the kitchen.

The dick frowned at the piece of paper. "I wasn't expecting to draw a blank here. I came here first. There's other names on this paper—Clara Fox, Michael Walsh, Michael spelled wrong, Hilda Lindquist, that's what it looks like, and a Marquis of Clivers. I don't suppose you—"

I horned in, shaking my head. "As I said, when this Harlan Scovil popped in here at half-past four today, I had never seen him before. Nor any of those others. Strangers to me. I'm sure Mr. Wolfe hadn't either. Had you, sir?"

"Seen them? No. But I believe I had heard of one of them. Wasn't it the Marquis of Clivers we were discussing yesterday?"

"Discussing? Yes, sir. When you dropped that javelin. That piece in the paper." I looked at Foltz helpfully. "There was an article in the *Times* yesterday, magazine section—"

He nodded. "I know all about that. The sergeant was telling me. This marquis seems to be something like a duke, he's immune by reason of a foreign power or something. It don't even have to be a friendly foreign power. The sergeant says this business might possibly be an international plot. Captain Devore is going to make arrangements to see this marquis and maybe warn him or protect him."

"Splendid." Wolfe nodded approvingly. "The police earn

the gratitude of all of us. But for them, Mr. Foltz, we private investigators might sit and wait for clients in vain."

"Yeah." Foltz got up. "Much obliged for the compliment, even if that's all I get. I mean, I haven't got much information. Except that telephone call, that may lead to something. Scovil was shot only four blocks from here, on 31st Street, only nine minutes after he got that phone call, at 5:35. He was walking along the sidewalk and somebody going by in a car reached out and plugged him, filled him full. He was dead right then. It was pretty dark around there, but a man near-by saw the license, and the car's already been found, parked on Ninth Avenue. Nobody saw anyone get out of it."

"Well, that's something." I was hopeful. "That ought to get you somewhere."

"Probably stolen. They usually are." The dick had his hat in his hand. "Gang stuff, it looks like. Much obliged to you folks anyhow."

"Don't mention it, Slim."

I went to the hall with him, and saw him out the front door, and shut it after him and slid the bolt. Before I returned to the office I stopped at the kitchen and told Fritz that I'd answer any doorbells that might ring for the rest of the evening.

I crossed to Wolfe's desk and grinned at him. "Ha ha. The damn police were here."

Wolfe looked at the clock, which said ten minutes past seven. He reached out and pushed the button, and when Fritz came, leaned back and sighed.

"Fritz."

"Yes, sir."

"A calamity. We cannot possibly dine at eight as usual. Not dine, that is. We can eat, and I suppose we shall have to. You have filets of beef with sauce Abano."

"Yes, sir."

Wolfe sighed again. "You will have to serve it in morsels, for five persons. By adding some of the fresh stock you can have plenty of soup. Open Hungarian *petits poissons*. You have plenty of fruit? Fill in as you can. It is distressing, but there's no help for it."

"The sauce is a great success, sir. I could give the others canned chicken and mushrooms—"

"Confound it, no! If there are to be hardships, I must share them. That's all. Bring me some beer."

Fritz went, and Wolfe turned to me: "Bring Clara Fox."

I unlocked the door to the front room. Fritz hadn't turned on all the lights, and it was dim. The two women were side by

43

side on the divan, and Mike Walsh was in a chair, blinking at me as if he had been asleep.

I said, "Mr. Wolfe would like to speak to Miss Fox."

Mike Walsh said, "I'm hungry."

Clara Fox said, "To all of us."

"First just you. Please. —There'll be some grub pretty soon, Mr. Walsh. If you'll wait in here."

Clara Fox hesitated, then got up and preceded me. I shut the door, and she went back to her chair in front of Wolfe, the one the dick had sat in. Wolfe had emptied a glass and was filling it up again.

"Will you have some beer, Miss Fox?"

She shook her head. "Thank you. But I don't like to discuss this with you alone, Mr. Wolfe. The others are just as much—"

"To be sure. Permit me." He wiggled a finger at her. "They shall join us presently. The fact is, I wish to touch on something else for a moment. Did you take that money from Mr. Muir's desk?"

She looked at him steadily. "We shouldn't let things get confused. Are you acting now as the agent of the Seaboard Products Corporation?"

"I'm asking you a question. You came here to consult me because you thought I had abilities. I have; I'm using them. Either answer my question or find abilities elsewhere. Did you take that money?"

"No."

"Do you know who took it?"

"No."

"Do you know anything about it?"

"No. I have certain suspicions, but nothing specific about the money itself."

"Do you mean suspicions on account of the attitude of Mr. Perry and Mr. Muir toward you personally?"

"Yes. Chiefly Mr. Muir."

"Good. Now this: Did you kill anyone this evening between five and six o'clock?"

She stared at him. "Don't be an idiot."

He drank some beer, wiped his lips, and leaned back in his chair. "Miss Fox. The avoidance of idiocy should be the primary and constant concern of every intelligent person. It is mine. I am sometimes successful. Take, for instance, your statement that you did not steal that money. Do I believe it? As a philosopher, I believe nothing. As a detective, I believe it enough to leave it behind me, but am prepared to glance back over my shoulder. As a man, I believe it utterly. I assure you,

44

my reason for the questions I am asking is not idiotic. For one thing, I am observing your face as you reply to them. Bear with me; we shall be getting somewhere, I think. Did you kill anyone this evening between five and six o'clock?"

"No."

"Did Mr. Walsh or Miss Lindquist do so?"

"Kill anyone?"

"Yes."

She smiled at him. "As a philosopher, I don't know. I'm not a detective. As a woman, they didn't."

"If they did, you have no knowledge of it?"

"No."

"Good. Have you a dollar bill?"

"I suppose I have."

"Give me one."

She shook her head, not in refusal, but in resigned perplexity at senseless antics. She looked in her bag and got out a dollar bill and handed it to Wolfe. He took it and unfolded it and handed it across to me.

"Enter it, please, Archie. Retainer from Miss Clara Fox. And get Mr. Perry on the phone." He turned to her. "You are now my client."

She didn't smile. "With the understanding, I suppose, that I may—"

"May sever the connection?" His creases unfolded. "By all means. Without notice."

I found Perry's number and dialed it. After giving my fingerprints by television to some dumb kluck I finally got him on, and nodded to Wolfe to take it.

Wolfe was suave. "Mr. Perry? This is Nero Wolfe. I have Mr. Goodwin's report of his preliminary investigation. He was inclined to agree with your own attitude regarding the probable innocence of Clara Fox, and he thought we might therefore be able to render some real service to you. But by a curious chance Miss Fox called at our office this evening—she is here now, in fact—and asked us to represent her interests in the matter. . . . No, permit me, please. . . . Well, it seemed to be advisable to accept her retainer. . . . Really, sir, I see nothing unethical . . ."

Wolfe hated to argue on the telephone. He cut it as short as he could, and rang off, and washed it down with beer. He turned back to Clara Fox.

"Tell me about your personal relations with Mr. Perry and Mr. Muir."

She didn't answer right away. She was sitting there frown-

45

ing at him. It was the first time I had seen her brow wrinkled, and I liked it better smoothed out. Finally she said, "I supposed you had already taken that case for Mr. Perry. I had gone to a lot of trouble deciding that you were the best man for us—Miss Lindquist and Mr. Walsh and Mr. Scovil and me—and I had already telephoned on Saturday and made the appointment with you, before I heard anything about the stolen money. I didn't know until two hours ago that Mr. Perry had engaged you, and since we had the appointment I thought we might as well go through with it. Now you tell Mr. Perry you're acting for me, not the Seaboard, and you say I've given you a retainer for that. That's not straight. If you want to call that a retainer, it's for the business I came to see you about, not that silly rot about the money. That's nonsense."

Wolfe inquired, "What makes you think it's nonsense?"

"Because it is. I don't know what the truth of it is, but as far as I'm concerned it's nonsense."

Wolfe nodded. "I agree with you. That's what makes it dangerous."

"Dangerous? How? If you mean I'll lose my job, I don't think so. Mr. Perry is the real boss there, and he knows I'm more than competent, and he can't possibly believe I took that money. If this other business is successful, and I believe it will be, I won't want the job anyhow."

"But you will want your freedom." Wolfe sighed. "Really, Miss Fox, we are wasting time that may be valuable. Tell me, I beg you, about Mr. Perry and Mr. Muir. Mr. Muir hinted this afternoon that Mr. Perry is enjoying the usufructs of gallantry. Is that true?"

"Of course not." She frowned, and then smiled. "Calling it that, it doesn't sound bad at all, does it? But he isn't. I used to go to dinner and the theater with Mr. Perry fairly frequently, shortly after I started to work for Seaboard. That was during my adventuress phase. I was going to be an adventuress."

"Did something interrupt?"

"Nothing but my disappointment. I have always been determined to get somewhere, not anywhere in particular, just somewhere. My father died when I was nine, and my mother when I was seventeen. She always said I was like my father. She paid for my schooling by sewing fat women's dresses. I loved my mother passionately, and hated the humdrum she was sunk in and couldn't get out of."

"She couldn't find George Rowley."

"She didn't try much. She thought it was fantastic. She

46

wrote once to Harlan Scovil, but the letter was returned. After she died I tried various things, everything from hat-check girl to a stenographic course, and for three years I studied languages in my spare time because I thought I'd want to go all over the world. Finally, by a stroke of luck, I got a good job at the Seaboard three years ago. For the first time I had enough money so I could spend a little trying to find George Rowley and the others mentioned in father's letter—I realized I'd have to find some of the others so there would be someone to recognize George Rowley. I guess mother was right when she said I'm like father; I certainly had fantastic ideas, and I'm terribly confident that I'm a very unusual person. My idea at that time was that I wanted to get money from George Rowley as soon as possible, so I could pay that old debt of my father's in California, and then go to Arabia. The reason I wanted to go to Arabia—"

She broke off abruptly, looked startled, and demanded, "What in the name of heaven started me on that?"

"I don't know." Wolfe looked patient. "You're wasting time again. Perry and Muir?"

"Well." She brushed her hair back. "Not long after I started to work for Seaboard, Mr. Perry began asking me to go to the theater with him. He said that his wife had been sick in bed for eight years and he merely wanted companionship. I knew he was a multi-millionaire, and I thought it over and decided to become an adventuress. If you think that sounds like a loony kid, don't fool yourself. For lots of women it has been a very exciting and satisfactory career. I never really expected to do anything much with Mr. Perry, because there was no stimulation in him, but I thought I could practice with him and at the same time keep my job. I even went riding with him, long after it got to be a bore. I thought I could practice with Mr. Muir, too, but I was soon sorry I had ever aroused his interest."

She drew her shoulders in a little, a shade toward the center of her, and let them out again, in delicate disgust. "It was Mr. Muir that cured me of the idea of being an adventuress, I mean in the classical sense. Of course I knew that to be a successful adventuress you have to deal with men, and they have to be rich, and seeing what Mr. Muir was like made me look around a little, and I realized it would be next to impossible to find a rich man it would be any fun to be adventurous with. Mr. Muir seemed to go practically crazy after he had had dinner with me once or twice. Once he came to my apartment and almost forced his way in, and he had an enormous pearl neck-

47

lace in his pocket! Of course it was disgusting in a way, but it was even more funny than it was disgusting, because I have never cared for pearls at all. But the worst thing about Mr. Muir is his stubbornness. He's a Scotsman, and apparently if he once gets an idea in his head he can't get it out again—"

Wolfe put in, "Is Mr. Muir a fool?"

"Why . . . yes, I suppose he is."

"I mean as a business man. A man of affairs. Is he a fool?"

"No. Not that way. In fact, he's very shrewd."

"Well, you are." Wolfe sighed. "You are quite an amazing fool, Miss Fox. You know that Mr. Muir, who is a shrewd man, is prepared to swear out a warrant against you for grand larceny. Do you think that he would consider himself prepared if preparations had not actually been made? Why does he insist on immediate action? So that the preparations may not be interfered with, by design, or by mischance. As soon as a warrant is in force against you, the police may search any property of yours, including that item of it where the $30,000 will be found. Couldn't Mr. Muir have taken it himself from his desk and put it anywhere he wanted to, with due circumspection?"

"Put it . . . " She stared at him. "Oh, no." She shook her head. "That would be too low. A man would have to be a dirty scoundrel to do that."

"Well? Who should know better than you, an ex-adventuress, that the race of dirty scoundrels has not yet been exterminated? By the eternal, Miss Fox, you should be tied in your cradle! Where do you live?"

"But, Mr. Wolfe . . . you could never persuade me . . . "

"I wouldn't waste time trying. Where do you live?"

"I have a little flat on East 61st Street."

"And what other items? We can disregard your desk at the office, that would not be conclusive enough. Do you have a cottage in the country? A trunk in storage? An automobile?"

"I have a little car. Nothing else whatever."

"Did you come here in it?"

"No. It's in a garage on 60th Street."

Wolfe turned to me. "Archie. What two can you get here at once?"

I glanced at the clock. "Saul Panzer in ten minutes. If Fred Durkin's not at the movies, him in twenty minutes. If he is, Orrie Cather in half an hour."

"Get them. Miss Fox will give you the key to her apartment and a note of authority, and also a note to the garage. Saul Panzer will search the apartment thoroughly. Tell him what he's looking for, and if he finds it bring it here. Fred will get

48

the automobile and drive it to our garage, and when he gets it there go through it, and leave it there. This alone will cost us twenty dollars, twenty times the amount of Miss Fox's retainer. Everything we undertake nowadays seems to be a speculation."

I got at the telephone. Wolfe opened his eyes on Clara Fox:

"You might learn if Miss Lindquist and Mr. Walsh will care to wash before dinner. It will be ready in five minutes."

She shook her head. "We don't need to eat. Or we can go out for a bite."

"Great hounds and Cerberus!" He was about as close to a tantrum as he ever got. "Don't need to eat! In heaven's name, are you camels, or bears in for the winter?"

She got up and went to the front room to get them.

• • • • 6 • • • •

MY DINNER was interrupted twice. Saul Panzer came before I had finished my soup, and Fred Durkin arrived while we were in the middle of the beef and vegetables. I went to the office both times and gave them their instructions and told them some hurry would do.

Wolfe made it a rule never to talk business at table, but we got a little forward at that, because he steered Hilda Lindquist and Mike Walsh into the talk and we found out things about them. She was the daughter of Victor Lindquist, now nearly 80 years old and in no shape to travel, and she lived with him on their wheat farm in Nebraska. Apparently it wasn't coffee cups she snapped in her fingers, it was threshing-machines. Clara Fox had finally found her, or rather her father, through Harlan Scovil, and she had come east for the clean-up on the chance that she might get enough to pay off a few dozen mortgages and perhaps get something extra for a new tractor, or at least a mule.

Walsh had gone through several colors before fading out to his present dim obscurity. He had made three good stakes in Nevada and California and had lost all of them. He had tried his hand as a building contractor in Colorado early in the century, made a pile, and dropped it when a sixty-foot dam had gone down the canyon three days after he had finished it. He had come back east and made a pass at this and that, but apparently had used up all his luck. At present he was night watchman on a construction job up at 55th and Madison, and he was inclined to be sore on account of the three dollars he was losing by paying a substitute in order to keep this appointment with Clara Fox. She had found him a year ago through an ad in the paper.

Wolfe was the gracious host. He saw that Mike Walsh got

50

two rye highballs and the women a bottle of claret, and like a gentleman he gave Walsh two extra slices of the beef, smothered with sauce, which he would have sold his soul for. But he wouldn't let Walsh light his pipe when the coffee came. He said he had asthma, which was a lie. Pipe smoke didn't bother him much, either. He was just sore at Walsh because he had had to give up the beef, and he took it out on him that way.

We hadn't any more than got back to the office, a little after nine o'clock, and settled into our chairs—the whole company present this time—when the doorbell rang. I went out to the front door and whirled the lock and slid the bolt, and opened it. Fred Durkin stepped in. He looked worried, and I snapped at him:

"Didn't you get it?"

"Sure I got it."

"What's the matter?"

"Well, it was funny. Is Wolfe here? Maybe he'd like to hear it too."

I glared at him, fixed the door, and led him to the office. He went across and stood in front of Wolfe's desk.

"I got the car, Mr. Wolfe. It's in the garage. But Archie didn't say anything about bringing a dick along with it, so I pushed him off. He grabbed a taxi and followed me. When I left the car in the garage just now and walked here, he walked too. He's out on the sidewalk across the street."

"Indeed." Wolfe's voice was thin; he disliked after-dinner irritations. "Suppose you introduce us to the dick first. Where did you meet him?"

Fred shifted his hat to his other hand. He never could talk to Wolfe without getting fussed up, but I must admit there was often enough reason for it. Fred Durkin was as honest as sunshine, and as good a tailer as I ever saw, but he wasn't as brilliant as sunshine. Warm and cloudy today and tomorrow. He said:

"Well, I went to the garage and showed the note to the guy, and he said all right, wait there and he'd bring it down. He went off and in a couple of minutes a man with a wide mouth came up and asked me if I was going for a ride. I'd never saw him before, but I'd have known he was a city feller if I'd had my eyes shut and just touched him with my finger. I supposed he was working on something and was just looking under stones, so I just answered something friendly. He said if I was going for a ride I'd better get a horse, because

51

the car I came for was going to remain there for the present."

Wolfe murmured, "So you apologized and went to a drug store to telephone here for instructions."

Fred looked startled. "No, sir, I didn't. My instructions was to get that car, and I got it. That dick had no documents or nothing, in fact he didn't have nothing but a wide mouth. I went upstairs with him after me. When the garage guy saw the kind of an argument it might be he just disappeared. I ran the car down on the elevator myself and got into the street and headed east. The dick jumped on the running-board, and when I reached around to brush a speck off the windshield I accidentally pushed the dick off. By that time we was at Third Avenue and he hopped a taxi and followed me. When I got to Tenth Avenue, inside your garage, I turned the car inside out, but there was nothing there but tools and an old lead pencil and a busted dog leash and a half a package of Omar cigarettes and—"

Wolfe put up a palm at him. "And the dick is now across the street?"

"Yes, sir. He was when I come in."

"Excellent. I hope he doesn't escape in the dark. Go to the kitchen and tell Fritz to give you a cyanide sandwich."

Fred shifted his hat. "I'm sorry, sir, if I—"

"Go! Any kind of a sandwich. Wait in the kitchen. If we find ourselves getting into difficulties here, we shall need you."

Fred went. Wolfe leaned back in his chair and got his fingers laced on his belly; his lips were moving, out and in, and out and in. At length he opened his eyes enough for Clara Fox to see that he was looking at her.

"Well. We were too late. I told you you were wasting time."

She lifted her brows. "Too late for what?"

"To keep you out of jail. Isn't it obvious? What reason could there be for watching your car except to catch you trying to go somewhere in it? And is it likely they would be laying for you if they had not already found the money?"

"Found it where?"

"I couldn't say. Perhaps, in the car itself. I am not a necromancer, Miss Fox. Now, before we—"

The phone rang, and I took it. It was Saul Panzer. I listened and got his story, and then told him to hold the wire and turned to Wolfe:

"Saul. From a pay station at 62nd and Madison. There was a dick playing tag with himself in front of Miss Fox's

52

address. Saul went through the apartment and drew a blank. Now he thinks the dick is sticking there, but he's not sure. It's possible he's being followed, and if so should he shake the dick and then come here, or what?"

"Tell him to come here. By no means shake the dick. He may know the one Fred brought, and in that case they might like to have a talk."

I told Saul, and hung up.

Wolfe was still leaning back, with his eyes half closed. Mike Walsh sat with his closed entirely, his head swaying on one side, and his breathing deep and even in the silence. Hilda Lindquist's shoulders sagged, but her face was flushed and her eyes bright. Clara Fox had her lips tight enough to make her look determined.

Wolfe said, "Wake Mr. Walsh. Having attended to urgencies —in vain—we may now at our leisure fill in some gaps. Regarding the fantastic business of · the Rubber Band. —Mr. Walsh, a sharp blow with your hand at the back of your neck will help. A drink of water? Very well. —Did I understand you to say, Miss Fox, that you have found George Rowley?"

She nodded. "Two weeks ago."

"Tell me about it."

"But Mr. Wolfe . . . those detectives . . ."

"To be sure. You remember I told you you should be tied in your cradle? For the present, this house is your cradle. You are safe here. We shall return to that little problem. Tell me about George Rowley."

She drew a breath. "Well . . . we found him. I began a long while ago to do what I could, which wasn't much. Of course I couldn't afford to go to England, or send someone, or anything like that. But I gathered some information. For instance, I learned the names of all the generals who had commanded brigades in the British army during the war, and as well as I could from this distance I began to eliminate them. There were hundreds and hundreds of them still alive, and of course I didn't know whether the one I wanted was alive or not. I did lots of things, and some of them were pretty bright if I am a fool. I had found Mike Walsh through an advertisement, and I got photographs of scores of them and showed them to him. Of course, the fact that George Rowley had lost the lobe of his right ear was a help. On several occasions, when I learned in the newspapers that a British general or ex-general was in New York, I managed to get a look at him, and sometimes Mike Walsh did too. Two weeks ago another one came, and in a photograph in the paper it looked as if the bottom of his right ear was off. Mike Walsh stood in front of his hotel all one afternoon when he should have been asleep, and saw him, and it was George Rowley."

Wolfe nodded. "That would be the Marquis of Clivers."

"How do you know that?"

"Not by divination. It doesn't matter. Congratulations, Miss Fox."

"Thank you. The Marquis of Clivers was going to Washington the next day, but he was coming back. I tried to see him that very evening, but couldn't get to him. I cabled a connection I had made in London, and learned that the marquis owned big estates and factories and mines and a yacht. I had been communicating with Hilda Lindquist and Harlan Scovil for some time, and I wired them to come on and sent them money for the trip. Mr. Scovil wouldn't take the money. He wrote me that he had never taken any woman-money and wasn't going to start." She smiled at Wolfe and me too. "I guess he was afraid of adventuresses. He said he would sell some calves. Saturday morning I got a telegram that he would get here Monday, so I telephoned your office for an appointment. When I saw him this noon I showed him two pictures of the Marquis of Clivers, and he said it was George Rowley. I had a hard time to keep him from going to the hotel after the marquis right then."

Wolfe wiggled a finger at her. "But what made you think you needed me? I detect no lack of confidence in your operations to date."

"Oh, I always thought we'd have to have a lawyer at the windup. I had read about you and admired you."

"I'm not a lawyer."

"I shouldn't think that would matter. I only know three lawyers, and if you saw them you would know why I chose you."

"You sound like a fool again." Wolfe sighed. "Do you wish me to believe that I was selected for my looks?"

"No, indeed. That would be . . . anyhow, I selected you. When I told you what your fee might be, I wasn't exaggerating. Let's say his estates and mines and so on are worth fifty million—"

"Pounds?"

"Dollars. That's conservative. He agreed to pay half of it. Twenty-five million. But there are two of the men I can't find. I haven't found a trace of Rubber Coleman, the leader,

54

or the man called Turtle-back. I have tried hard to find Rubber Coleman, because he had the papers, but I couldn't. On the twenty-five million take off their share, one-third, and that leaves roughly sixteen million. Make allowances for all kinds of things, anything you could think of—take off, say, just for good measure, fifteen million. That leaves a million dollars. That's what I asked him for a week ago."

"You asked who for? Lord Clivers?"

"Yes."

"You said you were unable to see him."

"That was before he went to Washington. When he came back I tried again. I had made an acquaintance . . . he has some assistants with him on his mission—diplomats and so on— and I had got acquainted with one two weeks ago, and through him I got to the marquis, thinking I might manage it without any help. He was very unpleasant. When he found out what I was getting at, he ordered me out. He claimed he didn't know what I was talking about, and when I wanted to show him the letter my father had written in 1918, he wouldn't look at it. He told the young man whom he called to take me away that I was an adventuress."

She wasn't through. But the doorbell rang, and I went to answer it. I thought it just possible that a pair might rush me, and there was no advantage in a roughhouse, so I left the bolt and chain on until I saw it was Saul Panzer. Then I opened up and let him in, and shut the door and slid the bolt again.

Saul is about the smallest practicing dick, public or private, that I've ever seen, and he has the biggest scope. He can't push over buildings because he simply hasn't got the size, but there's no other kind of a job he wouldn't earn his money on. It's hard to tell what he looks like, because you can't see his face for his nose. He had a big long cardboard box under his arm.

I took him to the office. As he sidled past a chair to get to Wolfe's desk he passed one sharp glance around, and I knew that gave him a print of those three sitting there which would fade out only when he did.

Wolfe greeted him. "Good evening, Saul."

"Good evening, Mr. Wolfe. Of course Archie told you my phone call. There's not much to add. When I arrived the detective was there on the sidewalk. His name is Bill Purvil. I saw him once about four years ago in Brooklyn, when we had that Moschenden case. He didn't recognize me on the sidewalk. But when I went in at that entrance he followed me. I

55

figured it was better to go ahead. There was a phone in the apartment. If I found the package I could phone Archie to come and get into the court from 60th Street, and throw it to him from a back window. When the detective saw I was going into that apartment with a key, he stopped me to ask questions, and I answered what occurred to me. He stayed out in the hall and I locked the door on the inside. I went through the place. The package isn't there. I came out and the detective followed me downstairs to the sidewalk. I phoned from a drug store. I don't think he tried to follow me, but I made sure it didn't work if he did."

Wolfe nodded. "Satisfactory. And your bundle?"

Saul got the box from under his arm and put it on the desk. "I guess it's flowers. It has a name on it, Drummond, the Park Avenue florist. It was on the floor of the hall right at the door of the apartment, apparently been delivered, addressed Miss Clara Fox. My instructions were to search only the apartment, so I hesitated to open this box, because it wasn't in the apartment. But I didn't want to leave it there, because it was barely possible that what you want was in it. So I brought it along."

"Good. Satisfactory again. May we open it, Miss Fox?"

"Certainly."

I got up to help. Saul and I pulled off the fancy gray tape and took the lid off. Standing, we were the only ones who could see in. I said:

"It's a thousand roses."

Clara Fox jumped up to look. I reached in the box and picked up an envelope and took a card from the envelope. I squinted at it—it was scrawly writing—and read it out:

"Francis Horrocks?"

She nodded. "That's my acquaintance. The man that ejected me from the Marquis of Clivers. He's a young diplomat with a special knowledge of the Far East. Aren't they beautiful? Look, Hilda. Smell. They are *very* nice." She carried them to Wolfe. "Aren't they a beautiful color, Mr. Wolfe? Smell." She looked at Mike Walsh, but he was asleep again, so she put the box back on the desk and sat down.

Wolfe was rubbing his nose which she had tickled with the roses. "Saul. Take those to the kitchen and have Fritz put them in water. Remain there. You must see my orchids, Miss Fox, but that can wait. Mr. Walsh! Archie, wake him, please."

I reached out and gave Walsh a dig, and he jerked up and glared at me. He protested, "Hey! It's too warm in here. I'm never as warm as this after supper."

56

Wolfe wiggled a finger at him. "If you please, Mr. Walsh. Miss Fox has been giving us some details, such as your recognition of the Marquis of Clivers. Do you understand what I'm saying?"

"Sure." Walsh pulled the tips of his fingers across his eyes, and stretched his eyes open. "What about it?"

"Did you recognize the Marquis of Clivers as George Rowley?"

"Sure I did. Who says I didn't?"

"As yet, no one. Are you positive it was the same man?"

"Yes. I told you at the table, I'm always positive."

"So you did. Among other things. You told me that through ancient habit, and on your post as a night watchman, you carry a gun. You also told me that you suspected Harlan Scovil of being an Englishman, and that all English blood was bad blood. Do you happen to have your gun with you? Could I see it?"

"I've got a license."

"Of course. Could I see it? Just as a favor?"

Walsh growled something to himself, but after a moment's hesitation he leaned forward and reached to his hip and pulled out a gat. He looked at it, and rubbed his left palm caressingly over the barrel, and then got up and poked the butt at Wolfe. Wolfe took it, glanced at it, and held it out to me. I gave it a mild inspection. It was an old Folwell .44. It was loaded, the cylinder full, and there was no smell of any recent activity around the muzzle. I glanced at Wolfe and caught his little nod, and returned the cannon to Mike Walsh, who caressed it again before he put it back in his pocket.

Clara Fox said, "Who's wasting time now, Mr. Wolfe? You haven't told us yet—"

Wolfe stopped her. "Don't begin again, Miss Fox. Please. Give me a chance to earn my share of that million. Though I must confess that my opinion is that you might all of you sell out for a ten dollar bill and call it a good bargain. What have you to go on? Really nothing. The paper which George Rowley signed was entrusted to Rubber Coleman, whom you have been unable to find. The only other basis for a legal claim would be a suit by the man called Turtle-back to recover the value of his horse, and since Mr. Walsh has told us that Turtle-back was over 50 years old in 1895, he is in all likelihood dead. There are only two methods by which you can get anything out of the Marquis of Clivers; one is to attempt to establish a legal claim by virtue of contract, for which you would need

57

a lawyer, not a detective. You have yourself already done the detective work, quite thoroughly. The other method is to attempt to scare the marquis into paying you, through threat of public exposure of his past. That is an ancient and often effective method, technically known as blackmail. It is not—"

She interrupted him, cool but positive. "It isn't blackmail to try to collect something from a man that he promised to pay."

Wolfe nodded. "It's a nice point. Morally he owes it. But where's the paper he signed? Anyway, let me finish. I, myself, am in a quandary. When you first told me the nature of the commission you were offering me, I was prepared to decline it without much discussion. Then another element entered in, of which you are still ignorant, which lent the affair fresh interest. Of course, interest is not enough; before that comes the question, who is going to pay me? I shall expect—"

Mike Walsh squawked, "Ten per cent!"

Clara Fox said, "I told you, Mr. Wolfe—"

"Permit me. I shall expect nothing exorbitant. It happens that my bank account is at present in excellent condition, and therefore my cupidity is comparatively dormant. Still, I have a deep aversion to working without getting paid for it. I have accepted you, Miss Fox, as my client. I may depend on you?"

She nodded impatiently. "Of course you may. What is the other element that entered in of which I am still ignorant?"

"Oh. That." Wolfe's half-closed eyes took in all three faces. "At twenty-five minutes to six this evening, less than five hours ago, on Thirty-first Street near Tenth Avenue, Harlan Scovil was shot and killed."

Mike Walsh jerked up straight in his chair. They all gaped at Wolfe. Wolfe said:

"He was walking along the sidewalk, and someone going by in an automobile shot him five times. He was dead when a passerby reached him. The automobile has been found, empty of course, on Ninth Avenue."

Clara Fox gasped incredulously, "Harlan Scovil!" Hilda Lindquist sat with her fists suddenly clenched and her lower lip pushing her upper lip toward her nose. Mike Walsh was glaring at Wolfe. He exploded suddenly:

"Ye're a howling idiot!"

Wolfe's being called an idiot twice in one evening was certainly a record. I made a note to grin when I got time. Clara Fox was saying: "But Mr. Wolfe . . . it can't . . . how can . . ."

Walsh went on exploding, "So you hear of some shooting,

and you want to smell my gun? Ye're an idiot! Of all the dirty—" He stopped himself suddenly and leaned on his hands on his knees, and his eyes narrowed. He looked pretty alert and competent for a guy seventy years old. "To hell with that. Where's Harlan? I want to see him."

Wolfe wiggled a finger at him. "Compose yourself, Mr. Walsh. All in time. As you see, Miss Fox, this is quite a complication."

"It's terrible. Why . . . it's awful. He's really *killed?*"

Hilda Lindquist spoke suddenly. "I didn't want to come here. I told you that. I thought it was a wild goose chase. My father made me. I mean, he's old and sick and he wanted me to come because he thought maybe we could get enough to save the farm."

Wolfe nodded. "And now, of course . . ."

Her square chin stuck out. "Now I'm glad I came. I've often heard my father talk about Harlan Scovil. He would have been killed anyway, whether I came or not, and now I'm glad I'm here to help. You folks will have to tell me what to do, because I don't know. But if that marquis thinks he can refuse to talk to us and then shoot us down on the street . . . we'll see."

"I haven't said the marquis shot him, Miss Lindquist."

"Who else did?"

I thought from her tone she was going to tell him not to be an idiot, but she let it go at that and looked at him. Wolfe said:

"I can't tell you. But I have other details for you. This afternoon Harlan Scovil came to this office. He told Mr. Goodwin that he came in advance of the time for the interview to see what kind of a man I was. At twenty-six minutes after five, while he was waiting to see me, he received a telephone call from a man. He left at once. You remember that shortly after you arrived this evening a caller came and you were asked to go to the front room. The caller was a city detective. He informed us of the murder, described the corpse, and said that in his pocket had been found a paper bearing my name and address, and also the names of Clara Fox, Hilda Lindquist, Michael Walsh and the Marquis of Clivers. Scovil had been shot just nine minutes after he received that phone call here and left the house."

Clara Fox said, "I saw him write those names on the paper. He did it while he was eating lunch with me."

"Just so. —Mr. Walsh. Did you telephone Scovil here at 5:26?"

"Of course not. How could I? That's a damn fool question. I didn't know he was here."

"I suppose not. But I thought possibly Scovil had arranged to meet you here. When Scovil arrived it happened that there was another man in the office, one of my clients, and Scovil approached him and told him he wasn't Mike Walsh."

"Well, was he? I'm Mike Walsh, look at me. The only arrangement I had to meet him was at six o'clock, through Miss Fox. Shut up about it. I asked you where Harlan is. I want to see him."

"In time, sir. —Miss Fox. Did you telephone Scovil here?"

She shook her head. "No. Oh, no. I thought you said it was a man."

"So it seemed. Fritz might possibly have been mistaken. Was it you who phoned, Miss Lindquist?"

"No. I haven't telephoned anyone in New York except Clara."

"Well." Wolfe sighed. "You see the little difficulty, of course. Whoever telephoned knew that Scovil was in New York and knew he was at this office. Who knew that except you three?"

Hilda Lindquist said, "The Marquis of Clivers knew it."

"How do you know that?"

"I don't know it. I see it. Clara had been to see him and he had threatened to have her arrested for annoying him. He had detectives follow her, and they saw her this noon with Harlan Scovil, and they followed Harlan Scovil here and then notified the Marquis of Clivers. Then he telephoned—"

"Possible, Miss Lindquist. I admit it's possible. If you substitute for the detective a member of the marquis's entourage, even more possible. But granted that we rather like that idea, do you think the police will? A British peer, in this country on a government mission of the highest importance, murdering Harlan Scovil on Thirty-first Street? I have known quite a few policemen, and I am almost certain that idea wouldn't appeal to them."

Mike Walsh said, "To hell with the dumb Irish cops."

Clara Fox asked, "The detective that was here . . . the one that told you about . . . about the shooting. Our names were on that paper. Why didn't he want to see us?"

"He did. Badly. But I observed that there were no addresses on the paper except my own, so he is probably having difficulty. I decided not to mention that all of you happened to be here at the moment, because I wanted to talk with you and I knew he would monopolize your evening."

"The detective at my apartment . . . he may have been there . . . about this . . ."

"No. There had hardly been time enough. Besides, there was one at the garage too."

Clara Fox looked at him, and took a deep breath. "I seem to be in a fix."

"Two fixes, Miss Fox." Wolfe rang for beer. "But it is possible that before we are through we may be able to effect a merger."

. . . . 7 . . . .

I ONLY half heard that funny remark of Wolfe's. Parts of
my brain were skipping around from this to that and finding
no place to settle down. As a matter of fact I had been getting
more uncomfortable all evening, ever since Slim Foltz had
told us the names on that paper and Wolfe had let him go
without telling him that the three people he was looking for
were sitting in our front room. He was working on a murder,
and the fact that the name of a bird like that marquis was on
that paper meant that they weren't going to let anything slide.
They would find those three people sooner or later, and when
they learned where they had been at the time Slim Foltz
called on us, they would be vexed. There were already two or
three devoted public servants who thought Wolfe was a little
tricky, and it looked as if this was apt to give them entirely
too much encouragement. I knew pretty well how Wolfe
worked, and when he let Foltz go I had supposed he was
going to have a little talk with our trio of visitors and then
phone someone like Cramer at Headquarters or Dick Morley
of the District Attorney's office, and arrange for some interviews. But here it was past ten o'clock, and he was just going
on with an interesting conversation. I didn't like it.

I heard his funny remark though, about two fixes and effect-
ing a merger. I got his idea, and that was one of the points my
brain skipped to. I saw how there might possibly be a connection between the Rubber Band business and Clara Fox
being framed for lifting the thirty grand. She had gone to
this British gent and spilled her hand to him, and he had
given her the chilly how now and had her put out. But he had
been badly annoyed what. You might even say scared if he

hadn't been a nobleman. And a few days later the frame-up reared its ugly head. It would be interesting to find out if the Marquis of Clivers was acquainted with Mr. Muir, and if so to what extent. Clara Fox had said Muir was a Scotsman, so you couldn't depend on him any more than you could an Englishman, maybe not as much. As usual, Wolfe was ahead of me, but he hadn't lost me, I was panting along behind.

Meanwhile I had to listen too, for the conversation hadn't stopped. At the end of Wolfe's remark about the merger, Mike Walsh suddenly stood up and announced:

"I'll be going."

Wolfe looked at him. "Not just yet, Mr. Walsh. Be seated."

But he stayed on his feet. "I've got to go. I want to see Harlan."

"Mr. Scovil is dead. I beg you, sir. There are one or two points I must still explain."

Walsh muttered, "I don't like this. You see I don't like it?" He glared at Wolfe, handed me the last half of it, and sat down on the edge of his chair.

Wolfe said, "It's getting late. We are confronted by three distinct problems, and each one presents difficulties. First, the matter of the money missing from the office of the Seaboard Products Corporation. So far that appears to be the personal problem of Miss Fox, and I shall discuss it with her later. Second, there is your joint project of collecting a sum of money from the Marquis of Clivers. Third, there is your joint peril resulting from the murder of Harlan Scovil."

"Joint hell." Walsh's eyes were narrowed again. "Say we divide the peril up, mister. Along with the money."

"If you prefer. But let us take the second problem first. I see no reason for abandoning the attack on the Marquis of Clivers because Mr. Scovil has met a violent death. In fact, that should persuade us to prosecute it. My advice would be this—Archie, your notebook. Take a letter to the Marquis of Clivers, to be signed by me. Salute him democratically, 'Dear Sir:'

"I have been engaged by Mr. Victor Lindquist and his daughter, Miss Hilda Lindquist, as their agent to collect an amount which you have owed them since 1895. In that year, in Silver City, Nevada, with your knowledge and consent, Mr. Lindquist purchased a horse from a man known as Turtle-back, and furnished the horse to you for your use in an urgent private emergency. You signed

63

a paper before your departure acknowledging the obligation, but of course your debt would remain a legal obligation without that.

"At that time and place good horses were scarce and valuable; furthermore, for reasons peculiar to your situation, that horse was of extraordinary value to you at that moment. Miss Lindquist, representing her father, states that that extraordinary value can be specified as $100,000. That amount is therefore due from you, with accrued interest at 6% to date.

"I trust that you will pay the amount due without delay and without forcing us to the necessity of legal action. I am not an attorney. If you prefer to make the payment through attorneys representing both sides, we shall be glad to make that arrangement."

Wolfe leaned back. "All right, Miss Lindquist?"

She was frowning at him. "He can't pay with money for murdering Harlan Scovil."

"Certainly not. But one thing at a time. I should explain that this claim has no legal standing, since it has expired by time, but the marquis might not care to proceed to that defense in open legal proceedings. We are on the fringe of blackmail, but our hearts are pure. I should also explain that at 6% compound interest money doubles itself in something like twelve years, and that the present value of that claim as I have stated it in the letter is something over a million dollars. A high price for a horse, but we are only using it to carry us to a point of vantage. This has your approval, Miss Fox?"

Clara Fox was looking bad. Sitting there with the fingers of one hand curled tight around the fingers of the other, she wasn't nearly as cool and sweet as she had been that afternoon when Muir had declared right in front of her that she was a sneak thief.

"No," she said. "I don't think we want . . . no, Mr. Wolfe. I'm just realizing . . . it's my fault Mr. Scovil was killed. I started all this. Just for that money . . . no! Don't send that letter. Don't do anything."

"Indeed." Wolfe drank some beer, and put the glass down with his usual deliberation. "It would seem that murder is sometimes profitable, after all."

Her fingers tightened. "Profitable?"

"Obviously. If, as seems likely, Harlan Scovil was killed by someone involved in this Rubber Band business, the

64

murderer probably had two ends in view: to remove Scovil, and to frighten the rest of you. To scare you off. He appears to have accomplished both purposes. Good for him."

"We're not scared off."

"You're ready to quit."

Hilda Lindquist put in, with her chin up, "Not me. Send that letter."

"Miss Fox?"

She pulled her shoulders in, and out again. "All right. Send it."

"Mr. Walsh?"

"Deal me out. You said you wanted to explain something."

"So I did." Wolfe emptied his glass. "We'll send the letter, then. The third problem remains. I must call your attention to these facts: First, the police are at this moment searching for all three of you—in your case, Miss Fox, two separate assignments of police. Second, the police are capable of concluding that the murderer of Harlan Scovil is someone who knew him or knew of him, and was in this neighborhood this evening. Third, it is probable that there is no one in New York who ever heard of Harlan Scovil except you three and Clivers; or, if there is such a one, it is not likely that the police will discover him—in fact, the idea will not occur to them until they have exhausted all possibilities in connection with you three. Fourth, when they find you and question you, they will suspect you not only of knowledge of Scovil's murder, but also of some preposterous plot against Lord Clivers, since his name was on that paper.

"Fifth. When they question you, there will be three courses open to you. You may tell the truth, in which case your wild and extravagant tale will reinforce their suspicions and will be enough to convict you of almost anything, even murder. Or you may try to tone your tale down, tell only a little and improvise to fill in the gaps, whereupon they will catch you in lies and go after you harder than ever. Or you may assert your constitutional rights and refuse to talk at all; if you do that they will incarcerate you as material witnesses and hold you without bail. As you see, it is a dilemma with three horns and none of them attractive. As Miss Fox put it, you're in a fix. And any of the three courses will render you *hors de combat* for any further molestation of the Marquis of Clivers."

Hilda Lindquist's chin was way up in the air. Mike Walsh was leaning forward with his eyes on Wolfe narrower than ever. Clara Fox had stopped squeezing her hand and had her lips pressed tight. She opened them to say:

"All right. We're game. Which do we do?"

"None." Wolfe sighed. "None of those. Confound it, I was born romantic and I shall never recover from it. But, as I have said, I expect to be paid. I hope I have made it clear that it will not do for the police to find you until we are ready for them to. Have I demonstrated that?"

The two women asked simultaneously, "Well?"

"Well . . . Archie, bring Saul."

I jumped from habit and not from enthusiasm. I was half sore. I didn't like it. I found Saul in the kitchen drinking port wine and telling Fred and Fritz stories, and led him to the office. He stood in front of Wolfe's desk.

"Yes, sir."

Wolfe spoke, not to him. "Miss Lindquist, this is Mr. Saul Panzer. I would trust him further than might be thought credible. He is himself a bachelor, but has acquaintances who are married and possibly even friends, with the usual living quarters—an apartment or a house. Have you anything to say to him?"

But the Lindquist mind was slow. She didn't get it. Clara Fox asked Wolfe:

"May I?"

"Please do."

She turned to Saul. "Miss Lindquist would like to be in seclusion for a while—a few days—she doesn't know how long. She thought you might know of a place . . . one of your friends . . ."

Saul nodded. "Certainly, Miss Lindquist." He turned to Wolfe:

"Is there a warrant out?"

"No. Not yet."

"Shall I give the address to Archie?"

"By no means. If I need to communicate with Miss Lindquist I can do so through General Delivery. She can notify me on the telephone what branch."

"Shall we go out the back way onto Thirty-fourth Street?"

"I was about to suggest it. When you are free again, return here. Tonight." Wolfe moved his eyes. "Is there anything of value in your luggage at the hotel, Miss Lindquist?"

She was standing up. She shook her head. "Not much. No."

"Have you any money?"

"I have thirty-eight dollars and my ticket home."

"Good. Opulence. Goodnight, Miss Lindquist. Sleep well."

Clara Fox was up too. She went to the other woman and

66

put her hands on her shoulders and kissed her on the mouth. "Goodnight, Hilda. It's rotten, but . . . keep your chin up."

Hilda Lindquist said in a loud voice, "Goodnight, everybody," and turned and followed Saul Panzer out of the room. In a few seconds I could hear their footsteps on the stairs leading down to the basement, where a door opened onto the court in the rear. We were all looking at Wolfe, who was opening a bottle of beer. I was thinking, the old lummox certainly fancies he's putting on a hot number, I suppose he'll send Miss Fox to board with his mother in Buda Pesth. It looked to me like he was stepping off over his head.

He looked at Mike Walsh. "Now, sir, your turn. I note your symptoms of disapproval, but we are doing the best we can. In the kitchen is a man named Fred Durkin, whom you have seen. Within his capacity, he is worthy of your trust and mine. I would suggest—"

"I don't want any Durkin." Walsh was on his feet again. "I don't want anything from you at all. I'll just be going."

"But Mr. Walsh." Wolfe wiggled a finger at him. "Believe me, it will not pay to be headstrong. I am not by nature an alarmist, but there are certain features of this affair—"

"So I notice." Walsh stepped up to the desk. "The features is what I don't like about it." He looked at Clara Fox, then at me, then at Wolfe, letting us know what the features were. "I may be past me prime, but I'm not in a box yet. What kind of a shenanigan would ye like to try on an old man, huh? I'm to go out and hide, am I? Do I get to ask a question or two?"

"That's three." Wolfe sighed. "Go ahead."

Walsh whirled on me. "You, Goodwin's your name? Was it you that answered the phone yesterday, the call that came for Harlan Scovil?"

"No." I grinned at him. "I wasn't here."

"Where was you?"

"At the office of the Seaboard Products Corporation, where Miss Fox works."

"Ha! Was you indeed. You wasn't here. I suppose it couldn't have been you that phoned here to Harlan."

"Sure it could have, but it wasn't. Listen, Mr. Walsh—"

"I've listened enough. I've been listening to this Clara Fox for a year and looking at her pretty face, and I had no reason to doubt her maybe, and this is what's come out of it, I've helped lead my old friend Harlan Scovil into an ambush to his death. My old friend Harlan." He stopped abruptly, and shut his lips tight, and looked around at us while a big fat tear suddenly popped out of each of his eyes and rolled on

67

down, leaving a mark across his wrinkles. He went on, "I ate a meal with you. A meal and three drinks. Maybe I'd like to puke it up some day. Or maybe you're all square shooters, I don't know, but I know somebody ain't, and I'm going to find out who it is. What's this about them being after Miss Fox for stealing money? I can find out about that too. And if I want anything collected from this English Marquis nobleman, I can collect it myself. Goodnight to ye all." He turned and headed for the door.

Wolfe snapped, "Get him, Archie."

Remembering the gun on his hip, I went and folded myself around him and locked him. He let out a snarl and tried some twisting and unloosed a couple of kicks at my shins, but in four seconds he had sense enough to see it was no go. He quivered a little and then stood quiet, but I kept him tight. He said:

"It's me now, is it?"

Wolfe spoke across the room at him. "You called me an idiot, Mr. Walsh. I return the compliment. What is worse, you are hotheaded. But you are an old man, so there is humanity's debt to you. You may go where you please, but I must warn you that every step you take may be a dangerous step. Furthermore, when you talk, every word may be dangerous not only to you but to Miss Fox and Miss Lindquist. I strongly advise you to adopt the precautions—"

"I'll do me own precautions."

"Mike!" Clara Fox came, her hand out. "Mike, you can't be thinking . . . what Mr. Wolfe says is right. Don't desert us now. Turn him loose, Mr. Goodwin. Shake hands, Mike."

He shook his head. "Did you see him grab me, and all I was doing was walking out on me own feet? I hate the damn detectives and always have, and what was he doing at your office? And if you're my enemy, Clara Fox, God help you, and if not then you can be my friend. Not now. When he turns me loose I'll be going."

Wolfe said, "Release him, Archie. Goodnight, Mr. Walsh."

I let my muscles go and stepped back. Mike Walsh put a hand up to feel his ribs, turned to look at me, and then to Wolfe. He said:

"But I'm no idiot. Show me that back way."

Clara Fox begged him, "Don't go, Mike."

He didn't answer her. I started for the kitchen, and he followed me after stopping in the hall for his hat and coat. I told Fred to see him through the court and the fence and the passage leading to 34th Street, and switched on the basement light for them. I stood and watched them go down. I hadn't cared much for Wolfe's hot number anyhow, and now it looked like worse than a flop, with that wild Irishman in his old age going out to do his own precautions. But I hadn't argued about letting him go, because I knew that kind as well as Wolfe did and maybe better.

When I went back to the office Clara Fox was still standing up. She asked, "Did he really go?"

I nodded. "With bells on."

"Do you think he meant what he said?" She turned to Wolfe. "I don't think he meant it at all. He was just angry and frightened and sorry. I know how he felt. He felt that Harlan Scovil was killed because we started this business, and now he doesn't want to go away and hide. I don't either. I don't want to run away."

"Then it is lucky you won't have to." Wolfe emptied his glass, returned it to the tray, and slid the tray around to the other side of the pen block. That meant that he had decided he had had enough beer for the day, and therefore that he would probably open only one more bottle before going upstairs, provided he went fairly soon. He sighed. "You understand, Miss Fox, this is something unprecedented. It has been many years since any woman has slept under this roof. Not that I disapprove of them, except when they attempt to function as domestic animals. When they stick to the vocations for which they are best adapted, such as chicanery, sophistry, self-adornment, cajolery, mystification and incubation, they are sometimes splendid creatures. Anyhow . . . you will find our south room, directly above mine, quite comfortable. I may add that I am foolishly fond of good form, good color, and fine texture, and I have good taste in those matters. It is a pleasure to look at you. You have unusual beauty. I say that to inform you that while the idea of a woman sleeping in my house is theoretically insupportable, in this case I am willing to put up with it."

"Thank you. Then I'm to hide here?"

"You are. You must keep to your room, with the curtains drawn. Elaborate circumspection will be necessary and will be explained to you. Mr. Goodwin will attend to that. Should your stay be prolonged, it may be that you can join us in the diningroom for meals; eating from a tray is an atrocious insult both to the food and the feeder; and in that case, luncheon is punctually at one and dinner at eight. But before we adjourn for the night there are one or two things I need still to know; for instance, where were you and Miss Lindquist and Mr. Walsh from five to six o'clock this evening?"

Clara Fox nodded. "I know. That's why you asked me if I had killed anybody, and I thought you were being eccentric. But of course you don't believe that. I've told you we were looking for Harlan Scovil."

"Let's get a schedule. Put it down, Archie. Mr. Goodwin informed me that you left the Seaboard office at a quarter past five."

She glanced at me. "Yes, about that. That was the time I was supposed to get Harlan Scovil at his hotel on Forty-fifth Street, and I didn't get there until nearly half-past five. He wasn't there. I looked around on the street and went a block to another hotel, thinking possibly he had misunderstood me, and then went back again and he still wasn't there. They said he had been out all afternoon as far as they knew. Hilda was at a hotel on Thirtieth Street, and I had told Mike Walsh to be there in the lobby at a quarter to six, and I was to call there for them. Of course I was late, it was six o'clock when I got there, and we decided to try Harlan Scovil's hotel once more, but he wasn't there. We waited a few minutes and then came on without him, and got here at six-thirty." She stopped, and chewed on her lip. "He was dead . . . then. While we were there waiting for him. And I was planning . . . I thought . . ."

"Easy, Miss Fox. We can't resurrect. So you know nothing of Miss Lindquist's and Mr. Walsh's whereabouts between five and six. —Easy, I beg you. Don't tell me again I'm an idiot or you'll have me believing it. I am merely filling in a picture. Or rather, a rough sketch. I think perhaps you should leave us here with it and go to bed. Remember, you are to keep to your room, both for your own safety and to preserve me from serious annoyance. Mr. Goodwin—"

"I know." She frowned at him and then at me. "I thought of that when you said I was to stay here. You mean what they call accessory after the fact—"

"Bosh." Wolfe straightened in his chair and his hand went forward by automatism, but there was no beer there. He sent a sharp glance at me to see if I noticed it, and sat back again. "I can't be an accessory after a fact that never existed. I am acting on the assumption that you are not criminally involved either in larceny or in murder. If you are, say so and get out. If you are not, go to bed. Fritz will show you your room." He pushed the button. "Well?"

70

"I'll go to bed." She brushed her hair back. "I don't think I'll sleep."

"I hope you will, even without appetite for it. At any rate, you won't walk the floor, for I shall be directly under you." The door opened, and Wolfe turned to it. "Fritz. Please show Miss Fox to the south room, and arrange towels and so on. In the morning, take her roses to her with breakfast, but have Theodore slice the stems first. —And by the way, Miss Fox, you have nothing with you. The niceties of your toilet you will have to forego, but I believe we can furnish a sleeping-garment. Mr. Goodwin owns some handsome silk pajamas which his sister sent him on his birthday, from Ohio. They are hideous, but handsome. I'm sure he won't mind. I presume, Fritz, you'll find them in the chest of drawers near the window. Unless . . . would you prefer to get them for Miss Fox yourself, Archie?"

I could have thrown my desk at him. He knew damn well what I thought of those pajamas. I was so sore I suppose it showed in my cheeks, because I saw Fritz pull in his lower lip with his teeth. I was slower on the come-back than usual, and I never did get to make one, for at that instant the doorbell rang, which was a piece of luck for Nero Wolfe. I got up and strode past them to the hall.

I was careless for two reasons. I was taking it for granted it was Saul Panzer, back from planting Hilda Lindquist in seclusion; and the cause of my taking something for granted when I shouldn't, since that's always a bad thing to do in our business, was that my mind was still engaged with Wolfe's vulgar attempt to be funny. Anyhow, the fact remains that I was careless. I whirled the lock and took off the bolt and pulled the door open.

They darned near toppled me off my pins with the edge of the door catching my shoulder. I saved myself from falling and the rest was reflex. There were two of them, and they were going right on past in a hurry. I sprang back and got in front and gave one of them a knee in the belly and used a stiff-arm on the other. He started to swing, but I didn't bother about it; I picked up the one that had stopped my knee and just used him for a whisk-broom and depended on speed and my 180 pounds. The combination swept the hall out. We went through the door so fast that the first guy stumbled and fell down the stoop, and I dropped the one I had in my arms and turned and pulled the door shut and heard the lock click. Then I pushed the bell-button three times. The guy that had fallen

71

down the stoop, the one who had tried to plug me, was on his feet again and coming up, with words.

"We're officers—"

"Shut up." I heard footsteps inside, and I called through the closed door. "Fritz? Tell Mr. Wolfe a couple of gentlemen have called and we're staying out on the porch for a talk. And hey! Those things are in the bottom drawer."

• • • • 8 • • • •

I SAID, "What do you mean, officers? Army or navy?"

He looked down at me. He was an inch taller than me to begin with, and he was stretching it. He made his voice hard enough to scare a schoolgirl right out of her socks. "Listen, bud. I've heard about you. How'd you like to take a good nap on some concrete?"

The other officer was back on his ankles too, but he was a short guy. He was built something like a whisk-broom, at that. I undertook to throw oil on the troubled waters. Ordinarily I might have enjoyed a nice rough cussing-match, but I wanted to find out something and get back inside. I summoned a friendly grin.

"What the hell, how did I know you had badges? Okay, thanks, sergeant. All I knew was the door bumping me and a cyclone going by. Is that a way to inspire confidence?"

"All right, you know we've got badges now." The sergeant humped up a shoulder and let it drop, and then the other one. "Let us in. We want to see Nero Wolfe."

"I'm sorry, he's got a headache."

"We'll cure it for him. Listen. A friend of mine warned me about you once. He said the time would come when you would have to be taken down. Maybe that's the very thing I came here for. But so far it's a matter of law. Open that door or I'll open it myself. I want to see Mr. Wolfe on police business."

"There's no law about that. Unless you've got a warrant."

"You couldn't read it anyhow. Let us in."

I got impatient. "What's the use wasting time? You can't go in. The floor's just been scrubbed. Wolfe wouldn't see you anyhow, at this time of night. Tell me what you want like a gentleman and a cop, and I'll see if I can help you."

73

He glared at me. Then he put his hand inside to his breast pocket and pulled out a document, and I had a feeling in my knees like a steering-wheel with a shimmy. If it was a search warrant the jig was up right there. He unfolded it and held it for me to look, and even in the dim light from the street lamp one glance was enough to start my heart off again. It was only a warrant to take into custody. I peered at it and saw among other things the name Ramsey Muir, and nodded.

The sergeant grunted, "Can you see the name? Clara Fox."

"Yeah, it's a nice name."

"We're going in after her. Open up."

I lifted the brows. "In here? You're crazy."

"All right, we're crazy. Open the door."

I shook my head, and got out a cigarette, and lit up. I said, "Listen, sergeant. There's no use wasting the night in repartee. You know damn well you've got no more right to go through that door than a cockroach unless you've got a search warrant. Ordinarily Mr. Wolfe is more than willing to cooperate with you guys; if you don't know that, ask Inspector Cramer. So am I. Hell, some of my best friends are cops. I'm not even sore because you tried to rush me and I got excited and thought you were mugs and pushed you. But it just happens that we don't want company of any kind at present."

He grunted and glared. "Is Clara Fox in there?"

"Now that's a swell question." I grinned at him. "Either she isn't, in which case I would say no, or she is and I don't want you to know it, in which case would I say yes? I might at that, if she was somewhere else and I didn't want you to go there to look for her."

"Is she in there?"

I just shook my head at him.

"You're harboring a fugitive from justice."

"I wouldn't dream of such a thing."

The short dick, the one I had swept the hall with, piped up in a tenor, "Take him down for resisting an officer."

I reproved him: "The sergeant knows better than that. He knows they wouldn't book me, or if they did I read about a man once that collected enough to retire on for false arrest."

The big one stood and stared into my frank eyes for half a minute, then turned and descended the stoop and looked up and down the street. I didn't know whether he expected to see the Russian army or a place to buy a drink. He called up to his brother in arms:

"Stay here, Steve. Cover that door. I'll go and phone a report and probably send someone to cover the rear. When that

74

bird turns his back to go in the house give him a kick in the ass."

I waved at him, "Goodnight, sergeant," pushed the button three shorts, took my key from my pocket, unlocked the door and went in. If that tenor had tickled me I'd have pulled his nose. I slid the bolt in place. Fritz was standing in the middle of the hall with my automatic in his hand. I said:

"Watch out, that thing's loaded."

He was serious. "I know it is, Archie. I thought possibly you might need it."

"No, thanks. I bit their jugulars. It's a trick."

Fritz giggled and handed me the gun, and went to the kitchen. I strolled into the office. Clara Fox was gone, and I was reflecting that she might be looking at herself in the mirror with my silk pajamas on. I had tried them on once, but had never worn them. I had no more than got inside the office when the doorbell rang. As I returned to the entrance and opened the door, leaving the bolt and chain on, I wondered if it was the tenor calling me back to get my kick. But this time it was Saul Panzer. He stood there and let me see him. I asked him through the crack:

"Did you find her?"

"No. I lost her. Lost the trail."

"You're a swell bird dog."

I opened up and let him in, and took him to the office. Wolfe was leaning back in his chair with his eyes closed. The tray had been moved back to its usual position, and there was a glass on it with fresh foam sticking to the sides, and two bottles. He was celebrating the hot number he was putting on.

I said, "Here's Saul."

"Good." The eyes stayed shut. "All right, Saul?"

"Yes, sir."

"Of course. Satisfactory. Can you sleep here?"

"Yes, sir. I stopped by and got a toothbrush."

"Indeed. Satisfactory. The north room, Archie, above yours. Tell Fred he is expected at eight in the morning, and send him home. If you are hungry, Saul, go to the kitchen; if not, take a book to the front room. There will be instructions shortly."

I went to the kitchen and pried Fred Durkin out of his chair and escorted him to the hall and let him out, having warned him not to stumble over any foreign objects that might be found on the stoop. But the dick had left the stoop and was propped against a fire plug down at the curb. He jerked himself up to take a stare at Fred, and I was hoping he'd be dumb enough to suspect it was Clara Fox with pants on, but that was really too much to expect. I barricaded again and returned to the office.

Saul had gone to the front room to curl up with a book. Wolfe stayed put behind his desk. I went to the kitchen and negotiated for a glass of milk, and then went back and got into my own swivel and started sipping. When a couple of minutes passed without any sign from Wolfe, I said indifferently:

"That commotion in the hall a while ago was the Mayor and the Police Commissioner calling to give you the freedom of the city prison. I cut their throats and put them in the garbage can."

"One moment, Archie. Be quiet."

"Okay. I'll gargle my milk. It'll probably be my last chance for that innocent amusement before they toss us in the hoosegow. I remember you told me once that there is no moment in any man's life too empty to be dramatized. You seem to think that's an excuse for filling life up with—"

"Confound you." Wolfe sighed, and I saw his eyelids flicker. "Very well. Who was it in the hall?"

"Two city detectives, one a sergeant no less, with a warrant for the arrest of Clara Fox sworn to by Ramsey Muir. They tried to take us by storm, and I repulsed them single-handed and single-footed. Satisfactory?"

Wolfe shuddered. "I grant there are times when there is no leisure for finesse. Are they camping?"

"One's out there on a fire plug. The sergeant went to telephone. They're going to cover the back. It's a good thing Walsh and Hilda Lindquist got away. I don't suppose—"

The phone rang. I circled on the swivel and put down my milk and took it. "Hello, this is the office of Nero Wolfe." Someone asked me to wait. Then someone else:

"Hello, Wolfe? Inspector Cramer."

I asked him to hold it and turned to Wolfe. "Cramer. Up at all hours of the night."

As Wolfe reached for the phone on his desk he tipped me a nod, and I kept my receiver and reached for a pencil and notebook.

Cramer was snappy and crisp, also he was surprised and his feelings were hurt. He had a sad tale. It seemed that Sergeant Heath, one of the best men in his division, in pursuance of his duty to make a lawful arrest, had attempted to call at the office of Nero Wolfe for a consultation and had been denied

76

admittance. In fact, he had been forcibly ejected. What kind of cooperation was that?

Wolfe was surprised too, at this protest. At the time that his assistant, Mr. Goodwin, had hurled the intruders into the street single-handed, he had not known they were city employees; and when that fact was disclosed, their actions had already rendered their friendly intentions open to doubt. Wolfe was sorry if there had been a misunderstanding.

Cramer grunted. "Okay. There's no use trying to be slick about it. What's it going to get you, playing for time? I want that girl, and the sooner the better."

"Indeed." Wolfe was doing slow motion. "You want a girl?"

"You know I do. Goodwin saw the warrant."

"Yes, he told me he saw a warrant. Larceny, he said it was. But isn't this unusual, Mr. Cramer? Here it is nearly midnight, and you, an inspector, in a vindictive frenzy over a larceny—"

"I'm not in a frenzy. But I want that girl, and I know you've got her there. It's no use, Wolfe. Less than half-an-hour ago I got a phone call that Clara Fox was at that moment in your office."

"It costs only a nickel to make a phone call. Who was it?"

"That's my business. Anyhow, she's there. Let's talk turkey. If Heath goes back there now, can he get her? Yes or no."

"Mr. Cramer." Wolfe cleared his throat. "I shall talk turkey. First, Heath or anyone else coming here now will not be permitted to enter the house without a search warrant."

"How the hell can I get a search warrant at midnight?"

"I couldn't say. Second, Miss Clara Fox is my client, and, however ardently I may defend her interests, I do not expect to violate the law. Third, I will not for the present answer any question, no matter what its source, regarding her whereabouts."

"You won't. Do you call that cooperation?"

"By no means. I call it common sense. And there is no point in discussing it."

There was a long pause, then Cramer again: "Listen, Wolfe. This is more important than you think it is. Can you come down to my office right away?"

"Mr. Cramer!" Wolfe was aghast. "You know I cannot."

"You mean you won't. Forget it for once. I shouldn't leave here. I tell you this is important."

"I'm sorry, sir. As you know, I leave my house rarely, and only when impelled by exigent personal considerations. The last time I left it was in the taxicab driven by Dora Chapin, for the purpose of saving the life of my assistant, Mr. Goodwin."

Cramer cussed a while. "You won't come?"

"No."

"Can I come there?"

"I should think not, under the circumstances. As I said, you cannot enter without a search warrant."

"To hell with a search warrant. I've got to see you. I mean, come and talk with you."

"Just to talk? You are making no reservations?"

"No. This is straight. I'll be there in ten minutes."

"Very well." I saw the creases in Wolfe's cheeks unfolding. "I'll try to restrain Mr. Goodwin."

We hung up. Wolfe pushed the button for Fritz. I shut my notebook and tossed it to the back of the desk, and picked up the glass and took a sip of milk. Then, glancing at the clock and seeing it was midnight, I decided I had better reinforce my endurance and went to the cabinet and poured myself a modicum of bourbon. It felt favorable going down, so I took another modicum. Fritz had brought Wolfe some beer, and it was already flowing to its destiny.

I said, "Tell me where Mike Walsh is and I'll go and wring his neck. He must have gone to the first drug store and phoned headquarters. We should have had Fred tail him."

Wolfe shook his head. "You always dive into the nearest pool, Archie. Some day you'll hit a rock and break your neck."

"Yeah? What now? Wasn't it Walsh that phoned him?"

"I have no idea. I'm not ready to dive. Possibly Mr. Cramer will furnish us a sounding. Tell Saul to go to bed and come to my room for instructions at eight o'clock."

I went to the front room and gave Saul the program, and bade him goodnight, and went back to my desk again. There was a little white card lying there, fallen out of my notebook, where I had slipped it some hours before and forgotten about it. I picked it up and looked at it. *Francis Horrocks*.

I said, "I wonder how chummy Clara Fox got with that acquaintance she made. The young diplomat that sent her the roses. It was him that got her in to see his boss. Where do you suppose he fits in?"

"Fits in to what?"

So that was the way he felt. I waved a hand comprehensively. "Oh, life. You know, the mystery of the universe. The scheme of things."

"I'm sure I don't know. Ask him."

"Egad, I shall. I just thought I'd ask you first. Don't be so

78

damn snooty. The fact is, I feel rotten. That Harlan Scovil that got killed was a good guy. You'd have liked him; he said no one could ever get to know a woman well enough to leave her around loose. Though I suppose you've changed your mind, now that there's a woman sleeping in your bed—"

"Nonsense. My bed—"

"You own all the beds in this house except mine, don't you? Certainly it's your bed. Is her door locked?"

"It is. I instructed her to open it only to Fritz's voice or yours."

"Okay. I'm apt to wander in there any time. Is there anything you want to tell me before Cramer gets here? Such as who shot Harlan Scovil and where that thirty grand is and what will happen when they pick Mike Walsh up and he tells them all about our convention this evening? Do you realize that Walsh was here when Saul took Hilda Lindquist away? Do you realize that Walsh may be in Cramer's office right now? Do you realize—"

"That will do, Archie. Definitely." Wolfe sat up and poured beer. "I realize up to my capacity. As I told Mr. Walsh, I am not an alarmist, but I certainly realize that Miss Fox is in more imminent danger than any previous client I can call to mind; if not danger of losing her life, then of having it irretrievably ruined. That is why I am accepting the hazard of concealing her here. As for the murder of Harlan Scovil, a finger of my mind points straight in one direction, but that is scarcely enough for my own satisfaction and totally insufficient for the safety of Miss Fox or the demands of legal retribution. We may learn something from Mr. Cramer, though I doubt it. There are certain steps to be taken without delay. Can Orrie Cather and Johnny Keems be here at eight in the morning?"

"I'll get them. I may have to pull Johnny off—"

"Do so. Have them here by eight if possible, and send them to my room." He sighed. "A riot for a levee, but there's no help for it. You will have to keep to the house. Before we retire certain arrangements regarding Miss Fox will need discussion. And by the way, the letter I dictated on behalf of our other client, Miss Lindquist, should be written and posted with a special delivery stamp before the early morning collection. Send Fritz out with it."

"Then I'd better type it now, before Cramer gets here."

"As you please."

I turned and got the typewriter up and opened my notebook, and rattled it off. I grinned as I wrote the "dear sir," but the grin was bunk, because if Wolfe hadn't told me to be democratic I would have been up a stump and probably would have had to try something like "dearest marquis." From the article I had read the day before I knew where he was, Hotel Portland. Wolfe signed it, and I got Fritz and let him out the front door and waited there till he came back. The short dick was still out there.

I was back in the office but not yet on my sitter again, when the doorbell rang. I wasn't taking any chances, since Fred had gone home and Saul was upstairs asleep. I pulled the curtain away from the glass panel to get a view of the stoop, including corners, and when I saw Cramer was there alone I opened up. He stepped in and I shut the door and bolted it and then extended a paw for his hat and coat. And it wasn't so silly that I kept a good eye on him either, since I knew he had been enforcing the law for thirty years.

He mumbled, "Hello, son. Wolfe in the office?"

"Yeah. Walk in."

• • • • 9 • • • •

WOLFE AND the inspector exchanged greetings. Cramer sat down and got out a cigar and bit off the end, and held a match to it. Wolfe got a hand up and pinched his nostrils between a thumb and a forefinger to warn the membranes of the assault that was coming. I was in my chair with my notebook on my knee, not bothering to camouflage.

Cramer said, "You know, you're a slick son-of-a-gun. Do you know what I was trying to decide on my way over here?"

Wolfe shook his head. "I couldn't guess."

"I bet you couldn't. I decided it was a toss-up. Whether you've got that Fox woman here and you're playing for time or waiting for daylight to spring something, or whether you've sent her away for her health and you're kidding us to make us think she's here so we won't start nosing for her trail. For instance, I don't suppose it could have been this Goodwin here that phoned my office at half-past eleven?"

"I shouldn't think so. Did you, Archie?"

"No, sir. On my honor I didn't."

"Okay." Cramer got smoke in his windpipe and coughed it out. "I know there's no use trying to play poker with you, Wolfe. I quit that years ago. I've come to lay some cards on the table and ask you to do the same. In fact, the Commissioner says we're not asking, we're demanding. We're taking no chances—"

"The Police Commissioner? Mr. Hombert?" Wolfe's brows were up.

"Right. He was in my office when I phoned you. I told you, this is more important than you think it is. You've stepped into something."

"You don't say so." Wolfe sighed. "I was sure to, sooner or later."

81

"Oh, I'm not trying to impress you. I've quit that too. I'm just telling you. As I told the Commissioner, you're tricky and you're hard to get ahead of, but I've never known you to slip in the mud. By and large, and of course making allowances, you've always been a good citizen."

"Thank you. Let us go on from there."

"Right." Cramer took a puff and knocked off ashes. "I said I'd show you some cards. First, there's the background, I'd better mention that. You know how it is nowadays, everybody's got it in for somebody else, and half of them have gone cuckoo. When a German ship lands here a bunch of Jews go and tear the flag off it and raise general hell. If a Wop professor that's been kicked out of Italy tries to give a lecture a gang of Fascists haul him down and beat him up. When you try your best to feed people that haven't got a job they turn Communist on you and start a riot. It's even got so that when a couple of bank presidents have lunch at the White House, the servants have to search the floor for banana peels that they may have put there for the President to slip on. Everyone has gone nuts."

Wolfe nodded. "Doubtless you are correct. I don't get around much. It sounds bewildering."

"It is. To get down to particulars, when any prominent foreigners come here, we have to watch our step. We don't want anything happening. For instance, you'd be surprised at the precautions we have to take when the German Ambassador comes up from Washington for a banquet. You might think there was a war on. As a matter of fact, there is! No one's ready for a scrap but everyone wants to hit first. Whoever lands at this port nowadays, you can be sure there's someone around that's got it in for him."

"It might be better if everybody stayed at home."

"Huh? Oh. That's their business. Anyway, that's the background. A couple of weeks ago a man called the Marquis of Clivers came here from England."

"I know. I've read about him."

"Then you know what he came for."

Wolfe nodded. "In a general way. A high diplomatic mission. To pass out slices of the Orient."

"Maybe. I'm not a politician, I'm a cop. I was when I pounded the pavement thirty years ago, and I still am. But the Marquis of Clivers seems to be as important as almost anybody. I understand we get the dope on that from the Department of State. When he landed here a couple of weeks

82

ago we gave him protection, and saw him off to Washington. When he came back, eight days ago, we did the same."

"The same? Do you mean you have men with him constantly?"

Cramer shook his head. "Not constantly. All public appearances, and a sort of general eye out. We have special men. If we notice anything or hear of anything that makes us suspicious, we're on the job. That's what I'm coming to. At 5:26 this afternoon, just four blocks from here, a man was shot and killed. In his pocket he had a paper—"

Wolfe showed a palm. "I know all about that, Mr. Cramer. I know the man's name, I know he had left my office only a few minutes before he was killed, and I know that the name of the Marquis of Clivers was on the paper. The detective that was here, Mr. Foltz I believe his name was, showed it to me."

"Oh. He did. Well?"

"Well . . . I saw the names on the paper. My own was among them. But, as I explained to Mr. Foltz, I had not seen the man. He had arrived at our office, unexpected and unannounced, and Mr. Goodwin had—"

"Yeah." Cramer took his cigar from his mouth and hitched forward. "Look here, Wolfe. I don't want to get into a chinning match with you, you're better at it than I am, I admit it. I've talked with Foltz, I know what you told him. Here's my position: there's a man in this town representing a foreign government on important business, and I'm responsible both for his safety and his freedom from annoyance. A man is shot down on the street, and on a paper in his pocket we find the name of the Marquis of Clivers, and other names. Naturally I wouldn't mind knowing who killed Harlan Scovil, but finding that name there makes it a good deal more than just another homicide. What's the connection and what does it mean? The Commissioner says we've got to find out damned quick or it's possible we'll have a first-rate mess on our hands. It's already been bungled a little. Like a dumb flatfoot rookie, Captain Devore went to see the Marquis of Clivers this evening without first consulting headquarters."

"Indeed. Will you have some beer, Mr. Cramer?"

"No. The marquis just stared at Devore as if he was one of the lower animals, which he was, and said that possibly the dead man was an insurance salesman and the paper was a list of prospects. Later on the Commissioner himself telephoned the marquis, and by that time the marquis had remembered that a week ago today a woman by the name of

Clara Fox had called on him with some kind of a wild tale, trying to get money, and he had had her put out. So there's a tie-up. It's some kind of a plot, no doubt about it, and since it's interesting enough so that someone took the trouble to bump off this Harlan Scovil, you couldn't call it tiddly-winks. Your name was on that paper. I know what you told Foltz. Okay. What I've got to do is find those other three, and I should have been in bed two hours ago. First let me ask you a plain straight question: what do you know about the connection between Clara Fox, Hilda Lindquist, Michael Walsh, and the Marquis of Clivers?"

Wolfe shook his head, slowly. "That won't do, Mr. Cramer."

"It'll do me. Will you answer it?" Cramer stuck his cigar in his mouth and tilted it up.

Wolfe shook his head again. "Certainly not. —Permit me, please. Let us frame the question differently, like this: What have I been told regarding the relations between those four people which would either solve the problem of the murder of Harlan Scovil, or would threaten the personal safety of the Marquis of Clivers or subject him to undeserved or illegal annoyance? Will you accept that as your question?"

Cramer scowled at him. "Say it again."

Wolfe repeated it. Cramer said:

"Well . . . answer it."

"The answer is, nothing."

"Huh? Bellywash. I'm asking you, Wolfe—"

Wolfe's palm stopped him, and Wolfe's tone was snappy. "No more. I've finished with that. I admit your right to call on me, as a citizen enjoying the opportunities and privileges of the City of New York, not to hinder—even to some extent assist—your efforts to defend a distinguished foreign guest against jeopardy and improper molestation. Also your efforts to solve a murder. But here are two facts for you. First, it is possible that your two worthy enterprises will prove to be incompatible. Second, as far as I am concerned, for the present at least, that question and answer are final. You may have other questions that I may be disposed to reply to. Shall we try?"

Cramer, chewing his cigar, looked at him. "You know something, Wolfe? Some day you're going to fall off and get hurt."

"You said those very words to me, in this room, eight years ago."

"I wouldn't be surprised if I did." Cramer put his dead half-chewed cigar in the ashtray, took out a fresh one, and sat

84

back. "Here's a question. What do you mean about incompatible? I suppose it was the Marquis of Clivers that pumped the lead in Harlan Scovil. There's a thought."

"I've already had it. It might very well have been. Has he an alibi?"

"I don't know. I guess the Commissioner forgot to ask him. You got any evidence?"

"No. No fragment." Wolfe wiggled a finger. "But I'll tell you this. It is important to me, also, that the murder of Harlan Scovil be solved. In the interest of a client. In fact, two."

"Oh. You've got clients."

"I have. I have told you that there are various questions I might answer if you cared to ask them. For instance, do you know who was sitting in your chair three hours ago? Clara Fox. And in that one? Hilda Lindquist. And in that? Michael Walsh. That, I believe, covers the list on that famous paper, except for the Marquis of Clivers. I am sorry to say he was absent."

Cramer had jerked himself forward. He leaned back again and observed, "You wouldn't kid me."

"I am perfectly serious."

Cramer stared at him. He scraped his teeth around on his upper lip, took a piece of tobacco from his tongue with his fingers, and kept on staring. Finally he said, "All right. What do I ask next?"

"Well . . . nothing about the subject of our conference, for that was private business. You might ask where Michael Walsh is now. I would have to reply, I have no idea. No idea whatever. Nor do I know where Miss Lindquist is. She left here about two hours ago. The commission I have undertaken for her is a purely civil affair, with no impingements on the criminal law. My other client is Clara Fox. In her case the criminal law is indeed concerned, but not the crime of murder. As I told you on the telephone, I will not for the present answer any question regarding her whereabouts."

"All right. Next?"

"Next you might perhaps permit me a question. You say that you want to see these people on account of the murder of Harlan Scovil, and in connection with your desire to protect the Marquis of Clivers. But the detectives you sent, whom Mr. Goodwin welcomed so oddly, had a warrant for her arrest on a charge of larceny. Do you wonder that I was, and am, a little skeptical of your good faith?"

"Well." Cramer looked at his cigar. "If you collected all

the good faith in this room right now you might fill a tea-spoon."

"Much more, sir, if you included mine." Wolfe opened his eyes at him. "Miss Fox is accused of stealing. How do you know, justly or unjustly? You thought she was in my house. Had you any reason to suppose that I would aid a person suspected of theft to escape a trial by law? No. If you thought she was here, could you not have telephoned me and arranged to take her into custody tomorrow morning, when I could have got her release on bail? Did you need to assault my privacy and insult my dignity by having your bullies burst in my door in order to carry off a sensitive and lovely young woman to a night in jail? For shame, sir! Pfui!" Wolfe poured himself a glass of beer.

Cramer shook his head, slowly back and forth. "By God, you're a world-beater. I hand it to you. You know very well, Wolfe, I wasn't interested in any larceny. I wanted to talk with her about murder and about this damned marquis."

"Bah. After your talk, would she or would she not have been incarcerated?"

"I suppose she would. Hell, millions of innocent people have spent a night in jail, and sometimes much longer."

"The people I engage to keep out of it don't. If what you wanted was a talk, why the warrant? Why the violent and hostile onslaught?"

Cramer nodded. "That was a mistake. I admit it. I'll tell you the truth, the Commissioner was there demanding action. And the phone call came. I don't know who it was. He not only told me that Clara Fox was in your house, he also told me that the same Clara Fox was wanted for stealing money from the Seaboard Products Corporation. I got in touch with another department and learned that a warrant for her arrest had been executed late this afternoon. It was the Commissioner's idea to get the warrant and use it to send here and get her in a hurry."

I went on and got the signs for that down in my notebook, but my mind wasn't on that, it was on Mike Walsh. It was fairly plain that Wolfe had let one get by when he had permitted Walsh to walk out with no supervision, considering that New York is full not only of telephones, but also of subways and railroad trains and places to hide. And for the first time I put it down as a serious speculation whether Walsh could have had a reason to croak his dear old friend Harlan Scovil. Seeing Wolfe's lips moving slowly out and in, I suspected that the taste in his mouth was about the same as mine. Cramer was saying:

"Come on, Wolfe, forget it. You know what most Police Commissioners are like. They're not cops. They think all you have to do is flash a badge and strong men burst into tears. Be a sport and help me out once. I want to see this Fox woman. I'll take your word for Walsh and Lindquist and keep after them, but help me out on Clara Fox. If you've got her here, trot her out. If you haven't, tell me where to find her. If you've turned her loose too, which isn't a bad trick, show me her trail. She may be your client, but I'm not kidding when I say that the best thing you can do for her right now, and damn quick, is to let me see her. I don't care anything about any larceny—"

Wolfe interrupted. "She does. I do." He shook his head. "The larceny charge is of course in charge of the District Attorney's office; you haven't the power to affect it one way or another. I know that. As for the Marquis of Clivers, he is in no danger from Clara Fox that you need to protect him from. And as regards the murder of Harlan Scovil, she knows as little about that as I do. In fact, even less, since it is barely possible that I know who killed him."

Cramer looked at him. He puffed his cigar and kept on looking. At length he said, "Well. It's a case of murder. I'm in charge of the Homicide Squad. I'm listening."

"That's all. I volunteered that."

Cramer looked disgusted. "It can't be all. It's either too much or not enough. You've said enough to make you a material witness. You know what we can do with material witnesses if we want to."

"Yes, I know." Wolfe sighed. "But you can't very well lock me up, for then I wouldn't be free to unravel this tangle for my client—and for you. I said, barely possible." He sat up straight, abruptly. "Barely possible, sir! Confound all of you! You marquises that need protection, you hyenas of finance, you upholders of the power to persecute and defame! And don't mistake this outburst as a display of moral indignation; it is merely the practical protest of a man of business who finds his business interfered with by ignorance and stupidity. I expect to collect a fee from my client, Miss Fox. To do that I need to prosecute a claim for her, for a legal debt, I need to clear her from the false accusation of larceny, and I fear I need to discover who murdered Harlan Scovil. Those are legitimate needs, and I shall pursue them. If you want to protect your precious marquis, for God's sake do so! Surround him with a ring of iron and steel, or immerse him in antiseptic jelly! But don't annoy me when I'm trying to work! It is past one o'clock, and I must be up shortly after six, and Mr. Goodwin and I have things to do. I have every right to advise Miss Fox to avoid unfriendly molestation. If you want her, search for her. I have said that I will answer no question regarding her whereabouts, but I will tell you this much: if you undertake to invade these premises with a search warrant, you won't find her here."

Wolfe's half a glass of beer was flat, but he didn't mind that. He reached for it and swallowed it. Then he took the handkerchief from his breast pocket and wiped his lips. "Well, sir?"

Cramer put his cigar stub in the tray, rubbed the palms of his hands together for a while, pulled at the lobe of his ear, and stood up. He looked down at Wolfe.

"I like you, you know. You know damn well I do. But this thing is to some extent out of my hands. The Commissioner was talking on the telephone this evening with the Department of Justice. That's the kind of a lay-out it is. They might really send and get you. That's a friendly warning."

"Thank you, sir. You're going? Mr. Goodwin will let you out."

I did. I went to the hall and held his coat for him, and when I pulled the curtain aside to survey the stoop before opening the door he chuckled and slapped me on the back. That didn't make me want to kiss him. Naturally he knew when an apple was too high to reach without a ladder, and naturally there's no use letting a guy know you're going to sock him until you're ready to haul off. I saw his big car with a driver there at the curb, and there was a stranger on the sidewalk. Apparently the tenor had been relieved.

I went back to the office and sat down and yawned. Wolfe was leaning back with his eyes wide open, which meant he was sleepy. We looked at each other. I said:

"So if he comes with a search warrant he won't find her here. That's encouraging. It's also encouraging that Mike Walsh is being such a big help. Also that you know who killed Harlan Scovil, like I know who put the salt in the ocean. Also that we're tied hand and foot with the Commissioner himself sore at us." I yawned. "I guess I'll prop myself up in bed tomorrow and read and knit."

"Not tomorrow, Archie. The day after, possibly. Your notebook."

I got it, and a pencil. Wolfe began:

"Miss Fox to breakfast with me in my room at seven o'clock. Delay would be dangerous. Do not forget the gong. You are not to leave the house. Saul, Fred, Orrie and Keems are to be sent to my room immediately upon arrival, but singly. Arrange tonight for a long distance connection with London at eight-thirty, Hitchcock's office. From Miss Fox, where does Walsh live and where is he employed as night watchman. As early as possible, call Morley of the District Attorney's office and I'll talk to him. Have Fritz bring me a copy of this when he wakes me at six-thirty. From Saul, complete information from Miss Lindquist regarding her father, his state of health, could he travel in an airplane, his address and telephone number in Nebraska. Phone Murger's—they open at eight-thirty— for copies of *Metropolitan Biographies*, all years available. Explain to Fritz and Theodore procedure regarding Miss Fox, as follows: . . ."

He went on, in the drawling murmur that he habitually used when giving me a set-up. I was yawning, but I got it down. Some of it sounded like he was having hallucinations or else trying to make me think he knew things I didn't know. I quit yawning for grinning while he was explaining the procedure regarding Miss Fox.

He went to bed. After I finished the typing and giving a copy to Fritz and a few other chores, I went to the basement to take a look at the back door, and looked out the front to direct a Bronx cheer at the gumshoe on guard. Up the stairs, I continued to the third floor to take a look at the door of the south room, but I didn't try it to see if it was locked, thinking it might disturb her. Down again, in my room, I looked in the bottom drawer to see if Fritz had messed it up getting out the pajamas. It was all right. I hit the hay.

•••• 10 ••••

WHEN I leave my waking up in the morning to the vagaries of nature, it's a good deal like other acts of God—you can't tell much about it ahead of time. So Tuesday at six-thirty I staggered out of bed and fought my way across the room to turn off the electric alarm clock on the table. Then I proceeded to cleanse the form and the phiz and get the figure draped for the day. By that time the bright October sun had a band across the top fronts of the houses across the street, and I thought to myself it would be a pity to have to go to jail on such a fine day.

At seven-thirty I was in my corner in the kitchen, with Canadian bacon, pancakes, and wild thyme honey which Wolfe got from Syria. And plenty of coffee. The wheels had already started to turn. Clara Fox, who had told Fritz she had slept like a log, was having breakfast with Wolfe in his room. Johnny Keems had arrived early, and he and Saul Panzer were in the dining-room punishing pancakes. With the telephone I had pulled Dick Morley, of the District Attorney's office, out of bed at his home, and Wolfe had talked with him. It was Morley who would have lost his job, and maybe something more, but for Wolfe pulling him out of a hole in the Banister-Schurman business about three years before.

With my pancakes I went over the stories of Scovil's murder in the morning papers. They didn't play it up much, but the accounts were fairly complete. The tip-off was that he was a Chicago gangster, which gave me a grin, since he looked about as much like a gangster as a prima donna. The essentials were there, provided they were straight: no gun had been found. The car had been stolen from where some innocent perfume salesman had parked it on 29th Street. The closest eyewitness had been a man who had been walking along about thirty feet behind Harlan Scovil, and it was he who had got the license number before he dived for cover when the bullets started flying. In the dim light he hadn't got a good view of the man in the car, but he was sure it was a man, with his hat pulled down and a dark overcoat collar turned up, and he was sure he had been alone in the car. The car had speeded off across 31st Street and turned at the corner. No one had been found who had noticed it stopping on Ninth Avenue, where it had later been found. No fingerprints . . . and so forth and so forth.

I finished my second cup of coffee and got up and stretched and from then on I was as busy as a pickpocket on New Year's Eve. When Fred and Orrie came I let them in, and after they had got their instructions from Wolfe I distributed expense money to all four of them and let them out again. The siege was still on. There were two dicks out there now, one of them about the size of Charles Laughton before he heard beauty calling, and every time anyone passed in or out he got the kind of scrutiny you read about. I got the long distance call through to London, and Wolfe talked from his room to Ethelbert Hitchcock, which I consider the all-time low for a name for a snoop, even in England. I phoned Murger's for the copies of *Metropolitan Biographies,* and they delivered them within a quarter of an hour and I took them up to the plant rooms, as Wolfe had said he would glance at them after nine o'clock. As I was going out I stopped where Theodore Horstmann was turning out some old *Cattleyas trianae* and growled at him:

"You're going to get shot in the gizzard."

I swear to God he looked pale.

I phoned Henry H. Barber, the lawyer that we could count on for almost anything except fee-splitting, to make sure he would be available on a minute's notice all day, and to tell him that he was to consider himself retained, through us, by Miss Clara Fox, in two actions: a suit to collect a debt from the Marquis of Clivers, and a suit for damages through false arrest against Ramsey Muir. Likewise, in the first case, Miss Hilda Lindquist.

It looked as if I had a minute loose, so I mounted the two flights to the south room and knocked on the door, and called out my name. She said come in, and I entered.

She was in the armchair, with books and magazines on the table, but none of them was opened. Maybe she had slept

like a log, but her eyes looked tired. She frowned at me.
I said:

"You shouldn't sit so close to the window. If they wanted
to bad enough they could see in here from that 34th Street
roof."

She glanced around. "I shouldn't think so, with those curtains."

"They're pretty thin. Let me move you back a little, anyhow." She got up, and I shoved the chair and table toward
the bed. "I'm not usually nervous, but this is a stunt we're
pulling."

She sat down again and looked up at me. "You don't like
it, do you, Mr. Goodwin? I could see last night you didn't
approve of it. Neither do I."

I grinned at her. "Bless your dear little heart, what difference does that make? Nero Wolfe is putting on a show
and we're in the cast. Stick to the script, don't forget that."

"I don't call it a show." She was frowning again. "A man
has been murdered and it was my fault. I don't like to hide,
and I don't want to. I'd rather—"

I showed her both palms. "Forget it. You came to get Wolfe
to help you, didn't you? All right, let him. He may be a nut,
but you're lucky that he spotted the gleam of honesty in
your eye or you'd be in one sweet mess this minute. You
behave yourself. For instance, if that phone there on the stand
is in any way a temptation . . ."

She shook her head. "If it is, I'll resist it."

"Well, there's no use leaving it here anyhow." I went and
pulled the connection out of the plug and gathered the cord
and instrument under my arm. "I learned about feminine
impulses in school. —There goes the office phone. Don't open
the door and don't go close to the windows."

I beat it and went down two steps at a time. It was Dick
Morley on the phone, with a tale. I offered to connect him
with Wolfe in the plant rooms, but he said not to disturb him,
he could give it to me. He had had a little trouble. The Clara
Fox larceny charge was being handled by an Assistant District Attorney named Frisbie whom Morley knew only fairly
well, and Frisbie hadn't seemed especially inclined to open
up, but Morley had got some facts. A warrant for Clara Fox's
arrest, and a search warrant for her apartment, had been
issued late Monday afternoon. The apartment had not been
searched because detectives under Frisbie's direction had gone
first to the garage where she kept her car, and had found in
it, wrapped in a newspaper under the back seat, a package

of hundred dollar bills amounting to $30,000. The case was considered airtight. Frisbie's men no longer had the warrant for arrest because it had been turned over to Inspector Cramer at the request of the Police Commissioner.

I thanked Morley and hung up and went upstairs to the plant rooms and told Wolfe the sad story. He was in the tropical room trimming wilts. When I finished he said:

"We were wrong, Archie. Not hyenas. Hyenas wait for a carcass. Get Mr. Perry on the phone, connect it here, and take it down."

I went back to the office. It wasn't so easy to get Perry. His secretary was reluctant, or he was, or they both were, but I finally managed to get him on and put him through to Wolfe. Then I began a fresh page of the notebook.

Perry said he was quite busy, he hoped Wolfe could make it brief. Wolfe said he hoped so too, that first he wished to learn if he had misunderstood Perry Monday afternoon. He had gathered that Perry had believed Miss Fox to be innocent, had been opposed to any precipitate action, and had desired a careful and complete investigation. Perry said that was correct.

Wolfe's tone got sharp. "But you did not know until after seven o'clock last evening that I was not going to investigate for you, and the warrant for Miss Fox's arrest was issued an hour earlier than that. You would not call that precipitate?"

Perry sounded flustered. "Well . . . precipitate . . . yes, it was. It was, yes. You see . . . you asked me yesterday if I am not the fount of justice in this organization. To a certain extent, yes. But there is always . . . well . . . the human element. I am not a czar, neither in fact nor by temperament. When you phoned me last evening you may have thought me irritable—as a matter of fact, I thought of calling you back to apologize. The truth is I was chagrined and deeply annoyed. I knew then that a warrant had been issued for the arrest at the instance of Mr. Muir. Surely you can appreciate my position. Mr. Muir is a high official of my corporation. When I learned later in the evening that the money had been found in Miss Fox's car, I was astounded . . . I couldn't believe it . . . but what could I do? I was amazed . . ."

"Indeed." Wolfe still snapped. "You've got your money back. Do you intend to proceed with the prosecution?"

"You don't need to take that tone, Wolfe." Perry sharpened a little. "I told you there is the human element. I'm not a czar. Muir makes an issue of it. I'm being frank with you. I can't talk him off. Granted that I could kick the first vice-president

93

out of the company if I wanted to, which is a good deal to grant, do you think I should? After all, he has the law—"

"Then you're with him on it?"

A pause. "No. No, I'm not. I . . . I have the strongest . . . sympathy for Clara—Miss Fox. I would like to see her get something . . . much more human than justice. For instance, if there is any difficulty about bail for her I would be glad to furnish it."

"Thank you. We'll manage bail. You asked me to be brief, Mr. Perry. First, I suggest that you arrange to have the charge against Miss Fox quashed immediately. Second, I wish to inform you of our intentions if that is not done. At ten o'clock tomorrow morning I shall have Miss Fox submit herself to arrest and shall have her at once released on bail. She will then start an action against Ramsey Muir and the Seaboard Products Corporation to recover one million dollars in damages for false arrest. We deal in millions here now. I think there is no question but that we shall have sufficient evidence to uphold our action. If they try her first, so much the better. She'll be acquitted."

"But how can . . . that's absurd . . . if you have evidence . . ."

"That's all, Mr. Perry. That's my brevity. Goodbye."

I heard the click of Wolfe hanging up. Perry was sputtering, but I hung up too. I tossed the notebook away and got up and stuck my hands in my pockets and walked around. Perhaps I was muttering. I was thinking to myself, if Wolfe takes that pot with nothing but a dirty deuce he's a better man than he thinks he is, if that was possible. On the face of it, it certainly looked as if his crazy conceit had invaded the higher centers of his brain and stopped his mental processes completely; but there was one thing that made such a supposition unlikely, namely, that he was spending money. He had four expensive men riding around in taxis and he had got London on the phone as if it had been a delicatessen shop. It was a thousand to one he was going to get it back.

Still another expenditure was imminent, as I learned when the phone rang again. I sat down to get it, half hoping it was Perry calling back to offer a truce. But what I heard was Fred Durkin's low growl, and he sounded peeved.

"That you, Archie?"

"Right. What have you got?"

"Nothing. Less than that. Look here. I'm talking from the Forty-seventh Street Station."

"The . . . what? What for?"

"What the hell do you suppose for? I got arrested a little."

94

I made a face and took a breath. "Good for you," I said grimly. "That's a big help. Men like you are the backbone of the country. Go on."

His growl went plaintive. "Could I help it? They hopped me at the garage when I went there to ask questions. They say I committed something when I took that car last night. I think they're getting ready to send me somewhere, I suppose Centre Street. What the hell could I do, run and let him tag me? I wouldn't be phoning now if it hadn't happened that a friend of mine is on the desk here."

"Okay. If they take you to the D. A.'s office keep your ears open and stick to the little you know. We'll get after it."

"You'd better. If I—hey! Will you phone the missis?"

I assured him he would see the missis as soon as she was expecting him, and hung up. I sat and scratched my nose a minute and then made for the stairs. It was looking as if being confined to the house wasn't going to deprive me of my exercise.

Wolfe was still in the tropical room. He kept on snipping stems and listened without looking around. I reported the development. He said, "These interruptions are abominable."

I said, "All right, let him rot in a dungeon."

Wolfe sighed. "Phone Mr. Barber. Can you pick Keems up? No, you can't. When you hear from him let me talk to him."

I went back down and got Barber's office and asked him to send someone out to make arrangements for Fred to sleep with his missis that night, and gave him the dope.

I had no idea when I might hear from Johnny Keems. They had all got their instructions direct from Wolfe, and as usual he was keeping my head clear of unnecessary obstructions. As I had let Orrie Cather out he had made some kind of a crack about being the only electrician in New York who understood directors' rooms, and of course I knew Saul Panzer had a contact on with Hilda Lindquist, but beyond that their programs were outside my circle. I guessed Fred had gone back to the garage to see if he could get a line on a plant, which made it appear that Wolfe didn't even have a dirty deuce, but of course he had talked with Clara Fox nearly an hour that morning, so that was all vague. But it did seem that Frisbie or someone around the District Attorney's office was busting with ardor over an ordinary larceny on which they already had the evidence, leaving a dick at the garage; but that was probably part of the net they were holding for Clara Fox. It might even have been one of Cramer's men.

I went on being a switchboard girl. A little before ten Saul Panzer called, and from upstairs Wolfe listened to him while I put down the details he had collected from Hilda Lindquist regarding her father in Nebraska. She thought that if riding in an airplane didn't kill him it would scare him to death. Apparently Saul had further instructions, for Wolfe told him to proceed. A little later Orrie phoned in, and what he reported to Wolfe gave me my first view of a new slant that hadn't occurred to me at all. Introducing himself to Sourface Vawter as an electrician, he had been admitted to the directors' room of the Seaboard Products Corporation, and had learned that besides the double door at the end of the corridor it had another door leading into the public hall. It had been locked but could be opened from the inside, and Orrie had himself gone out that way and around the hall to the elevators. Wolfe told Orrie to wait and talked to me:

"Don't type a note on that, Archie. Any that you do type, put them in the safe at once. Leave Orrie on with me and be sure the other line is open. A call I am expecting hasn't come. When Keems calls I'll talk to him, but I'll give Orrie Fred's assignment."

Taking the hint that he didn't want to burden my ears with Orrie's schedule, I hung up. I filed some notes in the safe and loaded Wolfe's pen and tested it, a chore that I hadn't been able to get around to before—absentmindedly, because I was off on a new track. I had no idea what had started Wolfe in that direction. It had beautiful possibilities, no doubt of that, but a 100 to 1 shot in a big handicap is a beautiful possibility too, and how often would you collect on it? After taxing the brain a few minutes, this looked more like a million to one. I would probably have gone on to add more ciphers to that if I hadn't been interrupted by the doorbell. Of course I was still on that job too. I went to the hall and pulled the curtain to see through the glass panel, and got a surprise. It was the first time Wolfe's house had ever been taken for a church, but there wasn't any other explanation, for either that specimen on the stoop was scheduled for best man at a wedding or Emily Post had been fooling me for years.

The two dicks were down on the sidewalk, looking up at the best man as if it was too much of a problem for them. They had nothing on me. I opened the door and let it come three inches, leaving the chain on, and said in a well bred tone: "Good morning."

He peered through at me. "I say, that crack is scarcely adequate. Really." He had a well trained voice but a little squawky.

"I'm sorry. This is a bad neighborhood and we have to be careful. What can I do for you?"

He went on peering. "Is this the house of Mr. Nero Wolfe?"

"It is."

He hesitated, and turned to look down at the snoops on the sidewalk, who were staring up at him in the worst possible taste. Then he came closer and pushed his face up against the crack and said in a tone nearly down to a whisper:

"From Lord Clivers. I wish to see Mr. Wolfe."

I took a second for consideration and then slid the bolt off and opened up. He walked in and I shut the door and shot the bolt again. When I turned he was standing there with his stick hung over his elbow, pulling his gloves off. He was six feet, spare but not skinny, about my age, fair-skinned with chilly blue eyes, and there was no question about his being dressed for it. I waved him ahead and followed him into the office, and he took his time getting his paraphernalia deposited on Wolfe's desk before he lowered himself into a chair. Meantime I let him know that Mr. Wolfe was engaged and would be until eleven o'clock, and that I was the confidential assistant and was at his service. He got seated and looked at me as if he would have to get around to admitting my right to exist before we could hope to make any headway.

But he spoke. "Mr. Goodwin? I see. Perhaps I got a bit ahead at the door. That is . . . I really should see Mr. Wolfe without delay."

I grinned at him. "You mean because you mentioned the Marquis of Clivers? That's okay. I wrote that letter. I know all about it. You can't see Mr. Wolfe before eleven. I can let him know you're here . . ."

"If you will be so good. Do that. My name is Horrocks—Francis Horrocks."

I looked at him. So this was the geezer that bought roses with three-foot stems. I turned on the swivel and plugged in the plant rooms and pressed the button. In a minute Wolfe was on and I told him:

"A man here to see you, Mr. Francis Horrocks. From the Marquis of Clivers. . . . Yeah, in the office. . . . Haven't asked him. . . . I told him, sure. . . . Okay."

I jerked the plugs and swivelled again. "Mr. Wolfe says he can see you at eleven o'clock, unless you'd care to try me. He suggests the latter."

"I should have liked to see Mr. Wolfe." The blue eyes were

going over me. "Though I merely bring a message. First, though, I should . . . er . . . perhaps explain . . . I am here in a dual capacity. It's a bit confusing, but really quite all right. I am here, as it were, personally . . . and also semi-officially. Possibly I should first deliver my message from Lord Clivers."

"Okay. Shoot."

"I beg your pardon? Oh, quite. Lord Clivers would like to know if Mr. Wolfe could call at his hotel. An hour can be arranged—"

"I can save you breath on that. Mr. Wolfe never calls on anybody."

"No?" His brows went up. "He is not . . . that is, bed-ridden?"

"Nope, only house-ridden. He doesn't like it outdoors. He never has called on anybody and never will."

"You don't say." His forehead showed wrinkles. "Well. Lord Clivers wishes very much to see him. You say you wrote that letter?"

I nodded. "Yeah, I know all about it. I suppose Mr. Wolfe would be glad to talk with the marquis on the telephone—"

"He prefers not to discuss it on the telephone."

"Okay. I was going to add, or the marquis can come here. Of course the legal part of it is being handled by our attorney."

The young diplomat sat straight with his arms folded and looked at me. "You have engaged a solicitor?"

"Certainly. If it comes to a lawsuit, which we hope it won't, we don't want to waste any time. We understand the marquis will be in New York another week, so we'd have to be ready to serve him at once."

He nodded. "Just so. That's a bit candid." He bit his lip and cocked his head a little. "We appear to have reached a dead end. Your position seems quite clear. I shall report it, that's all I can do." He hitched his feet back and cleared his throat. "Now, if you don't mind, I assume my private capacity. I remarked that I am here personally. My name is Francis Horrocks."

"Yeah. Your personal name."

"Just so. And I would like to speak with Miss Fox. Miss Clara Fox."

I felt myself straightening out my face and hoped he didn't see me. I said, "I can't say I blame you. I've met Miss Fox. Go to it."

He frowned. "If you would be so good as to tell her I am here. It's quite all right. I know she's having a spot of seclu-

98

sion, but it's quite all right. Really. You see, when she telephoned me this morning I insisted on knowing the address of her retreat. In fact, I pressed her on it. I confess she laid it on me not to come here to see her, but I made no commitment. Also, I didn't come to see her; I came semi-officially. What? Being here, I ask to see her, which is quite all right. What?"

My face was under control after the first shock. I said, "Sure it's quite all right. I mean, to ask. Seeing her is something else. You must have got the address wrong or maybe you were phoning in your sleep."

"Oh, no. Really." He folded his arms again. "See here, Mr. Goodwin, let's cut across. It's a fact, I actually must see Miss Fox. As a friend, you understand. For purely personal reasons. I'm quite determined about this."

"Okay. Find her. She left no address here."

He shook his head patiently. "It won't do, I assure you it won't. She telephoned me. Is she in distress? I don't know. I shall have to see her. If you will tell her—"

I stood up. "Sorry, Mr. Horrocks. Do you really have to go? I hope you find Miss Fox. Tell the Marquis of Clivers—"

He sat tight, shook his head again, and frowned. "Damn it all. I dislike this, really. I've never set eyes on you before. What? I've never seen this Mr. Wolfe. Could Miss Fox have been under duress when she was telephoning? You see the possibility, of course. Setting my mind at rest and all that. If you put me out, it will really be necessary for me to tell those policemen outside that Miss Fox telephoned me from this address at nine o'clock this morning. Also I should have to take the precaution of finding a telephone at once to repeat the information to your police headquarters. What?"

I stared down at him, and I admit he was too much for me. Whether he was deep and desperate or dumb and determined I didn't know. I said:

"Wait here. Mr. Wolfe will have to know about you. Kindly stay in this room."

I left him there and went to the kitchen and told Fritz to stand in the hall, and if an Englishman emerged from the office, yodel. Then I bounced up two flights to the south room, called not too loud, and when I heard the key turn, opened the door and entered. Clara Fox stood and brushed her hair back and looked at me half alarmed and half hopeful.

I said, "What time this morning did you phone that guy Francis Horrocks?"

99

She stared. It got her. She swallowed. "But I . . . he . . . he promised . . ."

"So you did phone him. Swell. You forgot to mention it when I asked you about it a while ago."

"But you didn't ask me if I *had* phoned?"

"Oh, didn't I? Now that was careless." I threw up my hands. "To hell with it. Suppose you tell me what you phoned him about. I hope it wasn't a secret."

"No, it wasn't." She came a step to me. "Must you be so sarcastic? There was nothing . . . it was just personal."

"As for instance?"

"Why, it was really nothing. Of course, he sent those roses. Then . . . I had had an engagement to dine with him Monday evening, and when I made the appointment with Mr. Wolfe I had to cancel the one with Mr. Horrocks, and when he insisted I thought that three hours would be enough with Mr. Wolfe, so I told Mr. Horrocks I would go with him at ten o'clock to dance somewhere, and probably he went to the apartment and waited around there I don't know how long, and this morning I supposed he would keep phoning there and of course there would be no answer, and he couldn't get me at the office either, and besides, I hadn't thanked him for the roses . . ."

I put up a palm. "Take a breath. I see, romance. It'd be still more romantic if he came to visit you in jail. You're quite an adventuress, being as you are over 90% nincompoop. I don't suppose you know that according to an article in yesterday's *Times* this Horrocks is the nephew of the Marquis of Clivers and next in line for the title."

"Oh yes. He explained to me . . . that is . . . that's all right. I knew that. And Mr. Goodwin, I don't like—"

"We'll discuss your likes later. Here's something you don't know. Horrocks is downstairs in the office saying that he's got to see you or he'll run and get the police."

"What! He isn't."

"Yep. Somebody is, and from his looks I'm willing to admit it's Horrocks."

"But he shouldn't . . . he promised . . . send him away!"

"He won't go away. If I throw him out he'll yell for a cop. He thinks you're here under duress and need to be rescued—that's his story. You're a swell client, you are. With the chances Nero Wolfe's taking for you—all right. Anyhow, whether he's straight or not, there's no way out of it now. I'm going to bring him up here, and for God's sake make it snappy and let him go back to his uncle."

"But I . . . good heavens!" She brushed her hair back. "I don't want to see him. Not now. Tell him . . . of course I could . . . yes, that's it . . . I'll go down and just tell him—"

"You will not. Next you'll be wanting to go and walk around the block with him. You stay here."

Outside in the hall I hesitated, uncertain whether to go up and tell Wolfe of the party we were having, but decided there was no point in riling him. I went back down, tossing Fritz a nod as I passed by, and found the young diplomat sitting in the office with his arms still folded. He put his brows up at me. I told him to come on, and let him go first. Behind him on the stairs I noticed he had good springs in his legs, and at the top his air-pump hadn't speeded up any. Keeping fit for dear old England and the bloody empire. I opened the door and bowed him in and followed him.

Clara Fox came across to him. He looked at her with a kind of sickening grin and put out his hand. She shook her head:

"No. I won't shake hands with you. Aren't you ashamed of yourself? You promised me you wouldn't. Causing Mr. Goodwin all this trouble . . ."

"Now, really. I say." His voice was different from what it had been downstairs, sort of sweet and concentrated. Silly as hell. "After all, you know, it was fairly alarming . . . with you gone and all that . . . couldn't find a trace of you . . . and you look frightful, very bad in the eyes . . ."

"Thank you very much." All of a sudden she began to laugh. I hadn't heard her laugh before. It showed her teeth and put color in her cheeks. She laughed at him until if I had been him I'd have thought up some kind of a remark. Then she stuck out her hand. "All right, shake. Mr. Goodwin says you were going to rescue me. I warned you to let American girls alone—you see the sort of thing it leads to?"

With his big paw he was hanging onto her hand as if he had a lease on it. He was staring at her. "You know, they do, though. I mean the eyes. You're really quite all right? You couldn't expect me—"

I butted in because I had to. I had left the door open and the sound of the front doorbell came up plain. I glanced at Francis Horrocks and decided that if he really was a come-on I would at least have the pleasure of seeing how long he looked lying down, before he got out of that house, and I got brusque to Clara Fox:

"Hold it. The doorbell. I'm going to shut this door and go down to answer it, and it would be a good idea to make no

101

sounds until I get back." The bell started ringing again. "Okay?"

Clara Fox nodded.

"Okay, Mr. Horrocks?"

"Certainly. Whatever Miss Fox says."

I beat it, closing the door behind me. Some smart guy was leaning on the button, for the bell kept on ringing as I went down the two flights. Fritz was standing in the hall, looking belligerent; he hated people that got impatient with the bell. I went to the door and pulled the curtain and looked out, and felt mercury running up my backbone. It was a quartet. Only four, and I recognized Lieutenant Rowcliff in front. It was him on the button. I hadn't had such a treat for a long while. I turned the lock and let the door come as far as the chain.

Rowcliff called through: "Well! We're not ants. Come on, open up."

I said: "Take it easy. I'm just the messenger boy."

"Yeah? Here's the message." He unfolded a paper he had in his hand. Having seen a search warrant before, I didn't need a magnifying glass. I looked through the crack at it. Rowcliff said:

"What are you waiting for? Do you want me to count ten?"

• • • • 11 • • • •

I SAID, "Hold your horses, lieutenant. If what you want is in here it can't get out, since I suppose you've got the rear and the roof covered. This isn't my house, it belongs to Nero Wolfe and he's upstairs. Wait a minute, I'll be right back."

I went up three steps at a time, paying no attention to Rowcliff yelling outside. I went in the south room; they were standing there. I said to Clara Fox, "They're here. Make it snappy. Take Horrocks with you, and if he's in on this I'll kill him."

Horrocks started, "Really—"

"Shut up! Go with Miss Fox. For God's sake—"

She might have made an adventuress at that; she was okay when it came to action. She darted to the table and grabbed her handbag and handkerchief, dashed back and got Horrocks by the hand, and pulled him through the door with her. I took a quick look around to make sure there were no lipsticks or powder puffs left behind, shoved the table towards the window where it looked more natural, and beat it. In the hall I stopped one second to shake myself. Noises of Rowcliff bellowing on the stoop floated up. Horrocks and Clara Fox had disappeared. I went down to the front door and slid the bolt and flung it open.

"Welcome," I grinned. "Mr. Wolfe says he wants the warrant for a souvenir."

They trooped in behind Rowcliff. He grunted. "Where's Wolfe?"

"Up with the plants. Until eleven o'clock. He told me to tell you this, that of course you have the legal right to search the entire premises, but that the city will pay for every nickel's worth of damage that's done if he has to go to City Hall himself to collect it."

103

"No! Don't scare me to death. Come on, boys. Where does that go to?"

"Front room." I pointed. "Office. Kitchen. Basement stairs. The rear door is down there, onto the court."

He turned, and then whirled to me again. "Look here, Goodwin. You've had your bluff called. Why not save time? Why don't you bring this Fox woman down here, or up here, and call it a trick? It'd save a lot of messing around."

I said, coldly, "Pish-tush. Which isn't for you, lieutenant; I know you've got orders. It's for Inspector Cramer, and you can take it to him. The horse-laugh he'll get over this will be heard at Bath Beach. Does he think Nero Wolfe is simple enough to try to hide a woman under his bed? Go on and finish your button-button-who's-got-the-button and get the hell out of here."

He grunted and started off with his army toward the door of the basement stairs. I followed. I wanted to keep an eye on them anyway, on general principles, but besides that, I had decided to ride him. Wolfe had told me to use my judgment, and I knew that was the best way to put a bird like Rowcliff in the frame of mind we wanted him in. So I was right behind them going down, and while they poked around all over the basement, pulling the curtains back from the shelves, opening trunks and looking into empty packing cartons, I exercised the tongue. Rowcliff tried to pass it back once or twice and then pretended not to hear me. I opened the door to the insulated bottle department, and kept jerking my head around at them as if I expected to catch them in a snatch at a quart of rye. They finished up down there by taking a look at the court out of the back door, and after I got the door locked again I followed them back up to the first floor.

Rowcliff stationed a man at the door to the basement stairs and then began at the kitchen and worked forward. I hung on his tail. I said, "Up here, now, you've got to take soundings. The place is lousy with trap-doors," and when he involuntarily looked down at his feet I turned loose a haw-haw. In the office I asked him, "Want me to open the safe? There's a piece of her in there. That's the way we worked it, cut her up and scattered her around." By the time we started for the second floor he was boiling and trying not to show it, and about 97% convinced. He left a man at the head of the stairs and tackled Wolfe's room. Fritz had come along to see that nothing got hurt, thinking maybe that my mind was on something else, for there was a lot of stuff in there. I'll admit they didn't get rough, though they were thorough. Wolfe's double

104

mattress looked pretty thick under its black silk coverlet, and one of them wiggled under it to have a look. Rowcliff went around the rows of bookshelves taking measurements with his eyes for a concealed closet, and where the poker-dart board was hanging on a screen he pulled the screen around to look behind it. All the time I was making remarks as they occurred to me.

In my room, as Rowcliff was looking back of the clothes in the closet, I said, "Listen, I've got a suggestion. I'll put on an old mother hubbard I won once at a raffle and you take me to Cramer and tell him I'm Clara Fox. After this performance there's no question but what he's too damn dumb to know the difference."

He backed out of the closet, straightened up, and glared at me. He bellowed, "You shut your trap, see? Or I will take you somewhere, and it won't be to Cramer!"

I grinned at him. "That's childish, lieutenant. Make saps out of yourselves and then try to take it out on citizens. Oh, wait! Baby, wait till this gets out!"

He tramped to the hall and started up the next flight with his army behind. I'll admit I was a little squeamish as they entered the south room; it's hard for anyone to stay in a room ten hours and not leave a trace; but they weren't looking for traces, they were looking for a live woman. Anyway, she had followed Wolfe's instructions to the letter and it looked all right. That only took a couple of minutes, and the same for the north room, where Saul Panzer had slept. When they came out to the hall again I opened the door to the narrow stairs going up, and held it for them.

"Plant rooms fourth and last stop. And take it from me, if you knock over a bench of orchid pots you'll find more trouble here than you brought with you."

Rowcliff was licked. He wasn't saying so, and he was trying not to look it, but he was. He growled:

"Wolfe up there?"

"He is."

"All right. Come along, Jack. You two wait here."

The three of us got to the top in single file and I called to him to push in. We entered and he saw the elevator standing there with the door gaping. He opened the door to the stairs and called down, "Hey, Al! Come up and give this elevator a go and look over the shaft!" Then he rejoined us.

Those plant rooms had been considered impressive by better men than Lieutenant Rowcliff—for example among many others, by Pierre Fracard, President of the Horticultural Society of France. I was in and out of them ten times a day and they impressed me, though I pretended to Theodore Horstmann that they didn't. Of course they were more startling in February than they were in October, but Wolfe and Horstmann had developed a technique of forcing that made them worth looking at no matter when it was. Inside the door of the first room, which had Odontoglossums, Oncidiums and Miltonia hybrids, Rowcliff and the dick stopped short. The angle-iron staging gleamed in its silver paint, and on the concrete benches and shelves three thousand pots of orchids showed greens and blues and yellows and reds. It looked spotty to me, since I had seen it at the top of its glory, but it was nothing to sniff at. I said:

"Well, do you think you're at the flower show? You didn't pay to get in. Get a move on, huh?"

Rowcliff led the way. He didn't leave the center aisle. Once he stopped to stoop for a peek under a bench, and I let a laugh bust out and then choked it and said, "Excuse me, lieutenant, I know you have your duty to perform." He went on with his shoulders up, but I knew the eager spirit of the chase had oozed down into his shoes.

In the next room, Cattleyas, Laelias, hybrids and miscellaneous, Theodore Horstmann was over at one side pouring fertilizer on a row of Cymbidiums, which are terrestrials, and Rowcliff took a look at him but didn't say anything. The dick in between us stopped to bend down and stick his nose against a big lilac hybrid, and I told him, "Nope. If you smell anything sweet, it's me."

We went on through the tropical room, where it was hot with the sun shining and the lath screens already off, and continued to the potting room. It had enough free space to move around in, and it also had inhabitants. Francis Horrocks, still unsoiled, stood leaning with his back against an angle-iron, talking to Nero Wolfe, who was using the pressure spray. A couple of boards had been laid along the top of a long low wooden box which was filled with osmundine, and on the boards had been placed 35 or 40 pots of Laeliocattleya Lustre. Wolfe was spraying them with high pressure, and it was pretty wet around there. Horrocks was saying:

"It really seems a devilish lot of trouble. What? Of course, you know, it's perfectly proper for every chap . . ."

Rowcliff looked around. There were sphagnum, sand, charcoal, crock for drainage, stacks of hundreds of pots. Rowcliff moved forward, and Wolfe shut off the spray and turned to him.

I closed in. "Mr. Nero Wolfe, Lieutenant Rowcliff."

Wolfe inclined his head one inch. "How do you do." He looked toward the door, where the dick stood. "And your companion?"

He was using his aloof tone, and it was good. Rowcliff said, "One of my men. We're here on business."

"So I understand. If you don't mind, introduce him. I like to know the names of people who enter my house."

"Yeah? His name's Loedenkrantz."

"Indeed." Wolfe looked at him and inclined his head an inch again. "How do you do, sir."

The dick said without moving, "Pleased to meetcha."

Wolfe returned to Rowcliff. "And you are a lieutenant. Reward of merit? Incredible." His voice deepened and accelerated. "Will you take a message for me to Mr. Cramer? Tell him that Nero Wolfe pronounces him to be a prince of witlings and an unspeakable ass! Pfui!" He turned on the spray, directed it on the orchids, and addressed Francis Horrocks. "But my dear sir, since all life is trouble, the only thing is to achieve a position where we may select varieties . . ."

I said to Rowcliff, "There's a room there at the side, the gardener's. You don't want to miss that."

He went with me and looked in, and I hand it to him that he had enough face left to enter and look under the bed and open the closet door. He came out again, and he was done. But as he moved for the door he asked me, "How do you get out to the roof?"

"You don't. This covers all of it. Anyhow you've got it spotted. Haven't you? Don't tell me you overlooked that."

We were returning the way we had come, and I was behind them again. He didn't answer. Mr. Loedenkrantz didn't stop to smell an orchid. There was a grin inside of me trying to burst into flower, but I was warning it, not yet, sweetheart, they're not out yet. We left the plant rooms and descended to the third floor, and Rowcliff said to the pair he had left there:

"Fall in."

One began, "I thought I heard a noise—"

"Shut up."

I followed them down, on down. After all the diversion I had been furnishing I didn't think it advisable to go suddenly dumb, so I manufactured a couple of nifties during the descent. In the lower hall, before I unlocked the door, I squared off to Rowcliff and told him:

"Listen. I've been free with the lip, but it was my day.

107

We all have to take it sometimes, and hey-nonny-nonny. I'm aware it wasn't you that pulled this boner."

But being a lieutenant, he was stern and unbending. "Much obliged for nothing. Open the door."

I did that, and they went. On the sidewalk they were joined by their brothers who had been left there. I shut the door, heard the lock snap, and put on the bolt. I turned and went to the office. I seldom took a drink before dark, but the idea of a shot of bourbon seemed pleasing, so I went to the cabinet and helped myself. It felt encouraging going down. In my opinion, there was very little chance that Rowcliff had enough eagerness left in him to try a turn-around, but I returned to the entrance and pulled the curtain and stood looking out for a minute. There was no one in sight that had the faintest resemblance to a city employee. So I mounted the stairs, clear to the plant rooms, and went through to the potting room. Wolfe and Horrocks were standing there, and Wolfe looked at me inquiringly.

I waved a hand. "Gone. Done."

Wolfe hung the spray tube on its hook and called, "Theodore!"

Horstmann came trotting. He and I together lifted the pots of Laeliocattleyas, which Wolfe had been spraying, from the boards, and put them on a bench. Then we removed the boards from the long box of osmundine; Horrocks took one. Wolfe said:

"All right, Miss Fox."

The mossy fibre, dripping with water, raised itself up out of the box, fell all around us, and spattered our pants. We began picking off patches of it that were clinging to Clara Fox's soaked dress, and she brushed back her hair and blurted:

"Thank God I wasn't born a mermaid!"

Horrocks put his fingers on the sleeve of her dress. "Absolutely saturated. Really, you know—"

He may have been straight, but he had no right to be in on it. I cut him off: "I know you'll have to be going. Fritz can attend to Miss Fox. If you don't mind?"

108

• • • • 12 • • • •

AT TWELVE o'clock noon Wolfe and I sat in the office. Fred Durkin was out in the kitchen eating pork chops and pumpkin pie. He had made his appearance some twenty minutes before, with the pork chops in his pocket, for Fritz to cook, and a tale of injured innocence. One of Barber's staff had found him in a detention room down at headquarters, put there to weigh his sins after an hour of displaying his ignorance to Inspector Cramer. The lawyer had pried him loose without much trouble and sent him on his way, which of course was West 35th Street. Wolfe hadn't bothered to see him.

Up in the tropical room was the unusual sight of Clara Fox's dress and other items of apparel hanging on a string to dry out, and she was up in the south room sporting the dressing gown Wolfe had given me for Christmas four years before. I hadn't seen her, but Fritz had taken her the gown. It looked as if we'd have to get her out of the house pretty soon or I wouldn't have a thing to put on.

Francis Horrocks had departed, having accepted my hint without any whats. Nothing had been explained to him. Wolfe, of course, wasn't openly handing Clara Fox anything, but it was easy to see that she was one of the few women he would have been able to think up a reason for, from the way he talked about her. He told me that when she and Horrocks had come running into the potting room she had immediately stepped into the osmundine box, which had been all ready for her, and standing there she had fixed her eyes on Horrocks and said to him, "No questions, no remarks, and you do what Mr. Wolfe says. Understand." And Horrocks had stood and stared with his mouth open as she stretched herself out in the box and

109

Horstmann had piled osmundine on her three inches deep while Wolfe got the spray ready. Then he had come to and helped with the boards and the pots.

In the office at noon, Wolfe was drinking beer and making random remarks as they occurred to him. He observed that since Inspector Cramer was sufficiently aroused to be willing to insult Nero Wolfe by having his house invaded with a search warrant, it was quite possible that he had also seen fit to proceed to other indefensible measures, such as tapping telephone wires, and that therefore we should take precautions. He stated that it had been a piece of outrageous stupidity on his part to let Mike Walsh go Monday evening before asking him a certain question, since he had then already formed a surmise which, if proven correct, would solve the problem completely. He said he was sorry that there was no telephone at the Lindquist prairie home in Nebraska, since it meant that the old gentleman would have to endure the rigors of a nine-mile trip to a village in order to talk over long distance; and he hoped that the connection with him would be made at one o'clock as arranged. He also hoped that Johnny Keems would be able to find Mike Walsh and escort him to the office without interference, fairly soon, since a few words with Walsh and a talk with Victor Lindquist should put him in a position where he could proceed with arrangements to clean up the whole affair. More beer. And so forth.

I let him rave on, thinking he might fill in a couple of gaps by accident, but he didn't.

The phone rang. I took it, and heard Keems' voice. I stopped him before he got started:

"I can't hear you, Johnny. Don't talk so close."

"What?"

"I said, don't talk so close."

"Oh. Is this better?"

"Yeah."

"Well . . . I'm reporting progress backwards. I found the old lady in good health and took care of her for a couple of hours, and then she got hit by a brown taxi and they took her to the hospital."

"That's too bad. Hold the wire a minute." I covered the transmitter and turned to Wolfe: "Johnny found Mike Walsh and tailed him for two hours, and a dick picked him up and took him to headquarters."

"Picked up Johnny?"

"No. Walsh."

110

Wolfe frowned, and his lips went out and in, and again. He sighed. "The confounded meddlers. Call him in."

I told the phone, "Come on in, and hurry," and hung up.

Wolfe leaned back with his eyes shut, and I didn't bother him. It was a swell situation for a tantrum, and I didn't feel like a dressing-down. If his observations had been anything at all more than shooting off, this was a bad break, and it might lead to almost anything, since if Mike Walsh emptied the bag for Cramer there was no telling what might be thought necessary for protecting the Marquis of Clivers from a sinister plot. I didn't talk, but got out the plant records and pretended to go over them.

At a quarter to one the doorbell rang, and I went and admitted Johnny Keems. I was still acting as hallboy, because you never could tell about Cramer. Johnny, looking like a Princeton boy with his face washed, which was about the only thing I had against him, followed me to the office and dropped into a chair without an invitation. He demanded:

"How did I come through on the code? Not so bad, huh?"

I grunted. "Perfectly marvelous. You're a wonder. Where did you find Walsh?"

He threw one leg over the other. "No trouble at all. Over on East 64th Street, where he boards. Your instructions were not to approach him until I had a line or in case of emergency, so I found out by judicious inquiry that he was in there and then I stuck around. He came out at a quarter to ten and walked to Second Avenue and turned south. West on 58th to Park. South on Park—"

Wolfe put in, "Skip the itinerary."

Johnny nodded. "We were about there anyhow. At 56th Street he went into the Hotel Portland."

"Indeed."

"Yep. And he stayed there over an hour. He used the phone and then took an elevator, but I stayed in the lobby because the house dick knows me and he saw me and I knew he wouldn't stand for it. I knew Walsh might have got loose because there are two sets of elevators, but all I could do was stick, and at a quarter past eleven he came down and went out. He headed south and turned west on 55th, and across Madison he went in at a door where it's boarded up for construction. That's the place you told me to try if I drew a blank at 64th Street, the place where he works as a night watchman. I waited outside, thinking I might get stopped if I went in, and hoping he wouldn't use another exit. But he didn't. In

111

less than ten minutes he came out again, but he wasn't alone any more. A snoop had him and was hanging onto him. They walked to Park and took a taxi, and I hopped one of my own and followed to Centre Street. They went in at the big doors, and I found a phone."

Wolfe, leaning back, shut his eyes. Johnny Keems straightened his necktie and looked satisfied with himself. I tossed my notebook to the back of the desk, with his report in it, and tried to think of some brief remark that would describe how I felt. The telephone rang.

I took it. A voice informed me that Inspector Cramer wished to speak to Mr. Goodwin, and I said to put him on and signalled to Wolfe to take his line.

The sturdy inspector spoke: "Goodwin? Inspector Cramer. How about doing me a favor?"

"Surest thing you know." I made it hearty. "I'm flattered."

"Yeah? It's an easy one. Jump in your wagon and come down to my office."

I shot a glance at Wolfe, who had his receiver to his ear, but he made no sign. I said, "Maybe I could, except for one thing. I'm needed here to inspect cards of admission at the door. Like search warrants, for instance. You have no idea how they pile in on us."

Cramer laughed. "All right, you can have that one. There'll be no search warrants while you're gone. I need you down here for something. Tell Wolfe you'll be back in an hour."

"Okay. Coming."

I hung up and turned to Wolfe. "Why not? It's better than sitting here crossing my fingers. Fred and Johnny are here, and together they're a fifth as good as me. Maybe he wants me to help him embroider Mike Walsh. I'd be glad to."

Wolfe nodded. "I like this. There's something about it I like. I may be wrong. Go, by all means."

I shook my pants legs down, put the notebook and plant record away in the drawers, and got going. Johnny came to bolt the door behind me.

I hadn't been on the sidewalk for nearly twenty hours, and it smelled good. I filled the chest, waved at Tony with a cart of coal across the street, and opened up my knees on the way to the garage. The roadster whinnied as I went up to it, and I circled down the ramp, scared the daylights out of a truck as I emerged, and headed downtown with my good humor coming in again at every pore. I doubt if anything could ever get me so low that it wouldn't perk me up to get

112

out and enjoy nature, anywhere between the two rivers from the Battery to 110th Street, but preferably below 59th.

I parked at the triangle and went in and took an elevator. They sent me right in to Cramer's little inside room, but it was empty except for a clerk in uniform, and I sat down to wait. In a minute Cramer entered. I was thinking he might have the decency to act a little embarrassed, but he didn't; he was chewing a cigar and he appeared hearty. He didn't go to his desk, but stood there. I thought it wouldn't hurt to rub it in, so I asked him:

"Have you found Clara Fox yet?"

He shook his head. "Nope. No Clara Fox. But we will. We've got Mike Walsh."

I lifted the brows. "You don't say. Congratulations. Where'd you find him?"

He frowned down at me. "I'm not going to try to bluff you, Goodwin. It's a waste of time. That's what I asked you to come down here for, this Mike Walsh. You and Wolfe have been cutting it pretty thin up there, but if you help me out on this we'll call it square. I want you to pick this Mike Walsh out for me. You won't have to appear, you can look through the panel."

"I don't get you. I thought you said you had him."

"Him hell." Cramer bit his cigar. "I've got eight of 'em."

"Oh," I grinned at him sympathetically. "Think of that, eight Mike Walshes! It's a good thing it wasn't Bill Smith or Abe Cohen."

"Will you pick him out?"

"I don't like to." I pulled a hesitation. "Why can't the boys grind it out themselves?"

"Well, they can't. We've got nothing at all to go on except that Harlan Scovil had his name on a piece of paper and he was at your place last night. We couldn't use a hose on all eight of them even if we were inclined that way. The last one was brought in less than an hour ago, and he's worse than any of the others. He's a night watchman and he's seventy if he's a day, and he says who he knows or doesn't know is none of our damn business, and I'm inclined to believe him. Look here, Goodwin. This Walsh isn't a client of Wolfe's. You don't owe him anything, and anyway we're not going to hurt him unless he needs it. Come on and take a look and tell me if we've got him."

I shook my head. "I'm sorry. It wouldn't go with the program. I'd like to, but I can't."

113

Cramer took his cigar from his mouth and pointed it at me. "Once more I'm asking you. Will you do it?"

I just shook my head.

He walked around the desk to his chair and sat down. He looked at me as if he regretted something. Finally he said, "It's too much, Goodwin. This time it's too much. I'm going to have to put it on to you and Wolfe both for obstructing justice. It's all set for a charge. Even if I hated to worse than I do, I've got upstairs to answer to."

He pushed a button on his desk. I said, "Go ahead. Then, pretty soon, go ahead and regret it for a year or two and maybe longer."

The door opened and a gumshoe came in. Cramer turned to him. "You'll have to turn 'em loose, Nick. Put shadows on all of them except the kid that goes to N. Y. U. and the radio singer. They're out. Take good men. If one of them gets lost you've got addresses to pick him up again. Any more they pick up, I'll see them after you've got a record down."

"Yes, sir. The one from Brooklyn, the McGrue Club guy, is raising hell."

"All right. Let him out. I'll phone McGrue later."

The gumshoe departed. Cramer tried to get his cigar lit. I said: "And as far as upstairs is concerned, to hell with the Commissioner. How does he know whether or not it's justice that Wolfe's obstructing? How about that cripple Paul Chapin and that bird Bowen? Did he obstruct justice that time? If you ask me, I think you had a nerve to ask me to come down here. Are we interfering with your legal right to look for these babies? You even looked for one of them under Wolfe's bed and under my bed. Do Wolfe and I wear badges, and do we line up on the first and fifteenth for a city check? We do not."

Cramer puffed. "I ought to charge you."

I lifted the shoulders and let them drop. "Sure. You're just sore. That's one way cops and newspaper reporters are all alike, they can't bear to have anyone know anything they won't tell." I looked at my wrist watch and saw it was nearly two o'clock. "I'm hungry. Where do I eat, inside or out?"

Cramer said, "I don't give a damn if you never eat. Beat it."

I floated up and out, down the hall, down in the elevator, and back to the roadster. I looked around comprehensively, reflecting that within a radius of a few blocks eight Mike Walshes were scattering in all directions, six of them with tails, and that I would give at least two bits to know where one of

114

them was headed for. But even if he had gone by my elbow that second I wouldn't have dared to take it up, since that would have spotted him for them, so I hopped in the roadster and swung north.

When I got back to the house Wolfe and Clara Fox were in the dining-room, sitting with their coffee. They were so busy they only had time to toss me a nod, and I sat down at my end of the table and Fritz brought me a plate. She had on my dressing-gown, with the sleeves rolled up, and a pair of Fritz's slippers with her ankles bare. Wolfe was reciting Hungarian poetry to her, a line at a time, and she was repeating it after him; and he was trying not to look pleased as she leaned forward with an ear cocked at him and her eyes on his lips, asking as if she was really interested, "Say it again, slower, please do."

The yellow dressing-gown wasn't bad on her, at that, but I was hungry. I waded through a plate of minced lamb kidneys with green peppers, and a dish of endive, and as Fritz took the plate away and presented me with a hunk of pie I observed to the room:

"If you've finished with your coffee and have any time to spare, you might like to hear a report."

Wolfe sighed. "I suppose so. But not here." He arose. "If Fritz could serve your coffee in the office? And you, Miss Fox . . . upstairs."

"Oh, my lord. Must I dig in again?"

"Of course. Until dinnertime." He bowed, meaning that he inclined his head two inches, and went off.

Clara Fox got up and walked to my end. "I'll pour your coffee."

"All right. Black and two lumps."

She screwed up her face. "With all this grand cream here? Very well. You know, Mr. Goodwin, this house represents the most insolent denial of female rights the mind of man has ever conceived. No woman in it from top to bottom, but the routine is faultless, the food is perfect, and the sweeping and dusting are impeccable. I have never been a housewife, but I can't overlook this challenge. I'm going to marry Mr. Wolfe, and I know a girl that will be just the thing for you, and of course our friends will be in and out a good deal. This place needs some upsetting."

I looked at her. The hem of the yellow gown was trailing the floor. The throat of it was spreading open, and it was interesting to see where her shoulders came to and how the yellow made her hair look. I said:

"You've already upset enough. Go upstairs and behave yourself. Wolfe has three wives and nineteen children in Turkey."

"I don't believe it. He has always hated women until he saw how nicely they pack in osmundine."

I grinned at her and got up. "Thanks for the coffee. I may be able to persuade Wolfe to let you come down for dinner."

I balanced my cup and saucer in one hand while I opened the door for her with the other, and then went to the office and got seated at my desk and started to sip. Wolfe had his middle drawer open and was counting bottle caps to see how much beer he had drunk since Sunday morning. Finally he closed it and grunted.

"I don't believe it for a moment. Bah. Statistics are notoriously unreliable. I had a very satisfactory talk with Mr. Lindquist over long distance, and I am more than ever anxious for a few words with Mr. Walsh. Did you see him?"

"No. I declined the invitation." I reported my session with Cramer in detail, mostly verbatim, which was the way he liked it. Wolfe listened, and considered.

"I see. Then Mr. Walsh is loose again."

"Yeah. Not only is he loose, but I don't see how we can approach him, since there's a tail on him. The minute we do they'll know it's him and grab him away from us."

"I suppose so." Wolfe sighed. "Of course it would not do to abolish the police. For nine-tenths of the prey that the law would devour they are the ideal hunters, which is as it should be. As for Walsh, it is essential that I see him . . . or that you do. Bring Keems."

I went to the front room, where Johnny was taking ten cents a game from Fred Durkin with a checkerboard, and shook him loose. He sat down next to the desk and Wolfe wiggled a finger at him.

"Johnny, this is important. I don't send Archie because he is needed here, and Saul is not available."

"Yes, sir. Shoot."

"The Michael Walsh whom you followed this morning has been released by the police because they don't know if he is the one they want. They have put a shadow on him, so it would be dangerous for you to pick him up even if you knew where to look. It is very important for Archie to get in touch with him. Since he is pretending to the police that he is not the man they seek, there is a strong probability that he will stick to the ordinary routine of his life; that is, that he will go to work this evening. But if he does that he will certainly

116

be followed there and a detective will be covering the entrance all evening; therefore Archie could not enter that way to see him. I am covering all details so that you will know exactly what we want. Is it true that when a building project is boarded up, there is boarding where the construction adjoins the sidewalk but not on the other sides, where there are buildings? I would think so; at least it may be so sometimes. Very well, I wish to know by what means Archie can enter that building project at, say, seven o'clock this evening. Explore them all. I understand from Miss Fox, who was there last Thursday evening to talk with Mr. Walsh, that they have just started the steel framework.

"Miss Fox also tells me that Mr. Walsh goes to work at six o'clock. I want to know if he does so today. You can watch the entrance at that time, or you may perhaps have found another vantage point for observing him from inside. Use your judgment and your wit. Should you phone here, use code as far as possible. Be here by six-thirty with your report."

"Yes, sir." Johnny stood up. "If I have to sugar anybody around the other buildings in order to get through, I'll need some cash."

Wolfe nodded with some reserve. I got four fives from the safe and passed them over and Johnny tucked them in his vest. Then I took him to the hall and let him out.

I went back to my desk and fooled around with some things, made out a couple of checks and ran over some invoices from Richardt. Wolfe was drinking beer and I was watching him out of the corner of my eye. I was keyed up, and I knew why I was, it was something about him. A hundred times I tried to decide just what it was that made it so plain to me when he had the feeling that he was closing in and was about ready for the blow-up. Once I would think that it was only that he sat differently in his chair, a little further forward, and another time I would guess that it was the way he made movements, not quicker exactly but closer together, and still another time I would light on something else. I doubt if it was any of those. Maybe it was electric. There was more of a current turned on inside of him, and somehow I felt it. I felt it that day, as he filled his glass, and drained it and filled it again. And it made me uncomfortable, because I wasn't doing anything, and because there was always the danger that Wolfe would go off half cocked when he was keeping things to himself. So at length I offered an observation:

"And I just sit here? What's the idea, do you think those

117

gorillas are coming back? I don't. They're not even watching the front. What was the matter with leaving Fred and Johnny here and letting me go to 55th Street to do my own scouting? That might have been sensible, if you want me to see Mike Walsh by seven o'clock. All I'm suggesting is a little friendly chat. I've heard you admit you've got lots of bad habits, but the worst one is the way you dig up odd facts out of phone calls and other sources when my back is turned and then expect me . . ." I waved a hand.

Wolfe said, "Nonsense. When have my expectations of you ventured beyond your capacity?"

"Never. How could they? But for instance, if it's so important for me to see Mike Walsh it might be a good idea for me to know why, unless you want him wrapped up and brought here."

Wolfe shook his head. "Not that, I think. I'll inform you, Archie. In good time." He reached out and touched the button, then sighed and pushed the tray away. "As for my sending Johnny and letting you sit here, you may be needed. While you were out Mr. Muir telephoned to ask if he might call here at half-past-two. It is that now—"

"The devil he did. Muir?"

"Yes. Mr. Ramsey Muir. And as for my keeping you in ignorance of facts, you already interfere so persistently with my mental processes that I am disinclined to furnish you further grounds for speculation. In the present case you know the general situation as well as I do. Chiefly you lack patience, and my exercise of it infuriates you. If I know who killed Harlan Scovil—and since talking with Mr. Lindquist over long distance I think I do—why do I not act at once? Firstly because I require confirmation, and secondly because our primary interest in this case is not the solution of a murder but the collection of a debt. If I expect to get the confirmation I require from Mr. Walsh, why do I not get him at once, secure my confirmation, and let the police have him? Because the course they would probably take, after beating his story out of him, would make it difficult to collect from Lord Clivers, and would greatly complicate the matter of clearing Miss Fox of the larceny charge. We have three separate goals to reach, and since it will be necessary to arrive at all of them simultaneously—but there is the doorbell. Mr. Muir is three minutes late."

I went to the hall and took a look through the panel. Sure enough, it was Muir. I opened up and let him in. From the way he stepped over the doorsill and snapped out that he wanted to see Wolfe. it was fairly plain that he was mad as hell. He had on a brown plaid topcoat cut by a tailor that was out of my class, but 25 years too young for him, and apparently he wasn't taking it off. I motioned him ahead of me into the office and introduced him, and allowed myself a polite grin when I saw that he wasn't shaking hands any more than Wolfe was. I pushed a chair around and he sat with his hat on his knees.

Wolfe said, "Your secretary, on the telephone, seemed not to know what you wished to see me about. My surmise was, your charge against Miss Clara Fox. You understand of course that I am representing Miss Fox."

"Yes. I understand that."

"Well, sir?"

The bones of Muir's face seemed to show, and his ears seemed to point forward, more than they had the day before. He kept his lips pressed together and his jaw was working from side to side as if all this emotion in his old age was nearly too much for him. I remembered how he had looked at Clara Fox the day before and thought it was remarkable that he could keep his digestion going with all the stew there must have been inside of him. He said:

"I have come here at the insistence of Mr. Perry." His voice trembled a little, and when he stopped his jaw slid around. "I want you to understand that I know she took that money. She is the only one who could have taken it. It was found in her car." He stopped a little to control his jaw. "Mr. Perry told me of your threat to sue for damages. The insinuation in it is contemptible. What kind of a blackguard are you, to protect a thief by hinting calumnies against men who . . . men above suspicion?"

He paused and compressed his lips. Wolfe murmured, "Well, go on. I don't answer questions containing two or more unsupported assumptions."

I don't think Muir heard him; he was only hearing himself and trying not to blow up. He said, "I'm here only for one reason, for the sake of the Seaboard Products Corporation. And not on account of your dirty threat either. That's not where the dirt is in the Seaboard Products Corporation that has got to be concealed." His voice trembled again. "It's the fact that the president of the corporation has to satisfy his personal sensual appetite by saving a common thief from what she deserves! That's why she can laugh at me! That's why she can stand behind your dirty threats! Because she knows what Perry wants, and she knows how—"

"Mr. Muir!" Wolfe snapped at him. "I wouldn't talk like that if I were you. It's so futile. Surely you didn't come here to persuade me that Mr. Perry has a sensual appetite."

Muir made a movement and his hat rolled from his knees to the floor, but he paid no attention to it. His movement was for the purpose of getting his hand into his inside breast pocket, from which he withdrew a square manila envelope. He looked in it and fingered around and took out a small photograph, glanced at it, and handed it to Wolfe. "There," he said, "look at that."

Wolfe did so, and passed it to me. It was a snapshot of Clara Fox and Anthony D. Perry seated in a convertible coupe with the top down. I laid it on the edge of the desk and Muir picked it up and returned it to the envelope. His jaw was moving. He said, "I have more than thirty of them. A detective took them for me. Perry doesn't know I have them. I want to make it clear to you that she deserves . . . that she has a hold on him . . ."

Wolfe put up a hand. "I'm afraid I must interrupt you again, Mr. Muir. I don't like photographs of automobiles. You say that Mr. Perry insisted on your coming here. I'll have to insist on your telling me what for."

"But you understand—"

"No. I won't listen. I understand enough. Perhaps I had better put a question or two. Is it true that you have recovered all the missing money?"

Muir glared at him. "You know we have. It was found under the back seat of her car."

"But if that was her car in the photograph, it has no back seat."

"She bought a new one in August. The photograph was taken in July. I suppose Perry bought it. Her salary is higher than any other woman in our organization."

"Splendid. But about the money. If you have it back, why are you determined to prosecute?"

"Why shouldn't we prosecute? Because she's guilty! She took it from my desk, knowing that Perry would protect her! With her body, with her flesh, with her surrender—"

"No, Mr. Muir." Wolfe's hand was up again. "Please. I put the question wrong, I shouldn't have asked why. I want to know, are you determined to prosecute?"

Muir clamped his lips. He opened them, and clamped them again. At last he spoke, "We were. I was."

"Was? Are you still?"

No reply. "Are you still, Mr. Muir?"

"I . . . no."

"Indeed." Wolfe's eyes narrowed. "You are prepared to withdraw the charge?"

"Yes . . . under certain circumstances."

"What circumstances?"

"I want to see her." Muir stopped because his voice was trembling again. "I have promised Perry that I will withdraw the charge provided I can see her, alone, and tell her myself." He sat up and his jaw tightened. "That . . . those are the circumstances."

Wolfe looked at him a moment and then leaned back. He sighed. "I think possibly that can be arranged. But you must first sign a statement exonerating her."

"Before I see her?"

"Yes."

"No. I see her first." Muir's lips worked. "I must see her and tell her myself. If I had already signed a statement, she wouldn't . . . no. I won't do that."

"But you can't see her first." Wolfe sounded patient. "There is a warrant in force against her, sworn to by you. I do not suspect you of treachery, I merely protect my client. You say that you have promised Mr. Perry that you will withdraw the charge. Do so. Mr. Goodwin will type the statement, you will sign it, and I will arrange a meeting with Miss Fox later in the day."

Muir was shaking his head. He muttered, "No. No . . . I won't." All at once he broke loose worse than he had in Perry's office the day before. He jumped up and banged his hand on the desk and leaned over at Wolfe. "I tell you I must see her! You damn blackguard, you've got her here! What for? What do you get out of it? What do you and Perry . . ."

I had a good notion to slap him one, but of course he was too old and too little. Wolfe, leaning back, opened his eyes to look at him and then closed them. Muir went on raving. I got out of my chair and told him to sit down, and he began yelling at me, something about how I had looked at her in Perry's office yesterday. That sounded as if he might really be going to have a fit, so I took a step and got hold of his shoulders with a fairly good grip and persuaded him into his chair, and he shut up as suddenly as he had started and pulled a handkerchief from his pocket and began wiping his face with his hand trembling.

As he did that and I stepped back, the doorbell rang. I wasn't sure about leaving Wolfe there alone with a maniac, but when I didn't move he lifted his brows at me, so I went to see who the customer was.

I looked through the panel. It was a rugged-looking guy well past middle age in a loose-hanging tweed suit, with a red face, straight eyebrows over tired gray eyes, and no lobe on his right ear. Even without the ear I would have recognized him from the *Times* picture. I opened the door and asked him what he wanted and he said in a wounded tone:

"I'd like to see Mr. Nero Wolfe. Lord Clivers."

···· 13 ····

I NODDED. "Right. Hop the sill."

I proceeded to tax the brain. Before I go on to describe that, I'll make a confession. I had not till that moment seriously entertained the idea that the Marquis of Clivers had killed Harlan Scovil. And why not? Because like most other people, and maybe especially Americans, there was a sneaky feeling in me that men with noble titles didn't do things like that. Besides, this bird had just been to Washington and had lunch at the White House, which cinched it that he wasn't a murderer. As a matter of fact, I suspect that noblemen and people who eat lunch at the White House commit more than their share of murders compared to their numerical strength in the total population. Anyhow, looking at this one in the flesh, and reflecting that he carried a pistol and knew how to use one, and considering how well he was fixed in the way of motive, and realizing that since Harlan Scovil had been suspicious enough to make an advance call on Nero Wolfe he might easily have done the same on the Marquis of Clivers, I revised some of the opinions I had been forming. It looked wide open to me.

That flashed through my mind. Also, as I disposed of his hat and stick and gloves for him, I wondered if it might be well to arrange a little confrontation between Muir and the marquis, but I didn't like to decide that myself. So I escorted him to a seat in the front room, telling him Wolfe was engaged, and then returned to the hall and wrote on a piece of paper, "Old man Clivers," and went to the office and handed the paper to Wolfe.

Wolfe glanced at it, looked at me, and winked his right eye. I sat down. Muir was talking, much calmer but just as

123

stubborn. They passed it back and forth for a couple of minutes without getting anywhere, until Wolfe said:

"Futile, Mr. Muir. I won't do it. Tell Mr. Perry that I shall proceed with the program I announced to him this morning. That's final. I'll accept nothing less than complete and unconditional exoneration of my client. Good day, sir; I have a caller waiting."

Muir stood up. He wasn't trembling, and his jaw seemed to be back in place, but he looked about as friendly as Mussolini talking to the world. He didn't say anything. He shot me a mean glance and looked at Wolfe for half a minute without blinking, and then stooped to pick up his hat and straightened up and steered for the door. I followed and let him out, and stood on the stoop a second watching him start off down the sidewalk as if he had half a jag on. He was like the mule in the story that kept running into trees; he wasn't blind, he was just so mad he didn't give a damn.

I stood shaking my head more in anger than in pity, and then went back to the office and said to Wolfe:

"I would say you hit bottom that time. He's staggering. If you called that foxy, what would you say if you saw a rat?"

Wolfe nodded faintly. I resumed, "I showed you that paper because I thought you might deem it advisable to let Clivers and Muir see each other. Unexpected like that, it might have been interesting. It's my social instinct."

"No doubt. But this is a detective bureau, not a fashionable salon. Nor a menagerie—since Mr. Muir is plainly a lecherous hyena. Bring Lord Clivers."

I went through the connecting door to the front room, and Clivers looked around surprised at my entering from a new direction. He was jumpy. I pointed him ahead and he stopped on the threshold and glanced around before venturing in. Then he moved spry enough and walked over to the desk. Wolfe took him in with his eyes half shut, and nodded.

"How do you do, sir." Wolfe indicated the chair Muir had just vacated. "Be seated."

Clivers did a slow motion circle. He turned all the way around, encompassing with his eyes the book shelves, the wall maps, the Holbein reproductions, more book shelves, the three-foot globe on its stand, the engraving of Brillat-Savarin, more book shelves, the picture of Sherlock Holmes above my desk. Then he sat down and looked at me with a frown and pointed a thumb at me.

"This young man," he said.

Wolfe said, "My confidential assistant, Mr. Goodwin. There

124

would be no point in sending him out, for he would merely find a point of vantage we have prepared, and set down what he heard."

"The devil he would." Clivers laughed three short blasts, haw-haw-haw, and gave me up. He transferred the frown to Wolfe. "I received your letter about that horse. It's preposterous."

Wolfe nodded. "I agree with you. All debts are preposterous. They are the envious past clutching with its cold dead fingers the throat of the living present."

"Eh?" Clivers stared at him. "What kind of talk is that? Rot. What I mean to say is, two hundred thousand pounds for a horse. And uncollectible."

"Surely not." Wolfe sighed. He leaned forward to press the button for Fritz, and back again. "The best argument against you is your presence here. If it is uncollectible, why did you come? Will you have some beer?"

"What kind of beer?"

"American. Potable."

"I'll try it. I came because my nephew gave me to understand that if I wanted to see you I would have to come. I wanted to see you because I had to learn if you are a swindler or a dupe."

"My dear sir." Wolfe lifted his brows. "No other alternatives? —Another glass and bottle, Fritz." He opened his, and poured. "But you seem to be a direct man. Let's not get mired in irrelevancies. Frankly, I am relieved. I feared that you might even dispute the question of identity and create a lot of unnecessary trouble."

"Dispute identity?" Clivers glared. "Why the devil should I?"

"You shouldn't, but I thought you might. You were, forty years ago in Silver City, Nevada, known as George Rowley?"

"Certainly I was. Thanks, I'll pour it myself."

"Good." Wolfe drank, and wiped his lips. "I think we should get along. I am aware that Mr. Lindquist's claim against you has no legal standing on account of the expiration of time. The same is true of the claim of various others; besides, the paper you signed which originally validated it is not available. But it is a sound and demonstrable moral obligation, and I calculated that rather than have that fact shown in open court you would prefer to pay. It would be an unusual case and would arouse much public interest. Not only are you a peer of England, you are in this country on an important and delicate diplomatic mission, and therefore such publicity would be especially undesirable. Would you not rather pay what you owe, or at least a fraction of it, than permit the publicity? I calculated that you would. Do you find the beer tolerable?"

Clivers put down his glass and licked his lips. "It'll do." He screwed up his mouth and looked at Wolfe. "By God, you know, you might mean that."

"Verily, sir."

"Yes, by God, you might. I'll tell you what I thought. I thought you were basing the claim on that horse with the pretense that it was additional to the obligation I assumed when I signed that paper. The horse wasn't mentioned in the paper. Not a bad idea, an excellent go at blackmail. It all sounds fantastic now, but it wasn't then. If I hadn't signed that paper and if it hadn't been for that horse I would have had a noose around my neck. Not so damn pleasant, eh? And of course that's what you're doing, claiming extra for the horse. But it's preposterous. Two hundred thousand pounds for a horse? I'll pay a thousand."

Wolfe shook his head. "I dislike haggling. Equally I dislike quibbling. The total claim is in question, and you know it. I represent not only Mr. and Miss Lindquist but also the daughter of Gilbert Fox, and indirectly Mr. Walsh; and I was to have represented Mr. Scovil, who was murdered last evening." He shook his head again. "No, Lord Clivers. In my letter I based the claim on the horse only because the paper you signed is not available. It is the total claim we are discussing, and, strictly speaking, that would mean half of your entire wealth. As I said, my clients are willing to accept a fraction."

Clivers had a new expression on his face. He no longer glared, but looked at Wolfe quietly intent. He said, "I see. So it's a serious game, is it? I would have paid a thousand for the horse, possibly even another thousand for the glass of beer. But you're on for a real haul by threatening to make all this public and compromise my position here. Go to hell." He got up.

Wolfe said patiently, "Permit me. It isn't a matter of a thousand or two for a horse. Precisely and morally, you owe these people half of your wealth. If they are willing—"

"Bah! I owe them nothing! You know damn well I've paid them."

Wolfe's eyes went nearly shut. "What's that? You've paid them?"

"Of course I have, and you know it. And I've got their receipt, and I've got the paper I signed." Clivers abruptly sat

126

down again. "Look here. Your man is here, and I'm alone, so why not talk straight? I don't resent your being a crook, I've dealt with crooks before, and more pretentious ones than you. But cut out the pretense and get down to business. You have a good lever for blackmail, I admit it. But you might as well give up the idea of a big haul, because I won't submit to it. I'll pay three thousand pounds for a receipt from the Lindquists for that horse."

Wolfe's forefinger was tapping gently on the arm of his chair, which meant he was dodging meteors and comets. His eyes were mere slits. After a moment he said, "This is bad. It raises questions of credibility." He wiggled the finger. "Really bad, sir. How am I to know whether you really have paid? And if you have, how are you to know whether I was really ignorant of the fact and acting in good faith? Have you any suggestions?" He pushed the button. "I need some beer. Will you join me?"

"Yes. It's pretty good. Do you mean to say you didn't know I had paid?"

"I do. I do indeed. Though the possibility should certainly have occurred to me. I was too intent on the path under my feet." He stopped to open bottles, pushed one across to Clivers, and filled his glass. "You say you paid them. What *them?* When? How much? What with? They signed a receipt? Tell me about it."

Clivers, taking his time, emptied his glass and set it down. He licked his lips, screwed up his mouth, and looked at Wolfe, considering. Finally he shook his head. "I don't know about you. You're clever. Do you mean that if I show evidence of having paid, and their receipt, you will abandon this preposterous claim for the horse on payment of a thousand pounds?"

"Satisfactory evidence?" Wolfe nodded. "I'll abandon it for nothing."

"Oh, I'll pay a thousand. I understand the Lindquists are hard up. The evidence will be satisfactory, and you can see it tomorrow morning."

"I'd rather see it today."

"You can't. I haven't got it. It will arrive this evening on the *Berengaria*. My dispatch bag will reach me tonight, but I shall be engaged. Come to my hotel any time after nine in the morning."

"I don't go out. I am busy from nine to eleven. You can bring your evidence here any time after eleven."

"The devil I can." Clivers stared at him, and suddenly

127

laughed his three blasts again. Haw-haw-haw. He turned it off. "You can come to my hotel. You don't look infirm."

Wolfe said patiently, "If you don't bring it here, or send it, I won't get to see it and I'll have to press the claim for the horse. And by the way, how does it happen to be coming on the *Berengaria*?"

"Because I sent for it. Monday of last week, eight days ago, a woman saw me. She got in to me through my nephew—it seems they had met socially. She represented herself as the daughter of Gil Fox and made demands. I wouldn't discuss it with her. I thought it was straight blackmail and I would freeze her out. She was too damned good-looking to be honest. But I thought it worth while to cable to London for these items from my private papers, in case of developments. They'll be here tonight."

"And this payment—when was it made?"

"Nineteen-six or seven. I don't know. I haven't looked at those papers for twenty years."

"To whom was the payment made?"

"I have the receipt signed by all of them."

"So you said. And you have the paper which you had signed. The man called Rubber Coleman had that paper. Did he get the money?"

Clivers opened his mouth and shut it again. Then he said, "I've answered enough questions. You'll see the check in the morning, signed by me, endorsed by the payee, and cancelled paid." He looked at his empty glass. "I hadn't tried American lager before. It's pretty good."

Wolfe pressed the button. "Then why not anticipate it by a few hours? I'm not attempting a cross-examination, Lord Clivers. I merely want information. Was it Coleman?"

"Yes."

"How much did he get?"

"Two hundred and some odd thousand pounds. A million dollars. He came to me—July I think it was—about a year after I succeeded to the title. It must have been nineteen-six. He made exorbitant demands. Much of my property was entail. He was unreasonable. We finally agreed on a million dollars. Of course I needed time to get that much cash together. He returned to the States and came back in a couple of months with a receipt signed by all of them. Besides, he was deputized in the original paper, which he surrendered. My solicitor wanted me to send over here and have the signatures verified, but Coleman said he had had difficulty in persuading them to agree to the amount and I was afraid to reopen the question. I paid him."

"Where is Coleman now?"

"I don't know. I've never seen him since, nor heard of him. I wasn't interested; it was a closed chapter. I'm not greatly interested now. If he swindled them and kept the money, they shouldn't have trusted him with their signatures." Clivers hesitated, then resumed, "It's a fact that when the Fox woman saw me a week ago I took it for blackmail, but when Harlan Scovil called to see me yesterday afternoon I had my doubts. Scovil was a square man, he was born square, and I didn't think even forty years could turn him into a blackmailer. When I learned from the police last evening that he had been killed, there was no longer any doubt about a stink in the wind, but I couldn't tell them what I didn't know, and what I did know was my own business."

"So Harlan Scovil saw you yesterday?" Wolfe rubbed his nose. "That's int—"

"He didn't see me. I was out. When I returned in the late afternoon I was told he had been there." Clivers drank his beer. "Then this morning your letter came and it looked like blackmail again. With a murder involved in it also, it appeared that publicity was inevitable if I consulted the official police. The only thing left was to deal with you. All you wanted was money, and I have a little of it left in spite of taxes and revolutions. I don't for a minute believe that you're prepared to drop it merely because I show evidence that I've paid. You want money. You present a front that shows you're not a damned piker." He pointed. "Look at that globe, the finest I ever saw, couldn't have cost less than a hundred pounds. Twice as big as the one in my library. I'll pay three thousand for Lindquist's receipt for that horse."

"Indeed." Wolfe sighed. "Back to three thousand again. I'm sorry, sir, that you persist in taking me for a horse trader. And I do want money. That globe was made by Gouchard and there aren't many like it." He suddenly straightened up. "By the way, was it Mr. Walsh who told you that the Lindquists are hard up?"

Clivers stared. "How the devil do you know that?" He looked around. "Is Walsh here?"

"No, he isn't here. I didn't know it, I asked. I was aware that Mr. Walsh had called at the Hotel Portland this morning, so you had a talk with him. You haven't been entirely frank, Lord Clivers. You knew when you came here that Mr.

Walsh never got any of that money, possibly that he never signed the receipt."

"I knew he said he hadn't."

"Don't you believe him?"

"I don't believe anybody. I know damn well I'm a liar. I'm a diplomat." He did his three blasts again, haw-haw-haw. "Look here. You can forget about Walsh, I'll deal with him myself. I have to keep this thing clear, at least as long as I'm in this country. I'll deal with Walsh. Scovil is dead, God rest his soul. Let the police do what they can with that. As for the Lindquists, I'll pay them two thousand for the horse, and you would get a share of that. The Fox woman can look after herself; anyone as young and handsome as she is doesn't need any of my money. As far as I'm concerned, that clears it up. If you can find Coleman and put a twist on him, go ahead, but that would take doing. He was hard and tricky, and it's a safe bet he still is. You may see the documents tomorrow morning, but I won't bring them here and I won't send them. If you can't come, send your man to look at them. I'll see him, and we can arrange for the payment to the Lindquists and their receipt. Actually, a thousand pounds should be enough for a horse. Eh?"

Wolfe shook his head. He was leaning back again, with his fingers twined on his belly, and if you didn't know him you might have thought he was asleep. Clivers sat and frowned at him. I turned a new page of my notebook and wondered if we would have to garnishee Clara Fox's wages to collect our fee. Finally Wolfe's eyelids raised enough to permit the conjecture that he was conscious.

"It would have saved a lot of trouble," he murmured, "if they had hanged you in 1895. Isn't that so? As it stands, Lord Clivers, I wish to assure you again of my complete good faith in this matter, and I suggest that we postpone commitments until your evidence of payment has been examined. Tomorrow, then." He looked at me. "Confound you, Archie. I have you to thank for this acarpous entanglement."

It was a new one, but I got the idea. He meant that he had drawn his sword in defense of Clara Fox because I had told him that she was the ideal of my dreams. I suppose it was me that sat and recited Hungarian poetry to her.

• • • • 14 • • • •

WHEN WOLFE came down to the office from the plant rooms at six o'clock, Saul Panzer and Orrie Cather were there waiting for him. Fred Durkin, who had spent most of the afternoon in the kitchen with the cookie jar, had been sent home at five, after I had warned him to cross the street if he saw a cop.

Nothing much had happened, except that Anthony D. Perry had telephoned a little after Fred had left, to say that he would like to call at the office and see Wolfe at seven o'clock. Since I would be leaving about that time to sneak up on Mike Walsh, I asked him if he couldn't make it at six, but he said other engagements prevented. I tried a couple of leading questions on him, but he got brusque and said his business was with Nero Wolfe. I knew Saul would be around, or Johnny Keems, so I said okay for seven.

There had been no word from Johnny. The outstanding event of the afternoon had been the arrival of another enormous box of roses from the Horrocks person, and he had had the brass to have the delivery label addressed to me, with a card on the inside scribbled "Thanks Goodwin for forwarding," so now in addition to acting as hallboy and as a second-hand ladies' outfitter, apparently I was also expected to be a common carrier.

I had lost sixty cents. At a quarter to four, a few minutes after Clivers had gone, Wolfe had suggested that since I hadn't been out much a little exercise wouldn't hurt me any. He had made no comments on the news from Clivers, and I thought he might if I went along with him, but I told him I couldn't see it at two bits. He said, all right, a dime. So I mounted the stairs while he took the elevator and we met in his room. He took his coat and vest off, exhibiting about

131

eighteen square feet of canary yellow shirt, and chose the darts with yellow feathers, which were his favorites. The first hand he got an ace and two bull's eyes, making three aces. By four o'clock, time for him to go to the plant rooms, it had cost me sixty cents and I had got nothing out of it because he had been too concentrated on the game to talk.

I went on up to the south room and was in there nearly an hour. There were three reasons for it: first, Wolfe had instructed me to tell Clara Fox about the visits from Muir and Clivers; second, she was restless and needed a little discipline; and third, I had nothing else to do anyhow. She had her clothes on again. She said Fritz had given her an iron to press with, but her dress didn't look as if she had used it much. I told her I supposed an adventuress wouldn't be so hot at ironing. When I told her about Muir she just made a face and didn't seem disposed to furnish any remarks, but she was articulate about Clivers. She thought he was lying. She said that she understood he was considered one of the ablest of British diplomats, and it was to be expected he would use his talents for private business as well as public. I said that I hadn't observed anything particularly able about him except that he could empty a glass of beer as fast as Nero Wolfe; that while he might not be quite as big a sap as his nephew Francis Horrocks he seemed fairly primitive to me, even for a guy who had spent most of his life on a little island.

She said it was just a difference in superficial mannerisms, that she too had thought Horrocks a sap at first, that I would change my mind when I knew him better, and that after all traditions weren't necessarily silly just because they weren't American. I said I wasn't talking about traditions, I was talking about saps, and as far as I was concerned saps were out, regardless of race, nationality or religion. It went on from there until she said she guessed she would go up and take advantage of Mr. Wolfe's invitation to look at the orchids, and I went down to send Fred home.

When Wolfe came down I was at my desk working on some sandwiches and milk, for I didn't know when I might get back from my trip uptown. I told him about the phone call from Perry. He went into the front room to get reports from Saul and Orrie, which made me sore as usual, but when he came back and settled into his chair and rang for beer I made no effort to stimulate him into any choice remarks about straining my powers of dissimulation, because he didn't give me a chance. Having sent Orrie home and Saul to the kitchen, he was ready for me, and he disclosed the nature of my mission with Mike Walsh. It wasn't precisely what I had expected, but I pretended it was by keeping nonchalant and casual. He drank beer and wiped his lips and told me:

"I'm sorry, Archie, if this bores you."

I said, "Oh, I expect it. Just a matter of routine."

He winked at me, and I turned and picked up my milk to keep from grinning back at him, and the telephone rang.

It was Inspector Cramer. He asked for Wolfe and I passed the signal, and of course kept my own line. Cramer said:

"What about this Clara Fox? Are you going to bring her down here, or tell me where to send for her?"

Wolfe murmured into the transmitter, "What is this, Mr. Cramer? A new tactic? I don't get it."

"Now listen, Wolfe!" Cramer sounded hurt and angry. "First you tell me you've got her hid because we tried to snatch her on a phoney larceny charge. Now that that's out of the way, do you think you're going to pull—"

"What?" Wolfe stopped him. "The larceny charge out of the way?"

"Certainly. Don't pretend you didn't know it, since of course you did it, though I don't know how. You can put over the damnedest tricks."

"No doubt. But please tell me how you learned this."

"Frisbie over at the District Attorney's office. It seems that a fellow named Muir, a vice-president up at that Seaboard thing where she worked, is a friend of Frisbie's. He's the one that swore out the warrant. Now he's backed up, and it's all off, and I want to see this Miss Fox and hear her tell me that she never heard of Harlan Scovil, like all the Mike Walshes we got." Cramer became sarcastic. "Of course this is all news to you."

"It is indeed." Wolfe sent a glance at me, with a lifted brow. "Quite pleasant news. Let's see. I suspect it would be too difficult to persuade you that I know nothing of Miss Fox's whereabouts, so I shan't try. It is now six-thirty, and I shall have to make some inquiries. Where can I telephone you at eight?"

"Oh, for God's sake." Cramer sounded disgusted. "I wish I'd let the Commissioner pull you in, as he wanted to. I don't need to tell you why I hate to work against you, but have a heart. Send her down here, I won't bite her. I was going to a show tonight."

"I'm sorry, Mr. Cramer." Wolfe affected his sweet tone, which always made me want to kick him. "I must first verify

133

your information about the larceny charge, and then I must get in touch with Miss Fox. You'll be there until eight o'clock."

Cramer grunted something profane, and we hung up.

"So." I tossed down my notebook. "Mr. Muir is yellow after all, and Mr. Perry is probably coming to find out how you knew he would be. Shake-up in the Seaboard Products Corporation. But where the devil is Johnny—ah, see that? All I have to do is pronounce his name and he rings the doorbell."

I went to the entrance and let him in. One look at his satisfied handsomeness was enough to show that he had been marvelous all over again. As a matter of fact, Johnny Keems unquestionably had an idea at the back of his head—and still has—that it would be a very fine thing for the detective business if he got my job. Which doesn't bother me a bit, because I know Wolfe would never be able to stand him. He puts slick stuff on his hair and he wears spats, and he would never get the knack of keeping Wolfe on the job by bawling him out properly. I know what I get paid high wages for, though I've never been able to decide whether Wolfe knows that I know.

I took Johnny to the office and he sat down and began pulling papers out of his pocket. He shuffled through them and announced:

"I thought it would be better to make diagrams. Of course I could have furnished Archie with verbal descriptions, but along with my shorthand I've learned—"

Wolfe put in, "Is Mr. Walsh there now?"

Johnny nodded. "He came a few minutes before six. I was watching from the back of a restaurant that fronts on 56th Street, because I knew he'd have a shadow and I didn't want to run a risk of being seen, a lot of those city detectives know me. By the way, there's only the one entrance to the boarding, on 55th." He handed the papers across to Wolfe. "I dug up nine other ways to get in. Some of them you couldn't use, but with two of them, a restaurant and a pet shop that's open until nine, it's a cinch."

Instead of taking the papers, Wolfe nodded at me. "Give them to Archie. Is there anyone in there besides Mr. Walsh?"

"I don't think so. It's mostly steel men on the job now, and they quit at five. Of course it was dark when I left, and it isn't lit up much. There's a wooden shed at one side with a couple of tables and a phone and so on, and a man was standing there talking to Walsh, a foreman, but he looked as if he was ready to leave. The reason I was a little late, after I got out of there I went around to 55th to see if there was a shadow on the job, and there was. I spotted him easy. He was standing there across the street, talking to a taxi-driver."

"All right. Satisfactory. Go over the diagrams with Archie."

Johnny explained to me how good the diagrams were, and I had to agree with him. They were swell. Five of them I discarded, because four of them were shops that wouldn't be open and the other was the Orient Club, which wouldn't be easy to get into. Of the remaining four, one was the pet shop, one a movie theater with a fire alley, and two restaurants. After Johnny's detailed description of the relative advantages and disadvantages, I picked one of the restaurants for the first stab. It seemed like a lot of complicated organization work for getting ready to stop in and ask a guy a question, but considering what the question led to in Wolfe's mental arrangements it seemed likely that it might be worth the trouble. By the time we were through with Johnny's battle maps it lacked only a few minutes till seven, and I followed my custom of chucking things in the drawers, plugging the phone for all the house connections, and taking my automatic and giving it a look and sticking it in my pocket. I got up and pushed my chair in.

I asked Johnny, "Can you hang around for a couple of hours' overtime?"

"I can if I eat."

"Okay. You'll find Saul in the kitchen. There's a caller expected at seven and he'll tend to the door. Stick around. Mr. Wolfe may want you to exercise your shorthand."

Johnny strode out. I think he practiced striding. I started to follow, but turned to ask Wolfe, "Are you going to grab time by the forelock? Will there be a party when I get back?"

"I couldn't say." Wolfe's hand was resting on the desk; he was waiting for the door to close behind me, to ring for beer. "We'll await the confirmation."

"Shall I phone?"

"No. Bring it."

"Okay." I turned.

The telephone rang. From force of habit I wheeled again and stepped to my desk for it, though I saw that Wolfe had reached for his receiver. So we both heard it, a voice that sounded far away but thin and tense with excitement:

"Nero Wolfe! Nero—"

I snapped, "Yes. Talking."

"I've got him! Come up here . . . 55th Street . . . Mike Walsh this is . . . I've got him covered . . . come up—"

It was cut off by the sound of a shot in the receiver—a

135

sound of an explosion so loud in my ear that it might have been a young cannon. Then there was nothing. I said "Hello, Walsh! Walsh!" a few times, but there was no answer.

I hung up and turned to Wolfe. "Well, by Godfrey. Did you hear anything?"

He nodded. "I did. And I don't understand it."

"Indeed. That's a record. What's the program, hop up there?"

Wolfe's eyes were shut, and his lips were moving out and in. He stayed that way a minute. I stood and watched him. Finally he said, "If Walsh shot someone, who was it? But if someone shot him, why now? Why not yesterday or a week ago? In any case, you might as well go and learn what happened. It may have been merely a steel girder crashing off its perch; there was enough noise."

"No. That was a gun."

"Very well. Find out. If you—ah! The doorbell. Indeed. You might attend to that first. Mr. Perry is punctual."

As I entered the hall Saul Panzer came out of the kitchen, and I sent him back. I turned on the stoop light and looked through the panel because it was getting to be a habit, and saw it was Perry. I opened the door and he stepped inside and put his hat and gloves on the stand.

I followed him into the office.

Wolfe said, "Good evening sir. —I have reflected, Archie, that the less one meddles the less one becomes involved. You might have Saul phone the hospital that there has been an accident. —Oh no, Mr. Perry, nothing serious, thank you."

I went to the kitchen and told Saul Panzer: "Go to Allen's on 34th Street and phone headquarters that you think you heard a shot inside the building construction on 55th near Madison and they'd better investigate at once. If they want to know who you are, tell them King George. Make it snappy."

That was a nickel wasted, but I didn't know it then.

• • • • 15 • • • •

PERRY GLANCED at me as I got into my chair and opened my notebook. He was saying, "I don't remember that anything ever irritated me more. I suppose I'm getting old. You mustn't think I bear any ill-will; if you preferred to represent Miss Fox, that was your right. But you must admit I played your hand for you; so far as I know there wasn't the faintest shred of evidence with which you could have enforced your threat." He smiled. "You think, of course, that my personal—er—respect for Miss Fox influenced my attitude and caused me to bring pressure on Muir. I confess that had a great deal to do with it. She is a charming young lady and also an extremely competent employee."

Wolfe nodded. "And my client. Naturally, I was pleased to learn that the charge had been dropped."

"You say you heard it from the police? I hoped I was bringing the good news myself."

"I got it from Inspector Cramer." Wolfe had got his beer. He poured some, and resumed, "Mr. Cramer told me that he had been advised of it by a Mr. Frisbie, an Assistant District Attorney. It appears that Mr. Frisbie is a friend of Mr. Muir."

"Yes. I am acquainted with Frisbie. I know Skinner, the District Attorney, quite well." Perry coughed, watched Wolfe empty his glass, and resumed, "So I'm not the bearer of glad tidings. But," he smiled, "that wasn't the chief purpose of my call."

"Well, sir?"

"Well . . . I think you owe me something. Look at it this way. By threatening me with a procedure which would have meant most distasteful publicity for my corporation, you forced me to exert my authority and compel Muir to drop his charge.

Muir isn't an employee; he is the highest officer of the corporation after myself and he owns a fair proportion of the stock. It wasn't easy." Perry leaned forward and got crisper. "I surrendered to you. Now I have a right to know what I surrendered to. The only possible interpretation of your threat was that Miss Fox had been framed, and you wouldn't have dared to make such a threat unless you had some sort of evidence for it." He sat back and finished softly, "I want to know what that evidence is."

"But, Mr. Perry." Wolfe wiggled a finger. "Miss Fox is my client. You're not."

"Ah." Perry smiled. "You want to be paid for it? I'll pay a reasonable amount."

"Whatever information I have gathered in the interest of Miss Fox is not for sale to others."

"Rubbish. It has served her well. She has no further use for it." He leaned forward again. "Look here, Wolfe. I don't need to try to explain Muir to you, you've talked with him. If he has got so bad that he tries to frame a girl out of senile chagrin and vindictiveness, don't you think I ought to know it? He is our senior vice-president. Wouldn't our stockholders think so?"

"I didn't know stockholders think." Wolfe sighed. "But to answer your first question: yes, sir, I do think you ought to know it. But you won't learn it from me. Let us not go on pawing the air, Mr. Perry. This is definite: I did have evidence to support my threat, but under no circumstances will you get from me any proof that you could use against Mr. Muir. So we won't discuss that. If there is any other topic . . ."

Perry insisted. He got frank. His opinion was that Muir was such an old goat that his active services were no longer of any value to the corporation. He wanted to deal fairly with Muir, but after all his first duty was to the organization and its stockholders. And so on. He had suspected from the first that there was something odd about the disappearance of that $30,000, and he reasserted his right to know what Wolfe had found out about it. Wolfe let him ramble on quite a while, but finally he sighed and sat up and got positive. Nothing doing.

Perry seemed determined to keep his temper. He sat and bit his lower lip and looked at me and back at Wolfe again.

Wolfe asked, "Was there anything else, sir?"

Perry hesitated. Then he nodded. "There was, yes. But I don't suppose . . . however . . . I want to see Miss Fox."

"Indeed." Wolfe's shoulders went up an inch and down

again. "The demand for that young woman seems to be universal. Did you know the police are still looking for her? They want to ask her about a murder."

Perry's chin jerked up. "Murder? What murder?"

"Just a murder. A man on the street with five bullets in him. I would have supposed Frisbie had told you of it."

"No. Muir said Frisbie said something . . . I forget what . . . but this sounds serious. How can she possibly be connected with it? Who was killed?"

"A man named Harlan Scovil. Murder is often serious. But I think you needn't worry about Miss Fox; she really had nothing to do with it. You see, she is still my client. At present she is rather inaccessible, so if you could just tell me what you want to see her about . . ."

I saw a spot of color on Perry's temple, and it occurred to me that he was the fourth man I had that day seen badly affected in the emotions by either the presence or the name of Clara Fox. She wasn't a woman, she was an epidemic. But obviously Perry wasn't going to repeat Muir's performance. I watched the spot of color as it faded. At length he said to Wolfe quietly:

"She is in this house. Isn't she?"

"The police searched this house today and didn't find her."

"But you know where she is?"

"Certainly." Wolfe frowned at him. "If you have a message for her, Mr. Goodwin will take it."

"Can you tell me when and where it will be possible to see her?"

"No. I'm sorry. Not at present. Tomorrow, perhaps . . ."

Perry arose from his chair. He stood and looked down at Wolfe, and all of a sudden smiled. "All right," he said. "I can't say that my call here has been very profitable, but I'm not complaining. Every man has a right to his own methods if he can get away with them. As you suggest, I'll wait till tomorrow; you may feel differently about it." He put out his hand.

Wolfe glanced at the outstretched hand, then opened his eyes to look directly at Perry's face. He shook his head. "No, sir. You are perfectly aware that in view of this . . . event, I am no friend of yours."

Perry's temple showed color again. But he didn't say anything. He turned and steered for the door. I lifted myself and followed him. He already had his hat and gloves by the time I got to the hall stand, and when I opened the door for him I saw that he had a car outside, one of the new Wether-

139

sill convertibles. I watched him climb in, and waited until he had glided off before I re-entered and slid the bolt to.

I stopped in the kitchen long enough to learn from Saul that he had phoned the message to headquarters but hadn't been able to convince them that he was King George and so had rung off.

In the office, Wolfe sat with his eyes closed and his lips moving. After sitting down and glancing over my notebook and putting it in the drawer, I observed aloud:

"He's wise."

No reply, no acknowledgment. I added, "Which is more than you are." That met with the same lack of encouragement. I waited a courteous interval and resumed, "The poor old fellow would give anything in the world to forestall unpleasant publicity for the Seaboard Products Corporation. Just think what he has sacrificed! He has spent the best part of his life building up that business, and I'll bet his share of the profits is no more than a measly half a million a year. But what I want to know—"

"Shut up, Archie." Wolfe's eyes opened. "I can do without that now." He grimaced at his empty glass. "I am atrociously uncomfortable. It is sufficiently annoying to deal with inadequate information, which is what one usually has, but to sit thus while surmises, the mere ghosts of facts, tumble idiotically in my brain, is next to insupportable. It would have been better, perhaps, if you had gone to 55th Street. With prudence. At any rate, we can try for Mr. Cramer. I told him I would telephone him by eight, and it lacks only ten minutes of that. I particularly resent this sort of disturbance at this time of day. I presume you know we are having guinea chicken *Braziliera*. See about Mr. Cramer."

That proved to be a job. Cramer's extension seemed to be permanently busy. After five or six tries I finally got it, and was told by someone that Cramer wasn't there. He had left shortly after seven o'clock, and it wasn't known where he was, and he had left no word about any expected message from Nero Wolfe. Wolfe received the information standing up, for Fritz had appeared to announce dinner. I reported Cramer's absence and added, "Why don't I go uptown now and see if something fell and broke? Or send Saul."

Wolfe shook his head. "No. The police are there, and if there is anything to hear we shall hear it later by reaching Mr. Cramer, without exposing ourselves." He moved to the door. "There is no necessity for Johnny to sit in the kitchen

140

at a dollar and a half an hour. Send him home. Saul may remain. Bring Miss Fox."

I performed the errands.

At the dinner table, of course, business was out. Nothing was said to Clara Fox about the call for help from Mike Walsh or Perry's visit. In spite of the fact that she had a rose pinned on her, she was distinctly down in the mouth and wasn't making any effort in the way of peddling charm, but even so, appraising her coolly, I could see that she might be a real problem for any man who was at all impressionable. She had been in the plant rooms with Wolfe for an hour before six o'clock, and during dinner he went on with a conversation which they had apparently started then, about folk dances and that sort of junk. He even hummed a couple of tunes for her, after the guinea chicken had been disposed of, which caused me to take a firm hold on myself so as not to laugh the salad out of my mouth. At that, it was better than when he tried to whistle, for he did produce some kind of a noise.

With the coffee he told her that the larceny charge had been dropped. She opened her eyes and her mouth both.

"No, really? Then I can go!" She stopped herself and put out a hand to touch his sleeve, and color came to her cheeks. "Oh, I don't mean . . . that was terrible, wasn't it? But you know how I feel, hiding . . ."

"Perfectly." Wolfe nodded. "But I'm afraid you must ask us to tolerate you a little longer. You can't go yet."

"Why not?"

"Because, first, you might get killed. Indeed, it is quite possible, though I confess not very likely. Second, there is a development that must still be awaited. On that you must trust me. I know, since Archie told you of Lord Clivers's statement that he has paid—"

I didn't hear the finish, because the doorbell rang and I wasn't inclined to delay about answering it. I was already on pins and I would soon have been on needles if something hadn't happened to open things up. I loped down the hall.

It was only Johnny Keems whom I had sent home over an hour before. Wondering what for, I let him in. He said, "Have you seen it?"

I said, "No, I'm blind. Seen what?"

He pulled a newspaper from his pocket and stuck it at me. "I was going to a movie on Broadway and they were yelling this extra, and I was nearby so I thought it would be better to run over with it than to phone—"

I had looked at the headlines. I said, "Go to the office. No,

141

go to the kitchen. You're on the job, my lad. Satisfactory."

I went to the dining-room and moved Wolfe's coffee cup to one side and spread the paper in front of him. "Here," I said, "here's that development you're awaiting." I stood and read it with him while Clara Fox sat and looked at us.

MARQUIS ARRESTED!
BRITAIN'S ENVOY
FOUND STANDING OVER MURDERED MAN!
Gazette Reporter
Witnesses Unprecedented Drama!

At 7:05 this evening the Marquis of Clivers, special envoy of Great Britain to this country, was found by a city detective, within the cluttered enclosure of a building under construction on 55th Street, Manhattan, standing beside the body of a dead man who had just been shot through the back of the head. The dead man was Michael Walsh, night watchman. The detective was Purley Stebbins of the Homicide Squad.

At seven o'clock a *Gazette* reporter, walking down Madison Avenue, seeing a crowd collected at 55th Street, stopped to investigate. Finding that it was only two cars with shattered windshields and other minor damages from a collision, he strolled on, turning into 55th. Not far from the corner he saw a man stepping off the curb to cross the street. He recognized the man as Purley Stebbins, a city detective, and was struck by something purposeful in his gait. He stopped, and saw Stebbins push open the door of a board fence where a building is being constructed.

The reporter crossed the street likewise, through curiosity, and entered the enclosure after the detective. He ventured further, and saw Stebbins grasping by the arm a man elegantly attired in evening dress, while the man tried to pull away. Then the reporter saw something else: the body of a man on the ground.

Advancing close enough to see the face of the man in evening dress and recognizing him at once, the reporter was quick-witted enough to call sharply, "Lord Clivers!"

The man replied, "Who the devil are you?"

The detective, who was feeling the man for a weapon, instructed the reporter to telephone headquarters and get Inspector Cramer. The body was lying in such a position that the reporter had to step over it to get at the tele-

142

phone on the wall of a wooden shed. Meanwhile Stebbins had blown his whistle and a few moments later a patrolman in uniform entered. Stebbins spoke to him, and the patrolman leaned over the body and exclaimed, "It's the night watchman, old Walsh!"

Having phoned police headquarters, the reporter approached Lord Clivers and asked him for a statement. He was brushed aside by Stebbins, who commanded him to leave. The reporter persisting, Stebbins instructed the patrolman to put him out, and the reporter was forcibly ejected.

The superintendent of the construction, reached on the telephone, said that the name of the night watchman was Michael Walsh. He knew of no possible connection between Walsh and a member of the British nobility.

No information could be obtained from the suite of Lord Clivers at the Hotel Portland.

At 7:30 Inspector Cramer and various members of the police force had arrived on the scene at 55th Street, but no one was permitted to enter the enclosure and no information was forthcoming.

There was a picture of Clivers, taken the preceding week on the steps of the White House.

I was raving. If only I had gone up there! I glared at Wolfe: "Be prudent! Don't expose ourselves! I could have been there in ten minutes after that phone call! Great God and Jehosaphat!"

I felt a yank at my sleeve and saw it was Clara Fox. "What is it? What—"

I took it out on her. I told her savagely, "Oh, nothing much. Just another of your playmates bumped off. You haven't got much of a team left. Mike Walsh shot and killed dead, Clivers standing there—"

Wolfe had leaned back and closed his eyes, with his lips working. I reached for the paper and pushed it at her. "Sure, go ahead, hope you enjoy it." As she leaned over the paper I heard her breath go in. I said, "Of all the goddam wonderful management—"

Wolfe cut in sharply, "Archie!"

I muttered, "Go to hell everybody," and sat down and bobbed my head from side to side in severe pain. The cockeyed thing had busted wide open and instead of going where I belonged I had sat and eaten guinea chicken Brazilisomething and listened to Wolfe hum folk tunes. Not only that, it had busted at the wrong place and Nero Wolfe had made a fool of himself. If I had gone I would have been there before Cramer or anyone else. . . .

Wolfe opened his eyes and said quietly, "Take Miss Fox upstairs and come to the office." He lifted himself from his chair.

So did Clara Fox. She arose with her face whiter than before and looked from one to the other of us. She announced, "I'm not going upstairs. I . . . I can't just stay here. I'm going . . . I'm going . . ."

"Yes." Wolfe lifted his brows at her. "Where?"

She burst out, "How do I know where? Don't you see I . . . I've got to do something?" She suddenly flopped back into her chair and clasped her hands and began to tremble. "Poor old Mike Walsh . . . why in the name of God . . . why did I ever . . ."

Wolfe stepped to her and put his hand on her shoulder. "Look here," he snapped. "Do you wonder I'd rather have ten thousand orchids than a woman in my house?"

She looked up at him, and shivered. "And it was you that let Mike Walsh go, when you knew—"

"I knew very little. Now I know even less. —Archie, bring Saul."

"Johnny is here—"

"No. Saul."

I went to the kitchen and got him. Wolfe asked him: "How long will it take to get Hilda Lindquist here?"

Saul considered half an instant. "Fifty minutes if I phone. An hour and a half if I go after her."

"Good. Telephone. You had better tell her on the phone that Mike Walsh has been killed, since if she sees a *Gazette* on the way she might succumb also. Is there someone to bring her?"

"Yes, sir."

"Use the office phone. Tell her not to delay unnecessarily, but there is no great urgency. Wipe the spot of grease off of the left side of your nose."

"Yes, sir," Saul went, pulling his handkerchief from his pocket.

Clara Fox said, in a much better tone, "I haven't succumbed." She brushed back her hair, but her hand was none too steady. "I didn't mean, when I said you let Mike Walsh go—"

"Of course not." Wolfe didn't relent any. "You weren't in a condition to mean anything. You still are not. Archie and I

144

have one or two things to do. You can't leave this house, certainly not now. Will you go upstairs and wait till Miss Lindquist gets here? And don't be conceited enough to imagine yourself responsible for the death of Michael Walsh. Your meddlings have not entitled you to usurp the fatal dignity of Atropos; don't flatter yourself. Will you go upstairs and command patience?"

"Yes." She stood up. "But I want . . . if someone should telephone for me I want to talk."

Wolfe nodded. "You shall. Though I fancy Mr. Horrocks will be too occupied with this involvement of his chief for social impulses."

But it was Wolfe's off day; he was wrong again. A phone call from Horrocks, for Clara Fox, came within fifteen minutes. In the interim Wolfe and I had gone to the office and learned from Saul that he had talked to Hilda Lindquist and she was coming, and Wolfe had settled himself in his chair, disposed of a bottle of beer, and repudiated my advances. Horrocks didn't mention the predicament of his noble uncle; he just asked for Clara Fox, and I sent Saul up to tell her to take it in Wolfe's room, since there was no phone in hers. I should have listened in as a matter of business, but I didn't, and Wolfe didn't tell me to.

Finally Wolfe sighed and sat up. "Try for Mr. Cramer."

I did so. No result. They talked as if, for all they knew, Cramer might be up in Canada shooting moose.

Wolfe sighed again. "Archie. Have we ever encountered a greater jumble of nonsense?"

"No, sir. If only I had gone—"

"Don't say that again, or I'll send you upstairs with Miss Fox. Could that have ordered the chaos? The thing is completely ridiculous. It forces us to measures no less ridiculous. We shall have to investigate the movements of Mr. Muir since six o'clock this evening, to trust Mr. Cramer with at least a portion of our facts, to consider afresh the motivations and activities of Lord Clivers, to discover how a man can occupy two different spots of space at the same moment, and to make another long distance call to Nebraska. I believe there is no small firearm that will shoot fifteen hundred miles, but we seem to be confronted with a determination and ingenuity capable of almost anything, and before we are through with this we may need Mr. Lindquist badly. Get that farm—the name is Donvaag?"

I nodded and got busy. At that time of night, going on ten o'clock, the lines were mostly free, and I had a connection with Plainview, Nebraska, in less than ten minutes. It was a person to person call and a good clear connection; Ed Donvaag's husky voice, from his farmhouse out on the western prairie, was in my ear as plain as Francis Horrocks' had been from the Hotel Portland. Wolfe took his line.

"Mr. Donvaag? This is Nero Wolfe . . . That's it. You remember I talked to you this afternoon and you were good enough to go after Mr. Lindquist for a conversation with me. . . . Yes, sir. I have to ask another favor of you. Can you hear me well? Good. It will be necessary for you to go again to Mr. Lindquist tonight or the first thing tomorrow morning. Tell him there is reason to suspect that someone means him injury and may attempt it. . . . Yes. We don't know how. Tell him to be circumspect—to be careful. Does he eat candy? He might receive a box of poisoned candy in the mail. Even, possibly, a bomb. Anything. He might receive a telegram saying his daughter has died—with results expected from the shock to him. . . . No, indeed. His daughter is well and there is nothing to fear for her. . . . Well, this is a peculiar situation; doubtless you will hear all about it later. Tell him to be careful and to suspect anything at all unusual. . . . You can go at once? Good. You are a good neighbor, sir. Goodnight."

Wolfe rang off and pushed the button for beer. He sighed. "That desperate fool has a good deal to answer for. Another four dollars. —Three? Oh, the night rate. —Bring another, Fritz. —Archie, give Saul the necessary facts regarding Mr. Muir and send him out. We want to know where he was from six to eight this evening."

I went to the kitchen and did that. Johnny Keems was helping Fritz with the dishes and Saul was in my breakfast corner with the remainder of the dish of ripe olives. He didn't write anything down; he never had to. He pointed his long nose at me and absorbed the dope, nodded, took a twenty for expenses, gathered up the last of the olives into a handful, and departed. I let him out.

Back in the office, I asked Wolfe if he wanted me to try for Cramer again. He shook his head. He was leaning back with his eyes closed, and the faint movement of his lips in and out informed me that he was in conference with himself. I sat down and put my feet on my desk. In a few minutes I got up again and went to the cabinet and poured myself a shot of bourbon, smelled it, and poured it back into the bottle. It wasn't whiskey I wanted. I went to the kitchen and asked

Johnny some more questions about the layout up at 55th Street, and drank a glass of milk.

It was ten o'clock when Hilda Lindquist arrived. There was a man with her, but when I told him Saul wasn't there he didn't come in. I told him Saul would fix it with him and he beat it. Hilda's square face and brown dress didn't look any the worse for wear during the twenty-four hours since she had gone off, but her eyes were solemn and determined. She said of course the thing was all off, since they had caught the Marquis of Clivers and he would be executed for murder, and her father would be disappointed because he was old and they would lose the farm, and would she be able to get her bag which she had left at the hotel, and she would like to start for home as soon as there was a train. I told her to drive in and park a while, there was still some fireworks left in the bag, but by the way she turned her eyes on me I saw that she might develop into a real problem, so I put her in the front room and asked her to wait a minute.

I ran up to the south room and said to Clara Fox: "Hilda Lindquist is downstairs and I'm going to send her up. She thinks the show is over and she has to go back home to her poor old dad with her sock empty, and by the look in her eye it will take more than British diplomacy to keep her off of the next train. Nero Wolfe is going to work this out. I don't know how and maybe he don't either this minute, but he'll do it. Nero Wolfe is probably even better than I think he is, and that's a mouthful. You wrote the music for this piece, and half your band has been killed, and it's up to you to keep the other half intact. Well?"

I had found her sitting in a chair with her lips compressed tight and her hands clenched. She looked at me. "All right. I will. Send her up here."

"She can sleep in here with you, or in the room in front on this floor. You know how to ring for Fritz."

"All right."

I went down and told Squareface that Clara Fox wanted to speak to her, and shooed her up, and heard them exchanging greetings in the upper hall.

There was nothing in the office but a gob of silence; Wolfe was still in conference. I would have tried some bulldozing if I had thought he was merely dreaming of stuffed quail or pickled pigs' feet, but his lips were moving a little so I knew he was working. I fooled around my desk, went over Johnny's diagrams again in connection with an idea that had occurred to me, checked over Horstmann's reports and entered them

147

in the records, reread the *Gazette* scoop on the affair at 55th Street, and aggravated myself into such a condition of uselessness that finally, at eleven o'clock sharp, I exploded:

"If this keeps up another ten minutes I'll get *Weltschmerz!*"

Wolfe opened his eyes. "Where in the name of heaven did you get that?"

I threw up my hands. He shut his eyes again.

The doorbell rang. I knew it couldn't be Johnny Keems with another extra, because he was in the kitchen with Fritz, since I hadn't been able to prod an instruction from Wolfe to send him home again. It was probably Saul Panzer with the dope on Muir. But it wasn't; I knew that when the bell started again as I entered the hall. It kept on ringing, so I leisurely pulled the curtain for a look through the panel, and when I saw there were four of them, another quartet, I switched on the stoop light to make a good survey. One of them, in evening dress, was leaning on the bell button. I recognized the whole bunch. I turned and beat it back to the office.

"Who the devil is ringing that bell?" Wolfe demanded. "Why don't you—"

I interrupted, grinning. "That's Police Commissioner Hombert. With him are Inspector Cramer, District Attorney Skinner, and my old friend Purley Stebbins of the Homicide Squad. Is it too late for company?"

"Indeed." Wolfe sat up and rubbed his nose. "Bring them in."

• • • • 16 • • • •

THEY ENTERED as if they owned the place. I tipped Purley a wink as he passed me, but he was too impressed by his surroundings to reciprocate, and I didn't blame him, as I knew he might get either a swell promotion or the opposite out of this by the time it was over. From the threshold I saw a big black limousine down at the curb, and back of it two other police cars containing city fellers. Well, well, I thought to myself as I closed the door, this looks pretty damned ominous. Cramer had asked me if Wolfe was in the office and I had waved him on, and now I brought up the rear of the procession.

I moved chairs around. Cramer introduced Hombert and Skinner, but Skinner and Wolfe had already met. At Cramer's request I took Purley Stebbins to the kitchen and told him to play checkers with Johnny Keems. When I got back Hombert was shooting off his mouth about defiance of the law, and I got at my desk and ostentatiously opened my notebook. Cramer was looking more worried than I had ever seen him. District Attorney Skinner, already sunk in his chair as if he had been there all evening, had the wearied cynical expression of a man who had some drinks three hours ago and none since.

Hombert was practically yelling. ". . . and you're responsible for it! If you had turned those three people over to us last night this wouldn't have happened! Cramer tells me they were here in this office! Walsh was here! This afternoon we had him at headquarters and your man wouldn't point him out! You are directly and legally responsible for his death!" The Police Commissioner brought his fist down on the arm of his chair and glared. Cramer was looking at him and shaking his head faintly.

149

"This sudden onslaught is overwhelming," Wolfe murmured. "If I am legally responsible for Mr. Walsh's death, arrest me. But please don't shout at me—"

"All right! You've asked for it!" Hombert turned to the inspector. "Put him under arrest!"

Cramer said quietly, "Yes, sir. What charge?"

"Any charge! Material witness! We'll see whether he'll talk or not!"

Cramer stood up. Wolfe said, "Perhaps I should warn you, Mr. Hombert. If I am arrested, I shall do no talking whatever. And if I do no talking, you have no possible chance of solving the problem you are confronted with." He wiggled a finger. "I don't shout, but I never say anything I don't mean. Proceed, Mr. Cramer."

Cramer stood still. Hombert looked at him, then looked grimly at Wolfe. "You'll talk or you'll rot!"

"Then I shall certainly rot." Wolfe's finger moved again. "Let me make a suggestion, Mr. Hombert. Why don't you go home and go to sleep and leave this affair to be handled by Mr. Cramer, an experienced policeman, and Mr. Skinner, an experienced lawyer? You probably have abilities of some sort, but they are obviously inappropriate to the present emergency. To talk of arresting me is childish. I have broken no law and I am a sufficiently respectable citizen not to be taken into custody merely for questioning. Confound it, sir, you can't go around losing your temper like this, it's outrageous! You are entangled in a serious difficulty, I am the only man alive who can possibly extricate you from it, and you come here and begin yelling inane threats at me! Is that sort of conduct likely to appeal either to my reason or my sympathy?"

Hombert glared at him, opened his mouth, closed it again, and looked at Cramer. District Attorney Skinner snickered. Cramer said to Hombert, "Didn't I tell you he was a nut? Let me handle him."

Wolfe nodded solemnly. "That's an idea, Mr. Cramer. You handle me."

Hombert, saying nothing, sat back and folded his arms and goggled. Cramer looked at Wolfe. "So you know about Walsh."

Wolfe nodded. "From the *Gazette*. That was unfortunate, the reporter happening on the scene."

"You're telling me," Cramer observed grimly. "Of course the marquis isn't arrested. He can't be. Diplomatic immunity. Washington is raising hell because it got in the paper, as if there was any way in God's world of keeping it out of that lousy sheet once that reporter got away from there." He waved a disgusted hand. "That's that. The fact is, the Commissioner's right. You're responsible. I told you yesterday how important this was. I told you it was your duty as a citizen to help us protect the Marquis of Clivers."

Wolfe lifted his brows. "Aren't you a little confused, Mr. Cramer? Or am I? I understood you wished to protect Lord Clivers from injury. Was it he who was injured this evening?"

"Certainly it was," Hombert broke in. "This Walsh was blackmailing him!"

Cramer said, "Let me. Huh?"

"Did Lord Clivers say that?" Wolfe asked.

"No." Cramer grunted. "He's not saying anything, except that he knew Walsh a long time ago and went there to see him this evening by appointment and found him lying there dead. But we didn't come here to answer questions for you, we came to find out what you know. We could have you pulled in, but decided it was quicker to come. It's time to spill it. What's it all about?"

"I suppose so." Wolfe sighed. "Frankly, I think you're wrong; I believe that while you may have information that will help me, I have none that will help you. But we'll get to that later. My connection with this affair arises from my engagement to press a civil claim on behalf of two young women. Also, to defend one of them from a trumped up charge of larceny brought against her by an official of the Seaboard Products Corporation. Since I have succeeded in having the larceny charge withdrawn—"

District Attorney Skinner woke up. He croaked in his deep bass, "Don't talk so much. What has that got to do with it? Come to the point."

Wolfe said patiently, "Interruptions can only waste time, by forcing me to begin my sentences over again. Since I have succeeded in having the larceny charge withdrawn, and since they cannot possibly be suspected of complicity in the murder of Mr. Walsh, I am willing to produce my clients, with the understanding that if I send for them to come here they will be questioned here only and will not be taken from this house. I will not have—"

"The hell you won't!" Hombert was ready to boil again. "You can't dictate to us—"

But the authority of Wolfe's tone and the assurance of his manner had made enough impression so that his raised palm

151

brought Hombert to a halt. "I'm not dictating," he snapped. "Confound it, let us get on or we shall be all night. I was about to say, I will not have the lives of my clients placed in possible jeopardy by releasing them from my own protection. Why should I? I can send for them and you can question them all you please—"

"All right, all right," Cramer agreed impatiently. "We won't take them, that's understood. How long will it take you to get them here?"

"One minute perhaps, if they are not in bed. Archie? If you please."

I arose grinning at Cramer's stare, stepped over Skinner's feet, and went up and knocked at the door of the south room. "Come in."

I entered. The two clients were sitting in chairs, looking as if they were too miserable to go to bed. I said, "Egad, you look cheerful. Come on, buck up! Wolfe wants you down in the office. There are some men down there that want to ask you some questions."

Clara Fox straightened up. "Ask us . . . now?" Hilda Lindquist tightened her lips and began to nod her head for I told you so.

"Certainly." I made it matter of fact. "They were bound to, sooner or later. Don't worry, I'll be right there, and tell them anything they want to know. There's three of them. The dressed-up one with the big mouth is Police Commissioner Hombert, the one with the thin nose and ratty eyes is District Attorney Skinner, and the big guy who looks at you frank and friendly but may or may not mean it is Inspector Cramer."

"My God." Clara Fox brushed back her hair and stood up.

"All right," I grinned. "Let's go."

I opened the door, and followed them out and down.

The three visitors turned their heads to look at us as we entered the office. Skinner, seeing Clara Fox, got up first, then Hombert also made it to his feet and began shoving chairs around. I moved some up, while Wolfe pronounced names. He had rung for beer while I was gone, and got it poured. I saw there was no handkerchief in his pocket and went and got him one out of the drawer.

Cramer said, "So you're Clara Fox. Where were you this morning?"

She glanced at Wolfe. He nodded. She said, "I was here."

"Here in this house? All morning?"

"Yes, last night and all day."

152

Cramer handed Wolfe a glassy stare. "What did you do to Rowcliff, grease him?"

"No, sir." Wolfe shook his head. "Mr. Rowcliff did his best, but Miss Fox was not easily discoverable. I beg you to attach no blame to your men. It is necessary for you to know that three of us are prepared to state on oath that Miss Fox has been here constantly, to make it at once obvious that she is in no way involved in Mr. Walsh's death."

"I'll be damned. What about the other one?"

"Miss Lindquist came here at ten o'clock this evening. But she has been secluded in another part of the city. You may as well confine yourself to events previous to half-past six yesterday. May I make a suggestion? Begin by asking Miss Fox to tell you the story which she recited to me at that hour yesterday, in the presence of Miss Lindquist and Mr. Walsh."

"Why . . . all right." Cramer looked at Clara Fox. "Go ahead."

She told the story. At first she was nervous and jerky, and I noticed that when she was inclined to stumble she glanced across at Wolfe as he leaned back, massive and motionless, with his fingers twined on his belly and his eyes nearly shut. She glanced at him and went ahead. They didn't interrupt her much with questions. She read the letter from her father, and when she finished and Cramer held out his hand for it, she glanced at Wolfe. Wolfe nodded, and she passed it over. Then she went on, with more detail even than she had told us. She spoke of her first letters with Harlan Scovil and Hilda Lindquist and her first meeting with Mike Walsh.

She got to the Marquis of Clivers and Walsh's recognition of him as he emerged from his hotel fifteen days back. From then on they were after her, not Cramer much, but Skinner and Hombert, and especially Skinner. He began to get slick, and of course what he was after was obvious. He asked her trick questions, such as where had her mother been keeping the letter from her father when she suddenly produced it on her deathbed. His way of being clever was to stay quiet and courteous and go back to one thing and then abruptly forward to another, and then after a little suddenly dart back again. Clara Fox was no longer nervous, and she didn't get mad. I remembered how the day before she had stood cool and sweet in front of Perry's desk. All at once Skinner began asking her about the larceny charge. She answered; but after a dozen questions on that Wolfe suddenly stirred, opened his eyes, and wiggled a finger at the District Attorney.

"Mr. Skinner. Permit me. You're wasting time. The larceny charge is indeed pertinent to the main issue, but there is very little chance that you'll ever discover why. The fact is that the line you have taken from the beginning is absurd."

"Thanks," Skinner said drily. "If, as you say, it is pertinent, why absurd?"

"Because," Wolfe retorted, "you're running around in circles. You have a fixed idea that you're an instrument of justice, being a prosecuting attorney, and that it is your duty to corner everyone you see. That idea is not only dangerous nonsense, in the present case it is directly contrary to your real interest. Why is this distinguished company," Wolfe extended a finger and bent a wrist, "present in my house? Because $30,000 was mislaid and two men were murdered? Not at all. Because Lord Clivers has become unpleasantly involved, the fact has been made public, and you are seriously embarrassed. You have wasted thirty minutes trying to trap Miss Fox into a slip indicating that she and Mr. Walsh and Mr. Scovil and Miss Lindquist hatched a blackmailing plot against Lord Clivers; you have even hinted that the letter written by her father to her mother seventeen years ago, of which Mr. Cramer now has her typewritten copy in his pocket, was invented by her. Is it possible that you don't realize what your real predicament is?"

"Thanks," Skinner repeated, more drily still. "I'll get to you—"

"No doubt. But let me—no, confound it, I'm talking! Let me orient you a little. Here's your predicament. An eminent personage, an envoy of Great Britain, has been discovered alone with a murdered man and the fact has been made public. Even if you wanted to you can't keep him in custody because of his diplomatic immunity. Why not, then, to avoid a lot of official and international fuss, just forget it and let him go? Because you don't dare; if he really did kill Mr. Walsh you are going to have to ask his government to surrender him to you, and fight to get him if necessary, or the newspapers will howl you out of office. You are sitting on dynamite, and so is Mr. Hombert, and you know it. I can imagine with what distaste you contemplate being forced into an effort to convict the Marquis of Clivers of murder. I see the complications; and the devil of it is that at this moment you don't at all know whether he did it or not. His story that he went to see Mr. Walsh and found him already dead may quite possibly be true.

"So, since an attempt to put Lord Clivers on trial for murder, and convict him, would not only create an international stink but might be disastrous for you personally, what should be your first and immediate concern? It seems obvious. You should swiftly and rigorously explore the possibility that he is not guilty. Is there someone else who wanted Harlan Scovil and Michael Walsh to die, and if so, who, and where is he? I know of only six people living who might help you in pursuing that inquiry. One of them is the murderer, another is an old man on a farm in Nebraska, and the other four are in this room. And, questioning one of them, what do you do? You put on an exhibition of your cunning at cross-examination in an effort to infer that she has tried to blackmail Lord Clivers, though he has had various opportunities to make such an accusation and has not done so. Again, you aim the weapon of your cunning, not at your own ignorance, but directly at Miss Fox, when you pounce on the larceny charge, though that accusation has been dismissed by the man who made it.

"Bah!" Wolfe looked around at them. "Do you wonder, gentlemen, that I have not taken you into my confidence in this affair? Do you wonder that I have no intention of doing so even now?"

Cramer grunted, gazing at a cigar he had pulled out of his pocket five minutes before. Skinner, scratching his ear, screwed up his mouth and looked sidewise at Clara Fox. Hombert let out a "Ha!" and slapped the arm of his chair. "So that's your game! You're not going to talk, eh? By God, you will talk!"

"Oh, I'll talk." Wolfe sighed. "You may know everything you are entitled to know. You are already aware that Mr. Scovil was in this room yesterday afternoon and got killed shortly after leaving it. Mr. Goodwin talked with him and will repeat the conversation if you wish it. You may hear everything from Miss Fox and Miss Lindquist that I have heard; and from Miss Fox regarding Mr. Walsh. You may know of the claim which I have presented to Lord Clivers on behalf of Miss Lindquist and her father, which he has offered to settle. But there are certain things you may not know, at least not from me; for instance, the details of a long conversation which I had with Lord Clivers when he called here this afternoon. He can tell you—"

"What's that?" Skinner sat up, croaking. Hombert goggled. Cramer, who had finally got his cigar lit, jerked it up with his lip so that the ash fell to the rug. Skinner went on, "What are you trying to hand us? Clivers called on you today?"

Wolfe nodded. "He was here over an hour. Perhaps I shouldn't say today, since it is nearly one o'clock Wednesday morning. Yes, Lord Clivers called. We drank eight bottles of beer, and he greatly admired that terrestrial globe you see there."

Without taking his cigar from his mouth, Cramer rumbled, "I'll be damned." Hombert still goggled. Skinner stared, and at length observed, "I've never heard of your being a plain liar, Wolfe, but you're dishing it up."

"Dishing it up?" Wolfe looked at me. "Does that mean lying, Archie?"

"Naw," I grinned, "it's just rhetoric."

"Indeed." Wolfe reached to push the button, and leaned back. "So you see, gentlemen, I not only have superior knowledge in this affair, I have it from a superior source. Lord Clivers gave me much interesting information, which of course I cannot consider myself free to reveal." He turned his eyes on the Police Commissioner. "I understand, Mr. Hombert, that Mr. Devore, Mr. Cramer and you were all in communication with him, protecting him, following the death of Mr. Scovil. It's too bad he didn't see fit to take you into his confidence. Maybe he will do so now, if you approach him properly."

Hombert sputtered, "I don't believe this. We'll check up on this."

"Do so." Wolfe opened the bottle and filled his glass. "Will you have beer, gentlemen? No? Water? Whiskey? Miss Fox? Miss Lindquist? —You haven't asked Miss Lindquist anything. Must she sit here all night?"

Skinner said, "I could use a good stiff highball. Listen, Wolfe, are you telling this straight?"

"Of course I am. —Fritz, serve what is required. —Why would I be so foolish as to invent such a tale? Let me suggest that the ladies be permitted to retire."

"Well . . ." Skinner looked at Hombert. Hombert, tight-lipped, shrugged his shoulders. Skinner turned and asked abruptly:

"Your name is Hilda Lindquist?"

Her strong square face looked a little startled at the suddenness of it, then was lifted by her chin. "Yes."

"You heard everything Clara Fox said. Do you agree with it?"

She stared. "What do you mean, agree with it?"

"I mean, as far as you know, is it true?"

"Certainly it's true."

156

"Where do you live?"

"Plainview, Nebraska. Near there."

"When did you get to New York?"

"Last Thursday. Thursday afternoon."

"All right. That's all. But understand, you're not to leave the city—"

Wolfe put in, "My clients will remain in this house until I have cleared up this matter."

"See that they do." Skinner grabbed his drink. "So you're going to clear it up. God bless you. If I had your nerve I'd own Manhattan Island." He drank.

The clients got up and went. I escorted them to the hall, and while I was out there the doorbell rang. It was Saul Panzer. I went to the kitchen with him and got his report, which didn't take long. Johnny Keems was there with his chair tipped back against the wall, half asleep, and Purley Stebbins was in a corner, reading a newspaper. I snared myself a glass of milk, took a couple of sips, and carried the rest to the office.

Hombert and Cramer had highballs and Fritz was arranging another one for Skinner. I said to Wolfe: "Saul's back. The subject left his office a few minutes before six and showed up at his apartment about a quarter after seven and dressed for dinner. Saul hasn't been able to trace him in between. Shall he keep after it tonight?"

"No. Send him home. Here at eight in the morning."

"Johnny too?"

"Yes. —No, wait." Wolfe turned. "Mr. Cramer. Perhaps I can simplify something for you. I know how thorough you are. Doubtless you have discovered that there are various ways of getting into that place on 55th Street, and I suppose you have had them all explored. You may even have learned that there was a man there this afternoon, investigating them."

Cramer was staring at him. "Now, somebody tell me, how did I know that? Yeah, we learned it, and we've got a good description, and there are twenty men looking for him . . ."

Wolfe nodded. "I thought I might save you some trouble. I should have mentioned it before. The man's out in the kitchen. He was up there for me."

Cramer went pop-eyed. "But good God! That was before Walsh was killed!" He put his drink down. "Now what kind of a—"

"We wanted to see Walsh, and knew you would have a man posted at the entrance. He was there to find a way. He

157

left a few minutes after six and was here from six-thirty until eight o'clock. You may talk with him if you wish, but it will be a waste of time. My word for it."

Cramer looked at him, and then at me. He picked up his drink. "To hell with it."

Wolfe said, "Send Johnny home."

Cramer said, "And tell Stebbins to go out front and tell Rowcliff to cancel that alarm and call those men in."

I went to perform those errands, and after letting the trio out I left the door open a crack and told Purley to shut it when he came back in. The enemy was inside anyhow, so there was no point in maintaining the barricade.

Back in the office, Skinner and Hombert were bombarding Wolfe. It had got now to where it was funny. Clivers was the bird they had been busy protecting, and the one they were trying to get out of hanging a murder onto, and here they were begging Wolfe to spill what Clivers had disclosed to him over eight bottles of beer! I sat down and grinned at Cramer, and darned if he didn't have decency enough to wink back at me. I thought that called for another highball, and went and got it for him.

Skinner, with an open palm outstretched, was actually wheedling. "But, my God, can't we work together on it? I'll admit we went at it wrong, but how did we know Clivers was here this afternoon? He won't tell us a damn thing, and as far as I personally am concerned I'd like to kick his rump clear across the Atlantic Ocean. And I'll admit we can't coerce you into telling us this vital information you say you got from Clivers, but we can ask for it, and we do. You know who I am. I'm not a bad friend to have in this county, especially for a man in your business. What's Clivers to you, anyhow, why the devil should you cover him up?"

"This is bewildering," Wolfe murmured. "Last night Mr. Cramer told me I should help him to protect a distinguished foreign guest, and now you demand the opposite!"

"All right, have your fun," Skinner croaked. "But tell us this, at least. Did Clivers say anything to indicate that he had it ready for Mike Walsh?"

Wolfe's eyelids flickered, and after a moment he turned to me. "Your notebook, Archie. You will find a place where I asked Lord Clivers, 'Don't you believe him?' I was referring to Mr. Walsh. Please read Lord Clivers' reply."

I had the notebook and was thumbing it. I looked too far front, and flipped back. Finally I had it, and read it out:

"Clivers: 'I don't believe anybody. I know damn well I'm a liar. I'm a diplomat. Look here. You can forget about Walsh. I'll deal with him myself. I have to keep this thing clear, at least as long as I'm in this country. I'll deal with Walsh. Scovil is dead, God rest his soul. Let the police do what they can with that. As for the Lindquists . . .'"

Wolfe stopped me with a finger. "That will do, Archie. Put the notebook away."

"He will not put it away!" Hombert was beating up the arm of his chair again. "With that in it? We want—"

He stopped to glare at Skinner, who had tapped a toe on his shin. Skinner was ready to melt with sweetness; his tone sounded like Romeo in the balcony scene. "Listen, Wolfe, play with us. Let us have that. Your man can type it, or he can dictate from his notes and I'll bring a man in to take it. Clivers is to sail for Europe Sunday. If we don't get this thing on ice there's going to be trouble."

Wolfe closed his eyes, and after a moment opened them again. They were all gazing at him, Cramer slowly chewing his cigar, Hombert holding in an explosion, Skinner looking innocent and friendly. Wolfe said, "Will you make a bargain with me, Mr. Skinner? Let me ask a few questions. Then, after considering the replies, I shall do what I can for you. I think it is more than likely you will find me helpful."

Skinner frowned. "What kind of questions?"

"You will hear them."

A pause. "All right. Shoot."

Wolfe turned abruptly to the inspector. "Mr. Cramer. You had a man following Mr. Walsh from the time you released him this afternoon, and that man was on post at the entrance of the boarding on 55th Street. I'd like to know what it was that caused him to cross the street and enter the enclosure, as reported in the *Gazette*. Did he hear a shot?"

"No." Cramer took his cigar from his mouth. "The man's out in the kitchen. Do you want to hear it from him?"

"I merely want to hear it."

"Well, I can tell you. Stebbins was away from his post for a few minutes, he's admitted it. There was a taxi collision at the corner of Madison, and he had to go and look it over, which was bright of him. He says he was away only two minutes, but he may have been gone ten, you know how that is. Anyhow, he finally strolled back, on the south side of 55th, and looking across at the entrance of the boarding he saw the door slowly opening, and the face of a man looked out and it

159

wasn't Walsh. There were predestrians going by, and the face went back in and the door closed. Stebbins got behind a parked car. In a minute the face looked out again, and there was a man walking by, and the face disappeared again. Stebbins thought it was time to investigate and crossed the street and went in, and it was just lousy luck that that damn newspaper cockroach happened to see him. It was Clivers all right, and Walsh's body was there on the ground—"

"I know." Wolfe sighed. "It was lying in front of the telephone. So Mr. Stebbins heard no shot."

"No. Of course, he was down at the corner and there was a lot of noise."

"To be sure. Was the weapon on Lord Clivers' person?"

"No." Cramer sounded savage. "That's one of the nice details. We can't find any gun, except one in Walsh's pocket that hadn't been fired. There's a squad of men still up there, combing it. Also there's about a thousand hollow steel shafts sticking up from the base construction, and it might have been dropped down one of those."

"So it might," Wolfe murmured. "Well . . . no shot heard, and no gun found." He looked around at them. "I can't help observing, gentlemen, that that news relieves me enormously. Moreover, I think you have a right to know that Mr. Goodwin and I heard the shot."

They stared at him. Skinner demanded, "You what? What the hell are you talking about?"

Wolfe turned to me. "Tell them, Archie."

I let them have my open countenance. "This evening," I said, and corrected it, "—last evening—Mr. Wolfe and I were in this office. At two minutes before seven o'clock the phone rang, and it happened that we both took off our receivers. A voice said, 'Nero Wolfe!' It sounded far off but very excited—it sounded—well, unnatural. I said, 'Yes, talking,' and the voice said, 'I've got him, come up here, 55th Street, this is Mike Walsh, I've got him covered, come up.' The voice was cut off by the sound of an explosion, very loud, as if a gun had been shot close to the telephone. I called Walsh's name a few times, but there was no answer. We sent a phone call to police headquarters right away."

I looked around respectfully for approval. Skinner looked concentrated, Hombert looked about ready to bust, and Cramer looked disgusted. The inspector, I could see, didn't have far to go to get good and sore. He burst out at Wolfe, "What else have you got? First you tell me the man I've got

160

the whole force looking for, thinking I've got a hot one, is one of your boy scouts acting as advance agent. Now you tell me that the phone call we're trying to trace about a shot being heard, and you can't trace a local call anyway with these damn dials, now you tell me you made that too." He stuck his cigar in his mouth and bit it nearly in two.

"But Mr. Cramer," Wolfe protested, "is it my fault if destiny likes this address? Did we not notify you at once? Did I not even restrain Mr. Goodwin from hastening to the scene, because I knew you would not want him to intrude?"

Cramer opened his mouth but was speechless. Skinner said, "You heard that shot on the phone at two minutes to seven. That checks. It was five after when Stebbins found Clivers there." He looked around sort of helpless, like a man who has picked up something he didn't want. "That seems to clinch it." He growled at Wolfe, "What makes you so relieved about not finding the gun and Stebbins not hearing the shot, if you heard it yourself?"

"In due time, Mr. Skinner." Wolfe's forefinger was gently tapping on the arm of his chair, and I wondered what he was impatient about. "If you don't mind, let me get on. The paper says that Mr. Stebbins felt Lord Clivers for a weapon. Did he find one?"

"No," Cramer grunted. "He got talkative enough to tell us that he always carries a pistol, but not with evening dress."

"But since Lord Clivers had not left the enclosure, and since no weapon can be found, how could he possibly have been the murderer?"

"We'll find it," Cramer asserted gloomily. "There's a million places in there to hide a gun, and we'll have to get into those shafts somehow. Or he might have thrown it over the fence. We'll find it. He did it, damn it. You've ruined the only outside leads I had."

Wolfe wagged his head at him. "Cheer up, Mr. Cramer. Tell me this, please. Since Mr. Stebbins followed Mr. Walsh all afternoon, I presume you know their itinerary. What was it?"

Skinner growled, "Don't start stalling, Wolfe. Let's get—"

"I'm not stalling, sir. An excellent word. Mr. Cramer?"

The inspector dropped his cigar in the tray. "Well, Walsh stopped at a lunch counter on Franklin near Broadway and ate. He kept looking around, but Stebbins thinks he didn't wise up. Then he took a surface car north and got off at 27th Street and walked west. He went in the Seaboard Building and took the elevator and got off at the 32nd floor and went into the executive offices of the Seaboard Products Corporation. Stebbins waited out in the hall. Walsh was in there nearly an hour. He took the elevator down again, and Stebbins didn't want to take the same one and nearly lost him. He walked east and went into a drug store and used a telephone in a booth. Then he took the subway and went to a boarding-house in East 64th Street, where he lived, and he left again a little after half-past five and walked to his job at 55th Street. He got there a little before six."

Wolfe had leaned back and closed his eyes. They all looked at him. Cramer got out another cigar and bit off the end and fingered his tongue for the shreds. Hombert demanded, "Well, are you asleep?"

Wolfe didn't move, but he spoke. "About that visit Mr. Walsh made at the Seaboard Products Corporation. Do you know who he saw there?"

"No, how could I? Stebbins didn't go in. Even if there had been any reason—the office was closed by the time I got Stebbins's report. What difference does it make?"

"Not much." Wolfe's tone was mild, but to me, who knew it so well, there was a thrill in it. "No, not much. There are cases when a conjecture is almost as good as a fact—even, sometimes, better." Suddenly he opened his eyes, sat up, and got brisk. "That's all, gentlemen. It is past two o'clock, and Mr. Goodwin is yawning. You will hear from me tomorrow—today, rather."

Skinner shook his head wearily. "Oh, no no no. Honest to God, Wolfe, you're the worst I've ever seen for trying to put over fast ones. There's a lot to do yet. Could I have another highball?"

Wolfe sighed. "Must we start yapping again?" He wiggled a finger at the District Attorney. "I offered you a bargain, sir. I said if I could get replies to a few questions I would consider them and would then do what I could for you. Do you think I can consider them properly at this time of night? I assure you I cannot. I am not quibbling. I have gone much further than you gentlemen along the path to the solution of this puzzle, and I am confronted by one difficulty which must be solved before anything can be done. When it will be solved I cannot say. I may light on it ten minutes from now, while I am undressing for bed, or it may require extended investigation and labor. Confound it, do you realize it will be dawn in less than four hours? It was past three when I retired last night." He put his hands on the edge of his desk and pushed his chair back, arose to his feet, and pulled at the corners of

162

his vest where a wide band of canary yellow shirt puffed out. "Daylight will serve us better. No more tonight, short of the rack and the thumbscrew. You will hear from me."

Cramer got up too, saying to Hombert, "He's always like this. You might as well stick pins in a rhinoceros."

···· 17 ····

WHEN, ABOUT a quarter after nine Wednesday morning, I went up to the plant rooms with a message, I thought that Wolfe's genius had at last bubbled over and he had gone nuts for good. He was in the potting room, standing by the bench, with a piece of board about four inches wide and ten inches long in each hand. He paid no attention to me when I entered. He held his hands two feet apart and then swiftly brought them together, flat sides of the two pieces of board meeting with a loud clap. He did that several times. He shook his head and threw one of the boards down and began hitting things with the other one, the top of the bench, one of its legs and then another one, the seat of a chair, the palm of his hand, a pile of wrapping paper. He kept shaking his head. Finally, deciding to admit I was there, he tossed the board down and turned his eyes on me with ferocious hostility.

"Well, sir?" he demanded.

I said in a resigned tone, "Cramer phoned again. That's three times. He says that District Attorney Skinner got tight after he left here and is now at his office with a hangover, cutting off people's heads. As far as that's concerned, I've had four hours sleep two nights in a row and I've got a headache. He says that the publisher of the *Gazette* told the Secretary of State to go to hell over long distance. He wants to know if we have seen the morning papers. He says that two men from Washington are in Hombert's office with copies of cables from London. He says that Hombert saw Clivers at his hotel half-an-hour ago and asked him about his visit to our office yesterday afternoon, and Clivers said it was a private matter and it will be a nice day if it don't rain. He says you have got to open up or he will open you. In addition to that, Miss Fox and Miss Lindquist are having a dogfight because their nerves are going back on them. In addition to that, Fritz is on the warpath because Saul and Johnny hang out in the kitchen too much and Johnny ate up some tambo shells he was going to put mushrooms into for lunch. In addition to that, I can't get you to tell me whether I am to go to the Hotel Portland to look at Clivers' documents which came on the *Berengaria*. In addition to that . . ."

I stopped for breath. Wolfe said, "You badger me. Those are all trivialities. Look at me—" he picked up the board and threw it down again "—I am sacrificing my hours of pleasure in an effort to straighten out the only tangle that remains in this knot, and you harass me with these futilities. Did the Secretary of State go to hell? If so, tell the others to join him there."

"Yeah, sure. I'm telling you, they're all going to be around here again. I can't hold them off."

"Lock the door. Keep them out. I will not be hounded!"

He turned away, definitely. I threw up my hands and beat it. On my way downstairs I stopped a second at the door of the south room, and heard the voices of the two clients still at it. In the lower hall I listened at the kitchen door and perceived that Fritz was still shrill with fury. The place was a madhouse.

Wolfe had been impossible from the time I first went to his room around seven o'clock, because he hadn't taken his phone when I buzzed him, to report the first call from Cramer. I had never seen him so actively unfriendly, but I didn't really mind that, knowing he was only peeved at himself on account of his genius not working right. What got me on edge was first, I had a headache; second, Fritz and the clients had to unload their troubles on me; and third, I didn't like all the cussings from outsiders on the telephone. It had been going on for over two hours and it was keeping up.

After taking another aspirin and doing a few morning chores around the office, I sat down at my desk and got out the plant records and entered some items from Horstmann's reports of the day before, and went over some bills and so on. There were circulars and lists from both Richardt and Hoehn in the morning mail, also a couple of catalogues from England, and I glanced over them and laid them aside. There was a phone call from Harry Foster of the *Gazette*, who had found out somehow that we were supposed to know something, and I kidded him and backed him off. Then, a little after ten o'clock, the phone rang again, and the first thing I knew I was talking to the Marquis of Clivers himself. I had half a mind to get Wolfe on, but decided to take the message instead, and after I rang off I gathered up the catalogues and circulars and reports and slipped a rubber band around them and proceeded upstairs.

Wolfe was standing at one side of the third room, frowning at a row of seedling hybrids in their second year. He looked plenty forbidding, and Horstmann, whom I had passed in the tropical room, had had the appearance of having been crushed to earth.

I sailed into the storm. I flipped the rubber band on my little bundle and said, "Here's those lists from Richardt and also some from Hoehn, and some catalogues from England. Do you want them or shall I leave them in the potting room? And Clivers just called on the telephone. He says those papers came, and if you want to go and look at them, or send me, okay. He didn't say anything about his little mix-up with the police last night, and of course I was too polite—"

I stopped because Wolfe wasn't listening. His lips had suddenly pushed out a full half-an-inch, and he had glued his eyes on the bundle in my hand. He stood that way a long while and I shut my mouth and stared at him.

Finally he murmured, "That's it. Confound you, Archie, did you know it? Is that why you brought it here?"

I asked courteously, "Have you gone cuckoo?"

He ignored me. "But of course not. It's your fate again." He closed his eyes and sighed a deep sigh, and murmured, "Rubber Coleman. The Rubber Band. Of course." He opened his eyes and flashed them at me. "Saul is downstairs? Send him up at once."

"What about Clivers?"

He went imperious. "Wait in the office. Send Saul."

Knowing there was no use pursuing any inquiries, I hopped back down to the kitchen door and beckoned Saul out into the hall. He stuck his nose up at me and I told him:

"Wolfe wants you upstairs. For God's sake watch your step, because he has just found the buried treasure and you know what to expect when he's like that. If he requests anything grotesque, consult me."

I went back to my desk, but of course plant records were out. I lit a cigarette, and took my pistol out of the drawer and looked it over and put it back again, and kicked over my wastebasket and let it lay.

There were steps on the stairs, and Saul's voice came from the door: "Let me out, Archie. I've got work to do."

"Let yourself out. What are you afraid of?"

I stuck my hands in my pockets and stretched out my legs and sat on my shoulder blades and scowled. Ten minutes after Saul had left the phone rang. I uttered a couple of expletives as I reached for it, thinking it was one of the pack with another howl, but Saul Panzer's voice was in my ear:

"Archie? Connect me with Mr. Wolfe."

I thought, now that was quick work, and plugged and buzzed. Wolfe's voice sounded:

"Nero Wolfe."

"Yes, sir. This is Saul. I'm ready."

"Good. Archie? You don't need to take this."

I hung up with a bang and a snort. My powers of dissimulation were being saved from strain again. But that kind of thing didn't really get me sore, for I knew perfectly well why Wolfe didn't always point out to me the hole he was getting ready to crawl through: he knew that half the time I'd be back at him with damn good proof that it couldn't be done, which would only have been a nuisance, since he intended to do it anyway. No guy who knows he's right because he's too conceited to be wrong can be expected to go into conference about it.

Five minutes after that phone call from Saul the fun began. I got a ring from Wolfe upstairs:

"Try for Lord Clivers."

I got the Hotel Portland and got through to him, and Wolfe spoke: "Good morning, sir. I received your message . . . Yes, so I understand . . . No, he can't go . . . If you will be so good—one moment—a very important development has taken place, and I don't like to discuss details on the telephone. You may remember that on the phone yesterday afternoon Mr. Walsh spoke to you regarding a certain person whom he had just seen . . . Yes, he is both dangerous and desperate; moreover, he is cornered, and there is only one person open to you that can possibly prevent the fullest and most distasteful publicity on the whole affair . . . I know that, that's why I want you to come to my office at once . . . No, sir, take my word for it, it won't do, I should have to expose him immediately and publicly . . . Yes, sir . . . Good. That's a sensible man. Be sure to bring those papers along. I'll expect you in fifteen minutes . . ."

Clivers rang off, but Wolfe stayed on.

"Archie. Try for Mr. Muir."

I got the Seaboard Products Corporation, and Miss Barish, and then Muir, and buzzed Wolfe.

"Mr. Muir? Good morning, sir. This is Nero Wolfe. . . .

167

One moment, sir, I beg you. I have learned, to my great discomfiture, that I did an act of injustice yesterday, and I wish to rectify it . . . Yes, yes, quite so, I understand . . . Yes, indeed. I prefer not to discuss it on the telephone, but I am sure you will find yourself as satisfied as you deserve to be if you will come to my office at half-past eleven this morning, and bring Mr. Perry with you . . . No, I'm sorry, I can't do that. Miss Fox will be here . . . Yes, she is here now . . . No, half-past eleven, not before, and it will be necessary to have Mr. Perry present . . . Oh, surely not, he has shown a most active interest . . . Yes, it's only a short distance . . ."

I heard Muir's click off, and said into my transmitter, "That will bring that old goat trotting up here without stopping either for Perry or his hat. Why didn't you—"

"Thanks, Archie. Try for Mr. Cramer."

I got headquarters, and Cramer's extension and his clerk. Then the inspector. Wolfe got on:

"Good morning, Mr. Cramer . . . Yes, indeed, I received your message, but I have been occupied to good purpose . . . So I understand, but could I help that? Can you be at my office at half-past eleven? I shall be ready for you at that time . . . The fact is, I do not intend merely to give you information, I hope to deliver a finished case . . . I can't help that either; do you think I have the Moerae running errands for me? . . . Certainly, if they wish to come, bring them, though I think it would be well if Mr. Hombert went back to diapers . . . Yes, eleven-thirty . . ."

Cramer was off. I said, "Shall I try for the Cabinet?"

"No, thanks." Wolfe was purring. "When Lord Clivers arrives, bring him up here at once."

•••• 18 ••••

I LET Saul Panzer in when he came. There was no longer any
reason why I shouldn't relinquish the job of answering the
door, which normally belonged to Fritz, but it seemed tactful
to give him time to cool off a little; and besides, if I left him
to his own devices in the kitchen a while longer without interruption, there was a chance that he would bounce a stewpan
on Johnny's bean, which would have done them both good.

So I let Saul in and parked him in the front room, and
also, a little later, I opened up for the Marquis of Clivers.
Whereupon I experienced a delightful surprise, for he had
his nephew along. Apparently there was no wedding on today;
Horrocks looked sturdy and wholesome in a sack suit that
hung like a dream, and I got so interested looking at it that I
almost forgot it was him inside of it. I suggested him towards
the office and said to Clivers:

"Mr. Wolfe would like to see you upstairs. Three flights.
Climb, or elevator?"

He was looking concentrated and sour. He said climb, and
I took him up to the plant rooms and showed him Wolfe and
left him there.

When I got back down Horrocks was still standing in the
hall.

"If you want to wait," I said, "there's a place in the office
to hold the back of your lap. You know, chair."

"The back of my lap?" He stared, and by gum, he worked
at it till he got it. "Oh, quite. Thanks awfully. But I . . . I
say, you know, Miss Fox got quite a wetting. Didn't she?"

"Yeah, she was good and damp."

"And I suppose she is still here, what?"

It was merely a question of which would be less irritating,
to let him go on and circle around it for a while, or cut the

169

knot for him and hand him the pieces. Deciding for the latter, I said, "Wait here," and mounted the stairs again. They seemed to have quieted down in the south room. I knocked and went in and told Clara Fox:

"That young diplomat is down below and wants to see you and I'm going to send him up. Keep him in here. We're going to be busy in the office, and it gives me the spirit of 'seventy-six to look at him."

She made a dive for her vanity case, and I descended to the hall again and told Horrocks he knew the way.

It was ten after eleven. There was nothing for me to do but sit down and suck my finger. There was one thing I would have liked to remind Wolfe of before the party began, but I didn't myself know how important it was, and anyway I had no idea how he intended to stage it. There was even a chance that this was to be only a dress rehearsal, a preliminary, to see what a little panic would do, but that wouldn't be like him. The only hint he condescended to give me was to ring me on the house phone and tell me he would come down with Clivers after the others had arrived, and until then I was to say nothing of Clivers' presence. I went in to see if Saul was talking, but he wasn't, so I went back and sat down and felt my pulse.

The two contingents, official and Seaboard, showed up within three minutes of each other. I let them in. The official came first. I took them to the office, where I had chairs pulled up. Skinner looked bilious, Hombert harassed, and Cramer moderately grim. When they saw Wolfe wasn't in the office they started to get exasperated, but I silenced them with a few well-chosen phrases, and then the bell rang again and I went for the second batch.

Muir and Perry were together. Perry smiled a tight smile at me and told me good morning, but Muir wasn't having any amenities; I saw his hand tremble a little as he hung his hat up, and he could have gone from that right on into permanent palsy without any tears wasted as far as I was concerned. I nodded them ahead.

They stopped dead inside the office door, at sight of the trio already there. Muir looked astonished and furious; Perry seemed surprised, looking from one to the other, and then turned to me:

"I thought . . . Wolfe said eleven-thirty, so I understood from Muir . . . if these gentlemen . . ."

"It's all right." I grinned at him. "Mr. Wolfe has arranged for a little conference. Have chairs. Do you know Mr. Hombert, the Police Commissioner? Inspector Cramer? Mr. Ramsey Muir. Mr. Anthony D. Perry."

I got to the house phone on my desk and buzzed the plant rooms. Wolfe answered, and I told him, "All here." The two bunches of eminent visitors were putting on a first-class exhibition of bad manners; neither had expected to see the other. Cramer looked around at them, slowly from one face to another, and then looked at me with a gleam in his eyes. Hombert was grumbling something to Perry. Skinner turned and croaked at me, "What kind of damn nonsense is this?" I just shook my head at him, and then I heard the creak of the elevator, and a moment later the door of the office opened and Wolfe entered with another visitor whom none of them had expected to see.

They approached. Wolfe stopped, and inclined his head. "Good morning, gentlemen. I believe some of you have met Lord Clivers. Not you, Mr. Perry? No. Mr. Muir. Mr. Skinner, our District Attorney. I want to thank all of you for being so punctual . . ."

I was seeing a few things. First, Clivers stood staring directly at Perry, reminding me of how Harlan Scovil had stared at him two days before, and Clivers had thrust his right hand into the side pocket of his coat and didn't take it out. Second, Perry was staring back, and his temples were moving and his eyes were small and hard. Third, Inspector Cramer had put his weight forward in his chair and his feet back under him, but he was sitting too far away, the other side of Skinner, to get anywhere quick.

I swiveled and opened a drawer unostentatiously and got out my automatic and laid it on the desk at my elbow. Hombert was starting to bellyache:

"I don't know, Wolfe, what kind of a high-handed procedure you think—"

Wolfe, who had moved around the desk and into his chair, put up a palm at him: "Please, Mr. Hombert. I think it is always advisable to take a short-cut when it is feasible. That's why I requested a favor of Lord Clivers." He looked at Clivers. "Be seated, sir. And tell us, have you ever met Mr. Perry before?"

Clivers, with his hand still in his pocket, lowered himself into his chair, which was between Hombert and me, without taking his eyes off of Perry. "I have," he said gruffly. "By gad, you were right. He's Coleman. Rubber Coleman."

Perry just looked at him.

Wolfe asked softly, "What about it, Mr. Perry?"

171

You could see from Perry's chin that his teeth were clamped. His eyes went suddenly from Clivers to Wolfe and stayed there; then he looked at me, and I returned it. His shoulders started going up, slowly up, high, as he took in a long breath, and then slowly they started down again. When they touched bottom he looked at Wolfe again and said:

"I'm not talking. Not just now. You go on."

Wolfe nodded. "I don't blame you, sir. It's a lot to give up, to surrender that old secret." He glanced around the circle. "You gentlemen may remember, from Miss Fox's story last night, that Rubber Coleman was the man who led that little band of rescuers forty years ago. That was Mr. Perry here. But you do not yet know that on account of that obligation Lord Clivers, in the year 1906, twenty-nine years ago, paid Coleman—Mr. Perry—the sum of one million dollars. Nor that this Coleman-Perry has never, to this day, distributed any of that sum as he agreed to do."

Cramer grunted and moved himself another inch forward. Skinner was sunk in his chair with his elbows on its arms and his finger-tips placed neatly together, his narrow eyes moving from Wolfe to Clivers to Perry and back again. Hombert was biting his lip and watching Clivers. Muir suddenly squeaked:

"What's all this about? What has this got to do—"

Wolfe snapped at him, "Shut up. You are here, sir, because that seemed the easiest way to bring Mr. Perry, and because I thought you should know the truth regarding your charge against Miss Fox. If you wish to leave, do so; if you stay, hold your tongue."

Clivers put in brusquely, "I didn't agree to this man's presence."

Wolfe nodded. "I think you may leave that to me. After all, Lord Clivers, it was you who originally started this, and if the hen has come home to roost and I am to pluck it for you, I must be permitted a voice in the method." He turned abruptly. "What about it, Mr. Perry? You've had a moment for reflection. You were Rubber Coleman, weren't you?"

"I'm not talking." Perry was gazing at him, and this time he didn't have to strain the words through his teeth. His lips compressed a little, his idea being that he was smiling. "Lord Clivers may quite possibly be mistaken." He tried the smile again. "It may even be that he will . . . will realize his mistake." He looked around. "You know me, Mr. Skinner. You too, Mr. Hombert. I am glad you are here. I have evidence to present to you that this man Wolfe is engaged in a malicious attempt to damage my reputation and that of my vice-president and the firm I direct. Mr. Muir will bear me out." He turned small hard eyes on Wolfe. "I'll give you rope. All you want. Go on."

Wolfe nodded admiringly. "Superlative." He leaned back and surveyed the group. "Gentlemen, I must ask you to listen, and bear with me. You will reach my conclusion only if I describe my progress toward it. I'll make it as brief as possible.

"It began some forty-five hours ago, when Mr. Perry called here and asked me to investigate a theft of $30,000 from the drawer of Mr. Muir's desk. Mr. Goodwin called at the Seaboard office and asked questions. He was there from 4:45 until 5:55, and for a period of 35 minutes, from 5:20 until 5:55, he saw neither Mr. Perry nor Mr. Muir, because they had gone to a conference in the directors' room. The case seemed to have undesirable features, and we decided not to handle it. I find I shall need some beer."

He reached to push the button, and leaned back again. "You know of Harlan Scovil's visit to this office Monday afternoon. Well, he saw Mr. Perry here. He not only saw him, he stared at him. You know of the phone call, at 5:26, which summoned Mr. Scovil to his death. Monday night, in addition to these things, I also knew the story which Miss Fox had related to us in the presence of Mr. Walsh and Miss Lindquist; and when, having engaged myself in Miss Fox's interest, it became necessary to consider the murder of Harlan Scovil, I scanned the possibilities as they presented themselves at that moment.

"Assuming, until disproven, that Harlan Scovil's murder was connected with the Rubber Band affair, the first possibility was of course Lord Clivers himself, but Tuesday morning he was eliminated, when I learned that the murderer was alone in the automobile. An article in Sunday's *Times*, which Mr. Goodwin had kindly read to me, stated that Lord Clivers did not know how to drive a car, and on Tuesday, yesterday, I corroborated that through an agent in London, at the same time acquiring various bits of information regarding Lord Clivers. The second possibility was Michael Walsh. I had talked with him and formed a certain judgment of him, and no motive was apparent, but he remained a possibility. The same applied to Miss Lindquist. Miss Fox was definitely out of it, because I had upon consideration accepted her as a client."

Somebody burst out, "Ha!" Hombert ventured a comment, while Wolfe poured beer and gulped, but it went unheeded. Wolfe wiped his lips and went on:

173

"Among the known possibilities, the most promising one was Anthony D. Perry. On account of the phone call which took Mr. Scovil to the street to die, it was practically certain that his murderer had known he was in this office; and because, so far as I was aware, Mr. Perry was the only person who had known that, it seemed at least worth while to accept it as a conjecture. Through *Metropolitan Biographies* and also through inquiries by one of my men, I got at least negative support for the conjecture; and I got positive support by talking over long distance to Nebraska, with Miss Lindquist's father. He remembered with considerable accuracy the appearance of the face and figure of Rubber Coleman, and while of course there could be no real identification by a telephone talk after forty years, still it was support. I asked Mr. Lindquist, in fact, for descriptions of all the men concerned in that affair, thinking there might be some complication more involved than this most obvious one, but it was his description of Rubber Coleman which most nearly approximated that of Mr. Perry. The next step—"

"Wait a minute, Wolfe." Skinner's croak was imperative. "You can't do this. Not this way. If you've got a case, I'm the District Attorney. If you haven't—"

Perry cut in, "Let him alone! Let him hang himself."

Hombert muttered something to Cramer, and the inspector rumbled back. Clivers spoke up: "I'm concerned in this. Let Wolfe talk." He used a finger of his left hand to point at Perry because his ring hand was still in his coat pocket. "That man is Rubber Coleman. Wolfe learned that, didn't he? What the devil have the rest of you done, except annoy me?"

Perry leveled his eyes at the marquis. "You're mistaken, Lord Clivers. You'll regret this."

Wolfe had taken advantage of the opportunity to finish his bottle and ring for another. Now he looked around. "You gentlemen may be curious why, if Mr. Perry is not Rubber Coleman, he does not express indignant wonderment at what I am talking about. Oh, he could explain that. Long ago, shortly after she entered Seaboard's employ, Miss Fox told him the story which you heard from her last night. He knows all about the Rubber Band, from her, and also about her efforts to find its surviving members. And by the way, as regards the identity—did Mr. Walsh telephone you around five o'clock yesterday afternoon, Lord Clivers, and tell you he had just found Rubber Coleman?"

Clivers nodded. "He did."

"Yes." Wolfe looked at Cramer. "As you informed me, immediately after leaving the Seaboard office, where he had gone on account of his unfortunate suspicions regarding Miss Fox and myself after Harlan Scovil had been killed, Mr. Walsh sought a telephone. There—as can doubtless be verified by inquiry, along with multitudinous other details—he had seen Mr. Perry. It is a pity he did not inform me, since in that case he would still be alive; but what he did do was to phone Lord Clivers, with whom he had had a talk in the morning. He had called at the Hotel Portland and Lord Clivers had considered it advisable to see him, had informed him of the payment which had been made to Rubber Coleman long before, and had declared his intention of giving him a respectable sum of money. Now, learning from Mr. Walsh over the telephone that he had found Rubber Coleman, Lord Clivers saw that immediate and purposeful action was required if publicity was to be avoided; and he told Mr. Walsh that around seven o'clock that evening, on his way to a dinner engagement, he would stop in at the place Mr. Walsh was working, which was a short distance from his hotel. I have been told these details within the last hour. Is that correct, sir?"

Clivers nodded. "It is."

Wolfe looked at Perry, but Perry's eyes were fixed on Clivers. Wolfe said, "So, for the identity, we have Mr. Lindquist's description, Mr. Walsh's phone call, and Lord Clivers' present recognition. Why, after forty years, Mr. Scovil and Mr. Walsh should have recognized Rubber Coleman is, I think, easily explicable. On account of the circumstances, their minds were at the moment filled with vivid memories of that old event, and alert with suspicion. They might have passed Mr. Perry a hundred times on the street without a second glance at him, but in the situations in which they saw him recollection jumped for them." He looked again at the Seaboard president, and again asked, "What about it now, Mr. Perry? Won't you give us that?"

Perry moved his eyes at him. He spoke smoothly. "I'm still not talking. I'm listening." He suddenly, spasmodically, jerked forward, and there was a stir around the circle. Cramer's bulk tensed in his chair. Skinner's hands dropped. Clivers stiffened. I got my hand to my desk, on the gun. I don't think Perry noticed any of it, for his gaze stayed on Wolfe, and he jerked back again and set his jaw. He said not quite so smoothly, "You go on."

Wolfe shook his head. "You're a stubborn man, Mr. Perry. However—as I started to say, the next step for me, yesterday

175

afternoon, was to get in touch with Mr. Walsh, persuade him of my good faith, show him a photograph of Mr. Perry, and substantiate my conjecture. That became doubly important and urgent after Lord Clivers called here and I learned of the payment that had been made to Coleman in 1906. I considered the idea of asking Lord Clivers for a description of Coleman, and even possibly showing him Perry's photograph, but rejected it. I was at that moment by no means convinced of his devotion to scruple, and even had I been, I would not have cared to alarm him further by showing him the imminence of Coleman's discovery—and the lid blown off the pot. First I needed Mr. Walsh, so I sent a man to 55th Street to reconnoitre.

"Of course, I had found out other things. For instance, one of my men had visited the directors' room of the Seaboard Products Corporation and learned that it has a second door, into the public hall, through which Mr. Perry might easily have departed at 5:20 or thereabouts Monday afternoon on some errand, and returned some thirty minutes later, without Mr. Goodwin's knowledge. Questions to his business associates who were present might elicit answers. For another instance, Miss Fox had breakfast with me yesterday morning—and I assure you, Mr. Skinner, I did not waste the time in foolish queries as to where her mother used to keep letters sixteen years ago.

"Combining information with conjecture, I get a fair picture of some of Mr. Perry's precautionary activities. In the spring of 1932 he saw an advertisement in a newspaper seeking knowledge of the whereabouts of Michael Walsh and Rubber Coleman. In a roundabout way he learned who had inserted it; and a month later Clara Fox was in the employ of the Seaboard Products Corporation. He could keep an eye on her, and did so. He cultivated her company, and earned a degree of her confidence. When she found Harlan Scovil, and later Hilda Lindquist, and still later Michael Walsh, he knew of it. He tried to convince her of the foolishness of her enterprise, but without success. Then suddenly, last Thursday, he learned she had found Lord Clivers, and he at once took measures to hamstring her. He may even then have considered murder and rejected it; at any rate, he decided that sending her to prison as a thief would completely discredit her and would be sufficient. He knew that her initiative was the only active force threatening him, and that with her removed there would be little danger. An opportunity was providentially at hand. Friday afternoon he himself took that $30,000 from Mr. Muir's

176

desk, and sent Miss Fox into that room with a cablegram to be copied. I don't know—"

Muir had popped up out of his chair and was squealing, "By God, I believe it! By God if I don't! And all the time you were plotting against her! You dirty sneak, you dirty—"

Cramer, agile on his feet, had a hand on Muir's shoulder. "All right, all right, you just sit down and we'll all believe it. Come on, now." He eased him down, Muir chattering.

Perry said contemptuously, bitingly, "So that's you, Muir." He whirled, and there was a quality in his movement that made me touch my gun again. "Wolfe, all this you're inventing, you'll eat it." He added slowly, "And it will finish you."

Wolfe shook his head. "Oh no, sir, I assure you." He sighed. "To continue: I don't know how and when Mr. Perry concealed the money in Miss Fox's automobile, but one of my men has uncovered a possibility which the police can easily follow. At any rate, it is certain that he did. That is unimportant. Another thing that moved him to action was the fact that Clara Fox had told him that, having heard him speak favorably of the abilities of Nero Wolfe, she had decided to engage me in the Rubber Band enterprise. Apparently Mr. Perry did give my competence a high rating, for he took the trouble to come here himself to get me to act for the Seaboard Products Corporation, which would of course have prevented me from taking Miss Fox as a client.

"But he had an unpleasant surprise here. He was sitting in that chair, the one he is in now, when a man walked into the room and said, 'My name's Harlan Scovil.' And the man stared at Mr. Perry. We cannot know whether he definitely recognized him as Rubber Coleman or whether Mr. Perry merely suspected that he did. In any event, it was enough to convince Mr. Perry that something more drastic than a framed-up larceny charge was called for without delay; for obviously it would not do for any living person to have even the remotest suspicion that there was any connection between Anthony D. Perry, corporation president, bank director, multi-millionaire, and eminent citizen, and the Rubber Band. Lord Clivers tells me that forty years ago Rubber Coleman was headstrong, sharp of purpose, and quick on the trigger. Apparently he has retained those characteristics. He went to his office and at once phoned Mr. Goodwin to come there. At 5:20 he went to the directors' room. A moment later he excused himself to his associates, left by the door to the public hall, descended to the ground floor and telephoned Harlan Scovil, saying what we can only guess at but certainly arranging a rendezvous,

177

went to the street and selected a parked automobile and took it, drove to where Scovil was approaching the rendezvous and shot him dead, abandoned the car on Ninth Avenue, and returned to the Seaboard Building and the directors' room. It was an action admirably quick-witted, direct and conclusive, with probably not one chance in a million of its being discovered but for the fact that Miss Fox had happened to pick me to collect a fantastic debt for her."

Wolfe paused to open and pour beer. Skinner said, "I hope you've got something, Wolfe. I hope to heaven you've got something, because if you haven't . . ."

Wolfe drank, and put his glass down. "I know. I can see the open jaws of the waiting beasts." He thumbed at Perry. "This one here in front. But let him wait a little longer. Let us go on to last evening. That is quite simple. We are not concerned with the details of how Mr. Walsh got to see Mr. Perry at his office yesterday afternoon; it is enough to know that he did, since he phoned Lord Clivers that he had found Rubber Coleman. Well, there was only one thing for Mr. Perry to do, and he did it. Shortly after half-past six o'clock he entered that building enclosure by one of the ways we know of—possibly he is a member of the Orient Club, another point for inquiry—crept up on old Mr. Walsh and shot him in the back of the head, probably muffling the sound of the shot by wrapping the gun in his overcoat or something else, moved the body to the vicinity of the telephone if it was not already there, left by the way he had come, and drove rapidly—"

"Wait a minute!" Cramer broke in, gruff. "How do you fit that? We know the exact time of that shot, two minutes to seven, when Walsh called you on the phone. And you heard the shot. We already know—"

"Please, Mr. Cramer." Wolfe was patient. "I'm not telling you what you already know; this, for you, is news. I was saying, Mr. Perry drove rapidly downtown and arrived at this office at exactly seven o'clock."

Hombert jerked up and snorted. Cramer stared at Wolfe, slowly shaking his head. Skinner, frowning, demanded, "Are you crazy, Wolfe? Yesterday you told us you heard the shot that killed Walsh, at 6:58. Now you say that Perry fired it, and then got to your office at seven o'clock." He snarled, "Well?"

"Precisely." Wolfe wiggled a finger at him. "Do you remember that last night I told you that I was confronted by a difficulty which had to be solved before anything could be done?

178

That was it. You have just stated it. —Archie, please tell Saul to go ahead."

I got up and went and opened the door to the front room. Saul Panzer was sitting there. I called to him, "Hey, Mr. Wolfe says to go ahead." Saul made for the hall and I heard him going out the front door.

Wolfe was saying, "It was ingenious and daring for Mr. Perry to arrange for Mr. Goodwin and me to furnish his alibi. But of course, strictly speaking, it was not an alibi he had in mind; it was a chronology of events which would exclude from my mind any possibility of his connection with Mr. Walsh's death. Such a connection was not supposed to occur to anyone, and above all not to me; for it is fairly certain that up to the time of his arrival here today Mr. Perry felt satisfactorily assured that no one had the faintest suspicion of his interest in this affair. There had been two chances against him: Harlan Scovil might have spoken to Mr. Goodwin between the time that Mr. Perry left here Monday afternoon and the time he phoned to summon Mr. Goodwin to his office; or Mr. Walsh might have communicated with me between five and six yesterday. But he thought not, for there was no indication of it from us; and he had proceeded to kill both of them as soon as he could reasonably manage it. So he arranged—"

Skinner growled, "Get on. He may not have had an alibi in mind, but he seems to have one. What about it?"

"As I say, sir, that was my difficulty. It will be resolved for you shortly. I thought it better—ah! Get it, Archie."

It was the phone. I swiveled and took it, and found myself exchanging greetings with Mr. Panzer. I told Wolfe, "Saul."

He nodded, and got brisk. "Give Mr. Skinner your chair. If you would please take that receiver, Mr. Skinner? I want you to hear something. And you, Mr. Cramer, take mine—here —the cord isn't long enough, I'm afraid you'll have to stand. Kindly keep the receiver fairly snug on your ear. Now, Mr. Skinner, speak into the transmitter, 'Ready.' That one word will be enough."

Skinner, at my phone, croaked, "Ready." The next development was funny. He gave a jump, and turned to glare at Wolfe, while Cramer, at Wolfe's phone, jerked a little too, and yelled into the transmitter, "Hey! Hey, you!"

Wolfe said, "Hang up, gentlemen, and be seated. —Mr. Skinner, please! That demonstration was really necessary. What you heard was Saul Panzer in a telephone booth at the

179

druggist's on the next corner. There, of course, the instrument is attached to the wall. What he did was this."

Wolfe reached into his pocket and took out a big rubber band. He removed the receiver from his French phone, looped the band over the transmitter end, stretched it out, and let it flip. He replaced the receiver.

"That's all," he announced. "That was the shot Mr. Goodwin and I heard over the telephone. The band must be three-quarters of an inch wide, and thick, as I learned from experiments this morning. On this instrument, of course, it is nothing; but on the transmitter of a pay-station phone, with the impact and jar and vibration simultaneous, the effect is startling. Didn't you find it so, Mr. Skinner?"

"I'll be damned," Cramer muttered. "I will be damned."

Skinner said, "It's amazing. I'd have sworn it was a gun."

"Yes." Wolfe's eyes, half shut, were on Perry. "I must congratulate you, sir. Not only efficient, but appropriate. Rubber Coleman. The Rubber Band. I fancy that was how the idea happened to occur to you. Most ingenious, and ludicrously simple. I wish you would tell us what old friend or employee you got to help you try it out, for surely you took that precaution. It would save Mr. Cramer a lot of trouble."

Wolfe was over one hurdle, anyway. He had Skinner and Hombert and Cramer with him, sewed up. When he had begun talking they had kept their eyes mostly on him, with only occasional glances at Perry; then, as he had uncovered one point after another, they had gradually looked more at Perry; and by now, while still listening to Wolfe, they weren't bothering to look at him much. Their gaze was on Perry, and stayed there, and, for that matter, so was mine and Muir's and Clivers'. Perry was obviously expecting too much of himself. He had waited too long for a convenient spot to open up with indignation or defiance or a counter-attack, and no doubt Wolfe's little act with the rubber band had been a complete surprise to him. He was by no means ready to break down and have a good cry, because he wasn't that kind of a dog, but you could see he was stretched too tight. Just as none of us could take our eyes off of him, he couldn't take his off of Wolfe. From where I sat I could see his temples moving, plain.

He didn't say anything.

Skinner's bass rumbled, "You've made up a good story, Wolfe. I've got a suggestion. How about leaving your man here to entertain Perry for a while and the rest of us go somewhere for a little talk? I need to ask some questions."

Wolfe shook his head. "Not at this moment, sir, if you

180

please. Patience; my reasons will appear. First, is the chronology clear to all of you? At or about 6:35 Mr. Perry killed Mr. Walsh, leaving his body near the telephone, and immediately drove downtown, stopping, perhaps, at the same drug store where Saul Panzer just now demonstrated for us. I think that likely, for that store has a side entrance through which the phone booths can be approached with little exposure to observation. From there he phoned here, disguising his voice, and snapping his rubber band. Two minutes later he was at my door, having established the moment at which Michael Walsh was killed. There was of course the risk that by accident the body had been discovered in the twenty minutes which had elapsed, but it was slight, and in any event there was nothing to point to him. As it happened, he had great luck, for not only was the body not discovered prematurely, it was discovered at precisely the proper moment, and by Lord Clivers himself! I think it highly improbable that Mr. Perry knew that Lord Clivers was expected there at that hour, or indeed at all; that was coincidence. How he must have preened himself last evening—for we are all vainer of our luck than of our merits—when he learned the news! The happy smile of Providence! Isn't that so, Mr. Perry?"

Perry smiled into Wolfe's face—a thin tight smile, but he made a go of it. He said, "I'm still listening . . . but it strikes me you're about through. As Mr. Skinner says, you've made up a good story." He stopped, and his jaw worked a little, then he went on: "Of course you don't expect me to reply to it, but I'm going to, only not with words. You're in a plot to blackmail Lord Clivers, but that's his business. I'm going back to my office and get my lawyer, and I'm going to come down on you for slander and for conspiracy, and also your man Goodwin. I am also going to swear out a warrant against Clara Fox, and this time there'll be no nonsense about withdrawing it." He clamped his jaw, and loosened it again. "You're done, Wolfe. I'm telling you, you're done."

Wolfe looked at the District Attorney. "I am aware, Mr. Skinner, that I have exasperated you, but in the end I think you will agree that my procedure was well-advised. First, on account of the undesirable publicity in connection with Lord Clivers, and the fact that he is soon to sail for home, prompt action was essential. Second, there was the advantage of showing Mr. Perry all at once how many holes he will have to plug up, for he is bound to get frantic about it and make a fool of himself. He was really sanguine enough to expect to keep his connection with this completely concealed. His leaving the directors' room Monday afternoon and returning; his access to Clara Fox's car for concealing the money, which is now being investigated by one of my men, Orrie Cather; the visit to him by Michael Walsh; his entrance into, and exit from, the building enclosure last evening; his overcoat, perhaps, which he wrapped around his pistol; his entering the corner drug store to telephone; all these and a dozen other details are capable of inquiry; and, finding himself confronted by so many problems all requiring immediate attention, he is sure to put his foot in it."

Skinner grunted in disgust. "Do you mean to say you've given us all you've got? And now you're letting him know it?"

"But I've got all that's necessary." Wolfe sighed. "For, since we are all convinced that Mr. Perry did kill Harlan Scovil and Michael Walsh, it is of no consequence whether he can be legally convicted and executed."

Cramer muttered, "Uh-huh, you're nuts." Skinner and Hombert stared, speechless.

"Because," Wolfe went on, "he is rendered incapable of further mischief anyway; and even if you regard the criminal law as an instrument of barbarous vengeance, he is going to pay. What is it that he has been trying so desperately to preserve, with all his ruthless cunning? His position in society, his high repute among his fellow men, his nimbus as a master biped. Well, he will lose all that, which should be enough for any law." He extended his hand. "May I have those papers, Lord Clivers?"

Clivers reached to his breast pocket and pulled out an envelope, and I got it and handed it to Wolfe. Wolfe opened the flap and extracted some pieces of paper, and unfolded them, with the usual nicety of his fingers.

"I have here," he said, "a document dated Silver City, Nevada, June 2, 1895, in which George Rowley agrees to make a certain future compensation for services rendered. It is signed by him, and attested by Michael Walsh and Rubber Coleman as witnesses. I also have another, same date, headed PLEDGE OF THE RUBBER BAND, containing an agreement signed by various persons. I also have one dated London, England, August 11, 1906, which is a receipt for two hundred thousand, seven hundred sixty-one pounds, signed by Rubber Coleman, Gilbert Fox, Harlan Scovil, Turtleback, Victor Lindquist and Michael Walsh. After the 'Turtleback,' in parentheses, appears the name William Mollen. I also have a check

182

for the same amount, dated September 19, drawn to the order of James N. Coleman and endorsed by him for payment."

Wolfe looked around at them. "The point here is, gentlemen, that none of those men except Coleman ever saw that receipt. He forged the names of all the others." He whirled suddenly to Perry, and his voice was a whip. "Well, sir? Is that slander?"

Perry held himself. But his voice was squeezed in his throat. "It is. They signed it."

"Ha! They signed it? So at last we have it that you're Rubber Coleman?"

"Certainly I'm Coleman. They signed it, and they got their share."

"Oh, no." Wolfe pointed a finger at him and held it there. "You've made a bad mistake, sir; you didn't kill enough men. Victor Lindquist is still alive and in possession of his faculties. I talked to him yesterday on the telephone, and I warned him against any tricks that might be tried. His testimony, with the corroboration we already have, will be ample for an English court. Slander? Pfui!" He turned to the others. "So you see, it isn't really so important to convict Mr. Perry of murder. He is now past sixty. I don't know the English penalty for forgery, but certainly he will be well over seventy when he emerges from jail, discredited, broken, a pitiable relic—"

Wolfe told me later that his idea was to work Perry into a state where he would then and there sign checks for Clara Fox and Victor Lindquist, and Walsh's and Scovil's heirs if any, for their share of the million dollars. I don't know. Anyhow, the checks didn't get signed, because dead men can't write even their names.

It happened like lightning, a bunch of reflexes. Perry jerked out a gun and turned it on Wolfe and pulled the trigger. Hombert yelled and Cramer jumped. I could never have got across in time to topple him, and anyway, as I say, it was reflex. I grabbed my gun and let him have it, but then Cramer was there and I quit. There was a lot of noise, Perry was down, sunk in his chair, and they were pawing him. I dived around the desk for Wolfe, who was sitting there looking surprised for once in his life, feeling with his right hand at his upper left arm.

Him protesting, I pulled his coat open and the sleeve off, and the spot of blood on the outside of the arm of the canary yellow shirt looked better to me than any orchid. I stuck my finger in the hole the bullet had made and ripped the sleeve and took a look, and then grinned into the fat devil's face. "Just

183

the meat, and not much of that. You don't use that arm much anyhow."

I heard Cramer behind me, "Dead as a doornail," and turned to see the major casualty. They had let it come on out of the chair and stretched it on the floor. The inspector was kneeling by it, and the others standing, and Clivers and Skinner were busy putting out a fire. Clivers was pulling and rubbing at the bottom front of one side of his coat, where the bullet and flame had gone through when he pulled the trigger with his hand still in his pocket, and Skinner was helping him. He must have plugged Perry one-tenth of a second before I did.

Cramer stood up. He said heavily, "One in the right shoulder, and one clear through him, through the heart. Well, he asked for it."

I said, "The shoulder was mine. I was high."

"Surely not, Archie." It was behind me, Wolfe murmuring. We looked at him; he was sopping blood off of his arm with his handkerchief. "Surely not. Do you want Lord Clivers' picture in the *Gazette* again? We must protect him. You can stand the responsibility of a justifiable homicide. You can—what do you call it, Mr. Cramer?—take the rap."

•••• 19 ••••

"FIVE THOUSAND pounds," Clivers said. "To be paid at once, and to be returned to me if and when recovery is made from Coleman's estate. That's fair. I don't say it's generous. Who the devil can afford to be generous nowadays?"

Wolfe shook his head. "I see I'll have to get you on the wing. You dart like a humming-bird from two thousand to ten to seven to five. We'll take the ten, under the conditions you suggest."

Clara Fox put in, "I don't want anything. I've told you that. I won't take anything."

It was nearly three o'clock and we were all in the office. There had been six of us at lunch, which had meant another pick-me-up. Muir had gone, sped on his way by a pronouncement from Wolfe to the effect that he was a scabrous jackass, without having seen Clara Fox. Cramer and Hombert and Skinner had departed, after accepting Wolfe's suggestion for protecting the marquis from further publicity, and I had agreed to it. Doc Vollmer had come and fixed up Wolfe's arm and had gone again. What was left of Rubber Coleman-Anthony D. Perry had been taken away under Cramer's supervision, and the office floor looked bare because the big red and yellow rug where Perry had sat and where they had stretched him out was down in the basement, waiting for the cleaners to call. The bolt was back on the front door and I was acting as hallboy again, because reporters were still buzzing around the entrance like flies on the screen on a cloudy day.

Wolfe said, "You're still my client, Miss Fox. You are under no compulsion to take my advice, but it is my duty to offer it. First, take what belongs to you; your renunciation would not resurrect Mr. Scovil or Mr. Walsh, nor even Mr. Perry. Almost certainly, a large sum can be collected from Mr. Perry's

185

estate. Second, remember that I have earned a fee and you will have to pay it. Third, abandon for good your career as an adventuress; you're much too soft-hearted for it."

Clara Fox glanced at Francis Horrocks, who was sitting there looking at her with that sickening sweet expression that you occasionally see in public and at the movies. It was a relief to see him glance at Wolfe and get his mind on something else for a brief moment. He blurted out:

"I say, you know, if she doesn't want to take money from that chap's estate, she doesn't have to. It's her own affair, what? Now, if my uncle paid your fee . . . it's all the same . . ."

"Shut up, Francis." Clivers was impatient. "How the devil is it all the same? Let's get this settled. I've already missed one engagement and shall soon be late for another. Look here, seven thousand."

Hilda Lindquist said, "I'll take what I can get. It doesn't belong to me, it's my father's." Her square face wasn't exactly cheerful, but I wouldn't say she looked wretched. She leveled her eyes at Clivers. "If you had been half way careful when you paid that money twenty-nine years ago, father would have got his share then, when mother was still alive and my brother hadn't died."

Clivers didn't bother with her. He looked at Wolfe. "Let's get on. Eight thousand."

"Come, come, sir." Wolfe wiggled a finger at him. "Make it dollars. Fifty thousand. The exchange favors you. There is a strong probability that you'll get it back when Perry's estate is settled; besides, it might be argued that you should pay my fee instead of Miss Fox. There is no telling how this might have turned out for you but for my intervention."

"Bah." Clivers snorted. "Even up there, I saved your life. I shot him."

"Oh, no. Read the newspapers. Mr. Goodwin shot him."

Clivers looked at me, and suddenly exploded with his three short blasts, haw-haw-haw. "So you did, eh? Goodwin's your name? Damned fine shooting!" He turned to Wolfe. "All right. Draw up a paper and send it to my hotel, and you'll get a check." He got up from his chair, glancing down at the mess he had made of the front of his coat. "I'll have to go there now and change. A fine piece of cloth ruined. I'm sorry not to see more of your orchids. You, Francis! Come on."

Horrocks was murmuring something in a molasses tone to Clara Fox and she was taking it in and nodding at him. He finished, and got up. "Right-o." He moved across and stuck out his paw at Wolfe. "You know, I want to say, it was devilish clever, the way you watered Miss Fox yesterday morning and they never suspected. It was the face you put on that stumped them, what?"

"No doubt." Wolfe got his hand back again. "Since you gentlemen are sailing Saturday, I suppose we shan't see you again. *Bon voyage.*"

"Thanks," Clivers grunted. "At least for myself. My nephew isn't sailing. He has spent a fortune on cables and got himself transferred to the Washington embassy. He's going to carve out a career. He had better, because I'm damned if he'll get my title for another two decades. Come on, Francis."

I glanced at Clara Fox, and my dreams went short on ideals then and there. If I ever saw a woman look smug and self-satisfied . . .

• • • • 20 • • • •

AT TWENTY minutes to four, with Wolfe and me alone in the office, the door opened and Fritz came marching in. Clamped under his left arm was the poker-dart board; in his right hand was the box of javelins. He put the box down on Wolfe's desk, crossed to the far wall and hung up the board, backed off and squinted at it, straightened it up, turned to Wolfe and did his little bow, and departed.

Wolfe emptied his glass of beer, arose from his chair, and began fingering the darts, sorting out the yellow ones.

He looked at me. "I suppose this is foolhardy," he murmured, "with this bullet-wound, to start my blood pumping."

"Sure," I agreed. "You ought to be in bed. They may have to amputate."

"Indeed." He frowned at me. "Of course, you wouldn't know much about it. As far as my memory serves, you have never been shot by a high-calibre revolver at close range."

"The lord help me." I threw up my hands. "Is that going to be the tune? Are you actually going to have the nerve to brag about that little scratch? Now, if Hombert's foot hadn't jostled his chair and he had hit what he aimed at . . ."

"But he didn't." Wolfe moved to the fifteen-foot mark. He looked me over. "Archie. If you would care to join me at this . . ."

I shook my head positively. "Nothing doing. You'll keep beefing about your bullet-wound, and anyway I can't afford it. You'll probably be luckier than ever."

He put a dignified stare on me. "A dime a game."

"No."

"A nickel."

"No. Not even for matches."

He stood silent, and after a minute of that heaved a deep

188

sigh. "Your salary is raised ten dollars a week, beginning last Monday."

I lifted the brows. "Fifteen."

"Ten is enough."

I shook my head. "Fifteen."

He sighed again. "Confound you! All right. Fifteen."

I arose and went to the desk to get the red darts.

THE
RED
BOX

Introduction

How many novels will you read this year that were published in 1937?

The odds are, not many.

But Rex Stout's *The Red Box* is a marvelous exception and with good reason. The fourth book in the immortal Nero Wolfe series, *The Red Box* is quintessential Stout. Every element so long adored by faithful fans is there, the brownstone on Thirty-fifth Street; Wolfe's monumental girth, which is exceeded only by his towering intellect; the ten thousand orchids (Archie keeps the records updated) in the glassed-over rooms on the roof (the orchids' caretaker, Theo Horstmann, sleeps up there in a small den); the quick wit and ready cynicism of good-looking, blunt-talking Archie Goodwin; the unmatched epicurean delights (on the heavy side, only good eaters invited) of chef Fritz Brenner; the great man's collection of beer bottle caps.

And therein lies much of the magic of this series, the creation of a world that readers come to know as well as the insides of their own households, from the yellow couch and double-width cherry desk in Wolfe's office-cum-living room to the climate-and-temperature-controlled plant rooms where Wolfe spends from nine to eleven and four to six every day.

Readers often are curious as to how much of the author can be found in a book's hero. In the case of Rex Stout and Nero Wolfe, the lack of correlation is perhaps more striking. Stout was tall, slender, scraggly bearded; Wolfe packed a seventh of a ton into a stocky five foot eleven inches. Stout radiated energy; Wolfe avoided physical exertion as if it were deleterious to his health. Stout enjoyed good food, but was quite willing to enjoy common fare; Wolfe was a gourmand who would rather skip a meal than eat junk food. Stout had a wide-ranging interest in the political life of his country; Wolfe was almost apolitical.

But what they had in common and the quality that accounts for the greatest charm of the Nero Wolfe series is a love of language. Stout used language with great precision and with great pleasure. Wolfe was surely his alter ego in this glorious pursuit.

As all Wolfe and Goodwin aficionados know, Wolfe's idea of heaven was life uninterrupted in his brownstone with the orderly progression of his day from plant room to meal to plant room. It was Archie who alternately bullied and cajoled the great man into taking cases, which Wolfe did only because he knew he had to earn enough money to maintain their life-style.

The Red Box is a shining example of Wolfe and Archie at their most entertaining and intriguing, and the banter between the great detective and his unquenchable sidekick will delight Stout fans.

The Red Box provides one of the few instances in the long history recorded by Archie (more than forty books) when Wolfe does indeed depart from the cozy confines of his brownstone, much to Wolfe's disgruntlement. Archie achieves this rare state of affairs through a clever ploy that takes advantage of Wolfe's orchidmania.

The sortie to the clothing enterprise on Fifty-second Street provides perspicacious Wolfe with the only ambiguity among the recorded statements on the murder of a model.

Wolfe is faced first with a seemingly insoluble crime—who was really the intended victim? When he correctly identifies the murderer's true objective and has within his grasp the opportunity to divine the perpetrator, murder once again intervenes—this time in Wolfe's own office, both an infuriating and ultimately tactless mistake by the murderer.

The cast of suspects includes:

—A gorgeous, rich model who knows too much about the candy.

—The caretaker of an estate who talks so much and so fast no one can get a word in edgewise.

—A self-possessed widow who certainly earned the ire of her husband.

—Wolfe's first client, who can't seem to make up his mind what he wants.

—An expatriate without visible means of support who seems to live quite comfortably.

Wolfe is frustrated because he decides early on who did the killing, but sees no way of bringing the suspect to justice. Wolfe solves this problem—with some artful legerdemain—when he unmasks a clever and calculating killer in the comfort and convenience of his lair.

Archie Goodwin is in top form, sassing police, suspects, and clients (as Archie remarks, this case "is just one damned client after another").

Introduction

Readers will delight in the intricacy of the plot, the repartee between Wolfe and his man-about-town, Archie, and they may be quite particular in their choice of candies should a box without provenance be offered.

—**Carolyn G. Hart**

Chapter 1

Wolfe looked at our visitor with his eyes wide open—a sign, with him, either of indifference or of irritation. In this case it was obvious that he was irritated.

"I repeat, Mr. Frost, it is useless," he declared. "I never leave my home on business. No man's pertinacity can coerce me. I told you that five days ago. Good day, sir."

Llewellyn Frost blinked, but made no move to acknowledge the dismissal. On the contrary, he settled back in his chair.

He nodded patiently. "I know, I humored you last Wednesday, Mr. Wolfe, because there was another possibility that seemed worth trying. But it was no good. Now there's no other way. You'll have to go up there. You can forget your build-up as an eccentric genius for once—anyhow, an exception will do it good. The flaw that heightens the perfection. The stutter that accents the eloquence. Good Lord, it's only twenty blocks, Fifty-second between Fifth and Madison. A taxi will take us there in eight minutes."

"Indeed." Wolfe stirred in his chair; he was boiling. "How old are you, Mr. Frost?"

"Me? Twenty-nine."

"Hardly young enough to justify your childish effrontery. So. You humored me! You speak of my build-up! And you undertake to stampede me into a frantic dash through the maelstrom of the city's traffic—in a taxicab! Sir, I would not enter a taxicab for a chance to solve the Sphinx's deepest riddle with all the Nile's cargo as my reward!" He sank his voice to an outraged murmur. "Good God. A taxicab."

I grinned a bravo at him, twirling my pencil as I sat at my desk, eight feet from his. Having worked for Nero Wolfe for nine years, there were a few points I wasn't skeptical about any more. For instance: That he was the best private detective north of the South Pole. That he was convinced that outdoor air was apt to clog the lungs. That it short-circuited his nervous system to be jiggled and jostled. That he would have starved to death if anything had happened to Fritz Brenner, on account of his firm belief that no one's cooking but Fritz's was fit to eat. There were other points too, of a different sort, but I'll pass them up since Nero Wolfe will probably read this.

Young Mr. Frost quietly stared at him. "You're having a grand time, Mr. Wolfe. Aren't you?" Frost nodded. "Sure you are. A girl has been murdered. Another one—maybe more—is in danger. You offer yourself as an expert in these matters, don't you? That part's all right, there's no question but that you're an expert. And a girl's been murdered, and others are in great and immediate peril, and you rant like Booth and Barrett about a taxicab in a maelstrom. I appreciate good acting; I ought to, since I'm in show business. But in your case I should think there would be times when a decent regard for human suffering and misfortune would make you wipe off the make-up. And if you're really playing it straight, that only makes it worse. If, rather than undergo a little personal inconvenience—"

"No good, Mr. Frost." Wolfe was slowly shaking his head. "Do you expect to bully me into a defense of my conduct? Nonsense. If a girl has been murdered, there are the police. Others are in peril? They have my sympathy, but they hold no option on my professional services. I cannot chase perils away with a wave of my hand, and I will not ride in a taxicab. I will not ride in anything, even my own car with Mr. Goodwin driving, except to meet my personal contingencies. You observe my bulk. I am not immovable, but my flesh has a constitutional reluctance to sudden, violent or sustained displacement. You spoke of 'decent regard.' How about a decent regard for the privacy of my dwelling? I use this room as an office, but this house is my home. Good day, sir."

The young man flushed, but did not move. "You won't go?" he demanded.

"I will not."

"Twenty blocks, eight minutes, your own car."

"Confound it, no."

Frost frowned at him. He muttered to himself, "They don't come any stubborner." He reached to his inside coat pocket and pulled out some papers, selected one and unfolded it and glanced at it, and returned the others. He looked at Wolfe:

"I've spent most of two days getting this thing signed. Now, wait a minute, hold your horses. When Molly Lauck was poisoned, a week ago today, it looked phony from the beginning. By Wednesday, two days later, it was plain that the cops were running around in circles, and I came to you. I know about you, I know you're the one and only. As you know, I tried to get McNair and the others down here to your office and they wouldn't come, and I tried to get you up there

and you wouldn't go, and I invited you to go to hell.
That was five days ago. I've paid another detective
three hundred dollars for a lot of nothing, and the cops
from the inspector down are about as good as Fanny
Brice would be for Juliet. Anyhow, it's a tough one,
and I doubt if *anyone* could crack it but you. I decided
that Saturday, and during the weekend I covered a lot
of territory." He pushed the paper at Wolfe. "What do
you say to that?"

Wolfe took it and read it. I saw his eyes go slowly
half-shut, and knew that whatever it was, its effect on
his irritation was pronounced. He glanced over it
again, looked at Llewellyn Frost through slits, and
then extended the paper toward me. I got up to take
it. It was typewritten on a sheet of good bond, plain,
and was dated New York City, March 28, 1936:

To MR. NERO WOLFE:

At the request of Llewellyn Frost, we, the
undersigned, beg you and urge you to investigate the death of Molly Lauck, who was poisoned on March 23 at the office of Boyden
McNair Incorporated on 52nd Street, New York.
We entreat you to visit McNair's office for that
purpose.

We respectfully remind you that once each
year you leave your home to attend the Metropolitan Orchid Show, and we suggest that the
present urgency, while not as great to you
personally, appears to us to warrant an equal
sacrifice of your comfort and convenience.

With high esteem,
WINOLD GLUECKNER
CUYLER DITSON
T. M. O'GORMAN

RAYMOND PLEHN
CHAS. E. SHANKS
CHRISTOPHER BAMFORD

I handed the document back to Wolfe and sat down and grinned at him. He folded it and slipped it under the block of petrified wood which he used for a paperweight. Frost said:

"That was the best I could think of, to get you. I had to have you. This thing has to be ripped open. I got Del Pritchard up there and he was lost. I had to get you somehow. Will you come?"

Wolfe's forefinger was doing a little circle on the arm of his chair. "Why the devil," he demanded, "did they sign that thing?"

"Because I asked them to. I explained. I told them that no one but you could solve it and you had to be persuaded. I told them that besides money and food the only thing you were interested in was orchids, and that there was nobody who could exert any influence on you but them, the best orchid-growers in America. I had letters of introduction to them. I did it right. You notice I restricted my list to the very best. Will you come?"

Wolfe sighed. "Alec Martin has forty thousand plants at Rutherford. He wouldn't sign it, eh?"

"He would if I'd gone after him. Glueckner told me that you regard Martin as tricky and an inferior grower. Will you come?"

"Humbug." Wolfe sighed again. "An infernal imposition." He wiggled a finger at the young man. "Look here. You seem to be prepared to stop at nothing. You interrupt these expert and worthy men at their tasks to get them to sign this idiotic paper. You badger me. Why?"

"Because I want you to solve this case."

"Why me?"

"Because no one else can. Wait till you see—"

"Yes. Thank you. But why your overwhelming interest in the case? The murdered girl—what was she to you?"

"Nothing." Frost hesitated. He went on, "She was nothing to me. I knew her—an acquaintance. But the danger—damn it, let me tell you about it. The way it happened—"

"Please, Mr. Frost." Wolfe was crisp. "Permit me. If the murdered girl was nothing to you, what standing will there be for an investigator engaged by you? If you could not persuade Mr. McNair and the others to come to me, it would be futile for me to go to them."

"No, it wouldn't. I'll explain that—"

"Very well. Another point. I charge high fees."

The young man flushed. "I know you do." He leaned forward in his chair. "Look, Mr. Wolfe. I've thrown away a lot of my father's money since I put on long pants. A good gob of it in the past two years, producing shows, and they were all flops. But now I've got a hit. It opened two weeks ago, and it's a ten weeks buy. *Bullets for Breakfast.* I'll have plenty of cash to pay your fee. If only you'll find out where the hell that poison came from—and help me find a way. . . ."

He stopped. Wolfe prompted him, "Yes, sir? A way—"

Frost frowned. "A way to get my cousin out of that murderous hole. My ortho-cousin, the daughter of my father's brother."

"Indeed." Wolfe surveyed him. "Are you an anthropologist?"

"No." Frost flushed again. "I told you, I'm in show business. I can pay your fee—within reason, or even without reason. But we ought to have an understanding about that. Of course the amount of the fee is up to you, but my idea would be to split it, half to find out where that candy came from, and the other half for getting my cousin Helen away from that place. She's as stubborn as you are, and you'll probably have to earn the first half of the fee in order to earn the second, but I don't care if you don't. If you get her out of there without clearing up Molly Lauck's death, half the fee is yours anyhow. But Helen won't scare, that won't work, and she has some kind of a damn fool idea about loyalty to this McNair, Boyden McNair. Uncle Boyd, she calls him. She's known him all her life. He's an old friend of Aunt Callie's, Helen's mother. Then there's this dope, Gebert—but I'd better start at the beginning and sketch it—hey! You going now?"

Wolfe had pushed his chair back and elevated himself to his feet. He moved around the end of his desk with his customary steady and not ungraceful deliberation.

"Keep your seat, Mr. Frost. It is four o'clock, and I now spend two hours with my plants upstairs. Mr. Goodwin will take the details of the poisoning of Miss Molly Lauck—and of your family complications if they seem pertinent. For the fourth time, I believe it is, good day, sir." He headed for the door.

Frost jumped up, sputtering. "But you're coming uptown—"

Wolfe halted and ponderously turned. "Confound you, you know perfectly well I am! But I'll tell you this, if Alec Martin's signature had been on that outlandish paper I would have thrown it in the wastebasket. He splits bulbs. Splits them! —Archie. We shall meet Mr. Frost at the McNair place tomorrow morning at ten minutes past eleven."

He turned and went, disregarding the client's

protest at the delay. Through the open office door I heard, from the hall, the grunt of the elevator as he stepped in it, and the bang of its door.

Llewellyn Frost turned to me, and the color in his face may have been from gratification at his success, or from indignation at its postponement. I looked him over as a client—his wavy light brown hair brushed back, his wide-open brown eyes that left the matter of intelligence to a guess, his big nose and broad jaw which made his face too heavy even for his six feet.

"Anyhow, I'm much obliged to you, Mr. Goodwin." He sat down. "You were clever about it, too, keeping that Martin out of it. It was a big favor you did me, and I assure you I won't forget—"

"Wrong number." I waved him off. "I told you at the time, I keep all my favors for myself. I suggested that round robin only to try to drum up some business, and for a scientific experiment to find out how many ergs it would take to jostle him loose. We haven't had a case that was worth anything for nearly three months." I got hold of a notebook and pencil, and swiveled around and pulled my desk-leaf out. "And by the way, Mr. Frost, don't you forget that you thought of that round robin yourself. I'm not supposed to think."

"Certainly," he nodded. "Strictly confidential. I'll never mention it."

"Okay." I flipped the notebook open to the next blank page. "Now for this murder you want to buy a piece of. Spill it."

Chapter 2

So the next morning I had Nero Wolfe braving the elements—the chief element for that day being bright warm March sunshine. I say I had him, because I had conceived the persuasion which was making him burst all precedents. What pulled him out of his front door, enraged and grim, with overcoat, scarf, gloves, stick, something he called gaiters, and a black felt pirate's hat size 8 pulled down to his ears, was the name of Winold Glueckner heading the signatures on the letter—Glueckner, who had recently received from an agent in Sarawak four bulbs of a pink Coellogyne pandurata, never seen before, and had scorned Wolfe's offer of three thousand bucks for two of them. Knowing what a tough old heinie Glueckner was, I had my doubts whether he would turn loose of the bulbs no matter how many murders Wolfe solved at his request, but anyhow I had lit the fuse.

Driving from the house on 35th Street near the Hudson River—where Wolfe had lived for over twenty years and I had lived with him—to the address on 52nd Street, I handled the sedan so as to keep it as smooth as a dip's fingers. Except for one I couldn't resist; on Fifth Avenue near Forty-third there was an ideal little hole about two feet across where I suppose someone had been prospecting for the twenty-six dollars they paid the Indians, and I maneuvered to hit it square at a good clip. I glanced in the mirror for a glimpse of Wolfe in the back seat and saw he was looking bitter and infuriated.

I said, "Sorry, sir, they're tearing up the streets." He didn't answer.

From what Llewellyn Frost had told me the day before about the place of business of Boyden McNair Incorporated—all of which had gone into my notebook and been read to Nero Wolfe Monday evening—I hadn't realized the extent of its aspirations in the way of class. We met Llewellyn Frost downstairs, just inside the entrance. One of the first things I saw and heard, as Frost led us to the elevator to take us to the second floor, where the offices and private showrooms were, was a saleswoman who looked like a cross between a countess and Texas Guinan, telling a customer that in spite of the fact that the little green sport suit on the model was of High Meadow Loom hand-woven material and designed by Mr. McNair himself, it could be had for a paltry three hundred. I thought of the husband and shivered and crossed my fingers as I stepped into the elevator. And I remarked to myself, "I'll say it's a sinister joint."

The floor above was just as elegant, but quieter. There was no merchandise at all in sight, no saleswomen and no customers. A long wide corridor had doors on both sides at intervals, with etchings and hunting prints here and there on the wood paneling, and in the large room where we emerged from the elevator there were silk chairs and gold smoking stands and thick deep-colored rugs. I took that in at a glance and then centered my attention on the side of the room opposite the corridor, where a couple of goddesses were sitting on a settee. One of them, a blonde with dark blue eyes, was such a pronounced pippin that I had to stare so as not to blink, and the other one, slender and medium-dark, while not as remarkable, was a cinch in a contest for Miss Fifty-second Street.

The blonde nodded at us. The slender one said, "Hello, Lew."

Llewellyn Frost nodded back. "'Lo, Helen. See you later."

As we went down the corridor I said to Wolfe, "See that? I mean, them? You ought to get around more. What are orchids to a pair of blossoms like that?"

He only grunted at me.

Frost knocked at the last door on the right, opened it, and stood aside for us to precede him. It was a large room, fairly narrow but long, and there was only enough let-up on the elegance to allow for the necessities of an office. The rugs were just as thick as up front, and the furniture was Decorators' Delight. The windows were covered with heavy yellow silk curtains, sweeping in folds to the floor, and the light came from glass chandeliers as big as barrels.

Frost said, "Mr. Nero Wolfe. Mr. Goodwin. Mr. McNair."

The man at the desk with carved legs got up and stuck out a paw, without enthusiasm. "How do you do, gentlemen. Be seated. Another chair, Lew?"

Wolfe looked grim. I glanced around at the chairs, and saw I'd have to act quick, for I knew that Wolfe was absolutely capable of running out on us for less than that, and having got him this far I was going to hold on to him if possible. I stepped around to the other side of the desk and put a hand on Boyden McNair's chair. He was still standing up.

"If you don't mind, sir. Mr. Wolfe prefers a roomy seat, just one of his whims. The other chairs are pretty damn narrow. If you don't mind?"

By that time I had it shoved around where Wolfe could take it. McNair stared. I brought one of the Decorators' Delights around for him, tossed him a grin, and went around and sat down by Llewellyn Frost.

McNair said to Frost, "Well, Lew, you know I'm busy. Did you tell these gentlemen I agreed to give them fifteen minutes?"

Frost glanced at Wolfe and then looked back at McNair. I could see his hands, with the fingers twined, resting on his thigh; the fingers were pressed tight. He said, "I told them I had persuaded you to see them. I don't believe fifteen minutes will be enough—"

"It'll have to be enough. I'm busy. This is a busy season." McNair had a thin tight voice and he kept shifting in his chair—that is, temporarily his chair. He went on, "Anyway, what's the use? What can I do?" He spread out his hands, glanced at his wrist watch, and looked at Wolfe. "I promised Lew fifteen minutes. I am at your service until 11:20."

Wolfe shook his head. "Judging from Mr. Frost's story, I shall need more. Two hours or more, I should say."

"Impossible," McNair snapped. "I'm busy. Now, fourteen minutes."

"This is preposterous." Wolfe braced his hands on the arms of the borrowed chair and raised himself to his feet. He stopped Frost's ejaculation by showing him a palm, looked down at McNair and said quietly, "I didn't need to come here to see you, sir. I did so in acknowledgment of an idiotic but charming gesture

conceived and executed by Mr. Frost. I understand
that Mr. Cramer of the police has had several conversations with you, and that he is violently dissatisfied
with the lack of progress in his investigation of the
murder of one of your employees on your premises.
Mr. Cramer has a high opinion of my abilities. I shall
telephone him within an hour and suggest that he
bring you—and other persons—to my office." Wolfe
wiggled a finger. "For much longer than fifteen minutes."

He moved. I got up. Frost started after him.

"Wait!" McNair called out. "Wait a minute, you
don't understand!" Wolfe turned and stood. McNair
continued, "In the first place, why try to browbeat
me? That's ridiculous. Cramer couldn't take me to
your office, or any place, if I didn't care to go, you
know that. Of course Molly—of course the murder was
terrible. Good God, don't I know it? And naturally I'll
do anything I can to help clear it up. But what's the
use? I've told Cramer everything I know, we've been
over it a dozen times. Sit down." He pulled a handkerchief from his pocket and wiped his forehead and
nose, started to return it to his pocket and then threw
it on the desk. "I'm going to have a breakdown. Sit
down. I worked fourteen hours a day getting the
spring line ready, enough to kill a man, and then this
comes on top of it. You've been dragged into this by
Lew Frost. What the devil does he know about it?" He
glared at Frost. "I've told it over and over to the police
until I'm sick of it. Sit down, won't you? Ten minutes
is all you'll need for what I know, anyhow. That's what
makes it worse, as I've told Cramer, nobody knows
anything. And Lew Frost knows less than that." He
glared at the young man. "You know damn well you're
just trying to use it as a lever to pry Helen out of
here." He transferred the glare to Wolfe. "Do you

expect me to have anything better than the barest courtesy for you? Why should I?"

Wolfe had returned to his chair and got himself lowered into it, without taking his eyes off McNair's face. Frost started to speak, but I silenced him with a shake of the head. McNair picked up the handkerchief and passed it across his forehead and threw it down again. He pulled open the top right drawer of his desk and looked in it, muttered, "Where the devil's that aspirin?" tried the drawer on the left, reached in and brought out a small bottle, shook a couple of tablets onto his palm, poured half a glass of water from a thermos carafe, tossed the tablets into his mouth, and washed them down.

He looked at Wolfe and complained resentfully, "I've had a hell of a headache for two weeks. I've taken a ton of aspirin and it doesn't help any. I'm going to have a breakdown. That's the truth—"

There was a knock, and the door opened. The intruder was a tall handsome woman in a black dress with rows of white buttons. She came on in, glanced politely around, and said in a voice full of culture:

"Excuse me, please." She looked at McNair: "That 1241 resort, the cashmere plain tabby with the medium oxford twill stripe—can that be done in two shades of natural shetland with basket instead of tabby?"

McNair frowned at her and demanded, "What?"

She took a breath. "That 1241 resort—"

"Oh. I heard you. It cannot. The line stands, Mrs. Lamont. You know that."

"I know. Mrs. Frost wants it."

McNair straightened up. "Mrs. Frost? Is she here?"

The woman nodded. "She's ordering. I told her you

were engaged. She's taking two of the Portsmouth ensembles."

"Oh. She *is*." McNair had suddenly stopped fidgeting, and his voice, though still thin, sounded more under command. "I want to see her. Ask if it will suit her convenience to wait till I'm through here."

"And the 1241 in two shades of shetland—"

"Yes. Of course. Add fifty dollars."

The woman nodded, excused herself again, and departed.

McNair glanced at his wrist watch, shot a sharp one at young Frost, and looked at Wolfe. "You can still have ten minutes."

Wolfe shook his head. "I won't need them. You're nervous, Mr. McNair. You're upset."

"What? You won't need them?"

"No. You probably lead too active a life, running around getting women dressed." Wolfe shuddered. "Horrible. I would like to ask you two questions. First, regarding the death of Molly Lauck, have you anything to add to what you have told Mr. Cramer and Mr. Frost? I know pretty well what that is. Anything new?"

"No." McNair was frowning. He picked up his handkerchief and wiped his forehead. "No. Nothing whatever."

"Very well. Then it would be futile to take up more of your time. The other question: may I be shown a room where some of your employees may be sent to me for conversation? I shall make it as brief as possible. Particularly Miss Helen Frost, Miss Thelma Mitchell, and Mrs. Lamont. I don't suppose Mr. Perren Gebert happens to be here?"

McNair snapped, "Gebert? Why the devil should he be?"

"I don't know." Wolfe lifted his shoulders half an

inch, and dropped them. "I ask. I understand he was here one week ago yesterday, the day Miss Lauck died, when you were having your show. I believe you call it a show?"

"I had a show, yes. Gebert dropped in. Scores of people were here. About talking with the girls and Mrs. Lamont—if you make it short you can do it here. I have to go down to the floor."

"I would prefer something less—more humble. If you please."

"Suit yourself." McNair got up. "Take them to one of the booths, Lew. I'll tell Mrs. Lamont. Do you want her first?"

"I'd like to start with Miss Frost and Miss Mitchell. Together."

"You may be interrupted, if they're needed."

"I shall be patient."

"All right. You tell them, Lew?"

He looked around, grabbed his handkerchief from the desk and stuffed it in his pocket, and bustled out.

Llewellyn Frost, rising, began to protest, "I don't see why you didn't—"

Wolfe stopped him. "Mr. Frost. I endure only to my limit. Obviously, Mr. McNair is sick, but you cannot make that claim to tolerance. Don't forget that you are responsible for this grotesque expedition. Where is this booth?"

"Well, I'm paying for it."

"Not adequately. You couldn't. Come, sir!"

Frost led us out and back down the corridor, and opened the door at the end on the left. He switched on lights, said he would be back soon, and disappeared. I moved my eyes. It was a small paneled room with a table, a smoking stand, full-length mirrors, and three dainty silk chairs. Wolfe stood and looked at the mess, and his lips tightened.

He said, "Revolting. I will not—I will not."

I grinned at him. "I know damn well you won't, and for once I don't blame you. I'll get it."

I went out and strode down the corridor to McNair's office, entered, heaved his chair to my shoulder, and proceeded back to the booth with it. Frost and the two goddesses were going in as I got there. Frost went for another chair, and I planked my prize down behind the table and observed to Wolfe, "If you get so you like it we'll take it home with us." Frost returned with his contribution, and I told him, "Go and get three bottles of cold light beer and a glass and an opener. We've got to keep him alive."

He lifted his brows at me. "You're crazy."

I murmured, "Was I crazy when I suggested that letter from the orchid guys? Get the beer."

He went. I negotiated myself into a chair with the blonde pippin on one side and the sylph on the other. Wolfe was sniffing the air. He suddenly demanded:

"Are all of these booths perfumed like this?"

"Yes, they are." The blonde smiled at him. "It's not us."

"No. It was here before you came in. Pfui. And you girls work here. They call you models?"

"That's what they call us. I'm Thelma Mitchell." The blonde waved an expert graceful hand. "This is Helen Frost."

Wolfe nodded, and turned to the sylph. "Why do you work here, Miss Frost? You don't have to. Do you?"

Helen Frost put level eyes on him, with a little crease in her brow between them. She said quietly, "My cousin told us you wished to ask us about—about Molly Lauck."

"Indeed." Wolfe leaned back, warily, to see if the

chair would take it. There was no creak, and he settled. "Understand this, Miss Frost: I am a detective. Therefore, while I may be accused of incompetence or stupidity, I may not be charged with impertinence. However nonsensical or irrelevant my questions may seem to you, they may be filled with the deepest significance and the most sinister implications. That is the tradition of my profession. As a matter of fact, I was merely making an effort to get acquainted with you."

Her eyes stayed level. "I am doing this as a favor to my cousin Lew. He didn't ask me to get acquainted." She swallowed. "He asked me to answer questions about last Monday."

Wolfe leaned forward and snapped, "Only as a favor to your cousin? Wasn't Molly Lauck your friend? Wasn't she murdered? You aren't interested in helping with that?"

It didn't jolt her much. She swallowed again, but stayed steady. "Interested—yes. Of course. But I've told the police—I don't see what Lew—I don't see why you—" She stopped herself and jerked her head up and demanded, "Haven't I said I'll answer your questions? It's awful—it's an awful thing—"

"So it is." Wolfe turned abruptly to the blonde. "Miss Mitchell. I understand that at twenty minutes past four last Monday afternoon, a week ago yesterday, you and Miss Frost took the elevator together, downstairs, and got out at this floor. Right?"

She nodded.

"And there was no one up here; that is, you saw no one. You walked down the corridor to the fifth door on the left, across the corridor from Mr. McNair's office, and entered that room, which is an apartment used as a rest room for the four models who work here. Molly Lauck was in there. Right?"

She nodded again. Wolfe said, "Tell me what happened."

The blonde took a breath. "Well, we started to talk about the show and the customers and so on. Nothing special. We did that about three minutes, and then suddenly Molly said she forgot, and she reached under a coat and pulled out a box—"

"Permit me. What were Miss Lauck's words?"

"She just said she forgot, she had some loot—"

"No. Please. What did she say? Her exact words."

The blonde stared at him. "Well, if I can. She said, let's see: 'Oh, I forgot, girls, I've got some loot. Swiped it as clean as a whistle.' While she was saying that she was pulling the box from under the coat—"

"Where was the coat?"

"It was her coat, lying on the table."

"Where were you?"

"Me? I was right there, standing there. She was sitting on the table."

"Where was Miss Frost?"

"She was—she was across by the mirror, fixing her hair. Weren't you, Helen?"

The sylph merely nodded. Wolfe said:

"And then? Exactly. Exact words."

"Well, she handed me the box and I took it and opened it, and I said—"

"Had it been opened before?"

"I don't know. It didn't have any wrapping or ribbon or anything on it. I opened it and I said, 'Gee, it's two pounds and never been touched. Where'd you get it, Molly?' She said, 'I told you, I swiped it. Is it any good?' She asked Helen to have some—"

"Her words."

Miss Mitchell frowned. "I don't know. Just 'Have some, Helen,' or 'Join the party, Helen'—something like that. Anyway, Helen didn't take any—"

"What did she say?"

"I don't know. What did you say, Helen?"

Miss Frost spoke without swallowing. "I don't remember. I just had had cocktails, and I didn't want any."

The blonde nodded. "Something like that. Then Molly took a piece and I took a piece—"

"Please." Wolfe wiggled a finger at her. "You were holding the box?"

"Yes. Molly had handed it to me."

"Miss Frost didn't have it in her hands at all?"

"No, I told you, she said she didn't want any. She didn't even look at it."

"And you and Miss Lauck each took a piece—"

"Yes. I took candied pineapple. It was a mixture; chocolates, bonbons, nuts, candied fruits, everything. I ate it. Molly put her piece in her mouth, all of it, and after she bit into it she said—she said it was strong—"

"Words, please."

"Well, she said, let's see: 'My God, it's 200 proof, but not so bad, I can take it.' She made a face, but she chewed it and swallowed it. Then . . . well . . . you wouldn't believe how quick it was—"

"I'll try to. Tell me."

"Not more than half a minute, I'm sure it wasn't. I took another piece and was eating it, and Molly was looking into the box, saying something about taking the taste out of her mouth—"

She stopped because the door popped open. Llewellyn Frost appeared, carrying a paper bag. I got up and took it from him, and extracted from it the opener and glass and bottles and arranged them in front of Wolfe. Wolfe picked up the opener and felt of a bottle.

"Umph. Schreirer's. It's too cold."

I sat down again. "It'll make a bead. Try it." He poured. Helen Frost was saying to her cousin:

"So that's what you went for. Your detective wants to know exactly what I said, my exact words, and he asks Thelma if I handled the box of candy . . ."

Frost patted her on the shoulder. "Now, Helen. Take it easy. He knows what he's doing . . ."

One bottle was empty, and the glass. Frost sat down. Wolfe wiped his lips.

"You were saying, Miss Mitchell, Miss Lauck spoke of taking the taste out of her mouth."

The blonde nodded. "Yes. And then—well—all of a sudden she straightened up and made a noise. She didn't scream, it was just a noise, a horrible noise. She got off the table and then leaned back against it and her face was all twisted . . . it was . . . twisted. She looked at me with her eyes staring, and her mouth went open and shut but she couldn't say anything, and suddenly she shook all over and grabbed for me and got hold of my hair . . . and . . . and . . ."

"Yes, Miss Mitchell."

The blonde gulped. "Well, when she went down she took me with her because she had hold of my hair. Then of course I was scared. I jerked away. Later, when the doctor . . . when people came, she had a bunch of my hair gripped in her fingers."

Wolfe eyed her. "You have good nerves, Miss Mitchell."

"I'm not a softy. I had a good cry after I got home that night, I cried it out. But I didn't cry then. Helen stood against the wall and trembled and stared and couldn't move, she'll tell you that herself. I ran to the

elevator and yelled for help, and then I ran back and
put the lid on the box of candy and held onto it until
Mr. McNair came and then I gave it to him. Molly was
dead. I could see that. She was crumpled up. She fell
down dead." She gulped again. "Maybe you could tell
me. The doctor said it was some kind of acid, and it
said in the paper potassium cyanide."

Lew Frost put in, "Hydrocyanic. The police say—
it's the same thing. I told you that. Didn't I?"

Wolfe wiggled a finger at him. "Please, Mr. Frost.
It is I who am to earn the fee, you to pay it. —Then
Miss Mitchell, you felt no discomfort from your two
pieces, and Miss Lauck ate only one."

"That's all." The blonde shivered. "It's terrible, to
think there's something that can kill you that quick.
She couldn't even speak. You could see it go right
through her, when she shook all over. I held onto the
box, but I got rid of it as soon as I saw Mr. McNair."

"Then, I understand, you ran away."

She nodded. "I ran to the washroom." She made a
face. "I had to throw up. I had eaten two pieces."

"Indeed. Most efficient." Wolfe had opened another
bottle, and was pouring. "To go back a little. You had
not seen that box of candy before Miss Lauck took it
from under the coat?"

"No. I hadn't."

"What do you suppose she meant when she said she
had swiped it?"

"Why—she meant—she saw it somewhere and
took it."

Wolfe turned. "Miss Frost. What do you suppose
Miss Lauck meant by that?"

"I suppose she meant what she said, that she
swiped it. Stole it."

"Was that customary with her? Was she a thief?"

"Of course not. She only took a box of candy. She did it for a joke, I suppose. She liked to play jokes—to do things like that."

"Had you seen the box before she produced it in that room?"

"No."

Wolfe emptied his glass in five gulps, which was par, and wiped his lips. His half-shut eyes were on the blonde. "I believe you went to lunch that day with Miss Lauck. Tell us about that."

"Well—Molly and I went together about one o'clock. We were hungry because we had been working hard— the show had been going on since eleven o'clock—but we only went to the drug store around the corner because we had to be back in twenty minutes to give Helen and the extras a chance. The show was supposed to be from eleven to two, but we knew they'd keep dropping in. We ate sandwiches and custard and came straight back."

"Did you see Miss Lauck swipe the box of candy at the drug store?"

"Of course I didn't. She wouldn't do that."

"Did you get it at the drug store yourself and bring it back with you?"

Miss Mitchell stared at him. She said, disgusted, "For the Lord's sake. No."

"You're sure Miss Lauck didn't get it somewhere while out for lunch?"

"Of course I'm sure. I was right with her."

"And she didn't go out again during the afternoon?"

"No. We were working together until half past three, when there was a let-up and she left to go upstairs, and a little later Helen and I came up and found her here. There in the restroom."

"And she ate a piece of candy and died, and you ate

two and didn't." Wolfe sighed. "There is of course the possibility that she had brought the box with her when she came to work that morning."

The blonde shook her head. "I've thought of that. We've all talked about it. She didn't have any package. Anyway, where could it have been all morning? It wasn't in the restroom, and there wasn't anyplace else . . ."

Wolfe nodded. "That's the devil of it. It's recorded history. You aren't really telling me your fresh and direct memory of what happened last Monday, you're merely repeating the talk it has been resolved into.— I beg you, no offense, you can't help it. I should have been here last Monday afternoon—or rather, I shouldn't have been here at all. I shouldn't be here now." He glared at Llewellyn Frost, then remembered the beer, filled his glass, and drank.

He looked from one girl to the other. "You know, of course, what the problem is. Last Monday there were more than a hundred people here, mostly women but a few men, for that show. It was a cold March day and they all wore coats. Who brought that box of candy? The police have questioned everyone connected with this establishment. They have found no one who ever saw the box or will admit to any knowledge of it. No one who saw Miss Lauck with it or has any idea where she got it. An impossible situation!"

He wiggled a finger at Frost. "I told you, sir, this case is not within my province. I can use a dart or a rapier, but I cannot set traps throughout the territory of the metropolitan district. Who brought the poison here? Whom was it intended for? God knows, but I am not prepared to make a call on Him, no matter how many orchid-growers are coerced into signing idiotic letters. I doubt if it is worthwhile for me to try even for the second half of your fee, since your cousin— your ortho-cousin—refuses to become acquainted with me. As for the first half, the solution of Miss Lauck's death, I could undertake that only through interviews with all of the persons who were in this place last Monday; and I doubt if you could persuade even the innocent ones to call at my office."

Lew Frost muttered, "It's your job. You took it. If you're not up to it—"

"Nonsense. Does a bridge engineer dig ditches?" Wolfe opened the third bottle. "I believe I have not thanked you for this beer. I do thank you. I assure you, sir, this problem is well within my abilities in so far as it is possible to apply them. In so far—for instance, take Miss Mitchell here. Is she telling the truth? Did she murder Molly Lauck? Let us find out." He turned and got sharp. "Miss Mitchell. Do you eat much candy?"

She said, "You're being smart."

"I'm begging your indulgence. It won't hurt you, with nerves like yours. Do you eat much candy?"

She drew her shoulders together, and released them. "Once in a while. I have to be careful. I'm a model, and I watch myself."

"What is your favorite kind?"

"Candied fruits. I like nuts too."

"You removed the lid from that box last Monday. What color was it?"

"Brown. A kind of gold-brown."

"What kind was it? What did it say on the lid?"

"It said . . . it said *Medley*. Some kind of a medley."

Wolfe snapped, "'Some kind?' Do you mean to say you don't remember what name was on the lid?"

She frowned at him. "No . . . I don't. That's funny. I would have thought—"

"So would I. You looked at it and took the lid off, and later replaced the lid and held onto the box, knowing there was deadly poison in it, and you weren't even curious enough—"

"Now wait a minute. You're not so smart. Molly was dead on the floor, and everybody was crowding into the room, and I was looking for Mr. McNair to give him the box, I didn't want the damn thing, and certainly I wasn't trying to think of things to be curious about." She frowned again. "At that, it *is* funny I didn't really see the name."

Wolfe nodded. He turned abruptly to Lew Frost. "You see, sir, how it is done. What is to be deduced from Miss Mitchell's performance? Is she cleverly pretending that she does not know what was on that lid, or is it credible that she really failed to notice it? I am merely demonstrating. For another example, take your cousin." He switched his eyes and shot at her, "You, Miss Frost. Do you eat candy?"

She looked at her cousin. "Is this necessary, Lew?"

Frost flushed. He opened his mouth, but Wolfe was in ahead:

"Miss Mitchell didn't beg off. Of course, she has good nerves."

The sylph leveled her eyes at him. "There's nothing wrong with my nerves. But this cheap—oh, well. I eat candy. I much prefer caramels, and since I work as a model and have to be careful too, I confine myself to them."

"Chocolate caramels? Nut caramels?"

"Any kind. Caramels. I like to chew them."

"How often do you eat them?"

"Maybe once a week."

"Do you buy them yourself?"

"No. I don't get a chance to. My cousin knows my preference, and he sends me boxes of Carlatti's. Too often. I have to give most of them away."

"You are very fond of them?"

She nodded. "Very."

"You find it hard to resist them when offered?"

"Sometimes, yes."

"Monday afternoon you had been working hard? You were tired? You had had a short and unsatisfactory lunch?"

She was tolerating it. "Yes."

"Then, when Miss Lauck offered you caramels, why didn't you take one?"

"She didn't offer me caramels. There weren't any in that—" She stopped. She glanced aside, at her cousin, and then put her eyes at Wolfe again. "That is, I didn't suppose—"

"Suppose?" Wolfe's voice suddenly softened. "Miss Mitchell couldn't remember what was on the lid of that box. Can you, Miss Frost?"

"No. I don't know."

"Miss Mitchell has said that you didn't handle the box. You were at the mirror, fixing your hair; you didn't even look at it. Is that correct?"

She was staring at him. "Yes."

"Miss Mitchell has also said that she replaced the lid on the box and kept it under her arm until she handed it to Mr. McNair. Is that correct?"

"I don't know. I . . . I didn't notice."

"No. Naturally, under the circumstances. But after the box was given to Mr. McNair, from that time until he turned it over to the police, did you see it at all? Did you have an opportunity to inspect it?"

"I didn't see it. No."

"Just one more, Miss Frost—this finishes the demonstration: you are sure you don't know what was on that lid? It was not a brand you were familiar with?"

She shook her head. "I have no idea."

Wolfe leaned back and sighed. He picked up the third bottle and filled his glass and watched the foam work. No one spoke; we just looked at him, while he drank. He put the glass down and wiped his lips, and opened his eyes on his client.

"There you are, Mr. Frost," he said quietly. "Even in a brief demonstration, where no results were expected, something is upturned. By her own testimony, your cousin never saw the contents of that box after Miss Lauck swiped it. She doesn't know what brand it was, so she could not have been familiar with its contents. And yet, she knew, quite positively, that there were no caramels in it. Therefore: she saw the contents of the box, somewhere, sometime, *before* Miss Lauck swiped it. That, sir, is deduction. That is what I meant when I spoke of interviews with all of the persons who were at this place last Monday."

Lew Frost, glaring at him, blurted, "You call this—what the hell do you call this? My cousin—"

"I told you, deduction."

The sylph sat, pale, and stared at him. She opened her mouth a couple of times, but closed it without speaking. Thelma Mitchell horned in:

"She didn't say she knew positively there were no caramels in it. She only said—"

Wolfe put up a palm at her. "You being loyal, Miss Mitchell? For shame. The first loyalty here is to the dead. Mr. Frost dragged me here because Molly Lauck died. He hired me to find out how and why. —Well, sir? Didn't you?"

Frost sputtered, "I didn't hire you to play damn

fool tricks with a couple of nervous girls. You damn fat imbecile—listen! I already know more about this business than you'd ever find out in a hundred years! If you think I'm paying you—now what? Where you going? What's the game now? You get back in that chair I say—"

Wolfe had arisen, without haste, and moved around the table, going sideways past Thelma Mitchell's feet, and Frost had jumped up and started the motions of a stiff arm at him.

I got upright and stepped across. "Don't shove, mister." I would just as soon have plugged him, but he would have had to drop on a lady. "Subside, please. Come on, back up."

He gave me a bad eye, but let that do. Wolfe had sidled by, towards the door, and at that moment there was a knock on it and it opened, and the handsome woman in the black dress with white buttons appeared. She moved in.

"Excuse me, please." She glanced around, composed, and settled on me. "Can you spare Miss Frost? She is needed downstairs. And Mr. McNair says you wish to speak with me. I can give you a few minutes now."

I looked at Wolfe. He bowed to the woman, his head moving two inches. "Thank you, Mrs. Lamont. It won't be necessary. We have made excellent progress; more than could reasonably have been expected— Archie. Did you pay for the beer? Give Mr. Frost a dollar. That should cover it."

I took out my wallet and extracted a buck and laid it on the table. A swift glance showed me that Helen Frost looked pale, Thelma Mitchell looked interested, and Llewellyn looked set for murder. Wolfe had left. I did likewise, and joined him outside where he was pushing the button for the elevator.

I said, "That beer couldn't have been more than two bits a throw, seventy-five cents for three."

He nodded. "Put the difference on his bill."

Downstairs we marched through the activity without halting. McNair was over at one side talking with a dark medium-sized woman with a straight back and a proud mouth, and I let my head turn for a second look, surmising it was Helen Frost's mother. A goddess I hadn't seen before was parading in a brown topcoat in front of a horsey jane with a dog, and three or four other people were scattered around. Just before we got to the street door it opened and a man entered, a big broad guy with a scar on his cheek. I knew all about that scar. I tossed him a nod.

"Hi, Purley."

He stopped and stared, not at me, at Wolfe. "In the name of God! Did you shoot him out of a cannon?"

I grinned and went on.

On the way home I made attempts at friendly conversation over my shoulder, but without success. I tried:

"Those models are pretty creatures. Huh?"

No sale. I tried:

"Did you recognize that gentleman we met coming out? Our old friend Purley Stebbins of the Homicide Squad. One of Cramer's hirelings."

No response. I started looking ahead for a good hole.

Chapter 3

The first telephone call from Llewellyn Frost came around half-past one, while Wolfe and I were doing the right thing by some sausage with ten kinds of herbs in it, which he got several times every spring from a Swiss up near Chappaqua who prepared it himself from home-made pigs. Fritz Brenner, the chef and household pride, was instructed to tell Llewellyn that Mr. Wolfe was at table and might not be disturbed. I wanted to go and take it, but Wolfe nailed me down with a finger. The second call came a little after two, while Wolfe was leisurely sipping coffee, and I went to the office for it.

Frost sounded concerned and aggravated. He wanted to know if he could expect to find Wolfe in at two-thirty, and I said yes, he would probably be in forevermore. After we hung up I stayed at my desk and fiddled around with some things, and in a few minutes Wolfe entered, peaceful and benign but ready to resent any attempt at turbulence, as he always was after a proper and unhurried meal.

He sat down at his desk, sighed happily, and looked around at the walls—the bookshelves, maps, Holbeins, more bookshelves, the engraving of Brilliat-

Savarin. After a moment he opened the middle drawer and began taking out beer-bottle caps and piling them on the desk. He remarked:

"A little less tarragon, and add a pinch of chervil. Fritz might try that next time. I must suggest it to him."

"Yeah," I agreed, not wanting to argue about that. He knew damn well I love tarragon. "But if you want to get those caps counted you'd better get a move on. Our client's on his way down here."

"Indeed." He began separating the caps into piles of five. "Confound it, in spite of those three outside bottles, I think I'm already four ahead on the week."

"Well, that's normal." I swirled. "Listen, enlighten me before Frost gets here. What got you started on the Frost girl?"

His shoulders lifted a quarter of an inch and dropped again. "Rage. That was a cornered rat squealing. There I was, cornered in that insufferable scented hole, dragooned into a case where there was nothing to start on. Or rather, too much. Also, I dislike murder by inadvertence. Whoever poisoned that candy is a bungling ass. I merely began squealing." He frowned at the piles of caps. "Twenty-five, thirty, thirty-three. But the result was remarkable. And quite conclusive. It would be sardonic if we should earn the second half of our fee by having Miss Frost removed to prison. Not that I regard that as likely. I trust, Archie, you don't mind my babbling."

"No, it's okay right after a meal. Go right ahead. No jury would ever convict Miss Frost of anything anyhow."

"I suppose not. Why should they? Even a juror must be permitted his tribute to beauty. But if Miss Frost is in for an ordeal, I suspect it will not be that.

Did you notice the large diamond on her finger? And the one set in her vanity case?"

I nodded. "So what? Is she engaged?"

"I couldn't say. I remarked the diamonds because they don't suit her. You have heard me observe that I have a feeling for phenomena. Her personality, her reserve—even allowing for the unusual circumstances—it is not natural for Miss Frost to war diamonds. Then there was Mr. McNair's savage hostility, surely as unnatural as it was disagreeable, however he may hate Mr. Llewellyn Frost—and why does he hate him? More transparent was the reason for Mr. Frost's familiarity with so strange a term as 'ortho-cousin,' strictly a word for an anthropologist, though it leaves room for various speculations. . . . Ortho-cousins are those whose parents are of the same sex—the children of two brothers or of two sisters; whereas cross-cousins are those whose parents are brother and sister. In some tribes cross-cousins may marry, but not ortho-cousins. Obviously Mr. Frost has investigated the question thoroughly. . . . Certainly it is possible that none of these oddities has any relation to the death of Molly Lauck, but they are to be noted, along with many others. I hope I am not boring you, Archie. As you are aware, this is the routine of my genius, though I do not ordinarily vocalize it. I sat in this chair one evening for five hours, thus considering the phenomena of Paul Chapin, his wife, and the members of that incredible League of Atonement. I talk chiefly because if I do not you will begin to rustle papers to annoy me, and I do not feel like being irritated. That sausage—but there's the bell. Our client. Ha! Still our client, though he may not think so."

Footsteps sounded from the hall, and soon again,

returning. The office door opened and Fritz appeared. He announced Mr. Frost, and Wolfe nodded and requested beer. Fritz went.

Llewellyn came bouncing in. He came bouncing, but you could tell by his eyes it was a case of dual personality. Back behind his eyes he was scared stiff. He bounced up to Wolfe's desk and began talking like a man who was already late for nine appointments.

"I could have told you on the phone, Mr. Wolfe, but I like to do business face to face. I like to see a man and let him see me. Especially for a thing like this. I owe you an apology. I flew off the handle and made a damn fool of myself. I want to apologize." He put out a hand. Wolfe looked at it, and then up at his face. He took his hand back, flushed, and went on, "You shouldn't be sore at me, I just flew off the handle. And anyway, you must understand this, I've got to insist on this, that that was nothing up there. Helen—my cousin was just flustered. I've had a talk with her. That didn't mean a thing. But naturally she's all cut up—she already was, anyhow—and we've talked it over, and I agree with her that I've got no right to be butting in up there. Maybe I shouldn't have butted in at all, but I thought—well—it doesn't matter what I thought. So I appreciate what you've done, and it was swell of you to go up there when it was against your rule . . . so we'll just call it a flop and if you'll just tell me how much I owe you . . ."

He stopped, smiling from Wolfe to me and back again like a haberdasher's clerk trying to sell an old number with a big spiff on it.

Wolfe surveyed him. "Sit down, Mr. Frost."

"Well . . . just to write a check . . ." He backed into a chair and got onto his sitter, pulling a check folder from one pocket and a fountain pen from another. "How much?"

"Ten thousand dollars."

He gasped and looked up. "What!"

Wolfe nodded. "Ten thousand. That would be about right for completing your commission; half for solving the murder of Molly Lauck and half for getting your cousin away from that hell-hole."

"But, my dear man, you did neither. You're loony." His eyes narrowed. "Don't think you're going to hold me up. Don't think—"

Wolfe snapped, "Ten thousand dollars. And you will wait here while the check is being certified."

"You're crazy." Frost was sputtering again. "I haven't got ten thousand dollars. My show's going big, but I had a lot of debts and still have. And even if I had it—what's the idea? Blackmail? If you're that kind—"

"Please, Mr. Frost. I beg you. May I speak?"

Llewellyn glared at him.

Wolfe settled back in his chair. "There are three things I like about you, sir, but you have several bad habits. One is your assumption that words are brick-bats to be hurled at people in an effort to stun them. You must learn to stop that. Another is your childish readiness to rush into action without stopping to consider the consequences. Before you definitely hired me to undertake an investigation you should have scrutinized the possibilities. But the point is that you hired me; and let me tell you, you burned all bridges when you goaded me into that mad sortie to Fifty-second Street. That will have to be paid for. You and I are bound by contract; I am bound to pursue a certain inquiry, and you are bound to pay my reasonable and commensurate charge. And when, for personal and peculiar reasons, you grow to dislike the contract, what do you do? You come to my office and try to knock me out of my chair by propelling words like 'blackmail' at me! Pfui! The insolence of a spoiled child!"

He poured beer, and drank. Llewellyn Frost watched him. I, after getting it into my notebook, nodded my head at him in encouraging approval of one of his better efforts.

The client finally spoke. "But look here, Mr. Wolfe. I didn't agree to let you go up there and . . . that is . . . I didn't have any idea you were going . . ." He stopped on that, and gave it up. "I'm not denying the contract. I didn't come here and start throwing brickbats. I just asked, if we call it off now, how much do I owe you?"

"And I told you."

"But I haven't got ten thousand dollars, not this minute. I think I could have it in a week. But even if I did, my God, just for a couple of hours' work—"

"It is not the work." Wolfe wiggled a finger at him. "It is simply that I will not permit my self-conceit to be bruised by the sort of handling you are trying to give it. It is true that I hire out my abilities for money, but I assure you that I am not to be regarded as a mere peddler of gewgaws or tricks. I am an artist or nothing. Would you commission Matisse to do a painting, and, when he had scribbled his first rough sketch, snatch it from him and crumple it up and tell him, 'That's enough, how much do I owe you?' No, you wouldn't do that. You think the comparison is fanciful? I don't. Every artist has his own conceit. I have mine. I know you are young, and your training has left vacant lots in your brain; you don't realize how offensively you have acted."

"For God's sake." The client sat back. "Well." He

looked at me as if I might suggest something, and then back at Wolfe. He spread out his hands, palms up. "All right, you're an artist. You're it. I've told you, I haven't got ten thousand dollars. How about a check dated a week from today?"

Wolfe shook his head. "You could stop payment. I don't trust you; you are incensed; the flame of fear and resentment is burning in you. Besides, you should get more for your money, and I should do more to earn it. The only sensible course—"

The ring of the telephone interrupted him. I swung around to my desk and got it. I acknowledged my identity to a gruff male inquiry, waited a minute, and heard the familiar tones of another male voice. What it said induced a grin.

I turned to Wolfe: "Inspector Cramer says that one of his men saw you up at McNair's place this morning, and nearly died of the shock. So did he when he heard it. He says it would be a pleasure to discuss the case with you a while on the telephone."

"Not for me. I am engaged."

I returned to the wire and had more talk. Cramer was as amiable as a guy stopping you on a lonely hill because he's out of gas. I turned to Wolfe again:

"He'd like to stop in at six o'clock to smoke a cigar. He says, to compare notes. He means S O S."

Wolfe nodded.

I told Cramer sure, come ahead, and rang off.

The client had stood up. He looked back and forth from me to Wolfe, and said with no belligerence at all, "Was that Inspector Cramer? He—he's coming here?"

"Yeah, a little later." I answered because Wolfe had leaned back and closed his eyes. "He often drops around for a friendly chat when he has a case so easy it bores him."

"But he . . . I . . ." Llewellyn was groggy. He straightened up. "Listen, goddam it. I want to use that phone."

"Help yourself. Take my chair."

I vacated and he moved in. He started dialing without having to look up the number. He was jerky about it, but seemed to know what he was doing. I stood and listened.

"Hello, hello! That you, Styce? This is Lew Frost. Is my father still there? Try Mr. McNair's office. Yes, please. . . . Hello, Dad? Lew . . . No. . . . No, wait a minute. Is Aunt Callie still there? Waiting for me? Yeah, I know . . . No, listen, I'm talking from Nero Wolfe's office, 918 West 35th Street. I want you and Aunt Callie to come down here right away. . . . There's no use explaining on the phone, you'll have to come. . . . I can't explain that . . . Well, bring her anyway. . . . Now, Dad, I'm doing the best I can. . . . Right. You can make it in ten minutes. . . . No, it's a private house. . . ."

Wolfe's eyes were closed.

Chapter 4

That conference was a lulu. On several occasions I have run through pages of my notebook where I took it down, just for the entertainment. Dudley Frost was one of the very few people who have sat in that office and talked Nero Wolfe to a frazzle. Of course, he did it more by volume than by vigor, but he did it.

It was after three when they got there. Fritz ushered them in. Calida Frost, Helen's mother, Lew's Aunt Callie—though I suppose it would be more genteel to introduce her as Mrs. Edwin Frost, since I never got to be cronies with her—she came first, and sure enough, she was the medium-sized woman with the straight back and proud mouth. She was good-looking and well made, with deep but direct eyes of an off color, something like the reddish brown of dark beer, and you wouldn't have thought she was old enough to be the mother of a grownup goddess. Dudley Frost, Lew's father, weighed two hundred pounds, from size rather than fat. He had gray hair and a trimmed gray moustache. Some rude collision had pushed his nose slightly off center, but only a close observer like me would have noticed it. He had on a beautiful gray pin-stripe suit and sported a red flower in his lapel.

Llewelyn went to the office door and brought them across and introduced them. Dudley Frost rumbled at Wolfe, "How do you do." He gave me one too. "How do you do." I was getting chairs under them. He turned to our client: "What's all this, now? What's the trouble, son? Look out, Calida, your bag's going to fall. What's up here, Mr. Wolfe? I was hoping to get in some bridge this afternoon. What's the difficulty? My son has explained to me—and to Mrs. Frost—my sister-in-law—we thought it best for him to come straight down here—"

Llewellyn blurted at him, "Mr. Wolfe wants ten thousand dollars."

He cackled. "God bless me, so do I. Though I've seen the time—but that's past." He gazed at Wolfe and in a change of pace ran all his words together: "What do you want ten thousand dollars for, Mr. Wolfe?"

Wolfe looked grim, seeing already that he was up against it. He said in one of his deeper tones, "To deposit in my bank account."

"Ha! Good. Damn good and I asked for it. Strictly speaking, that was the only proper reply to my question. I should have said, let me see, for what reason do you expect to get ten thousand dollars from anyone, and from whom do you expect it? I hope not from me, for I haven't got it. My son has explained to us that he engaged you tenta—tentatively for a certain kind of job in a fit of foolishness. My son is a donkey, but surely you don't expect him to give you ten thousand dollars merely because he's a donkey? I hope not, for he hasn't got it either. Nor has my sister-in-law—have you, Calida? What do you think,

Calida? Shall I go on with this? Do you think I'm getting anywhere?"

Mrs. Edwin Frost was looking at Wolfe, and didn't bother to turn to her brother-in-law. She said in a low pleasant tone, "I think the most important thing is to explain to Mr. Wolfe that he jumped to a wrong conclusion about what Helen said." She smiled at Wolfe. "My daughter Helen. But first, since Lew thought it necessary for us to come down here, perhaps we should hear what Mr. Wolfe has to say."

Wolfe aimed his half-shut eyes at her. "Very little, madam. Your nephew commissioned me to perform an inquiry, and persuaded me to take an unprecedented step which was highly distasteful to me. I no sooner began it than he informed me it was a flop and asked me how much he owed me. I told him, and on account of the unusual circumstances demanded immediate cash payment. In a panic, he telephone his father."

Her brow was wrinkled. "You asked for ten thousand dollars?"

Wolfe inclined his head, and raised it.

"But, Mr. Wolfe." She hesitated. "Of course I am not familiar with your business"—she smiled at him—"or is it a profession? But surely that is a remarkable sum. Is that your usual rate?"

"Now see here." Dudley Frost had been squirming in his chair. "After all, this thing is simple. There are just certain points. In the first place, the thing was purely tentative. It must have been tentative, because how could Mr. Wolfe tell what he might or might not be able to find out until he had gone up there and looked things over? In the second place, figure Mr. Wolfe's time at twenty dollars an hour, and Lew owes him forty dollars. I've paid good lawyers less than that. In the third place, there's no sense in talking

about ten thousand dollars, because we haven't got it."
He leaned forward and put a paw on the desk. "That's
being frank with you, Mr. Wolfe. My sister-in-law
hasn't got a cent, no one knows that better than I do.
Her daughter—my niece—has got all that's left of my
father's fortune. We're a pauper family, except for
Helen. My son here seems to think he has got something started, but he has thought that before. I doubt
if you could collect, but of course the only way to settle
that is a lawsuit. Then it would drag along, and
eventually you'd compromise on it—"

Our client had called at him several times—
"Dad! . . . Dad!" in an effort to stop him, but with no
success. Now Llewellyn reached across and gripped
his father's knee. "Listen to me a minute, will you? If
you'd give me a chance—Mr. Wolfe isn't letting it drag
along! Inspector Cramer is coming here at six o'clock
to compare notes with him. About this."

"Well? You don't need to crush my leg to a pulp.
Who the deuce is Inspector Cramer?"

"You know very well who he is. Head of the
Homicide Bureau."

"Oh, that chap. How do you know he's coming
here? Who said he was?"

"He telephoned. Just before I phoned you. That's
why I asked you and Aunt Callie to come down here."

I saw the glint in Dudley Frost's eye, as swift as it
was, and wondered if Wolfe caught it too. It disappeared as fast as it came. He asked his son, "Who
talked to Inspector Cramer? You?"

I put in, brusque, "No. Me."

"Ah." Dudley Frost smiled at me broadly, with
understanding; he transferred it to Wolfe, and then
back to me again. "You seem to have gone to a good
deal of trouble around here. Of course I can see that

that was the best way to get your threat in, to arrange for a call with my son in your office. But the point is—"

Wolfe snapped, "Put him out, Archie."

I laid the pencil and notebook on the desk and got up. Llewellyn arose and stood like a pigeon. I noticed that all his aunt did was lift one brow a little.

Dudley Frost laughed. "Now, Mr. Wolfe. Sit down boys." He goggled at Wolfe. "God bless me, I don't blame you for trying to make an impression. Quite a natural—"

"Mr. Frost." Wolfe wiggled a finger. "Your suggestion that I need to fake a phone call to impress your son is highly offensive. Retract it, or go."

Frost laughed again. "Well, let's say you did it to impress me."

"That, sir, is worse."

"Then my sister-in-law. Are you impressed, Calida? I must admit I am. This is what it looks like. Mr. Wolfe wants ten thousand dollars. If he doesn't get it he intends to see Inspector Cramer—where and when doesn't matter—and tell him that Helen has said she saw that box of candy before Molly Lauck did. Of course Helen didn't tell him that, but that won't keep the police from tormenting her, and possibly the rest of us, and it might even get into the papers. In my position as the trustee of Helen's property, my responsibility is as great as yours, Calida, though she is your daughter." He turned to goggle at his son. "It's your fault, Lew. Absolutely. You offered this man Wolfe his opportunity. Haven't you time and time again—"

Wolfe leaned far forward in his chair and reached until the tip of his finger hovered delicately within an inch of the brown tweed of Mrs. Frost's coat. He appealed to her: "Please. Stop him."

She shrugged her shoulders. Her brother-in-law

was going right on. Then abruptly she rose from her chair, stepped around behind the others, and approached me. She came close enough to ask quietly, "Have you any good Irish whiskey?"

"Sure," I said. "Is that it?"

She nodded. "Straight. Double. With plain water."

I went to the cabinet and found the bottle of Old Corcoran. I made it plenty double, got a glass of water, put them on a tray stand, and took it over and deposited it beside the orator's chair. He looked at it and then at me.

"What the deuce is it? What? Where's the bottle?" He lifted it to his off-center nose and sniffed. "Oh! Well." His eyes circled the group. "Won't anyone join me? Calida? Lew?" He sniffed the Irish again. "No? To the Frosts, dead and alive, God bless 'em!" He neither sipped it nor tossed it off, but drank it like milk. He lifted the glass of water and took a dainty sip, about half a teaspoonful, put it down again, leaned back in his chair and thoughtfully caressed his moustache with the tip of his finger. Wolfe was watching him like a hawk.

Mrs. Frost asked quietly, "What is that about Inspector Cramer?"

Wolfe shifted to her. "Nothing, madam, beyond what your nephew has told you."

"He is coming here to consult with you?"

"So he said."

"Regarding the . . . the death of Miss Lauck?"

"So he said."

"Isn't that . . ." She hesitated. "Is it usual for you to confer with the police about the affairs of your clients?"

"It is usual for me to confer with anyone who might have useful information." Wolfe glanced at the clock.

"Let's see if we can't cut across, Mrs. Frost. It is ten minutes to four. I permit nothing to interfere with my custom of spending the hours from four to six with my plants upstairs." As your brother-in-law said with amazing coherence, this thing is simple. I do not deliver an ultimatum to Mr. Llewellyn Frost, I merely offer him an alternative. Either he can pay me at once the amount I would have charged him for completing his commission—he knew before he came here that I ask high fees for my services—and dismiss me, or he can expect me to pursue the investigation to a conclusion and send him a bill. Of course it will be much more difficult for me if his own family tries to obstruct—"

Mrs. Frost shook her head. "We have no wish to obstruct," she said gently. "But it is apparent that you have misconstrued a remark my daughter Helen made while you were questioning her, and we . . . naturally, we are concerned about that. And then . . . if you are about to confer with the police, surely it would be desirable for you to understand."

"I understand, Mrs. Frost." Wolfe glanced at the clock. "You would like to be assured that I shall not inform Inspector Cramer of my misconstruction of your daughter's remark. I'm sorry, I can't commit myself on that, unless I am either dismissed from the case now with payment in full, or am assured by Mr. Llewellyn Frost—and, under the circumstances, by you and your brother-in-law also—that I am to continue the investigation for which I was engaged. I may add, you people are quite unreasonably alarmed, which is to be expected with persons of your station in society. It is highly unlikely that your daughter has any guilty connection with the murder of Miss Lauck; and if by chance she possesses an important bit of information which discretion has caused her to conceal, the sooner she discloses it the better, before the police do somehow get wind of it."

Mrs. Frost was frowning. "My daughter has no information whatever."

"Without offense—I would need to ask her about that myself."

"And you . . . wish to be permitted to continue. If you are not, you intend to tell Inspector Cramer—"

"I have not said what I intend."

"But you wish to continue."

Wolfe nodded. "Either that, or my fee now."

"Listen, Calida. I've been sitting here thinking." It was Dudley Frost. He sat up straight. I saw Wolfe get his hands on the arms of his chair. Frost was going on: "Why don't we get Helen down here? This man Wolfe is throwing a bluff. If we're not careful we'll find ourselves coughing up ten thousand dollars of Helen's money, and since I'm responsible for it, it's up to me to prevent it. Lew says he'll have it next week, but I've heard that before. A trustee is under the most sacred obligation to preserve the property under his care, and it couldn't be paid out of surplus income because you don't have any surplus. The only way is to call this fellow's bluff—"

I was about ready to go to the cabinet for some more Irish, since apparently the previous serving had all been assimilated, when I saw it wouldn't be necessary. Wolfe shoved back his chair and got up, moved around and stopped in front of Llewellyn, and spoke loud enough to penetrate the Dudley Frost noise:

"I must go. Thank God. You can tell Mr. Goodwin your decision." He started his progress to the door, and didn't halt when Dudley Frost called at him:

"Now here! You can't run away like that! All right, all right, sir! All right!" His target gone, he turned to his sister-in-law: "Didn't I say, Calida, we'd call his bluff? See that? All it needs in a case like this—"

Mrs. Frost hadn't bothered to turn in her chair to witness Wolfe's departure. Llewellyn had reached across for another grip on his father's knee and was expostulating: "Now, Dad, cut it out—now listen a minute—"

I stood up and said, "If you folks want to talk this over, I'll leave you alone a while."

Mrs. Frost shook her head. "Thank you, I don't believe it will be necessary." She turned to her nephew and sounded crisp: "Lew, you started this. It looks as if you'll have to continue it."

Llewellyn answered her, and his father joined in, but I paid no attention as I got at my desk and stuck a sheet of paper in the typewriter. I dated it at the top and tapped it off.

To NERO WOLFE:
    Please continue until further notice the in-
    vestigation into the murder of Molly Lauck
    for which I engaged you yesterday, Monday,
    March 30, 1936.

I whirled it out of the machine, laid it on a corner of Wolfe's desk, and handed Llewellyn my pen. He bent over the paper to read it. His father jumped up and pulled at him.

"Don't sign that! What is it? Let me see it! Don't sign anything at all—"

Llewellyn surrendered it to him, and he read it through twice, with a frown. Mrs. Frost stretched out a hand for it, and ran over it at a glance. She looked at me.

48 **Rex Stout**

"I don't believe my nephew will have to sign anything . . ."

"I believe he will." I was about as fed up as Wolfe had been. "One thing you people don't seem to realize, if Mr. Wolfe should feel himself relieved of his obligation to his client and tells Inspector Cramer his angle on that break of Miss Frost's, there won't be any argument about it. When Cramer has been working on a popular murder case for a week without getting anywhere, he gets so tough he swallows cigars whole. Of course he won't use a piece of hose on Miss Frost, but he'll have her brought to headquarters and snarl at her all night. You wouldn't want—"

"All right." Dudley Frost had his frown on me. "My son is willing for Wolfe to continue. I've thought all along that's the best way to handle it. But he won't sign this. He won't sign anything—"

"Yes, he will." I took the paper from Calida Frost and put it on the desk again. "What do you think?" I threw up my hands. "Holy heaven! You're three and I'm one. That's no good in case of bad memories. What is there to it, anyhow? It says 'until further notice.' Mr. Wolfe said you could tell me your decision. Well, I've got to have a record of it or so help me, I'll have a talk with Inspector Cramer myself."

Lew Frost looked at his aunt and his father, and then at me. "It certainly is one sweet mess." He grimaced in disgust. "If I had ten thousand dollars this minute, I swear to God . . ."

I said, "Look out, that pen drips sometimes. Go ahead and sign it."

While the other two frowned at him, he bent over the paper and scrawled his name.

Chapter 5

"**I** had a notion to call in a notary and make Stebbins swear to an affidavit." Inspector Cramer chewed on his cigar some more. "Nero Wolfe a mile away from home in broad daylight and in his right mind? Then it must be a raid on the United States Treasury and we'll have to call out the army and declare martial law."

It was a quarter past six. Wolfe was back in the office again, fairly placid after two hours with Horstmann among the plants, and was on his second bottle of beer. I was comfortable, with my feet up on the edge of the bottom drawer pulled out, and my notebook on my knees.

Wolfe, leaning back in his chair with his fingers twined at the peak of his middle, nodded grimly. "I don't wonder, sir. Some day I'll explain it to you. Just now the memory of it is too vivid; I'd rather not discuss it."

"Okay. What I thought, maybe you're not eccentric any more."

"Certainly I'm eccentric. Who isn't?"

"God knows I'm not." Cramer took his cigar from his mouth and looked at it and put it back again. "I'm too damn dumb to be eccentric. Take this Molly Lauck business, for instance. In eight days of intense effort, what do you think I've found out? Ask me." He leaned forward. "I've found out Molly Lauck's dead! No doubt about it! I screwed that out of the Medical Examiner." He leaned back again and made a face of disgust. at both of us. "By God, I'm a whirlwind. Now that I've emptied the bag for you, how about you doing the same for me? Then you'll have your fee, which is what you want, and I'll have an excuse for keeping my job, which is what I need."

Wolfe shook his head. "Nothing, Mr. Cramer. I am not even aware Miss Lauck is dead, except by hearsay. I have not seen the Medical Examiner."

"Oh, come on." Cramer removed his cigar. "Who hired you?"

"Mr. Llewellyn Frost."

"That one, eh?" Cramer grunted. "To keep somebody clear?"

"No. To solve the murder."

"You don't say. How long did it take you?"

Wolfe got himself forward to pour beer, and drank. Cramer was going on: "What got Lew Frost so worked up about it? I don't get it. It wasn't him that the Lauck girl was after, it was that Frenchman, Perren Gebert. Why is Lew Frost so anxious to spend good dough for a hunk of truth and justice?"

"I couldn't say." Wolfe wiped his lips. "As a matter of fact, there is nothing whatever I can tell you. I haven't the faintest notion—"

"You mean to say you went clear to 52nd Street just for the exercise?"

"No. God forbid. But I have no scrap of information, or surmise, for you regarding Miss Lauck's death."

"Well." Cramer rubbed a palm on his knee. "Of course, I know that the fact you've got nothing for me doesn't prove you have nothing for yourself. You going on with it?"

"I am."

"You're not committed to Lew Frost to dig holes for anybody?"

"If I understand you—I think I do—I am not."

Cramer stared at his worn-out cigar for a minute, then reached out and put it in the ashtray and felt in his pocket for a new one. He bit off the end and got the shreds off his tongue, socked his teeth into it again, and lit it. He puffed a thick cloud around him, got a new grip with his teeth, and settled back.

He said, "As conceited as you are, Wolfe, you told me once that I am better equipped to handle nine murder cases out of ten than you are."

"Did I?"

"Yeah. So I've been keeping count, and this Lauck case is the tenth since that rubber band guy, old man Perry. It's your turn again, so I'm glad you're already in it without me having to shove you. I know; you don't like to tell people things, not even Goodwin here. But since you've been up there, you might be willing to admit that you know how it happened. I understand that you've talked with McNair and the two girls who saw her eat it."

Wolfe nodded. "I've heard the obvious details."

"Okay. Obvious is right. I've gone over it ten times with those two. I've had sessions with everybody in the place. I've had twenty men out chasing after everyone who was there at the fashion show that day, and I've seen a couple of dozen of them myself. I've had half the force checking up all over town on sales of two-pound boxes of Bailey's Royal Medley during the past month, and the other half trying to trace purchases of potassium cyanide. I've sent two men out to Darby, Ohio, where Molly Lauck's parents live. I've had shadows on ten or twelve people where it looked like there was a chance of a tie-up."

"You see," Wolfe murmured, "as I said, you are better equipped."

"Go to hell. I use what I've got, and you know damn well I'm a good cop. But after these eight days, I don't even know for sure whether Molly Lauck was killed by poison that was intended for someone else. What if the Frost girl and the Mitchell girl did it together? You couldn't beat it for a set-up, and maybe they're that clever. Knowing Molly Lauck liked to play jokes, maybe they planted it for her to swipe, or maybe they just gave it to her and then told their story. But why? That's another item, I can't find anyone who had any reason at all to want to kill her. It seems she was mellow in the pump about this Perren Gebert and he couldn't see her, but there's no evidence that she was making herself a nuisance to him."

Wolfe murmured, "Mellow where?"

I put in, "Okay, boss. Soft-hearted."

"Gebert was there that day, too." Cramer went on, "but I can't get anywhere with him on that. There hasn't been another single nibble on motive, *if* the stuff was intended for Molly Lauck. In my opinion, it wasn't. It looks like she really did swipe it. And the minute you take that theory, what have you got? You've got the ocean. There were over a hundred people there that day, and it might have been intended for any one of them, and any of them might have brought it. You can see what a swell lay-out that is. We've traced over three hundred sales of two-pound boxes of Bailey's Royal Medley, and among that bunch of humans that was there at the show we've uncovered enough grudges and jealousies and bad blood and biliousness to account for twenty murders. What do we do with it now? We file it."

He stopped and chewed savagely on his cigar. I grinned at him: "Did you come here to inspect our filing system, Inspector? It's a beaut."

He growled at me, "Who asked you anything? I came here because I'm licked. What do you think of that? Did you ever hear me say that before? And no one else." He turned to Wolfe. "When I heard you were up there today, of course I didn't know for who or what, but I thought to myself, now the fur's going to fly. Then I thought I might as well drop in and you might give me a piece as a souvenir. I'll take anything I can get. This is one of those cases that can't cool off, because the damn newspapers keep the heat turned on indefinitely, and I don't mean only the tabloids. Molly Lauck was young and beautiful. Half of the dames that were there at the show that day are in the Social Register. H. R. Cragg was there himself, with his wife, and so on. The two girls that saw her die are also young and beautiful. They won't let it cool off, and every time I go into the Commissioner's office he beats the arm of his chair. You've seen him do that right here in your own office."

Wolfe nodded. "Mr. Hombert is a disagreeable noise. I'm sorry I have nothing for you, Mr. Cramer, I really am."

"Yeah, I am too. But you can do this, anyhow: give me a push. Even if it's in the wrong direction and you know it."

"Well . . . let's see." Wolfe leaned back with his eyes half closed. "You are blocked on motive. You can find none as to Miss Lauck, and too many in other directions. You can't trace the purchase either of the candy or the poison. In fact, you have traced or found nothing whatever, and you are without a starting-point. But you do really have one; have you used it?"

Cramer stared. "Have I used what?"

"The one thing that is indubitably connected with the murder. The box of candy. What have you done about that?"

"I've had it analyzed, of course."

"Tell me about it."

Cramer tapped ashes into the tray. "There's not much to tell. It was a two-pound box that's on sale pretty well all over town, at druggists and branch stores, put up by Bailey of Philadelphia, selling at a dollar sixty. They call it Royal Medley, and there's a mixture in it, fruits, nuts, chocolates, and so on. Before I turned it over to the chemist I got Bailey's factory on the phone and asked if all Royal Medley boxes were uniform. They said yes, they were packed strictly to a list, and they read the list to me. Then for a check I sent out for a couple of boxes of Royal Medley and spread them out and compared them with the list. Okay. By doing the same with the box Molly Lauck ate from, I found that three pieces were gone from it: candied pineapple, a candied plum, and a Jordan almond. That agreed with the Mitchell girl's story."

Wolfe nodded. "Fruits, nuts, chocolates—were there any caramels?"

"Caramels?" Cramer stared at him. "Why caramels?"

"No reason. I used to like them."

Cramer grunted. "Don't try to kid me. Anyhow, there aren't any caramels in a Bailey's Royal Medley. That's too bad, huh?"

"Perhaps. It certainly decreases the interest, for

me. By the way, these details regarding the candy—have they been published? Has anyone been told?"

"No. I'm telling you. I hope you can keep a secret. It's the only one we've got."

"Excellent. And the chemist?"

"Sure, excellent, and what has it got me? The chemist found that there was nothing wrong with any of the candy left in the box, except four Jordan almonds in the top layer. The top layer of a Royal Medley box has five Jordan almonds in it, and Molly Lauck had eaten one. Each of the four had more than six grains of potassium cyanide in it."

"Indeed. Only the almonds were poisoned."

"Yeah, it's easy to see why they were picked. Potassium cyanide smells and tastes like almonds, only more so. The chemist said they would taste strong, but not enough to scare you off if you liked almonds. You know Jordan almonds? They're covered with hard candy of different colors. Holes had been bored in them, or picked in, and filled with the cyanide, and then coated over again so that you'd hardly notice it unless you looked for it." Cramer hunched up his shoulders and dropped them again. "You say the box of candy was a starting-point? Well, I started, and where am I? I'm sitting here in your office telling you I'm licked, with that damn Goodwin pup there grinning at me."

"Don't mind Mr. Goodwin. Archie, don't badger him! But, Mr. Cramer, you didn't start; you merely made the preparations for starting. It may not be too late. If, for instance . . ."

Wolfe, leaning back, closed his eyes, and I saw the almost imperceptible movements of his lips—out and in, a pause, and out and in again. Then again . . .

Cramer looked at me and lifted his brows. I nodded and told him. "Sure, it'll be a miracle, wait and see."

Wolfe muttered, "Shut up, Archie."

Cramer glared at me and I winked at him. Then we just sat. If it had gone on long I would have had to leave the room for a bust, because Cramer was funny. He sat cramped, afraid to make a movement so as not to disturb Wolfe's genius working; he wouldn't even knock the ashes off his cigar. I'll say he was licked. He kept glaring at me to show he was doing something.

Finally Wolfe stirred, opened his eyes, and spoke. "Mr. Cramer. This is just an invitation to luck. Can you meet Mr. Goodwin at nine o'clock tomorrow morning at Mr. McNair's place, and have with you five boxes of that Royal Medley?"

"Sure. Then what?"

"Well . . . try this. Your notebook, Archie?"

I flipped to a fresh page.

Three hours later, after dinner, at ten o'clock that night, I went over to Broadway and hunted up a box of Bailey's Royal Medley, and sat in the office until midnight with my desk covered with pieces of candy, memorizing a code.

Chapter 6

At three minutes to nine the following morning, Wednesday, as I rolled the roadster to a stop on 52nd Street, in a nice open space evidently kept free by special police orders, I was feeling a little sorry for Nero Wolfe. He loved to stage a good scene and get an audience sitting on the edge of their chairs, and here was this one, his own idea, taking place a good mile from his plant rooms and his oversized chair. But, stepping onto the sidewalk in front of Boyden McNair Incorporated, I merely shrugged my shoulders and thought to myself, Well-a-day, you fat son-of-a-gun, you can't be a homebody and see the world too.

I walked across to the entrance, where the uniformed McNair doorman was standing alongside a chunky guy with a round red face and a hat too small for him pushed back on his forehead. As I reached for the door this latter moved to block me.

He put an arm out. "Excuse me, sir. Are you here by request? Your name, please?" He brought into view a piece of paper with a typewritten list on it.

I gazed down my nose at him. "Look here, my man. It was I who made the requests."

He squinted at me. "Yeah? Sure. The inspector says, nothing for you boys here. Beat it."

Naturally I would have been sore anyhow at being taken for a reporter, but what made it worse was that I had taken the trouble to put on my suit of quiet brown with a faint tan stripe, a light tan shirt, a green challis four-in-hand and my dark green soft-brim hat. I said to him:

"You're blind in one eye and can't see out of the other. Did you ever hear that one before? I'm Archie Goodwin of Nero Wolfe's office." I took out a card and stuck it at him.

He looked at it. "Okay. They're expecting you upstairs."

Inside was another dick, standing over by the elevator, and no one else around. This one I knew: Slim Foltz. We exchanged polite greetings, and I got in the elevator and went up.

Cramer had done pretty well. Chairs had been gathered from all over, and about fifty people, mostly women but a few men, were sitting there in the big room up front. There was a lot of buzz and chatter. Four or five dicks, city fellers, were in a group in a corner where the booths began. Across the room Inspector Cramer stood talking to Boyden McNair, and I walked over there.

Cramer nodded. "Just a minute, Goodwin." He went on with McNair, and pretty soon turned to me. "We got a pretty good crowd, huh? Sixty-two promised to come, and there's forty-one here. Not so bad."

"All the employees here?"

"All but the doorman. Do we want him?"

"Yeah, make it unanimous. Which booth?"

"Third on the left. Do you know Captain Dixon? I picked him for it."

"I used to know him." I walked down the corridor, counting three, and opened the door and went in. The room was a little bigger than the one we had used the day before. Sitting behind the table was a little squirt with a bald head and big ears and eyes like an eagle. There were pads of paper and pencils arranged neatly in front of him, and at one side was a stack of five boxes of Bailey's Royal Medley. I told him he was Captain Dixon and I was Archie Goodwin, and it was a nice morning. He looked at me by moving his eyes without disturbing his head, known as conservation of energy, and made a noise something between a hoot-owl and a bullfrog. I left him and went back to the front room.

McNair had gone around back of the crowd and found a chair. Cramer met me and said, "I don't think we'll wait for any more. They're going to get restless as it is."

"Okay, shoot." I went over and propped myself against the wall, facing the audience. They were all ages and sizes and shapes, and were about what you might expect. There are very few women who can afford to pay 300 bucks for a spring suit, and why do they have to be the kind you might as well wrap in an old piece of burlap for all the good it does? Nearly always. Among the exceptions present that morning was Mrs. Edwin Frost, who was sitting with her straight back in the front row, and with her were the two goddesses, one on each side. Llewellyn Frost and his father were directly behind them. I also noted a red-haired woman with creamy skin and eyes like stars, but later, during the test, I learned that her name was Countess von Rantz-Deichen of Prague, so I never tried to follow it up.

Cramer had faced the bunch and was telling them about it:

". . . First I want to thank Mr. McNair for closing his store this morning and permitting it to be used for this purpose. We appreciate his cooperation, and we realize that he is as anxious as we are to get to the bottom of this . . . this sad affair. Next I want to thank all of you for coming. It is a real pleasure and encouragement to know that there are so many good citizens ready to do their share in a . . . a sad affair like this. None of you had to come, of course. You are merely doing your duty—that is, you are helping out when it is needed. I thank you in the name of the Police Commissioner, Mr. Hombert, and the District Attorney, Mr. Skinner."

I wanted to tell him, "Don't stop there, what about the Mayor and the Borough Presidents and the Board of Aldermen and the Department of Plant and Structures . . ."

He was going on: "I hope that none of you will be offended or irritated at the simple experiment we are going to try. It wasn't possible for us to explain it to each of you on the telephone, and I won't make a general explanation now. I suppose some of you will regard it as absurd, and in the case of most of you, and possibly all of you, it will be, but I hope you'll just take it and let it go at that. Then you can tell your friends how dumb the police are, and we'll all be satisfied. But I can assure you we're not doing this just for fun or to try to annoy somebody, but as a serious part of our effort to get to the bottom of this sad affair.

"Now this is all there is to it. I'm going to ask you to go one at a time down that corridor to the third door on the left. I've organized it to take as little time as possible; that's why we asked you to write your name twice, on two different pieces of paper, when you came in. Captain Dixon and Mr. Goodwin will be in that room, and I'll be there with them. We'll ask you a question, and that's all. When you come out you are requested to leave the building, or stay here by the corridor if you want to wait for someone, without speaking to those who have not yet been in the booth. Some of you, those who go in last, will have to be patient. I want to thank you again for your cooperation in this . . . this sad affair."

Cramer took a breath of relief, wheeled, and called out toward the bunch of dicks: "All right, Rowcliff, we might as well start with the front row."

"Mr. Inspector!" Cramer turned again. A woman with a big head and no shoulders had arisen in the middle of the audience and stuck her chin forward. "I want to say, Mr. Inspector, that we are under no compulsion to answer any question you may think fit to ask. I am a member of the Better Citizens' League, and I came here to make sure that—"

Cramer put up a hand at her. "Okay, madam. No compulsion at all—"

"Very well. It should be understood by all that citizenship has its privileges as well as its duties—"

Two or three snickered. Cramer tossed me a glance, and I joined him and followed him down the corridor and into the room. Captain Dixon didn't bother to move even his eyes this time, probably having enough of us already in his line of vision to make a good guess at our identity. Cramer grunted and sat down on one of the silk affairs against the partition.

"Now that we're ready to start," he growled, "I think it's the bunk."

Captain Dixon made a noise something between a

pigeon and a sow with young. I had decided to wear
out the ankles so as to see better. I removed the four
top Royal Medleys from the stack and put them on the
floor under the table, out of sight, and picked up the
other one.

"As arranged?" I asked Cramer. "Am I to say it?"

He nodded. The door opened, and one of the dicks
ushered in a middle-aged woman with a streamlined
hat on the side of her head, and lips and fingernails the
color of the first coat of paint they put on an iron
bridge. She stopped and looked around without much
curiosity. I put out a hand at her.

"The papers, please?"

She handed me the slips of paper, and I gave one to
Captain Dixon and kept the other. "Now, Mrs. Ballin,
please do what I ask, naturally, as you would under
ordinary circumstances, without any hesitation or
nervousness—"

She smiled at me. "I'm not nervous."

• "Good." I took the cover from the box and held it
out to her. "Take a piece of candy."

Her shoulders lifted daintily, and fell. "I very
seldom eat candy."

"We don't want you to eat it. Just take it. Please."

She reached in without looking and snared a chocolate cream and held it up in her fingers and looked at
me. I said, "Okay. Put it back, please. That's all.
Thank you. Good day, Mrs. Ballin."

She glanced around at us, said, "Dear me," in a
tone of mild and friendly astonishment, and went.

I bent to the table and marked an X on a corner of
her paper, and the figure 6 beneath her name. Cramer
growled, "Wolfe said three pieces."

"Yeah. He said to use our judgment too. In my
judgment, if that dame was mixed up in anything,

even Nero Wolfe would never find it out. What did you think of her, Captain?"

Dixon made a noise something between a hartebeest and a three-toed sloth. The door opened and in came a tall slender woman in a tight-fitting long black coat and a silver fox that must have had giantism. She kept her lips tight and gazed at us with deepest concentrated eyes. I took her slips and gave one to Dixon.

"Now, Miss Claymore, please do what I ask, naturally, as you would under ordinary circumstances, without any hesitation or nervousness. Will you?"

She shrank back a little, but nodded. I extended the box.

"Take a piece of candy."

"Oh!" she gasped. She goggled at the candy. "That's the box . . ." She shuddered, backed off, held her clenched fist against her mouth, and let out a fairly good shriek.

I said icily, "Thank *you*. Good day, madam. All right, officer."

The dick touched her arm and turned her for the door. I observed, bending to mark her slip, "That scream was just shop talk. That's Beth Claymore, and she's as phony on the stage as she is off. Did you see her in *The Price of Folly?*"

Cramer said calmly, "It's a goddam joke." Dixon made a noise. The door opened and another woman came in.

We went through with it, and it took nearly two hours. The employees were saved till the last. What with one thing and another, some of the customers took three pieces, some two or one, and a few none at all. When the first box began to show signs of wear I began with a fresh one from the reserve. Dixon made a few more noises, but confined himself mostly to making notations on his slips, and I went ahead with mine.

There were a few ructions, but nothing serious. Helen Frost came in pale and stayed pale, and wasn't having any candy. Thelma Mitchell glared at me and took three pieces of candied fruit, with her teeth clinched on her lower lip. Dudley Frost said it was nonsense and started an argument with Cramer and had to be suggested out by the dick. Llewellyn said nothing and made three different selections. Helen's mother picked out a thin narrow chocolate, a Jordan almond, and a gum drop, and wiped her fingers delicately on her handkerchief after she put them back. One customer that interested me because I had heard a few things about him was a bird in a morning coat with the shoulders padded. He looked about forty but might have been a little older, and had a thin nose, slick hair, and dark eyes that never stopped moving. His slip said Perren Gebert. He hesitated a second about having refreshment, then smiled to show he didn't mind humoring us, and took at random.

The employees came last, and last of all was Boyden McNair himself. After I had finished with him, Inspector Cramer stood up.

"Thank you, Mr. McNair. You've done us a big favor. We'll be out of here now in two minutes, and you can open up."

"Did you . . . get anywhere?" McNair was wiping his face with his handkerchief. "I don't know what all this is going to do to my business. It's terrible." He stuck his hand in his pocket and pulled it out again. "I've got a headache. I'm going to the office and get some aspirin. I ought to go home, or go to a hospital. Did you . . . what kind of a trick was this?"

"This in here?" Cramer got out a cigar. "Oh, this was just psychology. I'll let you know later if we got anything out of it."

"Yes. Now I've got to go out there and see those women . . . well, let me know." He turned and went.

I left with Cramer, and Captain Dixon trailing behind. While we were leaving the establishment, with his men to gather up and straggling customers and the help around, he kept himself calm and dignified, but as soon as we were out on the sidewalk he turned loose on me and let me have it. I was surprised at how bitter he was, and then, as he went on getting warmer, I realized that he was just showing how high an opinion he had of Nero Wolfe. As soon as he gave me a chance I told him:

"Nuts, Inspector. You thought Wolfe was a magician, and just because he told us to do this someone was going to flop on their knees and claw at your pants and pull an I-done-it. Have patience. I'll go home and tell Wolfe about it, and you talk 'em over with Captain Dixon—that is, if he can talk—"

Cramer grunted. "I should have had more sense. If that fat rhinoceros is kidding me, I'll make him eat his license and then he won't have any."

I had climbed in the roadster. "He's not kidding you. Wait and see. Give him a chance." I slipped in the gear and rolled away.

Little did I suspect what was waiting for me at West 35th Street. I got there about half past eleven, thinking that Wolfe would have been down from the plant rooms for half an hour and therefore I would catch him in good humor with his third bottle of beer, which was so much to the good, since I was not exactly the bearer of glad tidings. After parking in front and depositing my hat in the hall, I went to the office, and found to my surprise that it was empty. I sought the bathroom, but it was empty too. I proceeded to the kitchen to inquire of Fritz, and as soon as I crossed the threshold I stopped and my heart sank to my feet and kept on right through the floor.

Wolfe sat at the kitchen table with a pencil in his hand and sheets of paper scattered around. Fritz stood across from him, with the gleam in his eye that I knew only too well. Neither paid any attention to the noise I had made entering. Wolfe was saying:

". . . but we cannot get good peafowl. Archie could try that place on Long Island, but it is probably hopeless. A peafowl's breast flesh will not be sweet and tender and properly developed unless it is well protected from all alarms, especially from the air, to prevent nervousness, and Long Island is full of airplanes. The goose for this evening, with the stuffing as arranged, will be quite satisfactory. The kid will be ideal for tomorrow. We can phone Mr. Salzenback at once to butcher one, and Archie can drive to Garfield for it in the morning. You can proceed with the preliminaries for the sauce. Friday is a problem. If we try the peafowl we shall merely be inviting catastrophe. Squabs will do for tidbits, but the chief difficulty remains. Fritz, I'll tell you. Let us try a new tack entirely. Do you know shish kabab? I have had it in Turkey. Marinate thin slices of tender lamb for several hours in red wine and spices. Here, I'll put it down: thyme, mace, peppercorns, garlic—"

I stood and took it in. It looked hopeless. There was no question but that it was the beginning of a major relapse. He hadn't had one for a long while, and it might last a week or more, and while that spell was on him you might as well try to talk business to a lamp post as to Nero Wolfe. When we were engaged on a case, I never liked to go out and leave him alone with Fritz, for this very reason. If only I had got home an hour earlier! It looked now as if it had gone too far to stop it. And this was one of the times when it seemed easy to guess what had brought it on: he hadn't really expected anything from the mess he had cooked up for Cramer and me, and he was covering up.

I gritted my teeth and walked over to the table. Wolfe went on talking, and Fritz didn't look at me. I said, "What's this, you going to start a restaurant?" No attention. I said, "I've got a report to make. Forty-five people ate candy out of those boxes, and they all died in agony. Cramer is dead. H. R. Cragg is dead. The goddesses are dead. I'm sick."

"Shut up, Archie. Is the car in front? Fritz will need a few things right away."

I knew if the delivery of supplies once started there wouldn't be a chance. I also knew that coaxing wouldn't do it, and bullying wouldn't do it. I was desperate, and I ran over Wolfe's weaknesses in my mind and picked one.

I butted in. "Listen. This cockeyed feast you're headed for, I know I can't stop it. I've tried that before. Okay—"

Wolfe said to Fritz, "But not the pimento. If you can find any of those yellow anguino peppers down on Sullivan Street—"

I didn't dare touch him, but I leaned down close to him. I bawled at him, "And what am I to tell Miss Frost when she comes here at two o'clock? I am empowered to make appointments, am I not? She is a lady, is she not? Of course, if common courtesy is overboard too—"

Wolfe stopped himself, pressed his lips together,

and turned his head. He looked me in the eye. After a moment he asked quietly, "Who? What Miss Frost?"

"Miss Helen Frost. Daughter of Mrs. Edwin Frost, cousin of our client, Mr. Llewellyn Frost, niece of Mr. Dudley Frost. Remember?"

"I don't believe it. This is trickery. Birdlime."

"Sure." I straightened up. "This is close to the limit. Very well. When she comes I'll tell her I exceeded my authority in venturing to make an appointment. —I won't be in for lunch, Fritz." I wheeled and strode out, to the office, and sat down at my desk and pulled the slips of paper from my pocket, wondering if it would work, and trying to decide what I would do if it did. I fooled with the slips pretending to arrange them, not breathing much so I could listen.

It was at least two minutes before I heard anything from the kitchen, and then it was Wolfe sliding back his chair. Next his footsteps approaching. I kept busy with the papers, and so didn't actually see him as he entered the office, crossed to his desk, and got lowered into his seat. I continued with my work.

Finally he said, in the sweet tone that made me want to kick him, "So I am to change all my plans at the whim of a young woman who, to begin with, is a liar. Or at the least, postpone them." He suddenly exploded ferociously, "Mr. Goodwin! Are you conscious?"

I said without looking up, "No."

Silence. After a while I heard him sigh. "All right, Archie." He had controlled himself back to his normal tone. "Tell me about it."

It was up to me. It was the first time I had ever stopped a relapse after it had got as far as the menu stage, but it looked as if it might turn out to be something like curing a headache by chopping off my head. I had to go through with it, and the only way that occurred to me was to take a slender thread that had dangled in front of me up at McNair's that morning, and try to sell it to Wolfe for a steel cable.

"Well," I said, and swiveled. "We went and did it."

"Go on."

He had half-shut eyes on me. I knew he suspected me, and I wouldn't be surprised if he had my number right then. But he wasn't starting back for the kitchen.

"It was pretty close to a washout." I picked up the slips. "Cramer's as sore as a boil on your nose. Of course, he didn't know I was keeping track of the kind of candy they picked; he thought we were just looking for a giveaway in their actions, and naturally that was a flop. A third of them were scared and half of them were nervous and some got mad and a few were just casual. That's all there was to that. According to instructions, I watched their fingers while Cramer and Dixon looked at their faces, and put down symbols for their selections." I flipped the slips. "Seven of them took Jordan almonds. One of them took two."

Wolfe reached out and rang for beer. "And?"

"And so I put it down that way. I'll tell you. I'm not slick enough for that sort of thing. You know it and I know it. Who is? It's a waste of time to say you are, on account of inertia. Nevertheless, I am slicker than glue. Six of those people who took Jordan almonds, on account of their expressions and who they are and the way they did it—I don't think it meant anything. But the seventh one—I don't know. It's true he's going to have a nervous breakdown, he told you that himself. He was taken by surprise at the request to have a piece of candy, just as all the rest were. Cramer handled it right; he had men there to see that no one knew what was going on before they got inside the room. And Mr. Boyden McNair acted funny. When I stuck the box at him and asked him to take a piece he drew back a little, but lots of others did that. Then he pulled himself up and reached and looked in, and his fingers went straight to a Jordan almond and then jerked away, and he took a chocolate. I asked him quick to take another without giving him a chance to get it decided, and this time he touched two other pieces first and then took a Jordan almond, a white one. The third try he went straight to a gum drop and took it."

Fritz had come with beer for Wolfe and a scowl for me, and Wolfe had opened a bottle and was pouring. He murmured, "It was you who saw it, Archie. Your conclusion?"

I tossed the slips onto my desk. "My conclusion is that McNair was Jordan almond-conscious. You know, the way a workingman like me is class-conscious or a guzzler like you is beer-conscious. I'll admit it's vague, but you sent me up there to see if any of that bunch would betray an idea that Jordan almonds are different from any other candy, and either Boyden McNair did just that or I've got the soul of a male stenographer. And I don't even use all my fingers."

"Mr. McNair. Indeed." Wolfe had emptied one and was leaning back. "Miss Helen Frost, according to her cousin, our client, calls him Uncle Boyd. Did you know that I am an uncle, Archie?"

He knew perfectly well that I knew it, since I typed the monthly letters to Belgrade for him, but of course he wasn't expecting an answer. He had shut his eyes and became motionless. His brain may have been working, but so was mine; I had to figure out some plausible way of getting out of there to hop in the roadster and run up to 52nd Street and kidnap Helen Frost. I wasn't worrying about the McNair thing. It was the one nibble I had got uptown, and I really thought there was a good chance that we might hook a fish from it; besides, I had given it to Wolfe straight and now it was up to him. But the two o'clock appointment I had mentioned, God help me . . .

I got an idea. I knew that with Wolfe's eyes shut for his genius to work, he was often beyond the reach of external stimuli. Several times I had even kicked over my wastebasket without getting a flicker from him. I sat and watched him a while, saw him breathing and that was all, and finally decided to risk it. I drew my feet in under me and lifted myself out of my chair without making it creak. I kept my eyes on Wolfe. Three short steps on the rubber tile took me to the first rug, and on that silence was a cinch. I tiptoed it, holding my breath, accelerating gradually as I approached the door. I made the threshold—a step in the hall—another—

Thunder rolled from the office behind me: "Mr. Goodwin!"

I had a notion to dash on out, snaring my hat on the fly, but an instant's reflection showed that would have been disastrous. He would have relapsed again during my absence, out of pure damn meanness. I turned and went back in.

He roared, "Where were you going?"

I tried to grin at him. "Nowhere. Just upstairs a minute."

"And why the furtive stealth?"

"I . . . why . . . egad, sir, I didn't want to disturb you."

"Indeed. You egad me, do you?" He straightened up in his chair. "Not disturb me? Ha! What else have you done but that during the past eight years? Who is it that violently disrupts any private plans which I may venture, on rare occasions, to undertake?" He wiggled a whole hand at me. "You were not going upstairs. You were going to sneak out of this house and rush through the city streets in a desperate endeavor to conceal the chicanery you practiced on me. You were going to try to get Helen Frost and bring her here. Did you think I was not aware of your mendacity, there in the kitchen? Have I not told you that your powers of dissimulation are wretched? Very well. I have three things to say to you. The first is a reminder: we are to have rice fritters with black currant jam, and endive with tarragon, for lunch. The second is a piece of information: you will not have time to lunch here. The third is an instruction: you are to proceed to the McNair establishment, get Miss Frost, and have her at this office by two o'clock. Doubtless you will find opportunity to get a greasy sandwich somewhere. By the time you arrive here with Miss Frost I shall have finished with the fritters and endive."

I said, "Okay. I heard every word. The Frost girl has a stubborn eye. Have I got a free hand? Strangle her? Wrap her up?"

"But, Mr. Goodwin." It was a tone he seldom used; I would call it a sarcastic whine. "She has an appointment here for two o'clock. Surely there should be no difficulty. If only common courtesy—"

I beat it to the hall for my hat.

Chapter 7

On the way uptown in the roadster I reflected that there was one obvious lever to use on Helen Frost to pry her in the direction I wanted her; and I'm a great one for the obvious, because it saves a lot of fiddling around. I decided to use it.

The only parking space I could find was a block away, and I walked from there to the McNair entrance. The uniformed doorman stood grinning at a woman across the street who was trying to feed sugar to a mounted cop's horse. I went up to him:

"Remember me? I was here this morning."

Being accosted by a gentleman, he started to straighten up to be genteel, then recollected that I was connected with the police, so he relaxed.

"Sure I remember. You're the one that passed out the candy."

"Right. Attention, please. I want to speak to Miss Helen Frost privately, but I don't want to make any more fuss in there. Has she gone to lunch yet?"

"No. She doesn't go until one' o'clock."

"Is she inside?"

"Sure." He glanced at his watch. "She won't go for nearly half an hour."

"Okay." I nodded thanks and moseyed off. I had a notion to hunt up some oats for a gobble, but decided it would be better to stick around. I lit a cigarette and strolled to the corner of Fifth Avenue, and across the street, and back toward Madison a ways. Apparently the public was still interested in the place where the beautiful model was poisoned, for I noticed people slowing up and looking at the McNair entrance as they passed by, and now and then some stopped. The mounted cop was hanging around. I went on sauntering in the neighborhood, not getting far away.

At five minutes after one she came out, alone, and headed east. I tripped along, and crossed the street, and got behind her. A little before she got to Madison I snapped out:

"Miss Frost!"

She whirled on a dime. I took off my hat.

"Remember me? My name's Archie Goodwin. I'd like to have a few words—"

"This is outrageous!" She turned and started off.

She was quite a sketch. As independent as a hog on ice. I took a hop, skip and jump, and planted the frame square in front of her. "Listen. You're more childish even than your cousin Lew. I merely need, in performance of my duty, to ask you a couple of questions. You're on your way to get something to eat. I'm hungry and have to eat myself sooner or later. I can't invite you to lunch, because I wouldn't be allowed to put it on my expense account, but I can sit at a table with you for four minutes and then go elsewhere to eat if that is your desire. I am a self-made man, and am a roughneck but not rowdy. I graduated from high school at the age of seventeen and only a few months ago I gave two dollars to the Red Cross."

On account of my firm aggressive talk people were

looking at us, and she knew it. She said, "I eat at Moreland's, around the corner on Madison. You can ask your questions there."

One trick in. Moreland's was one of those dumps where they slice roast beef as thin as paper and specialize in vegetable plates. I let Helen Frost find a table, and trailed along and slid into a chair opposite her after she had sat down.

She looked at me and said, "Well?"

I said, "The waitress will hover. Order your lunch."

"I can order later. What do you want?"

A sketch all right. But I stayed pleasant. "I want to take you to 918 West 35th Street for a conversation with Nero Wolfe."

She stared at me. "That's ridiculous. What for?"

I said mildly, "We have to be there at two o'clock, so we haven't much time. Really, Miss Frost, it would be much more human if you'd get something to eat and let me do the same, while I explain. I'm not something revolting, like a radio crooner or an agent for the Liberty League."

"I . . . I'm not hungry. I can see you're funny. A month ago I would have thought you were a scream."

I nodded. "I'm a knockout." I beckoned to a waitress and consulted the card. "What will you have, Miss Frost?"

She ordered some kind of goo, and hot tea, and I favored the pork and beans, with a glass of milk.

With the waitress gone, I said, "There are lots of ways I could do this. I could scare you. Don't think I couldn't. Or I could try to persuade you that since your cousin is our client, and since Nero Wolfe is as square with a client as you would be with your twin if you had one, it's to your own interest to go and see him. But there's a better reason for your going than either of those. Ordinary decency. Whether Wolfe was right or wrong about what you said yesterday at McNair's doesn't matter. The point is that we've kept it to ourselves. You saw this morning what terms we're on with the police; they had me handling that test for them. But have they been ragging you on what you said yesterday? They have not. On the other hand, are you going to have to discuss it with someone—sooner or later? You're darned tooting you are, there's no way out of it. Who do you want to discuss it with? If you take my advice, Nero Wolfe, and the sooner the better. Don't forget that Miss Mitchell heard you say it too, and although she may be a good friend of yours—"

"Please don't talk any more." She was looking at her fork, which she was sliding back and forth on the tablecloth, and I saw how tight her fingers gripped it. I sat back and looked somewhere else.

The waitress came and began depositing food in front of us. Helen Frost waited until she was through, and gone, and then said more to herself than to me, "I can't eat."

"You ought to." I didn't pick up my tools. "You always ought to eat. Try it, anyhow. I've already eaten, I was only keeping you company." I fished for a dime and a nickel and laid them on the table. "My car is parked on 52nd, halfway to Park Avenue, on the downtown side. I'll expect you there at a quarter to two."

She didn't say anything. I beat it and found the waitress and got my check from her, paid at the desk, and went out. Across the street and down a little I found a drug store with a lunch counter, entered, and consumed two ham sandwiches and a couple of glasses of milk. I wondered what they would do with the beans, whether they would put them back in the pot, and thought it would be a crime to waste them. I didn't wonder much about Helen Frost, because it looked to me like a pipe, all sealed up. There wasn't anything else for her to do.

There wasn't. She came up to me at ten minutes to two, as I stood on the sidewalk alongside the roadster. I opened the door and she got in, and I climbed in and stepped on the starter.

As we rolled off I asked her, "Did you eat anything?"

She nodded. "A little. I telephoned Mrs. Lamont and told her where I'm going and said I'd be back at three o'clock."

"Uh-huh. You may make it."

I drove cocky because I felt cocky. I had her on the way and the sandwiches hadn't been greasy and it wasn't two o'clock yet; and even down in the mouth and with rings under her eyes, she was the kind of riding companion that makes it reasonable to put the top down so the public can see what you've got with you. Being a lover of beauty, I permitted myself occasional glances at her profile, and observed that her chin was even better from that angle than from the front. Of course there was an off chance that she was a murderess, but you can't have everything.

We made it at one minute past two. When I ushered her into the office there was no one there, and I left her there in a chair, fearing the worst. But it was okay. Wolfe was in the dining-room with his coffee cup emptied, doing his post-prandial beaming at space. I stood on the threshold and said:

"I trust the fritters were terrible. Miss Frost regrets being one minute late for her appointment. We got to chatting over a delicious lunch, and the time just flew."

"She's here? The devil." The beam changed to a frown as he made preparations to rise. "Don't suppose for a moment that I am beguiled. I don't really like this."

I preceded him to open the office door. He moved across to his desk more deliberately even than usual, circled around Miss Frost in her chair, and before he lowered himself, inclined his head toward her without saying anything. She leveled her brown eyes at him, and I could see that by gum she was holding the fort and she was going to go on holding it. I got at ease in my chair with my notebook, not trying to camouflage it.

Wolfe asked her politely, "You wished to see me, Miss Frost?"

Her eyes bulged a little. She said indignantly, "I? You sent that man to bring me here."

"Ah, so I did." Wolfe sighed. "Now that you are here, have you anything in particular to say to me?"

She opened her mouth and shut it again, and then said simply, "No."

Wolfe heaved another sigh. He leaned back in his chair and made a movement to clasp his hands on his front middle, then remembered that it was too soon after lunch and let them drop on the arms of his chair. With half-shut eyes he sat comfortable, motionless.

At length he murmured at her, "How old are you?"

"I'll be twenty-one in May."

"Indeed. What day in May?"

"The seventh."

"I understand that you call Mr. McNair 'Uncle Boyd.' Your cousin told me that. Is he your uncle?"

"Why, no. Of course not. I just call him that."

"Have you known him a long while?"

"All my life. He is an old friend of my mother's."

"You would know his preferences then. In candy, for instance. What kind does he prefer?"

She lost color, but she was pretty good with her eyes and voice. She didn't bat a lash. "I . . . I don't know. Really. I couldn't say . . ."

"Come, Miss Frost." Wolfe kept his tone easy. "I am not asking you to divulge some esoteric secret guarded by you alone. On this sort of detail many people may be consulted—any of Mr. McNair's intimates, many of his acquaintances, the servants at his home, the shops where he buys candy if he does buy it. If, for example, he happens to prefer Jordan almonds, those persons could tell me. I happen at the moment to be consulting you. Is there any reason why you should try to conceal this point?"

"Of course not." She hadn't got her color back. "I don't need to conceal anything." She swallowed. "Mr. McNair does like Jordan almonds, that's perfectly true." Suddenly the color did appear, a spot on her cheek that showed how quick her blood was. "But I didn't come here to talk about the kinds of candy that people like. I came here to tell you that you were entirely wrong about what I said yesterday."

"Then you do have something in particular to say to me."

"Certainly I have." She was warming up. "That was just a trick and you know it. I didn't want my mother and my uncle to come down here, but my cousin Lew lost his head as usual, he's always getting scared about me anyhow, as if I didn't have brains enough to take care of myself. You merely tricked me into saying something—I don't know what—that gave you a chance to pretend—"

"But, Miss Frost." Wolfe had a palm up at her. "Your cousin Lew is perfectly correct. I mean, about your brains. —No, permit me! Let me save time. I won't repeat verbatim what was said yesterday; you know as well as I do. I shall merely assert that the words you said, and the way you said them, make it apodictical that you knew the contents of that particular box of candy before Miss Mitchell removed the lid."

"That isn't true! I didn't say—"

"Oh, but you did." Wolfe's tone sharpened. "Understand me. Confound it, do you think I'll squabble with a chit like you? Or do you expect your loveliness to paralyze my intelligence? —Archie. Take this on the typewriter, please. One carbon. Letter-size, headed at the top, Alternative Statements for Helen Frost."

I swiveled around and swung the machine up and got the paper in. "Shoot."

Wolfe dictated:

"1. I admit that I knew the contents of the box of candy, and am ready to explain to Nero Wolfe how I knew, truthfully and in detail.

"2. I admit that I knew the contents. I refuse for the present to explain, but am ready to submit to questioning by Nero Wolfe on any other matters, reserving the right to withhold replies at my discretion.

"3. I admit that I knew the contents, but refuse to continue the conversation.

"4. I deny that I knew the contents."

Wolfe sat up. "Thank you, Archie. No, I'll take the carbon; the original to Miss Frost." He turned to her. "Read them over, please. —You observe the distinctions? Here's a pen; I would like you to initial one of them. One moment. First I should tell you, I am willing to accept either number one or number two. I will not accept either of the others. If you choose number three or number four, I shall have to resign the commission I have undertaken for your cousin, and take certain steps at once."

She wasn't a goddess any more; she was too flustered for a goddess. But it took her only a few seconds to collect enough sense to see that she was only gumming the works by fiddling with the paper. She looked level at Wolfe: "I . . . I don't have to initial anything. Why should I initial anything?" The spots of color appeared again. "It's all a trick and you know it! Anybody that's clever enough can ask people questions and trick them around to some kind of an answer that sounds like—"

"Miss Frost! Please. Do you mean to stick to your absurd denial?"

"Certainly I stick to it, and there's nothing absurd about it. I can warn you, too, when my cousin Lew—"

Wolfe's head pivoted and he snapped, "Archie. Get Mr. Cramer."

I pulled my phone across and dialed the number. They switched me to the extension and I got the clerk and asked for Inspector Cramer. For the sake of Wolfe's cake that had to have a hot griddle right then, I was hoping he wouldn't be out, and he wasn't. His voice boomed at me in the receiver:

"Hello! Hello, Goodwin! You got something?"

"Inspector Cramer? Hold the wire. Mr. Wolfe wants to speak to you."

I gave Wolfe a nod and he reached for his instrument. But the chit was on her feet, looking mad enough to eat nettle salad. Before lifting his receiver Wolfe said to her:

"As a courtesy, you may have a choice. Do you wish Mr. Goodwin to take you to police headquarters, or shall Mr. Cramer send for you?"

Her voice at him was a croak: "Don't . . . don't . . ." She grabbed up the pen and wrote her name under statement number two on the paper. She was so mad her hand trembled. Wolfe spoke into the phone:

"Mr. Cramer? How do you do. I was wondering if you have arrived at any conclusions from this morning. . . . Indeed . . . I wouldn't say that . . . No, I haven't, but I've started a line of inquiry which may develop into something later. . . . No, nothing for you now; as you know, I fancy my own discretion in these matters. . . . You must leave that to me, sir. . . ."

When he hung up, Helen Frost was sitting down again, looking at him with her chin up and her lips pushed together. Wolfe picked up the paper and glanced at it, handed it across to me, and settled back in his chair. He reached forward to ring for beer, and settled back again.

"So. Miss Frost, you have acknowledged that you possess information regarding an implement of murder which you refuse to disclose. I wish to remind you that I have not engaged to keep that acknowledgment confidential. For the present I shall do so; I am not committing myself beyond that. Do you know the police mind? One of its first and most constant assumptions is that any withheld knowledge regarding a crime is guilty knowledge. It is a preposterous assumption, but they hug it to their bosoms. For instance, if they knew what you have just signed, they would proceed on the theory that you either put the poison in the candy or know who did. I shall not do that. But as a matter of form I shall ask the question: did you poison that candy?"

She was pretty good, at that. She answered in a calm voice that was only pinched a little, "No. I didn't."

"Do you know who did?"

"No."

"Are you engaged to be married?"

She compressed her lips. "That is none of your business."

Wolfe said patiently, "I shall have to ask you about many things which you will regard as none of my business. Really, Miss Frost, it is foolish of you to irritate me unnecessarily. The question I just asked is completely innocuous; any of your friends could probably answer it; why shouldn't you? Do you imagine this is a friendly chat we are having? By no means. It is a very one-sided affair. I am forcing you to reply to questions by threatening to turn you over to the police if you don't. Are you engaged to be married?"

She was cracking a little. Her fists were clenched in her lap, and she looked smaller, as if she had shrunk, and her eyes got so damp that finally a tear formed in the corner of each one and dripped out. Without paying any attention to them, she said to Wolfe, looking at him, "You're a dirty fat beast. You . . . you . . ."

He nodded. "I know. I ask questions of women only when it is unavoidable, because I abominate hysterics. Wipe your eyes."

She didn't move. He sighed. "Are you engaged to be married?"

Tears of rage were also in her voice. "I am not."

"Did you buy that diamond on your finger?"

She glanced at it involuntarily. "No."

"Who gave it to you?"

"Mr. McNair."

"And the one set in your vanity case—who gave you that one?"

"Mr. McNair."

"Astonishing. I wouldn't have supposed you cared for diamonds." Wolfe opened a bottle of beer and filled his glass. "You mustn't mind me, Miss Frost. I mean, my seeming inconsequence. A servant girl named Anna Fiore sat in that chair once and conversed with me for five hours. The Duchess of Rathkyn did so for most of a night. I am apt to poke into almost any corner, and I beg you to bear with me." He lifted the glass and emptied it in par. "For instance, this diamond business is curious. Do you like them?"

"I don't . . . not ordinarily."

"Is Mr. McNair fond of them? Does he make gifts of them more or less at random?"

"Not that I know of."

"And although you don't like them, you wear these out of . . . respect for Mr. McNair? Affection for an old friend?"

"I wear them because I happen to feel like it."

"Just so. You see, I know very little about Mr. McNair. Is he married?"

"As I told you, he is an old friend of my mother's. A lifelong friend. He had a daughter about my age, a month or so older, but she died when she was two years old. His wife had died before, when the baby was born. Mr. McNair is the finest man I have ever known. He is . . . he is my best friend."

"And yet he puts diamonds on you. You must forgive my harping on the diamonds; I happen to dislike them. —Oh, yes, I meant to ask, do you know anyone else who is fond of Jordan almonds?"

"Anybody else?"

"Besides Mr. McNair."

"No, I don't."

Wolfe poured more beer and, leaving the foam to settle, leaned back and frowned at his victim. "You know, Miss Frost, it is time something was said to you. In your conceit, you are assuming, for your youth and inexperience, a terrific responsibility. Molly Lauck died nine days ago, probably through bungling of someone's effort to kill another person. During all that time you have possessed knowledge which, handled with competence and dispatch, might do something much more important than wreak vengeance; it might save a life, and it is even possible that the life would be one worth saving. What do you think; isn't that responsibility pretty heavy for you? I have too much sense to try coercion. There's too much egotism and too much mule in you. But you really should consider it." He picked up his glass and drank.

She sat and watched him. Finally she said, "I have considered it. I'm not an egotist. I . . . I've considered."

Wolfe lifted his shoulders an inch and dropped them. "Very well. I understand that your father is dead. I gathered that from the statement of your uncle, Mr. Dudley Frost, that he is the trustee of your property."

She nodded. "My father died when I was only a few months old. So I've never had a father." She frowned. "That is . . ."

"Yes? That is?"

"Nothing." She shook her head. "Nothing at all."

"And what does your property consist of?"

"I inherited it from my father."

"To be sure. How much is it?"

She lifted her brows. "It is what my father left me."

"Oh, come, Miss Frost. Sizes of estates in trust are no secrets nowadays. How much are you worth?"

She shrugged. "I understand that it is something over two million dollars."

"Indeed. Is it intact?"

"Intact? Why shouldn't it be?"

"I have no idea. But don't think I am prying into affairs which your family considers too intimate for discussion with outsiders. Your uncle told me yesterday that your mother hasn't got a cent. His expression. Then your father's fortune was all left to you?"

She flushed a little. "Yes. It was. I have no brother or sister."

"And it will be turned over to you—excuse me. If you please, Archie."

It was the phone. I wheeled to my desk and got it. I recognized the quiet controlled voice before she gave her name, and made my own tones restrained and dignified as she deserved. I don't like hysterics any better than Wolfe does.

I turned to Helen Frost: "Your mother would like to speak to you." I got up and held my chair for her, and she moved over to it.

"Yes, mother . . . Yes . . . No, I didn't . . . I know you said that, but under the circumstances—I can't very well tell you now . . . I couldn't ask Uncle Boyd about it because he wasn't back from lunch yet, so I just told Mrs. Lamont where I was going. . . . No, mother, that's ridiculous, don't you think I'm old enough to know what I'm doing? . . . I can't do that, and I can't explain till I see you, and when I leave here I'll come straight home but I can't tell now when that will be. . . . Don't worry about that, and for heaven's

sake give me credit for having a little sense . . .
No . . . Good-bye . . ."

She had color in her face again as she rose and
returned to her seat. Wolfe had narrow eyes on her.
He murmured sympathetically: "You don't like people
fussing about you, do you, Miss Frost? Even your
mother. I know. But you must tolerate it. Remember
that physically and financially you are well worth
some fuss. Mentally you are—well—in the pupa stage.
I hope you don't mind my discussing you."

"It would do me no good to mind it."

"I didn't say it would. I only said I hoped you
didn't. About your inheritance; I presume it will be
turned over to you when you come of age on May
seventh."

"I presume it will."

"That is only five weeks off. Twenty-nine, thirty-
six—five weeks from tomorrow. Two million dollars.
Another responsibility for you. Will you continue to
work?"

"I don't know."

"Why have you been working? Not for income
surely."

"Of course not. I work because I enjoy it. I felt silly
not doing anything. And Uncle Boyd—Mr. McNair—it
happened that there was work there I could do."

"How long—confound it. Excuse me."

It was the telephone again. I swiveled and picked
it up and started my usual salutation, "Hello, this is
the office—"

"Hello! hello there! I want to speak to Nero Wolfe!"

I made a face at my desk calendar; this was a voice
I knew too. I turned on the aggressiveness: "Don't
bark like that. Mr. Wolfe is engaged. This is Goodwin,
his confidential assistant. Who—"

"This is Mr. Dudley Frost! I don't care if he is engaged, I want to speak to him at once! Is my niece there? Let me speak to her! Let me speak to Wolfe first! He's going to be sorry—"

I roughened up: "Listen, mister, if you don't turn off that valve a little I'll hang up on you. I mean it. Mr. Wolfe and Miss Frost are having a conversation, and I refuse to disturb them. If you want to leave a message—"

"I insist on speaking to Wolfe!"

"You C, A, N, apostrophe, T, can't. Don't be childish."

"I'll show you who's childish! You tell Wolfe—tell him that I am my niece's trustee. She is under my protection. I will not have her annoyed. I'll have Wolfe and you too arrested as nuisances! She is a minor! I'll have you prosecuted—"

"Listen, Mr. Frost. *Will* you listen? What you say is okay. Let me suggest that you have Inspector Cramer do the arresting, because he's been here often and knows the way. Furthermore, I'm going to hang up now, and if you aggravate me by keeping this phone ringing, I'll hunt you up and straighten your nose for you. I mean that with all my heart."

I cradled the instrument, picked up my notebook and turned and said curtly, "More fuss."

Helen Frost said in a strained voice, because she didn't like to have to ask, "My cousin?"

"No. Your uncle. Your cousin comes next."

Which was truer and more imminent than I knew. Her mouth opened at me as if for another question, but she decided against it. Wolfe resumed:

"I was about to ask, how long have you been working?"

"Nearly two years." She leaned forward at him.

"I'd like to ask . . . is this . . . going on indefinitely? You're just trying to provoke me . . ."

Wolfe shook his head. "I'm trying not to provoke you. I'm collecting information, possibly none of it germane, but that's my affair." He glanced at the clock. "It's a quarter past three. At four o'clock I shall ask you to accompany me to my plant rooms on the roof; you'll find the orchids diverting. I should guess we shall be finished by six. I assure you, I'm going through with this. I intend to invite Mr. McNair to call on me this evening. If he finds that inconvenient, then tomorrow. If he refuses, Mr. Goodwin will go to his place in the morning and see what can be done. By the way, I need to be sure that you will be there tomorrow. You will?"

"Of course. I'm there every— Oh! No. I won't be there. The place will be closed."

"Closed? A Thursday? April second?"

She nodded. "Yes. April second. That's why. That's the date Mr. McNair's wife died."

"Indeed. And his daughter born?"

She nodded again. "He . . . he always closes up."

"And visits the cemetery?"

"Oh, no. His wife died in Europe, in Paris. Mr. McNair is a Scotsman. He only came to this country about twelve years ago, a little after mother and I came."

"Then you spent part of your childhood in Europe?"

"Most of it. The first eight years. I was born in Paris, but my father and mother were both Americans." She tilted up her chin. "I'm an American girl."

"You look it." Fritz brought more beer, and Wolfe poured some. "And after twenty years Mr. McNair still shuts up shop on April second in memory of his wife. A steadfast man. Of course, he lost his daughter also—when she was two, I believe you said—which completed his loss. Still he goes on dressing women . . . well. Then you won't be there tomorrow."

"No, but I'll be with Mr. McNair. I . . . do that for him. He asked it a long time ago, and mother let me, and I always do it. I'm almost exactly the same age his daughter was. Of course I don't remember her, I was too young."

"So you spend that day with him as a vicar for his daughter." Wolfe shivered. "His mourning day. Ghoulish. And he puts diamonds on you. However . . . you are aware, of course, that your cousin, Mr. Llewellyn Frost, wants you to quit your job. Aren't you?"

"Perhaps I am. But that isn't even any of my business, is it? It's his."

"Certainly. Hence mine, since he is my client. Do you forget that he hired me?"

"I do not." She sounded scornful. "But I can assure you that I am not going to discuss my cousin Lew with you. He means well. I know that."

"But you don't like the fuss." Wolfe sighed. The foam had gone from his beer, and he tipped a little more in the glass, lifted it, and drank. I sat and tapped with my pencil on my notebook and looked at Miss Frost's ankles and the hint of shapeliness ascending therefrom. I wasn't exactly bored, but I was beginning to get anxious, wondering if the relapse germ was still working on Wolfe's nerve centers. Not only was he not getting anywhere with this hard-working heiress, it didn't sound to me as if he was half trying. Remembering the exhibitions I had seen him put on with others—for instance, Nyura Pronn in the Diplomacy Club business—I was beginning to harbor a suspicion that he was only killing time. At anything like his top form, he should have had this poor little rich girl herded into a corner long ago. But here he was . . .

I was diverted by the doorbell buzz and the sound of Fritz's footsteps in the hall going to answer it. The idea popped into my head that Mr. Dudley Frost, not liking the way I had hung up on him, might be dropping around to get his nose straightened, and in a sort of negligent way I got solider in my chair, because I knew Wolfe was in no mood to be wafted away again by that verbal cyclone, and I damn well wasn't going to pass out any more of the Old Corcoran.

But it wasn't the cyclone, it was only the breeze, his son. Our client. Fritz came in and announced him, and at Wolfe's nod went back and brought him in. He wasn't alone. He ushered in ahead of him a plump little duck about his own age, with a round pink face and quick smart eyes. Lew Frost escorted this specimen forward, then dropped it and went to his cousin.

"Helen! You shouldn't have done this—"

"Now, Lew, for heaven's sake, why did you come here? Anyway, it's your fault that I had to come." She saw the plump one. "You too, Bennie?" She looked mad and grim. "Are you armed?"

Lew Frost turned to Wolfe, looking every inch a football player. "What the hell are you trying to pull? Do you think you can get away with this kind of stuff? How would you like it if I pulled you out of that chair—"

His plump friend grasped his arm, with authority. He was snappy: "None of that, Lew. Calm down. Introduce me."

Our client controlled himself with an effort. "But, Ben . . . all right. That's Nero Wolfe." He glared at

Wolfe. "This is Mr. Benjamin Leach, my attorney. Try some tricks on him."

Wolfe inclined his head. "How do you do, Mr. Leach. I don't know any tricks, Mr. Frost. Anyway, aren't you getting things a little complicated? First you hire me to do a job for you, and now, judging from your attitude, you have hired Mr. Leach to circumvent me. If you keep on with that—"

"Not to circumvent you." The lawyer sounded friendly and smooth. "You see, Mr. Wolfe, I'm an old friend of Lew's. He's a little hot-headed. He has told me something about this business . . . the, er, unusual circumstances, and I just thought it would be all right if he and I were present at any conversations you may have with Miss Frost. In fact, it would have been quite proper if you had arranged for us to be here from the beginning." He smiled pleasantly. "Isn't that so? Two of you and two of us?"

Wolfe had on a grimace. "You speak, sir, as if we were hostile armies drawn up for battle. Of course that's natural, since bad blood is for lawyers what a bad tooth is for a dentist. I mean nothing invidious; detectives live on trouble too. But they don't stir it up where there is none—at least, I don't. I don't ask you to sit down, because I don't want you here. I fancy that on that point we shall have to consult—yes, Fritz?"

Fritz had knocked and entered, and now walked across to the desk with his company gait, bearing the pewter tray. He bent at the waist and extended it.

Wolfe picked up the card and looked at it. "Still not the right one. Tell him . . . no. Show him in."

Fritz bowed and departed. The lawyer wheeled to face the door and Llewellyn turned his head, but Miss Frost just sat. The newcomer entered, and at sight of his thin nose and slick hair and dark darting eyes I squelched a grin and muttered to myself, "Still more fuss."

I stood up. "Over here, Mr. Gebert."

Lew Frost took a step and busted out at him, "You? What the hell do you want here?"

Wolfe spoke sharply, "Mr. Frost! This is my office!"

The lawyer took hold of our client—his too, of course—and held on. Perren Gebert paid no attention to either of them. He went past them before he stopped to incline his torso in Wolfe's direction. "Mr. Wolfe? How do you do? Permit me." He turned and bowed again, at Helen Frost, with a different technique. "So there you are! How are you? You've been crying! Forgive me, I have no tact, I shouldn't have mentioned that. How are you? All right?"

"Certainly I'm all right! For heaven's sake, Perren, why did *you* come?"

"I came to take you home." Gebert turned and shot the dark eyes at Wolfe. "Permit me, sir. I came to escort Miss Frost home."

"Indeed," Wolfe murmured. "Officially? Forcibly? In spite of anything?"

"Well . . ." Gebert smiled. "Semi-officially. How shall I say it . . . Miss Frost is almost my fiancée."

"Perren! That isn't true! I've told you not to say that!"

"I said 'almost,' Helen." He raised his palms to deprecate himself. "I put in the 'almost,' and I permit myself to say it only in hope—"

"Well, don't say it again. Why did you come?"

Gebert got in another bow. "The truth is, your mother suggested it."

"Oh. She did." Miss Frost glanced around at all her

protectors. She looked plenty exasperated. "I suppose she suggested it to you too, Lew. And you, Bennie?"

"Now, Helen." The lawyer sounded persuasive. "Don't start on me. I came here because when Lew told me about it, it seemed the best thing to do. —Be quiet, Lew! It seems to me that if we just discuss this thing quietly . . ."

The telephone rang, and I got back in my chair for it. Leach went on talking, spreading oil. As soon as I learned who it was on the phone I got discreet. I pronounced no names and kept my words down. It appeared to me likely that this time it was the right one. I asked him to hold the wire a minute, and choked the transmitter, and wrote on a piece of paper, *McN wants to pay us a call*, and handed it across to Wolfe.

Wolfe glanced at it and stuck it in his pocket and said softly, "Thank you, Archie. That's more like it. Tell Mr. Brown to telephone again in fifteen minutes."

I had trouble with that. McNair was urgent and wasn't going to be put off. The others had stopped talking. I made it reassuring but firm, and finally managed it. I hung up and told Wolfe:

"Okay."

He was making preparations to rise. He shoved his chair back, got his hands on its arms for levers, and up came the mountain. He stood and distributed a glance and put on his crispest tone:

"Gentlemen. It is nearly four o'clock and I must leave you. —No, permit me. Miss Frost has kindly accepted my invitation to come to my plant rooms and see my orchids. She is . . . she and I have concluded a little agreement. I may say that I am not an ogre and I resent your silly invasion of my premises. You gentlemen are leaving now, and certainly she is free to accompany you if she chooses to do that. —Miss Frost?"

She stood up. Her lips were compressed, but she opened them to say, "I'll look at the orchids."

They all began yapping at once. I got up and prepared for traffic duty in case of a jam. Llewellyn broke loose from his lawyer and started toward her, ready to throw her behind his saddle and gallop off. She gave them a good brave stare:

"For heaven's sake, shut up! Don't you think I'm old enough to take care of myself? Lew, stop that!"

She started off with Wolfe. All they could do was take it and look foolish. The lawyer friend pulled at his little pink nose. Perren Gebert stuck his hands in his pockets and stood straight. Llewellyn strode to the door, after the orchid lovers had passed through, and all we could see was his fine strong back. The sound of the elevator door closing came from the hall, and the whirr of its ascending.

I announced, "That'll be all for the present, and I don't like scenes. They get on my nerves."

Lew Frost whirled and told me, "Go to hell."

I grinned at him. "I can't plug you, because you're our client. But you might as well beat it. I've got work to do."

The plump one said, "Come on, Lew, we'll go to my office."

Perren Gebert was already on the move. Llewellyn stood aside and glared him full of holes as he passed. Then Leach went and nudged his friend along. I tripped by to open the front door for them; Llewellyn was continuing with remarks, but I disdained them. He and his attorney went down the stoop to the sidewalk and headed east; Gebert had climbed into a neat little convertible which he had parked back of the roadster and was stepping on the starter. I shut the door and went back in.

I switched on the house phone for the plant room and pressed the button. In about twenty seconds Wolfe answered, and I told him:

"It's quiet and peaceful down here now. No fuss at all."

His murmur came at me: "Good. Miss Frost is in the middle room, enjoying the orchids . . . reasonably well. When Mr. McNair phones, tell him six o'clock. If he insists on coming earlier, let him, and keep him. Let me know when he is there, and have the office door closed. She left her vanity case on my desk. Send Fritz up with it."

"Okay."

I switched off and settled to wait for McNair's call, reflecting on the relative pulling power of beauty in distress and two million iron men and how it probably depended on whether you were the romantic type or not.

Chapter 8

T wo hours later, at six o'clock, I sat at my desk pounding the typewriter with emphasis and a burst of speed, copying off the opening pages of one of Hoehn's catalogues. The radio was turned on, loud, for the band of the Hotel Portland Surf Room. Together the radio and I made quite a din. Boyden McNair, with his right elbow on his knee and his bent head resting on the hand which covered his eyes, sat near Wolfe's desk in the dunce's chair, yclept that by me on the day that District Attorney Anderson of Westchester sat in it while Wolfe made a dunce of him.

McNair had been there nearly an hour. He had done a lot of sputtering on the phone and had refused to wait until six o'clock, and had finally appeared a little after five, done some sputtering, and then settled down because there wasn't anything else to do. He had his bottle of aspirin along in his pocket and had already washed a couple of them down, me furnishing the water and also offering phenacetin tablets as an improvement, without any sale. He wouldn't take a drink, though he certainly looked as if he needed one.

The six o'clock radio and typewriter din was for the purpose of covering any sound of voices that might come from the hall as Nero Wolfe escorted his guest, Miss Frost, from the elevator to the front door and let her out to the taxi which Fritz had ordered from the kitchen phone. Of course I couldn't hear anything either, so I kept glancing at the office door without letting my fingers stop, and at length it opened and Wolfe entered. Observing the *mise en scène*, he winked at me with his right eye and steered for his desk. He got across and deposited in his chair before the visitor knew he was there. I arose and turned off the radio and quiet descended on us. McNair's head jerked up. He saw Wolfe, blinked, stood up and looked around.

"Where's Miss Frost?" he demanded.

Wolfe said, "I'm sorry to have kept you waiting, Mr. McNair. Miss Frost has gone home."

"What?" McNair gaped at him. "Gone home? I don't believe it. Who took her? Gebert and Lew Frost were here . . ."

"They were indeed." Wolfe wiggled a finger at him. "I entreat you, sir. This room has been filled with idiots this afternoon, and I would enjoy some sanity for a change. I am not a liar. I put Miss Frost into a cab not ten minutes ago, and she was going straight home."

"Ten minutes . . . but I was here! Right here in this chair! You knew I wanted to see her! What kind of a trick—"

"I know you wanted to see her. But I didn't want you to, and she is perfectly safe if she gets through the traffic. I do not intend that you shall see Miss Frost until I've had a talk with you. It was a trick, yes, but I've a right to play tricks. What about your own tricks? What about the outright lies you have been telling the police since the day Molly Lauck was murdered? Well, sir? Answer me!"

McNair started twice to speak, but didn't. He looked at Wolfe. He sat down. He pulled his handkerchief from his pocket and then put it back again without using it. Sweat showed on his forehead.

Finally he said, in a thin cool voice, "I don't know what you're talking about."

"Of course you know." Wolfe pinned him down with his eyes. "I'm talking about the box of poisoned candy. I know how Miss Frost became aware of its contents. I know that you have known from the beginning, and that you have deliberately withheld vital information from the police in a murder case. Don't be an idiot, Mr. McNair. I have a statement signed by Helen Frost; there was nothing else for her to do. If I told the police what I know you would be locked up. For the present I don't tell them, because I wish to earn a fee, and if you were locked up I couldn't get at you. I pay you the compliment of assuming that you have some brains. If you poisoned that candy, I advise you to say nothing, leave here at once, and beware of me; if you didn't, talk to the point, and there will be no dodging the truth." Wolfe leaned back and murmured, "I dislike ultimatums, even my own. But this has gone far enough."

McNair sat motionless. Then I saw a shiver in his left shoulder, a quick little spasm, and the fingers of his left hand, on the arm of his chair, began twitching. He looked down at them, and reached over with his other hand and gripped and twisted them, and the shoulder had another spasm, and I saw the muscles jerking in the side of his neck. His nerves were certainly shot. His eyes moved around and fell on the empty glass standing on the edge of Wolfe's desk, and he turned to me and asked as if it were a big favor:

"Could I have a little more water?"

I took the glass and went and filled it and brought it back, and when he didn't lift his hand to take it I put it down on the desk again. He paid no attention to it.

He muttered aloud, but to no one in particular. "I've got to make up my own mind. I thought I had, but I didn't expect this."

Wolfe said, "If you were a clever man you'd have done that before the unexpected forced you."

McNair took out his handkerchief and this time wiped off the sweat. He said quietly, "Good God, I'm not clever. I'm the most complete fool that was ever born. I've ruined my whole life." His shoulder twitched again. "It wouldn't do any good to tell the police what you know, Mr. Wolfe. I didn't poison that candy."

Wolfe said, "Go on."

McNair nodded. "I'll go on. I don't blame Helen for telling you about it, after the way you trapped her yesterday morning. I can imagine what she was up against here today, but I don't hold that against you either. I've got beyond all the ordinary resentments, they don't mean anything. You notice I'm not even trying to find out what Helen told you. I know if she told you anything she told you the truth."

He lifted his head to get Wolfe straighter in the eye. "I didn't poison the candy. When I went upstairs to my office about twelve o'clock that day, to get away from the crowd for a few minutes, the box was there on my desk. I opened it and looked in it, but didn't take any because I had a devil of a headache. When Helen came in a little later I offered her some, but thank God she didn't take any either, because there

were no caramels in it. When I went back downstairs
I left it on my desk, and Molly must have seen it there
later, and took it. She . . . liked to play pranks."

He stopped and wiped his brow again. Wolfe
asked:

"What did you do with the paper and twine the box
was wrapped with?"

"There wasn't any. It wasn't wrapped."

"Who put it on your desk?"

"I don't know. Twenty-five or thirty people had
been in and out of there before 11:30, looking at some
Crenuit models I didn't want to show publicly."

"Who do you think put it there?"

"I haven't any idea about it."

"Who do you think might want to kill you?"

"No one would want to kill me. That's why I'm
sure it was meant for someone else and was left there
by mistake. Anyway, there's no more reason to
suppose—"

"I'm not supposing." Wolfe sounded disgusted.
"You are certainly on solid ground when you say
you're not clever. But surely you're not halfwitted.
Consider what you're telling me: you found the box on
your desk, you have no suspicion as to who put it
there, you are convinced it was not intended for you
and have no idea who it was meant for, and yet you
have carefully concealed from the police the fact that
you saw it there. I have never heard such nonsense; a
babe in arms would laugh at you." Wolfe sighed
deeply. "I shall have to have beer. I imagine this will
require all my patience. Will you have some beer?"

McNair ignored the invitation. He said quietly.
"I'm a Scotsman, Mr. Wolfe. I've admitted I'm a fool.
In some vital ways I'm weak. But maybe you know
how stubborn a weak man can be sometimes? I can be

stubborn." He leaned forward a little and his voice got thinner. "What I've just told you about that box of candy is what I'm going to tell until I die."

"Indeed." Wolfe surveyed him. "So that's it. But you don't seem to realize that while nothing more formidable than my patience may confront you, something more disagreeable is sure to. If I do not clear this thing up reasonably soon I shall have to tell what I know to the police; I shall owe that to Mr. Cramer, since I have accepted his cooperation. If you stick to the absurd rigamarole you have told me, they will assume you are guilty; they will torment you, they will take you to their dungeon and harass you endlessly, they may even beat you with their fists, though that is not likely with a man of your standing, they will destroy your dignity, your business, and your digestion. In the end, with luck and perseverance, they might even electrocute you. I doubt if you're fool enough to be as stubborn as all that."

"I'm stubborn enough," McNair asserted. He leaned forward again. "But look here. I'm not fool enough not to know what I'm doing. I'm tired and I'm worn out and I'm all in, but I know what I'm doing. You think you've forced me to admit something by getting Helen here and bullying her, but I would just as soon as have admitted that to you anyhow. Then here's another thing. I've just practically told you that part of my story about that box isn't true, but that I'm going to stick to it. I didn't need to do that, I could have told you the story and made you think I expected you to believe it. I did it because I didn't want you to think I'm a bigger fool than I am. I wanted you to have as good an opinion of me as possible under the circumstances, because I want to ask you to do me a very important favor. I came here to see Helen, that's true, and to see how . . . how she was, but I also came to ask this favor of you. I want you to accept a legacy in my will."

Wolfe didn't surprise easily, but that got him. He stared. It got me too; it sounded offhand, as if McNair was actually going to try to bribe Nero Wolfe to turn off the heat, and that was such a novel idea that I began to admire him. I focused my lamps on him with renewed interest.

McNair went on, "What I want to leave you is a responsibility. A . . . a small article, and a responsibility. It's astonishing that I have to ask this of you. I've lived in New York for twelve years, and I realized the other day, when I had occasion to consider it, that I have not one friend I can trust. Oh, trust ordinarily, sure, several of them, but not trust with something vital, something more important than my life. But today at my lawyer's I had to name such a person, and I named you. That's astonishing, because I've only met you once, for a few minutes yesterday morning. But you seemed to me to be the kind of man that . . . that will be needed if I die. Last night and this morning I made some inquiries, and I think you are. It has to be a man with nerve, and one that can't be made a fool of, and he has to be honest clear through. I don't know anyone as good as that, and it had to be done today, so I decided to take a chance and name you."

McNair slid forward in his chair and put both hands on the edge of Wolfe's desk, gripping it, and I saw the muscles in his neck moving again. "I made provisions for you to get paid for it, and it will be a fair-sized estate, my business is in good shape, and I've been careful with investments. For you it will just be another job, but for me, if I'm dead, it will be of the most vital importance. If I could only be sure . . .

sure . . . Mr. Wolfe, that would let my spirit rest. I went to my lawyer's office this afternoon and made my will over, and I named you. I left you . . . this job. I should have come to you first, but I didn't want to take any chance of not having it down in black and white and signed. Of course I can't leave it that way without your consent. You've got to give it, then I'll be all right." His shoulder began to jerk, and he gripped the edge of the desk tighter. "Then let it come."

Wolfe said, "Sit back in your chair, Mr. McNair. No? You'll work yourself into a fit. Then let what come? Death?"

"Anything."

Wolfe shook his head. "A bad state of mind. But apparently your mind has practically ceased to function. You are incoherent. Of course you have now made completely untenable your position in regard to the poisoned candy. Obviously—"

McNair broke in, "I've named you. Will you do it?"

"Permit me, please." Wolfe wiggled a finger at him. "Obviously you know who poisoned the candy, and you know it was meant for you. You are obsessed with fear that this unfriendly person will proceed to kill you in spite of the fatal bungling of that effort. Possibly others are in danger also; yet, instead of permitting someone with a little wit to handle the affair by giving him your confidence, you sit there and drivel and boast to me of your stubbornness. More than that, you have the gall to request me to agree to undertake a commission although I am completely ignorant of its nature and have no idea how much I shall get for it. Pfui!—No, permit me. Either all this is true, or you are yourself a murderer and are attempting so elaborate a gullery that it is no wonder you have a headache. You ask, will I do it. If you mean, will I agree to do an unknown job for an unknown wage, certainly not."

McNair still had his hold of the edge of the desk, and kept it there while Wolfe poured beer. He said, "That's all right. I don't mind your talking like that. I expected it. I know that's the kind of a man you are, and that's all right. I don't expect you to agree to do an unknown job. I'm going to tell you about it, that's what I came here for. But I'd feel easier . . . if you'd just say . . . you'll do it if there's nothing wrong with it . . . if you'd just say that . . ."

"Why should I?" Wolfe was impatient. "There is no great urgency; you have plenty of time; I do not dine until eight o'clock. You need not fear your nemesis is in ambush for you in this room; death will not stalk you here. Go on and tell me about it. But let me advise you: it will be taken down, and will need your signature."

"No." McNair got energetic and positive. "I don't want it written down. And I don't want this man here."

"Then I don't want to hear it." Wolfe pointed a thumb at me. "This is Mr. Goodwin, my confidential assistant. Whatever opinion you have formed of me includes him of necessity. His discretion is the twin of his valor."

McNair looked at me. "He's young. I don't know him."

"As you please." Wolfe shrugged. "I shan't try to persuade you."

"I know. You know you don't have to. You know I can't help myself, I'm in a corner. But it must not be written down."

"On that I'll concede something." Wolfe had got

himself patient again. "Mr. Goodwin can record it, and then, if it is so decided, it can be destroyed."

McNair had abandoned his clutch on the desk. He looked from Wolfe to me and back again and, seeing the look in his eyes, if it hadn't been during business hours—Nero Wolfe's business hours—I would have felt sorry for him. He certainly was in no condition to put over a bargain with Nero Wolfe. He slid back on his seat and clasped his hands together, then after a moment separated them and took hold of the arms of the chair. He looked back and forth at us again.

He said abruptly, "You'll have to know about me or you wouldn't believe what I did. I was born in 1885 in Camfirth, Scotland. My folks had a little money. I wasn't much in school and was never very healthy, nothing really wrong, just craichy. I thought I could draw, and when I was twenty-two I went to Paris to study art. I loved it and worked at it, but never really did anything, just enough to keep me in Paris wasting the little money my parents had. When they died a little later my sister and I had nothing, but I'll come to that." He stopped and put his hands up to his temples and pressed and rubbed. "My head's going to bust."

"Take it easy," Wolfe murmured. "You'll feel better pretty soon. You're probably telling me something you should have told somebody years ago."

"No," McNair said bitterly. "Something that should never have happened. And I can't tell it now, not all of it, but I can tell enough. Maybe I'm really crazy, maybe I've lost my balance, maybe I'm just destroying all that I've safeguarded for so many years of suffering, I don't know. Anyhow, I can't help it, I've got to leave you the red box, and you would know then.

"Of course I knew lots of people in Paris. One I

knew was an American girl named Anne Crandall, and
I married her in 1913 and we had a baby girl. I lost
both of them. My wife died the day the baby was born,
April second, 1915, and I lost my daughter two years
later." McNair stopped, looking at Wolfe, and demanded fiercely, "Did you ever have a baby daughter?"

Wolfe merely shook his head. McNair went on,
"Some other people I knew were two wealthy American brothers, the Frosts, Edwin and Dudley. They
were around Paris most of the time. There was also a
girl there I had known all my life, in Scotland, named
Calida Buchan. She was after art too, and got about as
much of it as I did. Edwin Frost married her a few
months after I married Anne, though it looked for a
while as if his older brother Dudley was going to get
her. I think he would have, if he hadn't been off
drinking one night."

McNair halted and pressed at his temples again. I
asked him, "Phenacetin?"

He shook his head. "These help a little." He got the
aspirin bottle from his pocket, jiggled a couple of
tablets onto his palm, tossed them in his mouth, took
the glass of water and gulped. He said to Wolfe,
"You're right. I'm going to feel better after this is
over. I've been carrying too big a load of remorse and
for too many years."

Wolfe nodded. "And Dudley Frost went off drinking . . ."

"Yes. But that wasn't important. Anyway, Edwin
and Calida were married. Soon after that Dudley
returned to America, where his son was. His wife had
died like mine, in childbirth, some six years before. I
don't think he went back to France until more than
three years later, when America entered the war.

Edwin was dead; he had entered the British aviation corps and got killed in 1916. By that time I wasn't in Paris any more. They wouldn't take me in the army on account of my health. I didn't have any money. I had gone down to Spain with my baby daughter—"

He stopped, and I looked up from my notebook. He was bending over a little, with both hands, the fingers spread out, pressed against his belly, and his face was enough to tell you that something had suddenly happened that was a lot worse than a headache.

I heard Wolfe's voice like a whip: "Archie! Get him!"

I jumped up and across and reached for him. But I missed him, because he suddenly went into a spasm, a convulsion all over his body, and shot up out of his chair and stood there swaying.

He let out a scream: "Christ Jesus!" He put his hands, the fists doubled up, on Wolfe's desk, and tried to push himself back up straight. He screamed again, "Oh, Christ!" Then another convulsion went over him and he gasped at Wolfe: "The red box—the number— God, let me tell him!" He let out a moan that came from his guts and went down.

I had hold of him, but I let him go to the floor because he was out. I knelt by him, and saw Wolfe's shoes appear beyond him. I said, "Still breathing. No. I don't think so. I think he's gone."

Wolfe said, "Get Doctor Vollmer. Get Mr. Cramer. First let me have that bottle from his pocket."

As I moved for the phone I heard a mutter behind me, "I was wrong. Death did stalk him here. I'm an imbecile."

Chapter 9

Late the following morning, Thursday, April 2nd, I sat at my desk and folded checks and put them in envelopes as Wolfe signed them and passed them over to me. The March bills were being paid. He had come down from the plant rooms punctually at eleven, and we were improving our time as we awaited a promised visit from Inspector Cramer.

McNair had been dead when Doc Vollmer got there from his home only a block away, and still dead when Cramer and a couple of dicks arrived. An assistant medical examiner had come and done routine, and the remains had been carted away for a post mortem. Wolfe had told Cramer everything perfectly straight, without holding out on him, but had refused his request for a typed copy of my notes on the session with McNair. The aspirin bottle, which had originally held fifty tablets and still contained fourteen, was turned over to the inspector. Toward the end with Cramer, after eight o'clock, Wolfe got a little short with him, because it was past dinnertime. I had formerly thought that his inclination to eat when the time came in spite of hell and homicide was just another detail of his build-up for eccentricity, but it wasn't; he was just hungry. Not to mention that it was Fritz Brenner's cuisine that was waiting for him.

I had made my usual diplomatic advances to Wolfe Wednesday evening after dinner, and again this morning when he got down from the plant rooms, but all I had got was a few assorted rebuffs. I hadn't pressed him much, because I saw it was a case where a little thoughtless enthusiasm might easily project me out of bounds. He was about as touchy as I had ever seen him. A neat and complete murder had had its finale right in his own office, in front of his eyes, less than ten minutes after he had grandly assured the victim that nemesis was verboten on those premises. So I wasn't surprised he wasn't inclined to talk, and I made no effort to sink the spurs in him. All right, I thought, go ahead and be taciturn, you're in it up to your neck now anyway, and you'll have to stop treading water and head for a shore sooner or later.

Inspector Cramer arrived as I inserted the last check in its envelope. Fritz ushered him in. He looked busy but not too harassed; in fact, he tipped me a wink as he sat down, knocked ashes from his cigar, returned it to the corner of his mouth and started off conversationally.

"You know, Wolfe, I was just thinking on the way up here, this time I've got a brand new excuse for coming to see you. I've been here for a lot of different reasons, to try to pry something loose from you, to find out if you were harboring a suspect, to charge you with obstructing justice, and so on and so on, but this is the first time I've ever had the excuse that it's the scene of the crime. In fact, I'm sitting right on it. Wasn't he in this chair? Huh?"

I told Wolfe consolingly, "It's all right, boss. That's just humor. The light touch."

"I hear it." Wolfe was grim. "I have merited even Mr. Cramer's humor. You may exhaust your supply, sir." It had eaten into him even worse than I thought.

"Oh, I've got more." Cramer chuckled. "You know Lanzetta of the D.A.'s office? Hates your epidermis ever since that Fairmount business three years ago? He phoned the Commissioner this morning to warn him there was a chance you were putting over a fast one. The Commissioner told me about it, and I told him you're rapid all right, but not faster than light." Cramer chuckled again, removed his cigar, and slipped his briefcase from the desk onto his knees and unclasped it. He grunted. "Well. Here's this murder. I've got to get back before lunch. You had any inspiration?"

"No." Wolfe remained grim. "I've almost had indigestion." He wiggled a finger at the briefcase. "Have you papers of Mr. McNair's?"

Cramer shook his head. "This is just a lot of junk. There may be one or two items worth something. I've followed up your line, that it's sure to be hooked up with the Frosts, on account of the way McNair started his story to you. The Frosts and this fellow Gebert are being investigated from every angle, up, down, and across. But there's two other bare possibilities I don't like to lose sight of. First, suicide. Second, this woman, this Countess von Rantz-Deichen, that's been after McNair lately. There's a chance—"

"Tommyrot!" Wolfe was explosive. "Excuse me, Mr. Cramer. I am in no mood for fantasy. Get on."

"Okay." Cramer grunted. "Sore, huh? Okay. Fantasy. Notwithstanding, I'll leave two men on the Countess." He was shuffling through the papers from the briefcase. "First for the bottle of aspirin. There were fourteen tablets in it. Twelve of them were perfectly all right. The other two consisted of potassium cyanide tablets, approximately five grains each, with a thin coating of aspirin on the outside, apparently put on as a dry dust and carefully tapped down all over. The chemist says the coating was put on skillfully and thoroughly, so there would have been no cyanide taste for the few seconds before the tablet was swallowed. There was no cyanide smell, the bitter almond smell, in the bottle, but of course it was bone dry."

Wolfe muttered, "And yet you talk of suicide."

"I said bare possibility. Okay, forget it. The preliminary on the autopsy says cyanide of potassium, but they can't tell whether the tablets he took were loaded or not, because that stuff evaporates fast as soon as it's moist. I don't suppose he's worrying much about whether it was one or two tablets, so I'm not either. Next, who put the phonies in with the aspirins? Or anyway, who had a chance to? I've had three good men on that, and they're still on it. The answer so far is, most anyone. For the past week and more McNair has been taking aspirin the way a chicken takes corn. There has been a bottle either on his desk or in a drawer all the time. There's none there now, so when he went out yesterday he must have stuck it in his pocket. Thirty-six are gone from that fifty, and if you figure he took twelve a day that would mean that bottle has been in use three days, and in that time dozens of people have been in and out of his office where the bottle was kept. Of course all the Frosts have, and this Gebert. By the way—" Cramer thumbed to find a paper and stopped at one—"what's a camal . . . camallot doo something in French?"

Wolfe nodded. "*Camelot du roi.* A member of a Parisian royalist political gang."

"Oh. Gebert used to be one. I cabled Paris last night and had one back this morning. Gebert was one of those. He has been around New York now over three years, and we're after him. The preliminary reports I've had are vague. N.V.M.S. Paris says so too."

Wolfe lifted a brow. "N.V.M.S."

I told him, "Police gibberish. No visible means of subsistence. Bonton for bum."

Wolfe sighed. Cramer went on, "We're doing all the routine. Fingerprints on the bottle, on the drawers of McNair's desk and so on. Purchases of potassium cyanide—"

Wolfe stopped him: "I know. Pfui. Not for this murderer, Mr. Cramer. You'll have to do better than routine."

"Sure I will. Or you will." Cramer discarded his cigar and got into his pocket for a new one. "But I'm just telling you. We've discovered one or two things. For instance, yesterday afternoon McNair asked his lawyer if there was any way of finding out whether Dudley Frost, as trustee of the property of his niece, had squandered any of it, and he told the lawyer to do that in a hurry. He said that when Edwin Frost died twenty years ago he cut off his wife without a cent and left everything to his daughter Helen, and made his brother Dudley the trustee under such condition that no one, not even Helen, could demand an accounting of Dudley, and Dudley has never made any accounting. According to McNair. We're on that too. Do you get anywhere with it? If Dudley Frost is short a million or so as trustee, what good does it do him to bump off McNair?"

"I couldn't say. Will you have some beer?"

"No thanks." Cramer got his cigar lit and his teeth

sunk in it. He puffed it just short of a conflagration.
"Well, we may get somewhere on that." He thumbed
at the papers again. "Next is an item that you ought to
find interesting. It happens that McNair's lawyer is a
guy that can be approached, within reason, and after
your tip last night I was after him early this morning.
He gave me that dope on Dudley Frost, and he
admitted McNair made a will yesterday. In fact, after
I explained to him how serious murder is, he let me
see it and copy it. McNair gave it to you straight. He
named you all right."

"Without my consent." Wolfe was pouring beer.
"Mr. McNair was not my client."

Cramer grunted. "He is now. You wouldn't turn
down a dead man, would you? He left a few little
bequests, and the residuary estate to a sister, Isabel
McNair, living in Scotland in a place called Camfirth.
There's a mention of private instructions which he had
given his sister regarding the estate." Cramer turned
a sheet over. "Then you begin to come in. Paragraph
six names you as executor, without remuneration. The
next paragraph reads:

7. To Nero Wolfe, of 918 West 35th Street,
New York City, I bequeath my red leather box
and its contents. I have informed him where it
is to be found, and the contents are to be
considered as his sole property, to be used
by him at his will and his discretion. I direct
that any bill he may render, for a reasonable
amount, for services performed by him in
this connection, shall be considered a just and
proper debt of my estate, which shall be
promptly paid.

"Well." Cramer coughed up smoke. "He's your client now. Or he will be as soon as this is probated."

Wolfe shook his head. "I did not consent. I offer two comments: first, note the appalling caution of the Scotch. When Mr. McNair wrote that he was in a frenzy of desperation, he was engaging me for a job so vital to him that it had to be done right or his spirit could not rest, and yet he inserted, *for a reasonable amount.*" Wolfe sighed. "Obviously, that too was necessary for the repose of his spirit. Second, he has left me a pig in a poke. Where is the red leather box?"

Cramer looked straight at him and said quietly, "I wonder."

Wolfe opened his eyes for suspicion. "What do you mean, sir, by that tone? You wonder what?"

"I wonder where the red box is." Cramer upturned a palm. "Why shouldn't I? It's a hundred to one that what's in it will solve this case." He looked around, and back at Wolfe. "I don't suppose there's any chance it could be right here in this office this minute, for instance in the safe or in one of the drawers of Goodwin's desk." He turned to me. "Mind looking, son?"

I grinned at him. "I don't have to. I've got it in my shoe."

Wolfe said, "Mr. Cramer. I told you last evening how far Mr. McNair got with his tale. Do you mean to say that you have the effrontery to suspect—"

"Now listen." Cramer got louder and firmer. "Don't dump that on me. If I had any effrontery I wouldn't bother to bring it here with me, I'd just borrow some. I've seen your indignant innocence too often. I remind you of the recent occasion when I ventured to suggest that that Fox woman might be hiding in your house. I also remind you that McNair said yesterday in his will—here, I'll read it—*I have informed him where it is to be found*. Get it? Past tense. Sure, I know, you've told me everything McNair said yesterday afternoon, but where did he get that past tense idea before he saw you yesterday? You saw him Tuesday, too—"

"Nonsense. Tuesday was a brief first interview—"

"All right, I've known you to get further than that at a first interview. All right, I know I'm yelling and I'm going to keep on yelling. For once I'll be damned if I'm going to stand in line out on the sidewalk until you decide to open the doors and let us in to see the show. There's no reason in God's world why you shouldn't produce that red box right now and let me have a hand in it. I'm not trying to shove you off from a fee; go to it; I'm for you. But I'm the head of the Homicide Squad of the City of New York, and I'm sick and tired of you playing Godalmighty with any evidence and any clues and any facts and any witnesses—and anything you may happen to think you need for a while—nothing doing! Not this time! Not on your life!"

Wolfe murmured mildly, "Let me know when you're through."

"I'm not going to be through."

"Yes, you are. Sooner than you think. You're playing in bad luck, Mr. Cramer. In demanding that I produce Mr. McNair's red box, you have chosen the worst possible moment for bringing up your reserves and battering down the fort. I confess that I have on occasions quibbled with you and played with double meanings, but you have never known me to tell you a direct and categorical lie. Never, sir. I tell you now that I have never seen Mr. McNair's red box, I have no idea where it is or was, and I have no knowledge whatever of its contents. So please don't yell at me like that."

Cramer was staring, with his jaw loose. Being that he was usually so masterful, he looked so remarkable with his jaw hanging that I thought it wouldn't hurt him any for me to show him how sympathetic I felt, so with my pencil in one hand and the notebook in the other, I raised them both high above my head, opened my mouth and expanded my chest, and executed a major yawn. He saw me, but he didn't throw his cigar at me, because he actually was stunned. Finally he shaped words for Wolfe:

"You mean that straight? You haven't got it?"

"I have not."

"You don't know where it is? You don't know what's in it?"

"I do not."

"Then why did he say yesterday in his will he had told you where it was?"

"He intended to. He was anticipating."

"He never told you?"

Wolfe frowned. "Confound it, sir! Leave redundancy to music and cross-examinations. I am not playing you a tune, and I don't like to be badgered."

Ash fell from Cramer's cigar to the rug. He paid no attention to it. He muttered, "I'll be damned," and sank back in his chair. I considered it a good spot for another yawn, but almost got startled into lockjaw in the middle of it when Cramer suddenly exploded at me savagely: "For God's sake fall in it, you clown!"

I expostulated with him: "Good heavens, Inspector, a fellow can't help it if he has to—"

"Shut up!" He sat and looked silly. That was about to get monotonous when he went plaintive with Wolfe: "This is a healthy smack, all right. I didn't know you had me buffaloed as bad as that. I've got so used to you having rabbits in your hat that I was taking two things

for granted as a sure bet. First, that the answer to
this case is in that red box. Second, that you had it or
knew where it was. Now you tell me number two is
out. All right, I believe you. How about number one?"

Wolfe nodded. "I would agree. A sure bet, I think,
that if we had the contents of the red box we would
know who tried to kill Mr. McNair a week ago
Monday, and who did kill him yesterday." Wolfe
compressed his lips a moment and then added, "Killed
him here. In my office. In my presence."

"Yeah. Sure." Cramer poked his cigar in the tray.
"For you that's what makes it a crime instead of a
case." He turned abruptly to me: "Would you get my
office on the phone?"

I swiveled to my desk and pulled the instrument
across and dialed. I got the number, and the extension, and asked them to hold it, and vacated my chair.
Cramer went over and got it.

"Burke? Cramer. Got a pad? Put this down: red
leather box, don't know size or weight or old or new.
Probably not very big, because the chances are it
contains only papers, documents. It belonged to Boyden McNair. One: Give ten men copies of McNair's
photograph and send them to all the safe deposit
vaults in town. Find any safe deposit box he had, and
as soon as it's found get a court order to open it. Send
Haskins to that bird at the Midtown National that's so
damn cocky. Two: Phone the men that are going
through McNair's apartment and his place of business
and tell them about the box and the one who finds it
can have a day off. Three: Start all over again with
McNair's friends and acquaintances and ask if they
ever saw McNair have such a box and when and where
and what does it look like. Ask Collinger, McNair's
lawyer, too. I was so damn sure—I didn't ask him

that. Four: Send another cable to Scotland and tell them to ask McNair's sister about the box. Did an answer come to the one you sent this morning? . . . No, hardly time. Got it? . . . Good. Start it quick. I'll be down pretty soon."

He rang off. Wolfe murmured. "Ten men . . . a hundred . . . a thousand . . . Really, Mr. Cramer, with such an outfit as that, you should catch at least ten culprits for every crime committed."

"Yeah. We do." Cramer looked around. "Oh, I guess I left my hat in the hall. I'll let you know when we find the box, since it's your property. I may look into it first, just to make sure there's no bombs in it. I'd hate like the devil to see Goodwin here get hurt. You going to do any exploring?"

Wolfe shook his head. "With your army of terriers scratching at every hole? There would be no room. I'm sorry, sir, for your disappointment here; if I knew where the red box was you would be the first to hear of it. I trust that we are still brothers-in-arms? That is to say, in this present affair?"

"Absolutely. Pals."

"Good. Then I'll make one little suggestion. See that the Frosts, all of them, are acquainted with the terms of Mr. McNair's will immediately. You needn't bother about Mr. Gebert; I surmise that if the Frosts know it he soon will. You are in a better position than I am to do this without trumpets."

"Right. Anything else?"

"That's all. Except that if you do find the box I wouldn't advise you to tack its contents to your bulletin board. I imagine they will need to be handled with restraint and delicacy. The person who put those coated poison tablets in the bottle of aspirin is fairly ingenious."

"Uh-huh. Anything else?"

"Just better luck elsewhere than you have had here."

"Thanks. I'll need *that* all right."

He departed.

Wolfe rang for beer. I went to the kitchen for a glass of milk and came back to the office with it and stood by the window and started sipping. A glance at Wolfe had showed me that things were at a standstill, because he was sitting up with his eyes open, turning the pages of a Richardt folder which had come in the morning mail. I shrugged negligently. After I had finished the milk I sat at my desk and sealed the envelopes containing checks, and stamped them, went to the hall for my hat and moseyed out and down to the corner to drop them in a mailbox. When I got back again Wolfe was still having recess; he had taken a *laeliocattleya luminosa aurea* from the vase on his desk and was lifting the anthers to look at the pollinia with his glass. But at least he hadn't started on the atlas. I sat down and observed:

"It's a nice balmy spring day outdoors. April second. McNair's mourning day. You said yesterday it was ghoulish. Now he's a ghoul himself."

Wolfe muttered indifferently. "He is not a ghoul."

"Then he's inert matter."

"He is not inert matter. Unless he has been embalmed with uncommon thoroughness. The activity of decomposition is tremendous."

"All right, then he's a banquet. Anything you say. Might I inquire, have you turned the case over to Inspector Cramer? Should I go down and ask him for instructions?"

No response. I waited a decent interval, then went on, "Take this red leather box, for instance. Say

Cramer finds it and opens it and learns all the things it would be fun to know, and hitches up his horse and buggy and goes and gets the murderer, *with* evidence. There would go the first half of your fee from Llewellyn. The second half is already gone, since McNair is dead and of course that heiress won't work there any more. It begins to look as if you not only had the discomfort of seeing McNair die right in front of you, you're not even going to be able to send anyone a bill for it. You've taught me to be tough in money matters. Do you realize that Doc Vollmer will charge five bucks for the call he made here yesterday? You could have him send the bill to McNair's estate, but you'd have the trouble and expense of handling it anyhow, since you're the executor without remuneration. And by the way, what about that executor stuff? Aren't you supposed to bustle around and do something?"

No response.

I said, "And besides, Cramer hasn't really got any right to the red box at all. Legally it's yours. But if he gets hold of it he'll plunder it, don't think he won't. Then of course you could have your lawyer write him a letter—"

"Shut up, Archie." Wolfe put down the glass. "You are talking twaddle. Or perhaps you aren't; do you mean business? Would you go out with your pistol and shoot all the men in Mr. Cramer's army? I see no other way to stop their search. And then find the red box yourself?"

I grinned at him condescendingly. "I wouldn't do that, because I wouldn't have to. If I was the kind of man you are, I would just sit calmly in my chair with my eyes shut, and use psychology on it. Like you did with Paul Chapin, remember? First I would decide what the psychology of McNair was like, covering every point. Then I would say to myself, if my psychology was like that, and if I had a very important article like a red box to hide, where would I hide it? Then I would say to someone else, Archie, please go at once to such and such a place and get the red box and bring it here. That way you would get hold of it before any of Cramer's men—"

"That will do." Wolfe was positive but unperturbed. "I'll tolerate the goad, Archie, only when it is needed. In the present case I don't need that, I need facts; but I refuse to waste your energies and mine in assembling a collection of them which may be completely useless once the red box is found. As for finding it, we're obviously out of that, with Cramer's terriers at every hole." He got a little acid. "I choose to remind you of what my program contemplated yesterday: supervising the cooking of a goose. Not watching a man die of poison. And yours for this morning: driving to Mr. Salzenbach's place at Garfield for a freshly butchered kid. Not pestering me with inanities. And for this afternoon—yes, Fritz?"

Fritz approached. "Mr. Llewellyn Frost to see you."

"The devil." Wolfe sighed. "Nothing can be done now. Archie, if you—no. After all, he's our client. Show him in."

Chapter 10

Apparently Llewellyn hadn't come this time, as he had the day before, to pull fat men out of chairs. Nor did he have his lawyer along. He looked a little squashed, and amenable, and his necktie was crooked. He told both of us good morning as if he was counting on our agreeing with him and was in need of that support, and even thanked Wolfe for inviting him to sit down. Then he sat and glanced from one to the other of us as if it was an open question whether he could remember what it was he had come for.

Wolfe said, "You've had a shock, Mr. Frost. So have I: Mr. McNair sat in the chair you're in now when he swallowed the poison."

Lew Frost nodded. "I know. He died right here."

"He did indeed. They say that three grains have been known to kill a man in thirty seconds. Mr. McNair took five, or ten. He had convulsions almost immediately, and died within a minute. I offer you condolence. Though you and he were not on the best of terms, still you had known him long. Hadn't you?"

Llewellyn nodded again. "I had known him about twelve years. We . . . we weren't exactly on bad terms . . ." He halted, and considered. "Well, I suppose we were. Not personal, though. I mean, I don't think we disliked each other. The fact is, it was nothing but a misunderstanding. I've learned only this morning that I was wrong in the chief thing I had against him. I thought he wanted my cousin to marry that fellow Gebert, and now I've learned that he didn't at all. He was dead against it." Llewellyn considered again. "That . . . that made me think . . . I mean, I was all wrong about this. You see, when I came to see you Monday . . . and last week too . . . I thought I knew some things. I didn't say anything about it to you, or Mr. Goodwin here when I was telling him, because I knew I was prejudiced. I didn't want to accuse anyone. I just wanted you to find out. And I want to say . . . I want to apologize. My cousin has told me she did see that box of candy, and how and where. It would have been better if she had told you all about it, I can see that. She can too. But the hell of it was I had my mind on another . . . another . . . I mean to say, I thought I knew something . . . ."

"I understand, sir." Wolfe sounded impatient. "You knew that Molly Lauck was enamored of Mr. Perren Gebert. You knew that Mr. Gebert wanted to marry your cousin Helen, and you thought that Mr. McNair favored that idea. You were more than ready to suspect that the genesis of the poisoned candy was that eroto-matrimonial tangle, since you were vitally concerned in it because you wished to marry your cousin yourself."

Llewellyn stared at him. "Where did you get that idea?" His face began to get red, and he sputtered, "Me marry her? You're crazy! What kind of a damn fool—"

"Please don't do that." Wolfe wiggled a finger at him. "You should know that detectives do sometimes detect—at least some of them do. I don't say that you intended to marry your cousin, merely that you wanted to. I knew that early in our conversation last Monday afternoon, when you told me that she is your ortho-cousin. There was no reason why so abstruse and unusual a term should have been in the forefront of your mind, as it obviously was, unless you had been so preoccupied with the idea of marrying your cousin, and so concerned as to the custom and propriety of marriage between first cousins, that you had gone into it exhaustively. It was evident that canon law and the Levitical decrees had not been enough for you; you had even ventured into anthropology. Or possibly that had not been enough for someone else—herself, her mother, your father . . ."

Lew Frost blurted, his face still red, "You didn't detect that. She told you. Yesterday . . . did she tell you?"

Wolfe shook his head. "No, sir. I did detect it. Among other things. It wouldn't surprise me to know that when you called here three days ago you were fairly well convinced that either Mr. McNair or Mr. Gebert had killed Molly Lauck. Certainly you were in no condition to discriminate between nonsense and likelihood."

"I know I wasn't. But I wasn't convinced of . . . anything." Llewellyn chewed at his lip. "Now, of course, I'm up a tree. This McNair business is terrible. The newspapers have started it up all over again. The police have been after us this morning—us Frosts—as if we . . . as if we knew something about it. And of course Helen is all cut up. She wanted to go to see McNair's body this morning, and had to be told that she couldn't because they were doing a post mortem, and that was pleasant. Then she wanted to come to see you, and finally I drove her down here. I came in first because I didn't know who might be in here. She's out front in my car. May I bring her in?"

Wolfe grimaced. "There's nothing I can do for her, at this moment. I suspect she's in no condition—"

"She wants to see you."

Wolfe lifted his shoulders an inch, and dropped them. "Get her."

Lew Frost rose and strode out. I went along to manipulate the door. Parked at the curb was a gray coupe, and from it emerged Helen Frost. Llewellyn escorted her up the stoop and into the hall, and I must say she didn't bear much resemblance to a goddess. Her eyes were puffed up and her nose was blotchy and she looked sick. Her ortho-cousin led her on to the office, and I followed them in. She gave Wolfe a nod and seated herself in the dunce's chair, then looked at Llewellyn, at me, and at Wolfe, as if she wasn't sure she knew us.

She looked at the floor, and up again. "It was right here," she said in a dead tone. "Wasn't it? Right here."

Wolfe nodded. "Yes, Miss Frost. But if that is what you came here for, to shudder at the spot where your best friend died, that won't help us any." He straightened up a little. "This is a detective bureau, not a nursery for morbidity. Yes, he died here. He swallowed the poison sitting in that chair; he staggered to his feet and tried to keep himself upright by putting his fists on my desk; he collapsed to the floor in a convulsion and died; if he were still there you could reach down and touch him without moving from your chair."

Helen was staring at him and not breathing;

Llewellyn protested: "For God's sake, Wolfe, do you think—"

Wolfe showed him a palm. "I think I had to sit here and watch Mr. McNair being murdered in my office. —Archie. Your notebook, please. Yesterday I told Miss Frost it was time something was said to her. What did I say then? Read it."

I got the book and flipped back the pages and found it and read it out:

> . . . In your conceit, you are assuming, for your youth and inexperience, a terrific responsibility. Molly Lauck died nine days ago, probably through bungling of someone's effort to kill another person. During all that time you have possessed knowledge which, handled with competence and dispatch, might do something much more important than wreak vengeance; it might save a life, and it is even possible that the life would be one worth saving. What do you—

"That will do." Wolfe turned to her. "That, mademoiselle, was a courteous and reasonable appeal. I do not often appeal to anyone like that; I am too conceited. I did appeal to you, without success. If it is painful to you to be reminded that your best friend died yesterday, in agony, on the spot now occupied by your chair, do you think it was agreeable to me to sit here and watch him do it?" He shifted abruptly to Llewellyn. "And you, sir, who engaged me to solve a problem and then proceeded to hamper me as soon as I made the first step—now you are quick on the trigger to resent it if I do not show tenderness and consideration for your cousin's remorse and grief. I know none because I have none. If I offer anything for sale in this office that is worth buying, it certainly is not a warm heart and maudlin sympathy for the distress of spoiled obtuse children." He turned to Helen. "Yesterday, in your pride, you asked for nothing and offered nothing. What information you gave was forced from you by a threat. What did you come for today? What do you want?"

Llewellyn had risen and moved to her chair. He was holding himself in. "Come on, Helen," he entreated her. "Come on, get out of here . . ."

She reached up and touched his sleeve, and shook her head without looking at him. "Sit down, Lew," she told him. "Please. I deserve it." There was a spot of color on the cheek I could see.

"No. Come on."

She shook her head again. "I'm going to stay."

"I'm not." He shot out his chin in Wolfe's direction. "Look here, I apologized to you. All right, I owed you that. But now I want to say . . . that thing I signed here Tuesday . . . I'm giving you notice I'm done with that. I'm not paying you ten thousand dollars, because I haven't got it and you haven't earned it. I can pay a reasonable amount whenever you send a bill. The deal's off."

Wolfe nodded and murmured, "I expected that, of course. The suspicions you hired me to substantiate have evaporated. The threat of molestation of your cousin, caused by her admission that she had seen the box of candy, no longer exists. Half of your purpose is accomplished, since your cousin will not work any more—at least, not at Mr. McNair's. As for the other half, to continue the investigation of the murder of Molly Lauck would mean of necessity an inquiry into Mr. McNair's death also, and that might easily result in something highly distasteful to a Frost. That's the logic of it, for you, perfectly correct; and if I expected to collect even a fair fraction of my fee I shall probably have to sue you for it." He sighed, and leaned back. "And you stampeded me to 52nd Street with that confounded letter. Good day, sir. I don't blame you; but I shall certainly send you a bill for ten thousand dollars. I know what you are thinking: that you won't be sued because I won't go to a courtroom to testify. You are correct; but I shall certainly send you a bill."

"Go ahead. Come on, Helen."

She didn't budge. She said quietly, "Sit down, Lew."

"What for? Come on! Did you hear what he said about distasteful to a Frost? Don't you see it's him that has started the police after us as if we were all a bunch of murderers? And that he started it on account of something that McNair said to him yesterday before—before it happened? Just as Dad said, and Aunt Callie too? Do you wonder they wouldn't let you come down here unless I came along? I'm not saying McNair told him any lies, I'm just saying—"

"Lew! Stop it!" She wasn't loud, but determined. She put a hand on his sleeve again. "Listen, Lew. You know very well that all the misunderstandings we've ever had have been about Uncle Boyd. Don't you think we might stop having them, now that he's dead? I told Mr. Wolfe yesterday . . . he . . . he was the finest man I have ever known. . . . I don't expect you to agree with that . . . but it's true. I know he didn't like you, and I honestly thought that was the only thing he was wrong about." She stood up and put a hand on each of his arms. "You're a fine man, too, Lew. You have lots of fine things in you. But I loved Uncle Boyd." She shut her lips tight and nodded her head up and down several times. Finally she swallowed, and went on, "He was a grand person . . . he was. He gave me what common sense I've got, and it was him that kept me from being just a complete silly fool. . . ." She tightened her lips again, and then again went on, "He always used to say . . . whenever I . . . I . . ."

She turned away abruptly and sat down, lowered her face into her palms, and began to cry.

Llewellyn started at her: "Now, Helen, for God's sake, I know how you feel—"

I growled at him, "Sit down and shut up. Can it!"

He was going to keep on comforting her. I bounced up and grabbed his shoulder and whirled him. "You're not a client here any more. Don't argue. Didn't I tell you scenes make me nervous?" I left him glaring and went to the cabinet and got a shot of brandy and a glass of cold water, and went and stood alongside Helen Frost's chair. Pretty soon she got quieter, and then fished a handkerchief out of her bag and began dabbing. I waited until she could see to tell her:

"Brandy. 1890 Guarnier. Shall I put water in it?"

She shook her head and reached for it and gulped it down nicely. I offered her the water and she took a swallow of that. Then she looked at Nero Wolfe and said, "You'll have to excuse me. I'm not asking for any tenderness, but you'll have to excuse me." She looked at her cousin. "I'm not going to talk to you about Uncle Boyd any more. It doesn't do any good, does it? It's foolish." She dabbed at her eyes again, took in a long trembling breath and let it out, and turned back to Wolfe.

She said, "I don't care what Uncle Boyd told you about us Frosts. It couldn't have been anything very terrible, because he wouldn't tell lies. I don't care if you're working with the police, either. There couldn't be anything more . . . more distasteful to a Frost than what has happened. Anyway, the police never found out anything at all about Molly Lauck, and you did."

Her tears had dried. She went on, "I'm sorry I didn't tell you . . . of course I'm sorry. I thought I was keeping a secret for Uncle Boyd, but I'm sorry anyway. I only wish there was anything else I could tell you . . . but anyway . . . I can do this. This is the only time I've been truly glad I have lots of money. I'll pay you anything to find out who killed Uncle Boyd. Anything, and . . . and you won't have to sue me for it."

I got her glass and went to the cabinet to get her some more brandy. I grinned at the bottle as I poured, reflecting that this case was turning out to be just one damned client after another.

Chapter 11

Llewellyn was expostulating. "But, Helen, it's a police job. Not that he could be any more offensive than the police are, but it's a police job and let them do it. Anyway, Dad and Aunt Callie will be sore as the devil, you know they will, you know how they went after me when I . . . Tuesday."

Helen said, "I don't care if they're sore. It's not their money, it's mine. I'm doing this. Of course I won't be of age until next month—does that matter, Mr. Wolfe? Is that all right?"

"Quite all right."

"Will you do it?"

"Will I accept your commission? In spite of my experience with another Frost as a client, yes."

She turned to her ortho-cousin. "You do as you please, Lew. Go on home and tell them if you want to. But I . . . I'd like to have you . . ."

He was frowning at her. "Are you set on this?"

"Yes. Good and set."

"Okay." He settled back in his chair. "I stick here. I'm for the Frosts, but you're the first one on the list. You're . . . Oh, nothing." He flushed a little. "Go to it."

"Thank you, Lew." She turned to Wolfe. "I suppose you want me to sign something?"

Wolfe shook his head. "That won't be necessary." He had leaned back and his eyes were half closed. "My charge will be adequate, but not exorbitant. I shan't attempt to make you pay for your cousin's volatility. But one thing must be clearly understood. You are engaging me for this job because of your affection and esteem for Mr. McNair and your desire that his murderer should be discovered and punished. You are at present under the spell of powerful emotions. Are you sure that tomorrow or next week you will still want this thing done? Do you want the murderer caught and tried and convicted and executed if it should happen to be, for instance, your cousin, your uncle, your mother—or Mr. Perren Gebert?"

"But that . . . that's ridiculous . . ."

"Maybe, but it remains a question to be answered. Do you want to pay me for catching the murderer, no matter who it is?"

She gazed at him, and said finally, "Yes. Whoever killed Uncle Boyd—yes, I do."

"You won't go back on that?"

"No."

"Good for you. I believe you. I'll try the job for you. Now I want to ask you some questions, but it is possible that your reply to the first one will make others unnecessary. When did you last see Mr. Mc-Nair's red leather box?"

"His what?" She frowned. "Red leather box?"

"That's it."

"Never. I never did see it. I didn't know he had one."

"Indeed. —You, sir, are you answering questions?"

Lew Frost said, "I guess I am. Sure. But not about a red leather box. I've never seen it."

Wolfe sighed. "Then I'm afraid we'll have to go on. I may as well tell you, Miss Frost, that Mr. McNair foresaw—at least, feared—what was waiting for him. While you were here yesterday he was at his lawyer's executing his will. He left his property to his sister Isabel, who lives in Scotland. He named me executor of his estate, and bequeathed me his red leather box and its contents. He called here to ask me to accept the trust and the legacy."

"He named you executor?" Llewellyn was gazing at him incredulously. "Why, he didn't know you. Day before yesterday he didn't even want to talk to you. . . ."

"Just so. That shows the extent of his desperation. But it is evident that the red box holds the secret of his death. As a matter of fact, Miss Frost, I was glad to see you here today. I hoped for something from you—a description of the box, if nothing more."

She shook her head. "I never saw it. I didn't know . . . but I don't understand . . . if he wanted you to have it, why didn't he tell you yesterday . . ."

"He intended to. He didn't get that far. His last words—his last futile struggle against his fate—were an effort to tell me where the red box is. I should inform you: Inspector Cramer has a copy of the will, and at this moment scores of police are searching for the box, so if you or your cousin can give me any hint there is no time to lose. It is desirable for me to get the box first. Not to protect the murderer, but I have my own way of doing things—and the police have no client but the electric chair."

Llewellyn said, "But you say he left it to you, it's your property . . ."

"Murder evidence is no one's property, once the law touches it. No, if Mr. Cramer finds it, the best we can hope for is the role of privileged spectator. So turn your minds back, both of you. Look back at the days, weeks, months, years. Resurrect, if you can, some remark of Mr. McNair's, some forgotten gesture, perhaps of irritation or embarrassment at being interrupted, perhaps the hurried closing of a drawer, or the unintentional disclosure of a hiding-place. A remark by someone else who may have had knowledge of it. Some action of Mr. McNair's, unique or habitual, at the time unexplained . . ."

Llewellyn was slowly shaking his head. Helen said, "Nothing. I'll try to think, but I'm sure there's nothing I can remember like that."

"That's too bad. Keep trying. Of course the police are ransacking his apartment and his place of business. Had he preempted any other spot of earth or water? A garage, a boat, a place in the country?"

Llewellyn was looking at his cousin with inquiring brows. She nodded. "Yes. Glennanne. A little cottage with a few acres of land up near Brewster."

"Glennanne?"

"Yes. His wife's name was Anne and his daughter's was Glenna."

"Did he own it?"

"Yes. He bought it about six years ago."

"What and where is Brewster?"

"It's a little village about fifty miles north of New York."

"Indeed." Wolfe sat up. "Archie. Get Saul, Orrie, Johnny and Fred here immediately. If they cannot all be prompt, send the first two to search Glennanne, and let the others join them when they come. The

cottage, first, swiftly and thoroughly, then the grounds.
Is there a garden, Miss Frost? Tools?"

She nodded. "He . . . he grew some flowers."

"Good. They can take the sedan. Get extra things
for digging if they need them, and they should have
lights to continue after dark. The cottage is most
likely—a hole in the wall, a loose floor-board. Get
them. Wait. First your notebook; take this and type it
on a letterhead:

I hereby authorize the bearer, Saul Panzer,
to take complete charge of the house and grounds
of Glennanne, property of Boyden McNair,
deceased, and to undertake certain activities
there in accordance with my instructions.

"Leave room for my signature above the designa-
tion, 'Executor of the estate of Boyden McNair.' I
have not yet qualified, but we can tie the red tape
later." He nodded me off. "Now, Miss Frost, perhaps
you can tell me—"

I moved to the phone and started dialing. I got
Saul and Orrie right off the bat, and they said they
would come pronto. Fred Durkin was out, but his wife
said she knew where to get hold of him and would have
him call in ten minutes. Johnny Keems, when he
wasn't on a job for us, had formed the habit of phoning
every day at nine to give me his program, and had told
me that morning that he was still on a watchdog
assignment for Del Pritchard, so I tried that office.
They had Johnny booked for the day, but before I
finished typing the authorization for Saul, Fred called,
so I had three anyhow.

Saul Panzer arrived first and Wolfe had Fritz show
him into the office. He came in with his hat in his hand,

shot me a wink, asked Wolfe how he did, got himself an everlasting blueprint of the two Frosts in one quick glance, and pointed his big nose inquiringly at Wolfe.

Wolfe gave him the dope and told him what he was supposed to find. Helen Frost told him how to get to Glennanne from the village of Brewster. I handed him the signed authorization and forty bucks for expenses, and he pulled out his old brown wallet and deposited them in it with care. Wolfe told him to get the car from the garage and wait in front to pick up Fred and Orrie as they arrived.

Saul nodded. "Yes, sir. If I find the box, do I leave Fred or Orrie at the place when I come away?"

"Yes. Until notified. Fred."

"If any strangers offer to help me look, do I let them?"

Wolfe frowned. "I was about to mention that. Surely there can be no objection if we show a preference for law and order. With all courtesy, you can ask to see a search warrant."

"Is there something hot in the box?" Saul blushed. "I mean, stolen property?"

"No. It is legally mine. Defend it."

"Right." Saul went. I reflected that if he ever got his mitts on the box I wouldn't like to be the guy to try to take it away from him, small as he was. He didn't think any more of Nero Wolfe than I do of my patrician nose and big brown intelligent eyes.

Wolfe had pushed the button for Fritz, the long push, not the two shorts for beer. Fritz came, and stood.

Wolfe frowned at him. "Can you stretch lunch for us? Two guests?"

"No," Llewellyn broke in, "really—we'll have to get back—I promised Dad and Aunt Callie—"

"You can phone them. I would advise Miss Frost to stay. At any moment we may hear that the box has been found, and that would mean a crisis. And to provide against the possibility that it will not be found, I shall need a great deal of information. Miss Frost?"

She nodded. "I'll stay. I'm not hungry. I'll stay. You'll stay with me, Lew?"

He grumbled something at her, but stayed put. Wolfe told Fritz:

"The fricandeau should be ample. Add lettuce to the salad if the endive is short, and of course increase the oil. Chill a bottle of the '28 Marcobrunner. As soon as you are ready." He wiggled Fritz away with a finger, and settled back in his chair. "Now, Miss Frost. We are engaged in a joint enterprise. I need facts. I am going to ask you a lot of foolish questions. If one of them turns out to be wise or clever you will not know it, but let us hope that I will. Please do not waste time in expostulation. If I ask you whether your mother has recently sent you to the corner druggist for potassium cyanide tablets, just say no, and listen to the next one. I once solved a difficult case by learning from a young woman, after questioning her for five hours, that she had been handed a newspaper with a piece cut out. Your inalienable rights of privacy are temporarily suspended. Is that understood?"

"Yes." She looked straight at him. "I don't care. Of course I know you're clever, I want you to be. I know how easily you caught me in a lie Tuesday morning. But you ought to know . . . you can't catch me in one now, because I haven't anything to lie about. I don't see how anything I know can help you . . ."

"Possibly it can't. We can only try. Let us first straighten out the present a little, and work back. I

should inform you: Mr. McNair did tell me a few things
yesterday before he was interrupted. I have a little
background to start with. Now—for instance—what
did Mr. Gebert mean yesterday when he said you were
almost his fiancée?"

She compressed her lips, but then spoke right to it:
"He didn't mean anything, really. He has—several
times he has asked me to marry him."

"Have you encouraged him?"

"No."

"Has anyone?"

"Why . . . who could?"

"Lots of people. Your maid, the pastor of his
church, a member of your family—has anyone?"

She said, after a pause, "No."

"You said you had nothing to lie about."

"But I—" She stopped, and tried to smile at him. It
was then that I began to think she was a pretty good
kid, when I saw her try to smile to show that she
wasn't meaning to cheat on him. She went on, "This is
so very personal . . . I don't see how . . ."

Wolfe wiggled a finger at her. "We are proceeding
on this theory, that in any event whatever, we wish to
discover the murderer of Mr. McNair. Even—merely
for instance—if it should mean dragging your mother
into a courtroom to testify against someone she likes.
If that is our aim, you must leave the method of
pursuit to me; and I beg you, don't balk and shy at
every little pebble. Who encouraged Mr. Gebert?"

"I won't do it again," she promised. "No one really
encouraged him. I've known him all my life, and
mother knew him before I was born. Mother and
father knew him. He has always been . . . attentive,
and amusing, and in some ways he is interesting and I
like him. In other ways I dislike him extremely.

Mother has told me I should control my dislike on account of his good points, and she said that since he was such an old friend I shouldn't wound his feelings by cutting him off, that it wouldn't hurt to let him think he was still in the field as long as I hadn't decided."

"You agreed to that?"

"Well, I . . . I didn't fight it. My mother is very persuasive."

"What was the attitude of your uncle? Mr. Dudley Frost. The trustee of your property."

"Oh, I never discussed things like that with him. But I know what it would have been. He didn't like Perren."

"And Mr. McNair?"

"He disliked Perren more than I did. Outwardly they were friends, but . . . anyway, Uncle Boyd wasn't two-faced. Shall I tell you . . ."

"By all means."

"Well, one day about a year ago Uncle Boyd sent for me to go upstairs to his office, and when I went in Perren was there. Uncle Boyd was standing up and looking white and determined. I asked him what was the matter, and he said he only wanted to tell me, in Perrens's presence, that any influence his friendship and affection might have on me was unalterably opposed to my marriage with Perren. He said it very . . . formally, and that wasn't like him. He didn't ask me to promise or anything. He just said that and then told me to go."

"And in spite of that, Mr. Gebert has persisted with his courtship."

"Of course he has. Why wouldn't he? Lots of men have. I'm so rich it's worth quite an effort."

"Dear me." Wolfe's eyes flickered open at her and

half shut again. "As cynical as that about it? But a brave cynicism which is of course proper. Nothing is more admirable than the fortitude with which millionaires tolerate the disadvantages of their wealth. What is Mr. Gebert's profession?"

"He hasn't any. That's one of the things I don't like about him. He doesn't do anything."

"Has he an income?"

"I don't know. Really, I don't know a thing about it. I suppose he has . . . I've heard him make vague remarks. He lives at the Chesebrough, and he drives a car."

"I know. Mr. Goodwin informed me he drove it here yesterday. At all events, a man of courage. You knew him in Europe; what did he do there?"

"No more than here, as far as I remember—of course I was young then. He was wounded in the war, and afterwards came to visit us in Spain—that is, my mother, I was only two years old—and he went to Egypt with us a little later, but when we went on to the Orient he went back—"

"One moment, please." Wolfe was frowning. "Let us tidy up the chronology. There seems to have been quite a party in Spain; almost Mr. McNair's last words were that he had gone to Spain with his baby daughter. We'll start when your life started. You were born, you told me yesterday, in Paris—on May 7th, 1915. Your father was already in the war, as a member of the British Aviation Corps, and he was killed when you were a few months old. When did your mother take you to Spain?"

"Early in 1916. She was afraid to stay in Paris, on account of the war. We went first to Barcelona and then to Cartagena. A little later Uncle Boyd and Glenna came down and joined us there. He had no

money and his health was bad, and mother . . .
helped him. I think Perren came, not long after, partly
because Uncle Boyd was there—they had both been
friends of my father's. Then in 1917 Glenna died, and
soon after that Uncle Boyd went back to Scotland, and
mother took me to Egypt because they were afraid of
a revolution or something in Spain, and Perren went
with us."

"Good. I own a house in Egypt which I haven't seen
for twenty years. It has Rhages and Veramine tiles on
the doorway. How long were you in Egypt?"

"About two years. In 1919, when I was four years
old—of course mother has told me all this—three
English people were killed in a riot in Cairo, and
mother decided to leave. Perren went back to France.
Mother and I went to Bombay, and later to Bali and
Japan and Hawaii. My uncle, who was the trustee of
my property, kept insisting that I should have an
American education, and finally, in 1924—I was nine
years old then—we left Hawaii and came to New
York. It was from that time on, really, that I knew
Uncle Boyd, because of course I didn't remember him
from Spain, since I had been only two years old."

"He had his business in New York when you got
here?"

"No. He has told me—he started designing for
Wilmerding in London and was very successful and
became a partner, and then he decided New York was
better and came over here in 1925 and went in for
himself. Of course he looked mother up first thing, and
she was a little help to him on account of the people
she knew, but he would have gone to the top anyway
because he had great ability. He was very talented.
Paris and London were beginning to copy him. You
would never have thought, just being with him, talk-

ing with him . . . you would never have thought . . ."

She faltered, and stopped. Wolfe began to murmur something at her to steady her, but an interruption saved him the trouble. Fritz appeared to announce lunch. Wolfe pushed back his chair:

"Your coat will be all right here, Miss Frost. Your hat? But permit me to insist, as a favor; to eat with a hat on, except in a railroad station, is barbarous. Thank you. Restaurant? I know nothing of restaurants; short of compulsion, I would not eat in one were Vatel himself the chef."

Then, after we were seated at the table, when Fritz came to pass the relish platter, Wolfe performed the introduction according to his custom with guests who had not tasted that cooking before:

"Miss Frost, Mr. Frost, this is Mr. Brenner."

Also according to custom, there was no shop talk during the meal. Llewellyn was fidgety, but he ate; and the fact appeared to be that our new client was hungry as the devil. Probably she had had no breakfast. Anyway, she gave the fricandeau a play which made Wolfe regard her with open approval. He carried the burden of the conversation, chiefly about Egypt, tiles, the uses of a camel's double lip, and the theory that England's colonizing genius was due to her repulsive climate, on account of which Britons with any sense and willpower invariably decided to go somewhere else to work. It was two-thirty when the salad was finished, so we went back to the office and had Fritz serve coffee there.

Helen Frost telephoned her mother. Apparently there was considerable parental protest from the other end of the wire, for Helen sounded first persuasive, then irritated, and finally fairly sassy. During that performance Llewellyn sat and scowled at her, and I couldn't tell whether the scowl was for her or the opposition. It had no effect on our client either way, for she was sitting at my desk and didn't see it.

Wolfe started in on her again, resuming the Perren Gebert tune, but for the first half hour or so it was spotty because the telephone kept interrupting. Johnny Keems called to say that he could leave the Pritchard job if we needed him, and I told him that we'd manage to struggle along somehow. Dudley Frost phoned to give his son hell, and Llewellyn took it calmly and announced that his cousin Helen needed him where he was, whereupon she kept a straight face but I smothered a snicker. Next came a ring from Fred Durkin, to say that they had arrived and taken possession of Glennanne, finding no one there, and had begun operations; the phone at the cottage was out of order, so Saul had sent Fred to the village to make that report. A man named Collinger phoned and insisted on speaking to Wolfe, and I listened in and took it down as usual; he was Boyden McNair's lawyer, and wanted to know if Wolfe could call at his office right away for a conference regarding the will, and of course the bare idea set Wolfe's digestion back at least ten minutes. It was arranged that Collinger would come to 35th Street the following morning. Then, a little after three o'clock, Inspector Cramer got us, and reported that his army was making uniform progress on all fronts: namely, none. No red box and no information about it; no hide or hair of motive anywhere; nothing among McNair's papers that could be stretched to imply murder; no line on a buyer of potassium cyanide; no anything.

Cramer sounded a little weary. "Here's a funny item, too," he said in a wounded tone, "we can't find the young Frosts anywhere. Your client, Lew, isn't at his home or his office in the Portland Theatre or anywhere else, and Helen, the daughter, isn't around either. Her mother says she went out around eleven o'clock, but she doesn't know where, and I've learned that Helen was closer to McNair than anyone else, very close friends, so she's our best chance on the red box. Then what's she doing running around town, with McNair just croaked? There's just a chance that something's got too hot for them and they've faded. Lew was up at the Frost apartment on 65th Street and they went out together. We're trying to trail—"

"Mr. Cramer. Please. I've mumbled at you twice. Miss Helen Frost and Mr. Llewellyn Frost are in my office; I'm conversing with them. They had lunch—"

"Huh? They're there now?"

"Yes. They got here this morning shortly after you left."

"I'll be damned." Cramer shrilled a little. "What are you trying to do, lick off some cream for yourself? I want to see them. Ask them to come down—or wait, let me talk to her. Put her on."

"Now, Mr. Cramer." Wolfe cleared his throat. "I do not lick cream; and this man and woman came to see me unannounced and unexpected. I am perfectly willing that you should talk with her, but there is no point—"

"What do you mean, willing? What's that, humor? Why the devil shouldn't you be willing?"

"I should. But it is appropriate to mention it, since Miss Frost is my client, and is therefore under my—"

"Your client? Since when?" Cramer was boiling. "What kind of a shenanigan is this? You told me Lew Frost hired you!"

"So he did. But that—er—we have changed that. I have—speaking as a horse—I have changed riders in the middle of the stream. I am working for Miss Frost. I was about to say there is no point in a duplication of effort. She has had a bad shock and is under a strain. You may question her if you wish, but I have done so and am not through with her, and there is little likelihood that her interests will conflict with yours in the end. She is as anxious to find Mr. McNair's murderer as you are; that is what she hired me for. I may tell you this: neither she nor her cousin has any knowledge of the red box. They have never seen it or heard of it."

"The devil." There was a pause on the wire. "I want to see her and have a talk with her."

Wolfe sighed. "In that infernal den? She is tired, she has nothing to say that can help you, she is worth two million dollars, and she will be old enough to vote before next fall. Why don't you call at her home after dinner this evening? Or send one of your lieutenants?"

"Because I—Oh, the hell with it. I ought to know better than to argue with you. And she doesn't know where the red box is?"

"She knows nothing whatever about it. Nor does her cousin. My word for that."

"Okay. I'll get her later maybe. Let me know what you find, huh?"

"By all means."

Wolfe hung up and pushed the instrument away, leaned back and locked his fingers on his belly, and slowly shook his head as he murmured, "That man talks too much. —I'm sure, Miss Frost, that you won't be offended at missing a visit to police headquarters. It is one of my strongest prejudices, my disinclination to permit a client of mine to appear there. Let us hope that Mr. Cramer's search for the red box will keep him entertained."

Llewellyn put in, "In my opinion, that's the only thing to do anyway, wait till it's found. All this hash of ancient history—if you were as careful to protect your client from your own annoyance as you are—"

"I remind you, sir, you are here by sufferance. Your cousin has the sense, when she hires an expert, to permit him his hocus-pocus. —What were we saying, Miss Frost? Oh, yes. You were telling me that Mr. Gebert came to New York in 1931. You were then sixteen years old. You said that he is forty-four, so he was then thirty-nine, not an advanced age. I presume he called upon your mother at once, as an old friend?"

She nodded. "Yes. We knew he was coming; he had written. Of course I didn't remember him; I hadn't seen him since I was four years old."

"Of course not. Did he perhaps come on a political mission? I understand that he was a member of the *camelots du roi.*"

"I don't think so. I'm sure he didn't—but that's silly, certainly I can't be sure. But I think not."

"At any rate, as far as you know, he doesn't work, and you don't like that."

"I don't like that in anyone."

"Remarkable sentiment for an heiress. However. If Mr. Gebert should marry you, that would be a job for him. Let us abandon him to that slim hope for his redemption. It is getting on for four o'clock, when I must leave you. I need to ask you about a sentence you left unfinished yesterday, shortly after I made my unsuccessful appeal to you. You told me that your father died when you were only a few months old, and that therefore you had never had a father, and then you said, 'That is,' and stopped. I prodded you, but you said it was nothing, and we let it go at that. It may in fact be nothing, but I would like to have it—

whatever was ready for your tongue. Do you remember?"

She nodded. "It really was nothing. Just something foolish."

"Let me have it. I've told you, we're combing a meadow for a mustard seed."

"But this was nothing at all. Just a dream, a childish dream I had once. Then I had it several times after that, always the same. A dream about myself . . ."

"Tell me."

"Well . . . the first time I had it I was about six years old, in Bali. I've wondered since if anything had happened that day to make me have such a dream, but I couldn't remember anything. I dreamed I was a baby, not an infant but big enough to walk and run, around two I imagine, and on a chair, on a napkin, there was an orange that had been peeled and divided into sections. I took a section of the orange and ate it, then took another one and turned to a man sitting there on a bench, and handed it to him, and I said plainly, 'For daddy.' It was my voice, only it was a baby talking. Then I ate another section, and then took another one and said 'For daddy' again, and kept on that way till it was all gone. I woke up from the dream trembling and began to cry. Mother was sleeping in another bed—it was on a screened veranda—and she came to me and asked what was the matter, and I said, 'I'm crying because I feel so good.' I never did tell her what the dream was. I had it quite a few times after that—I think the last time was when I was about eleven years old, here in New York. I always cried when I had it."

Wolfe asked, "What did the man look like?"

She shook her head. "That's why it was just foolish.

It wasn't a man, it just looked like a man. There was one photograph of my father which mother had kept, but I couldn't tell if it looked like him in the dream. It just . . . I just simply called it daddy."

"Indeed." Wolfe's lips pushed out and in. At length he observed, "Possibly remarkable, on account of the specific picture. Did you eat sections of orange when you were young?"

"I suppose so. I've always liked oranges."

"Well. No telling. Possibly, as you say, nothing at all. You mentioned a photograph of your father. Your mother had kept only one?"

"Yes. She kept that for me."

"None for herself?"

"No." A pause, then Helen said quietly. "There's no secret about it. And it was perfectly natural. Mother was bitterly offended at the terms of father's will, and I think she had a right to be. They had a serious misunderstanding of some sort, I never knew what, about the time I was born, but no matter how serious it was . . . anyway, he left her nothing. Nothing whatever, not even a small income."

Wolfe nodded. "So I understand. It was left in trust for you, with your uncle—your father's brother Dudley—as trustee. Have you ever read the will?"

"Once, a long while ago. Not long after we came to New York my uncle had me read it."

"At the age of nine. But you waded through it. Good for you. I also understand that your uncle was invested with sole power and authority, without any right of oversight by you or anyone else. I believe the usual legal phrase is 'absolute and uncontrolled discretion.' So that, as a matter of fact, you do not know how much you will be worth on your twenty-first birthday;

it may be millions and it may be nothing. You may be in debt. If any—"

Lew Frost got in. "What are you trying to insinuate? If you mean that my father—"

Wolfe snapped, "Don't do that! I insinuate nothing; I merely state the fact of my client's ignorance regarding her property. It may be augmented; it may be depleted; she doesn't know. Do you, Miss Frost?"

"No." She was frowning. "I don't know. I know that for over twenty years the income has been paid in full, promptly every quarter. Really, Mr. Wolfe, I think we're getting—"

"We shall soon be through; I must leave you shortly. As for irrelevance, I warned you that we might wander anywhere. Indulge me in two more questions about your father's will: do you enter into complete possession and control on May seventh?"

"Yes, I do."

"And in case of your death before your twenty-first birthday, who inherits?"

"If I were married and had a child, the child. If not, half to my uncle and half to his son, my cousin Lew."

"Indeed. Nothing to your mother even then?"

"Nothing."

"So. Your father fancied his side of that controversy." Wolfe turned to Llewellyn. "Take good care of your cousin for another five weeks. Should harm befall her in that time, you will have a million dollars and the devil will have his horns on your pillow. Wills are noxious things. Frequently. It is astonishing, the amount of mischief a man's choler may do long after the brain-cells which nourished the choler have rotted away." He wiggled a finger at our client. "Soon, of course, you yourself must make a will, to dispose of the pile in case you should die on—say—May eighth, or subsequently. I suppose you have a lawyer?"

"No. I've never needed one."

"You will now. That's what a fortune is for, to support the lawyers who defend it for you against depredation." Wolfe glanced at the clock. "I must leave you. I trust the afternoon has not been wasted; I suppose you feel that it has. I don't think so. May I leave it that way for the present? I thank you for your indulgence. And while we continue to mark time, waiting for that confounded box to be found, I have a little favor to ask. Could you take Mr. Goodwin home to tea with you?"

Llewellyn's scowl, which had been turned on for the past hour, deepened. Helen Frost glanced at me and then back at Wolfe.

"Why," she said, "I suppose . . . if you want . . ."

"I do want. I presume it would be possible to have Mr. Gebert there?"

She nodded. "He's there now. Or he was when I phoned mother. Of course . . . you know . . . mother doesn't approve . . ."

"I'm aware of that. She thinks you're poking a stick in a hornet's nest. But the fact is the police are the hornets; you've avoided them, and she hasn't. Mr. Goodwin is a discreet and wholesome man and not without acuity. I want him to talk with Mr. Gebert, and with your mother too if she will permit it. You will soon be of age, Miss Frost; you have chosen to attempt a difficult and possibly dangerous project; surely you can prevail on your family and close friends for some consideration. If they are ignorant of any circumstance regarding Mr. McNair's death, all the more should they be ready to establish that point and help us to stumble on a path that will lead us away from

ignorance. So if you would invite Mr. Goodwin for a
cup of tea . . ."

Llewellyn said sourly, "I think Dad's there, too, he
was going to stay till we got back. It'll just be a big
stew—if it's Gebert you want, why can't we send him
down here? He'll do anything Helen tells him to."

"Because for two hours I shall be engaged with my
plants." Wolfe looked at the clock again, and got up
from his chair.

Our client was biting her lip. She quit that, and
looked at me. "Will you have tea with us, Mr. Goodwin?"

I nodded. "Yeah. Much obliged."

Wolfe, moving toward the door, said to her, "It is a
pleasure to earn a fee from a client like you. You can
come to a yes or no without first encircling the globe.
I hope and believe that when we are finished you will
have nothing to regret." He moved on, and turned at
the threshold. "By the way, Archie, if you will just get
that package from your room before you leave. Put it
on my bed."

He went to the elevator. I rose and told my
prospective hostess I would be back in a minute, left
the office and hopped up the stairs. I didn't stop at the
second floor, where my room was, but kept going to
the top, and got there almost as soon as the elevator
did with the load it had. At the door to the plant rooms
Wolfe stood, awaiting me.

"One idea," he murmured, "is to observe the reac-
tions of the others upon the cousins' return from our
office before there has been an opportunity for the
exchange of information. Another is to get an accurate
opinion as to whether any of them has ever seen the
red box or has possession of it now. The third is a
general assault on reticence."

"Okay. How candid are we?"

"Reasonably so. Bear in mind that with all three there, the chances are many to one that you will be talking to the murderer, so the candor will be one-sided. You, of course, will be expecting cooperation."

"Sure, I always do, because I'm wholesome."

I ran back downstairs and found that our client had on her hat and coat and gloves and her cousin was standing beside her, looking grave but a little doubtful.

I grinned at them. "Come on, children."

Chapter 12

Strictly speaking, that wasn't my job. I know pretty well what my field is. Aside from my primary function as the thorn in the seat of Wolfe's chair to keep him from going to sleep and waking up only for meals, I'm chiefly cut out for two things: to jump and grab something before the other guy can get his paws on it, and to collect pieces of the puzzle for Wolfe to work on. This expedition to 65th Street was neither of those. I don't pretend to be strong on nuances. Fundamentally I'm the direct type, and that's why I can never be a really fine detective. Although I keep it down as much as I can, so it won't interfere with my work, I always have an inclination in a case of murder to march up to all the possible suspects, one after the other, and look them in the eye and ask them, "Did you put that poison in the aspirin bottle?" and just keep that up until one of them says, "Yes." As I say, I keep it down, but I have to fight it.

The Frost apartment on 65th Street wasn't as gaudy as I had expected, in view of my intimate knowledge of the Frost finances. It was a bit shiny, with one side of the entrance hall solid with mirrors, even the door to the closet where I hung my hat, and, in the living room, chairs and little tables with chromium chassis, a lot of red stuff around in upholsteries and drapes, a metal grille in front of the fireplace, which apparently wasn't used, and oil paintings in modern silver frames.

Anyway, it certainly was cheerfuller than the people that were in it. Dudley Frost was in a big chair at one side, with a table at his elbow holding a whiskey bottle, a water carafe, and a couple of glasses. Perren Gebert stood near a window at the other end, with his back to the room and his hands in his pockets. As we entered he turned, and Helen's mother walked toward us, with a little lift to her brow as she saw me.

"Oh," she said. To her daughter: "You've brought . . ."

Helen nodded firmly. "Yes, mother." She was holding her chin a little higher than natural, to keep the spunk going. "You—all of you have met Mr. Goodwin. Yesterday morning at . . . that candy business with the police. I've engaged Nero Wolfe to investigate Uncle Boyd's death, and Mr. Goodwin works for him—"

Dudley Frost bawled from his chair, "Lew! Come here! Damn it, what kind of nonsense—"

Llewellyn hurried over there to stem it. Perren Gebert had approached us and was smiling at me:

"Ah! The fellow that doesn't like scenes. You remember I told you, Calida?" He transferred the smile to Miss Frost. "My dear Helen! You've engaged Mr. Wolfe? Are you one of the Erinyes? Alecto? Megaera? Tisiphone? Where's your snaky hair? So one can really buy anything with money, even vengeance?"

Mrs. Frost murmured at him, "Stop it, Perren."

"I'm not buying vengeance." Helen colored a little. "I told you this morning, Perren, you're being especially hateful. You'd better not make me cry again, or I'll . . . well, don't. Yes, I've engaged Mr. Wolfe, and Mr. Goodwin has come here and he wants to talk to you."

"To me?" Perren shrugged. "About Boyd? If you ask it, he may, but I warn him not to expect much. The police have been here most of the day, and I've realized how little I really knew about Boyd, though I've known him more than twenty years."

I said, "I stopped expecting long ago. Anything you tell me will be velvet. —I'm supposed to talk to you, too, Mrs. Frost. And your brother-in-law. I have to take notes, and it gives me a cramp to write standing up . . ."

She nodded at me, and turned. "Over here, I think." She started toward Dudley Frost's side of the room, and I joined her. Her straight back was graceful, and she was unquestionably streamlined for her age. Llewellyn started carrying chairs, and Gebert came up with one. As we got seated and I pulled out my notebook and pencil, I noticed that Helen still had to keep her chin up, but her mother didn't. Mrs. Frost was saying:

"I hope you understand this, Mr. Goodwin. This is a terrible thing, an awful thing, and we were all very old friends of Mr. McNair's, and we don't enjoy talking about it. I knew him all my life, from childhood."

I said, "Yeah. You're Scotch?"

She nodded. "My name was Buchan."

"So McNair told us." I jerked my eyes up quick from my notebook, which was my habit against the handicap of not being able to keep a steely gaze on the victim. But she wasn't recoiling in dismay; she was just nodding again.

"Yes. I gathered from what the policemen said that Boyden had told Mr. Wolfe a good deal of his early life. Of course you have the advantage of knowing what it was he had to say to Mr. Wolfe. I knew, naturally, that Boyden was not well . . . his nerves . . ."

Gebert put in, "He was what you call a wreck. He was in a very bad condition. That is why I told the police, they will find it was suicide."

"The man was crazy!" This was a croak from Dudley Frost. "I've told you what he did yesterday! He instructed his lawyer to demand an accounting on Edwin's estate! On what grounds? On the ground that he is Helen's godfather? Absolutely fantastic and illegal! I always thought he was crazy—"

That started a general rumpus. Mrs. Frost expostulated with some spirit, Llewellyn with respectful irritation, and Helen with a nervous outburst. Perren Gebert looked around at them, nodded at me as if he and I shared an entertaining secret, and got out a cigarette. I didn't try to put it all down, but just surveyed the scene and listened. Dudley Frost was surrendering no ground:

". . . crazy as a loon! Why shouldn't he commit suicide? Helen, my dear, I adore you, you know damned well I do, but I refuse to assume respect for your liking for that nincompoop merely because he is no longer alive! He had no use for me and I had none for him! So what's the use pretending about it? As far as your dragging this man in here is concerned—"

"Dad! Now, Dad! Cut it out—"

Perren Gebert said to no one, "And half a bottle gone." Mrs. Frost, sitting with her lips tight and patient, glanced at him. I leaned forward to get closer to Dudley Frost and practically yelled at him:

"What is it? Where does it hurt?"

He jerked back and glared at me. "Where does what hurt?"

I grinned. "Nothing. I just wanted to see if you could hear. I gather you would just as soon I'd go. The best way to manage that, for all of you, is to let me ask a few foolish questions, and you answer them briefly and maybe honestly."

"We've already answered them. All the foolish questions there are. We've been doing that all day. All because that nincompoop McNair—"

"Okay. I've already got it down that he was a nincompoop. You've made remarks about suicide. What reason did McNair have for killing himself?"

"How the devil do I know?"

"Then you can't think one up offhand?"

"I don't have to think one up. The man was crazy. I've always said so. I said so over twenty years ago, in Paris, when he used to paint rows of eggs strung on wires and call it The Cosmos."

Helen started to burst, "Uncle Boyd was never—" She was seated at my right, and I reached and tapped her sleeve with the tips of my fingers and told her, "Swallow it. You can't crack every nut in the bag." I turned to Perren Gebert:

"You mentioned suicide first. What reason did McNair have for killing himself?"

Gebert shrugged. "A specific reason? I don't know. He was very bad in his nerves."

"Yeah. He had a headache. How about you, Mrs. Frost? Have you got a reason?"

She looked at me. You couldn't take that woman's eyes casually; you had to make an effort. She said,

"You make your question a little provocative. Don't you? If you mean, do I know a concrete motive for Boyden to commit suicide, I don't."

"Do you think he did?"

She frowned. "I don't know what to think. If I think of suicide, it is only because I knew him quite intimately, and it is even more difficult to believe that there was anyone who . . . that someone killed him."

I started to sigh, then realized that I was imitating Nero Wolfe, and choked it off. I looked around at them. "Of course, you all know that McNair died in Nero Wolfe's office. You know that Wolfe and I were there, and naturally we know what he had been telling us about and how he was feeling. I don't know how carefully the police are with their conclusions, but Mr. Wolfe is very snooty about his. He has already made one or two about this case, and the first one is that McNair didn't kill himself. Suicide is out. So if you have any idea that that theory will be found acceptable, either now or eventually, obliterate it. Guess again."

Perren Gebert extended a long arm to crush his cigarette in a tray. "For my part," he said, "I don't feel compelled to guess. I made one to be charitable. Suppose you tell us why it wasn't suicide."

Mrs. Frost said quietly, "I asked you to sit down in my house, Mr. Goodwin, because my daughter brought you. But I wonder if you know when you are being offensive? We . . . I have no theory to advance . . ."

Dudley Frost started to croak: "Take no notice of him, Calida. Disregard him. I refuse to speak to him." He reached for the whiskey bottle.

I said, "If you ask me, I could be even more offensive and still hope to make the grade to heaven."

I got Mrs. Frost's eyes again. "For instance, I might remark on your phony la-de-da about asking me to sit down in your house. It isn't your house, it's your daughter's, unless she gave it to you—" There was a gasp at my right from the client, and Mrs. Frost's mouth opened, but I went on ahead of the rush:

"Just to show you how offensive I can be if I work at it. What kind of ninnies do you think we are? Even the cops aren't as thick as you seem to believe. It's time you folks pinched yourselves and woke up. Boyden McNair gets bumped off, and Helen Frost here happens to have enough regard for him to want to know who did it, and enough gumption to get the right man for the job, and enough jack to pay him. She's your daughter and niece and cousin and almost fiancée. She brings me here. I already know enough to be aware that you've got vital information which you don't intend to cough up, and you know I know it. And look at the kindergarten stuff you hand me! McNair had a headache, so he went to Nero Wolfe's office to poison himself! You might at least have the politeness to tell me straight that you refuse to discuss the matter because you don't intend to get involved if you can help it, then we can proceed with the involving." I pointed my pencil at Perren Gebert's long thin nose. "For instance, you! Did you know that Dudley Frost might tell us where the red box is?"

I concentrated on Gebert, but Mrs. Frost was off line only a little to the left of him, so I was having a glimpse of her too. Gebert fell for it absolutely. His head jerked around to look at Dudley Frost and then back at me. Mrs. Frost jerked too, first at Gebert, then back into steadiness. Dudley Frost was sputtering at me:

"What's that? What red box? That idiotic thing in

McNair's will? Damn you, are you crazy too? Do you dare—"

I grinned at him. "Hold it. I just said you might. Yeah, the thing McNair left to Wolfe in his will. Have you got it?"

He turned to his son and growled, "I refuse to speak to him."

"Okay. But the truth is, I'm a friend of yours. I'm tipping you off. Did you know that there's a way for the District Attorney to force an accounting from you of your brother's estate? And did you ever hear of a search warrant? I suppose when the cops went with one to your apartment this afternoon to look for the red box, there was a maid there to let them in. Didn't she phone you? And of course in looking for the box they would have occasion to glance at anything that might be around. Or maybe they didn't get there yet; they may be on the way now. And don't go blaming your maid, she can't help it—"

Dudley Frost had scrambled to his feet. "They wouldn't—that would be an outrage—"

"Sure it would. I'm not saying they've done it, I'm just telling you, in a case of murder they'll do anything—"

Dudley Frost had started across the room. "Come on, Lew—by Gad, we'll see—"

"But, Dad, I don't—"

"Come on, I say! Are you my son?" He had turned at the far end of the room. "Thank you for the refreshment, Calida, let me know if there is anything I can do. Lew, damn it, come on! Helen, my dear, you are a fool, I've always said so. Lew!"

Llewellyn stopped to murmur something to Helen, nodded to his aunt, ignored Gebert, and hurried after his father to assist in the defense of their castle. There were rumblings from the entrance hall, and then the door opening and closing.

Mrs. Frost stood up and looked down at her daughter. She spoke to her quietly: "This is frightful, Helen. That this should come . . . and just now, just when you will soon be a woman and ready for your life as you want it. I know what Boyd was to you, and he was a great deal to me, too. Just now you're holding things against me that time will make you forget . . . you're remembering that I thought it wise to temper the affection you had for him. I thought it best; you were a girl, and girls should look to youth. Helen, my dear child . . ."

She bent down and touched her daughter's shoulder, touched her hair and straightened up again. "You have strong impulses, like your father, and sometimes you don't quite manage them. I don't agree with Perren when he sneers at you for trying to buy vengeance. Perren loves to sneer; it's his favorite pose; he would call it being sardonic . . . but you know him. I think the impulse that led you to hire this detective was a generous one. Certainly I have every reason to know that you are generous." Her voice stayed low, but it got more of a ring in it, a music of metal. "I'm your mother, and I don't believe you really want to bring people here who tell me that I refuse to discuss . . . this matter . . . because I don't intend to get involved. I'm sorry I was brusque with you today on the telephone, but my nerves were on edge. Policemen were here, and you were away, just making more trouble for us to no good purpose. Really . . . really, don't you see that? Cheap insults and bullying for your own family won't help any. I think you've learned, in twenty-one years, that you can depend on me, and I'd like to feel that I can depend on you too . . ."

Helen Frost stood up. Seeing her face, with no color in it and her mouth twisted, it looked shaky to me, and I considered butting in, but decided to keep my trap shut. She stood straight, with her hands, fists, hanging at her sides, and her eyes were dark with trouble but held level at Mrs. Frost, which was why I didn't speak. Gebert took a couple of steps toward her and stopped.

She said, "You can depend on me, Mother. But so can Uncle Boyd. That's all right, isn't it? Oh, isn't it?" She looked at me and said in a funny tone like a child, "Don't insult my mother, Mr. Goodwin." Then she turned abruptly and ran out on us, skipped the she-bang. She left by a door on the right, not toward the hall, and closed it behind her.

Perren Gebert shrugged his shoulders and thrust his hands into his pockets, then pulled one out to rub the side of his thin nose with his forefinger. Mrs. Frost, with a couple of teeth clamped on her lower lip, looked at him and then back at the door where her daughter had gone.

I said brightly, "I don't think she fired me. I didn't understand it that way. What do you think?"

Gebert showed me a thin smile. "You leave now. No?"

"Maybe." I still had my notebook open in my hand. "But you folks might as well understand that we mean business. We're not just having fun, we do this for a living. I don't believe you can talk her out of it. This place belongs to her. I'm willing to have a showdown right now; say we go to her bedroom or wherever she went, and ask if I'm kicked out." I directed my gaze at Mrs. Frost. "Or have a little chat right here. You know, they might find that red box at Dudley Frost's, at that. How would that set with you?"

She said, "Stupid senseless tricks."

I nodded. "Yeah, I guess so. Even Steven. If you bounced me, Inspector Cramer would send me right back here with a man if Wolfe asked him to, and you're in no position to ritz the cops, because they're sensitive and they would only get suspicious. At present they're not actually suspicious, they just think you're hiding something because people like you don't want any publicity except in society columns and cigarette ads. For instance, they believe you know where the red box is. You know, of course, it's Nero Wolfe's property; McNair left it to him. We really would like to have it, just for curiosity."

Gebert, after listening to me politely, cocked his head at Mrs. Frost. He smiled at her: "You see, Calida, this fellow really believes we could tell him something. He's perfectly sincere about it. The police, too. The only way to get rid of them is to humor them. Why not tell them something?" He waved a hand inclusively. "All sorts of things."

She looked at him without approval. "This is nothing to be playful about. Certainly not your kind of playfulness."

He lifted his brows. "I don't mean to be playful. They want information about Boyd, and unquestionably we have it, quantities of it." He looked at me. "You do shorthand in that book? Good. Put this down: McNair was an inveterate eater of snails, and he preferred Calvados to cognac. His wife died in childbirth because he was insisting on being an artist and was too poor and incompetent to provide proper care for her. —What, Calida? But the fellow wants facts! —Edwin Frost once paid McNair two thousand francs—at that time four hundred dollars—for one of his pictures, and the next day traded it to a flower girl for a violet—not a bunch, a violet. McNair named his daughter Glenna because it means valley, and she came out of the valley of death, since her mother died at her birth—just a morsel of Calvinistic merriment. A light-hearted man, Boyd was! Mrs. Frost here was his oldest friend and she once rescued him from despair and penury; yet, when he became the foremost living designer and manufacturer of women's woolen garments, he invariably charged her top prices for everything she bought. And he never—"

"Perren! Stop it!"

"My dear Calida! Stop when I've just started? Give the fellow what he wants and he'll let us alone. It's a pity we can't give him his red box; Boyd really should have told us about that. But I realize that his chief interest is in Boyd's death, not his life. I can be helpful on that too. Knowing so well how Boyd lived, surely I should know how he died. As a matter of fact, when I heard of his death last evening, I was reminded of a quotation from Norboisin—the girl Denise gasps it as she expires: '*Au moins, je meurs ardemment!*' Might not Boyd have used those very words, Calida? Of course, with Denise the adverb applied to herself, whereas with Boyd it would have been meant for the agent—"

"Perren!" It was not a protest this time, but a command. Mrs. Frost's tone and look together refrigerated him into silence. She surveyed him: "You are a babbling fool. Would you make a jest of it? No one but a fool jests at death."

Gebert made her a little bow. "Except his own, perhaps, Calida. To keep up appearances."

"You may. I am Scotch, too, like Boyd. It is no joke

to me." She turned her head and let me have her eyes again. "You may as well go. As you say, this is my daughter's house; we do not put you out. But my daughter is still a minor—and anyway, we cannot help you. I have nothing whatever to say, beyond what I have told the police. If you enjoy Mr. Gebert's vaudeville I can leave you with him."

I shook my head. "No, I don't like it much." I stuck my notebook in my pocket. "Anyhow, I've got an appointment downtown, to squeeze blood out of a stone, which will be a cinch. It's just possible Mr. Wolfe will phone to invite you to his office for a chat. Have you anything on for this evening?"

She froze me. "Mr. Wolfe's taking advantage of my daughter's emotional impulse is abominable. I don't wish to see him. If he should come here—"

"Don't let that worry you." I grinned at her. "He's done all his traveling for this season and then some. But I expect I'll be seeing you again." I started off, and after a few steps turned. "By the way, if I were you I wouldn't make much of a point of persuading your daughter to fire us. It would just make Mr. Wolfe suspicious, and that turns him into a fiend. I can't handle him when he's like that."

It didn't look as if even that one was going to cause her to burst into sobs, so I beat it. In the entrance hall I tried to open up the wrong mirror, then found the right one and got my hat. The etiquette seemed to be turned off, so I let myself out and steered for the elevator.

I had to flag a taxi to take me home, because I had ridden up with our client and her cousin, not caring to leave them alone together at that juncture.

It was after six o'clock when I got there. I went to the kitchen first and commandeered a glass of milk, took a couple of sniffs at the goulash steaming gently on the simmer plate, and told Fritz it didn't smell much like freshly butchered kid to me. I slid out when he brandished a skimming spoon.

Wolfe was at his desk with a book, *Seven Pillars of Wisdom*, by Lawrence, which he had already read twice, and I knew what mood he was in when I saw that the tray and glass were on his desk but no empty bottle. It was one of his most childish tricks, every now and then, especially when he was ahead of his quota more than usual, to drop the bottle into the wastebasket as soon as he emptied it, and if I was in the office he did it when I wasn't looking. It was that sort of thing that kept me skeptical about the fundamental condition of his brain, and that particular trick was all the more foolish because he was unquestionably on the square with the bottle caps; he faithfully put every single one in the drawer; I know that, because I've checked up on him time and time again. When he was ahead on quota he made some belittling remark about statistics with each cap he dropped in, but he never tried to get away with one.

I tossed my notebook on my desk and sat down and sipped at the milk. There was no use trying to explode him off of that book. But after a while he picked up the thin strip of ebony he used for a bookmark, inserted it, closed the book, laid it down, and reached out and rang for beer. Then he leaned back and admitted I was alive.

"Pleasant afternoon, Archie?"

I grunted. "That was one hell of a tea. Dudley Frost was the only one who had any, and he wasn't inclined to divvy so I sent him home. I only got one real hot piece of news, that no one but a fool jests at death. How does that strike you?"

Wolfe grimaced. "Tell me about it."

I read it to him from the notebook, filling in the gaps from memory, though I didn't need much because I've condensed my symbols until I can take down the Constitution of the United States on the back of an old envelope, which might be a good place for it. Wolfe's beer arrived, and met its fate. Except for time out for swallowing, he listened, as usual, settled back comfortably with his eyes closed.

I tossed the notebook to the back of my desk, swiveled, and pulled the bottom drawer out and got my feet up. "That's the crop. That one's in the bag. What shall I start on now?"

Wolfe opened his eyes. "Your French is not even ludicrous. We'll return to that. Why did you frighten Mr. Frost away by talk of a search warrant? Is there a subtlety there too deep for me?"

"No, just momentum. I asked him that question about the red box to get a line on the other two, and as I went along it occurred to me it might be fun to find out if he had anything at home he didn't want anyone to see, and anyway what good was he? I got rid of him."

"Oh. I was about to credit you with superior finesse. It would have been that, to get him away on the chance that there might be a remark, a glance, a gesture, not to be expected in his presence. In fact, that is exactly what happened. I congratulate you anyhow. As for Mr. Frost—everyone has something at home they don't want anyone to see; that is one of the functions of a home, to provide a spot to keep such things. —And you say they haven't the red box and don't know where it is."

"I offer that opinion. The look Gebert shot at Frost when I hinted Frost had it, and the look Mrs. Frost gave Gebert, as I told you. It's a cinch that what they think is in the box means something important to them. It's a good guess that they haven't got it and don't know where it is, or they wouldn't have been so quick on the trigger when I hinted that. As for Frost, God knows. That's the advantage a guy has that always explodes no matter what you say, there's no symptomatic nuances for an observer like me."

"You? Ha! I am impressed. I confess I am surprised that Mrs. Frost didn't find a pretext as soon as you entered, to take her daughter to some other room. Is the woman immune to trepidation? Even common curiosity . . ."

I shook my head. "If it's common, she hasn't got it. That dame has got a steel spine, a governor on her main artery that prevents acceleration, and a patent air-cooling system for her brain. If you wanted to prove she murdered anyone you'd have to see her do it and be sure to have a camera along."

"Dear me." Wolfe came forward in his chair to pour beer. "Then we must find another culprit, which may be a nuisance." He watched the foam subside. "Take your book and look at your notes on Mr. Gebert's vaudeville. Where he quoted Norboisin; read that sentence."

"You'd like some more fun with my French?"

"No, indeed; it isn't fun. Since your shorthand is phonetic, do as well as you can with your symbols. I think I know the quotation, but I want to be sure. It has been years since I read Norboisin, and I haven't his books."

I read the whole paragraph, beginning "My dear Calida." I took the French on high and sailed right through it, ludicrous or not, having had three lessons in it altogether: one from Fritz in 1930, and two from a girl I met once when we were working on a forgery case.

"Want to hear it again?"

"No, thanks." Wolfe's lips were pushing in and out. "And Mrs. Frost calls it babbling. It would have been instructive to be there, for the tone and the eyes. Mr. Gebert was indeed sardonic, to tell you in so many words who killed Mr. McNair. Was it a lie, to be provoking? Or the truth, to display his own alertness? Or a conjecture, for a little subtlety of his own? I think, the second. I do indeed. It runs with my surmises, but he could not know that. And granted that we know the murderer, what the devil is to be done about it? Probably no amount of patience would suffice. If Mr. Cramer gets his hands on the red box and decides to act without me, he is apt to lose the spark entirely and leave both of us with fuel that will not ignite." He drank his beer, put the glass down, and wiped his lips. "Archie. We need that confounded box."

"Yeah. I'll go get it in just a minute. First, just to humor me, exactly when did Gebert tell us who killed McNair? You wouldn't by any chance be talking just to hear yourself?"

"Of course not. Isn't it obvious? But I forget—you don't know French. *Ardemment* means ardently. The quotation translates, 'At least, I die ardently.'"

"Really?" I elevated the brows. "The hell you say."

"Yes. And therefore—but I forget again. You don't know Latin. Do you?"

"Not intimately. I'm shy on Chinese too." I aimed a Bronx cheer in a sort of general direction. "Maybe we ought to turn this case over to the Heinemann School of Languages. Did Gebert's quotation fix us up on evidence too, or do we have to dig that out for ourselves?"

I overplayed it. Wolfe compressed his lips and eyed me without favor. He leaned back. "Some day, Archie, I shall be constrained . . . but no. I cannot remake the universe, and must therefore put up with this one. What is, is, including you." He sighed. "Let the Latin go. Information for your records: this afternoon I telephoned Mr. Hitchcock in London; expect it on the bill. I asked him to send a man to Scotland for a talk with Mr. McNair's sister, and to instruct his agent, either in Barcelona or in Madrid, to examine certain records in the town of Cartagena. That means an expenditure of several hundred dollars. There has been no further report from Saul Panzer. We need that red box. It was already apparent to me who killed Mr. McNair, and why, before Mr. Gebert permitted himself the amusement of informing you; he really didn't help us any, and of course he didn't intend to. But what is known is not necessarily demonstrable. Pfui! To sit here and wait upon the result of a game of hide-and-seek, when all the difficulties have in fact been surmounted! Please type out a note of that statement of Mr. Gebert's while it is fresh; conceivably it will be needed."

He picked up his book again, got his elbows on the arms of his chair, opened to his page, and was gone.

He read until dinnertime, but even *Seven Pillars of Wisdom* did not restrain his promptness in responding to Fritz's summons to table. During the meal he kindly explained to me the chief reason for Lawrence's amazing success in keeping the Arabian tribes together for the great revolt. It was because Lawrence's personal attitude toward women was the same as the classic and traditional Arabian attitude. The central fact about any man, in respect to his activities as a social animal, is his attitude toward women; hence the Arabs felt that essentially Lawrence was one of them, and so accepted him. His native ability for leadership and finesse did the rest. A romantic they would not have understood, a puritan they would have rudely ignored, a sentimentalist they would have laughed at, but the contemptuous realist Lawrence, with his false humility and his fierce secret pride, they took to their bosoms. The goulash was as good as any Fritz had ever made.

It was after nine o'clock when we finished with coffee and went back to the office. Wolfe resumed with his book. I got at my desk with the plant records. I figured that after an hour or so of digestion and this peaceful family scene I would make an effort to extract a little Latin lesson out of Wolfe, and find out whether Gebert really had said anything or if perchance Wolfe was only practicing some fee-faw-fum, but an interruption came before I had even decided on a method of attack. At nine-thirty the phone rang.

I reached for it. "Hello, this is the office of Nero Wolfe."

"Archie? Fred. I'm talking from Brewster. Better put Mr. Wolfe on."

I told him to hold it and turned to Wolfe. "Fred calling from Brewster. Fifteen cents a minute."

At that, he stopped to put in his bookmark. Then he got his receiver up, and I told Fred to proceed, and opened my notebook.

"Mr. Wolfe? Fred Durkin. Saul sent me to the village to phone. We haven't found any red box, but there's been a little surprise at that place. We finished with the house, covered every inch, and started outdoors. It's the worst time of year for it, because when it thaws in the spring it's the muddiest time of the year. After it got dark we were working with flashlights, and we saw the lights of a car coming down the road and Saul had us put our lights out. It's a narrow dirt road and you can't go fast. The car turned in at the gate and stopped on the driveway. We had put the sedan in the garage. The lights went out and the engine stopped and a man got out. There was only one of him, so we kept still, behind some bushes. He went to a window and turned a flashlight on it and started trying to open it, and Orrie and I stepped out between him and the car, and Saul went toward him and asked him why he didn't go in the door. He took it cool, he said he forgot his key, then he said he didn't know he'd be interrupting anyone and started off. Saul stopped him and said he'd better come in first and have a drink and a little talk. They guy laughed and said he would and they went in, and Orrie and I went in after them, and we turned on the lights and sat down. The guy's name is Gebert, G-E-B-E-R-T, a tall slender dark guy with a thin nose—"

"Yeah, I know him. What did he say?"

"Not a hell of a lot of anything. He talks but he don't say anything. He says this McNair was a friend of his, and there's some things belonging to him in the place, and he thought he might as well drive out and get them. He ain't scared and he ain't easy. He's a great smiler."

"Yeah, I know. Where is he now?"

"Why, he's out there. Saul and Orrie have got him. Saul sent me to ask what you want us to do with him—"

"Turn him loose. What else can you do? Unless you're hungry and want to make soup of him. Saul won't get anywhere with that bird. You can't keep him—"

"The hell we can't keep him. I ain't through, wait till I tell you. We had been in there with that Gebert ten or fifteen minutes, when there was a noise out front and I hopped out to take a look. It was two cars, and they stopped by the gate. They piled out and came in the yard after me, and by God if they didn't pull guns. You might have thought I was Dillinger. I saw state troopers' uniforms. I let out a yell to warn Saul to lock the door and then I met the attack. I was surrounded by who do you think? Rowcliff, that mutt of a lieutenant from the Homicide Squad, and three other dicks, and two troopers, and a little runt with spectacles that told me he was an assistant district attorney of Putnam County. Huh? Was I surrounded?"

"Yes. At last. Did they shoot you?"

"Sure, but I caught the bullets and tossed them back. Well, it seems that what they came for was to look for that red box. They went to the door and wanted in. Saul left Orrie there inside the door and went to a window and talked to them through the glass. Of course he asked to see a search warrant and they didn't have any. There was some gab back and forth, then the troopers announced they were going in after Saul because he was trespassing, and he held the paper that Mr. Wolfe signed up against the window and they put a flashlight on it. There was more talk, and then Saul told me to drive to the village and phone you, and Rowcliff said nothing doing until he searched me for the red box, and I told him if he touched me I'd skin him and hang him up to dry. But I couldn't get the sedan out because Gebert's car was in the driveway and the others blocked the road at the gate, so we declared a truce and Rowcliff took his car and we both came to Brewster in it. It's only about three miles. We left the rest of the gang sitting there on the porch. I'm in a booth in a restaurant and Rowcliff's down the street in a drug store phoning headquarters. I've got a notion to grab his car and go back without him."

"Okay. Damn good idea. Does he know Gebert's there?"

"No. If Gebert's shy about cops, of course he don't want to leave. What do we do? Toss him out? Let the cops in? We can't go out and dig, all we can do is sit there and watch Gebert smile, and it's as cold as an Englishman's heart and we haven't got a fire. Good God, you ought to hear those troopers talk, I guess out there in the wilds they catch bears and lions with their hands and eat 'em raw."

"Hold it." I turned to Wolfe. "I suppose I go for a drive?"

He shuddered. I presume he calculated that there must be at least a thousand jolts between 35th Street and Brewster, and ten thousand cars to meet and pass. The lurking dangers of the night. He nodded at me.

I told Fred, "Go on back. Keep Gebert, and don't let them in. I'll be there as soon as I can make it."

Chapter 13

It was a quarter to ten by the time I got away and around the corner to the garage on Tenth Avenue and was sailing down the ramp in the roadster, and it was 11:13 when I rolled into the village of Brewster and turned left—following the directions I had heard Helen Frost give Saul Panzer. An hour and twenty-eight minutes wasn't bad, counting the curves on the Pines Bridge Road and the bum stretch between Muscoot and Croton Falls.

I followed the pavement a little over a mile and then turned left again onto a dirt road. It was as narrow as a bigot's mind, and I got in the ruts and stayed there. My lights showed me nothing but the still bare branches of trees and shrubbery close on both sides, and I began to think that Fred's jabber about the wilds hadn't been so dumb. There was an occasional house, but they were dark and silent, and I went on bumping so long, a sharp curve to the left and one to the right and then to the left again, that I began wondering if I was on the wrong road. Then, finally, I saw a light ahead, stuck to the ruts around another curve, and there I was.

Besides a few rapid comments from Wolfe before I

started, I had trotted the brain around for a survey of
the situation during the drive, and there didn't seem
to be anything very critical about it except that it
would be nice to keep the news of Gebert's expedition
to ourselves for a while. They were welcome to go in
and look for the red box all they wanted to, since Saul,
with the whole afternoon to work undisturbed, hadn't
found it. But Gebert was worth a little effort, not to
mention the item that we had our reputation to
consider. So I stopped the roadster alongside the two
cars that were parked at the edge of the road and
leaned out and yelled:

"Come and move this bus! It's blocking the gate
and I want to turn in!"

A gruff shout came from the porch: "Who the hell
are you?" I called back:

"Haile Selassie. Okay, I'll move it myself. If it
makes a ditch, don't blame me."

I got out and climbed into the other car, open with
the top down, a state police chariot. I heard, and saw
dimly in the dark, a couple of guys leave the porch and
come down the short path. They jumped the low
palings. The front one was in uniform and I made out
the other one for my old friend Lieutenant Rowcliff.
The trooper was stern enough to scare me silly:

"Come out of that, buddie. Move that car and I'll
tie you in a knot."

I said, "You will not. Get it? It's a pun. My name is
Archie Goodwin, I represent Mr. Nero Wolfe, I belong
in there and you don't. If a man finds a car blocking his
own gate he has plenty of right to move it, which is
what I'm going to do, and if you try to stop me it will
be too bad because I'm mad as hell and I mean it."

Rowcliff growled, "All right, get out, we'll move

the damn thing." He muttered at the cossack. "You might as well. This bird's never been tamed yet."

The trooper opened the door. "Get out."

"You going to move it?"

"Why the hell shouldn't I move it? Get out."

I descended and climbed back in the roaster. The trooper started his car and eased it ahead, into the road, and off again beyond the entrance. My lights were on him. I put my gear in, circled through the gate onto the driveway, stopped back of a car there which I recognized for the convertible Gebert had parked in front of Wolfe's house the day before, and got out and started for the porch. There was a mob there sitting along the edge of it. One of them got smart and turned on a flash and spotted it on my face as I approached. Rowcliff and the trooper came up and stood at the foot of the steps.

I demanded, "Who's in charge of this gang? I know you're not, Rowcliff, we're outside the city limits. Who's got any right to be here on private property?"

They looked at each other. The trooper stuck out his chin at me, and asked, "Have you?"

"You're darned tooting I have. You've seen a paper signed by the executor of the estate that owns this. I've got another one in my pocket. Well, come on, who's in charge? Who's responsible for this outrage?"

There was a cackle from the porch, a shadow in the corner. "I've got a right to be here, ain't I, Archie?"

I peered at it. "Oh, hi, Fred. What are you doing out here in the cold?"

He ambled toward me. "We didn't want to open the door, because this bunch of highbinders might take a notion—"

I snorted. "Where would they get it from? —All right, nobody's in charge, is that it? Fred, call Saul—"

"I'll take the responsibility!" A little squirt had popped up and I saw his spectacles. He squealed, "I'm the Assistant District Attorney of this county! We have a legal right—"

I did some towering over him. "You have a legal right to go home and go to bed. Have you got a warrant or a subpoena or even a cigarette paper?"

"No, there wasn't time—"

"Then shut up." I turned to Rowcliff and the trooper. "You think I'm being tough? Not at all, I'm just indignant and I have a right to be. You've got a nerve, to come to a private house in the middle of the night and expect to go through it, without any evidence that there has ever been anything or anyone criminal in it. What do you want, the red box? It's Nero Wolfe's property, and if it's in there I'll get it and put it in my pocket and walk out with it, and don't try to play tag with me, because I'm sensitive about coming in contact with people." I brushed past them and mounted the porch, crossed to the door and rapped on it:

"Come here, Fred. Saul!"

I heard his voice from inside: "Hello, Archie! Okay?"

"Sure, okay. Open the door! Stand by, Fred."

The gang had stood up and edged toward us a little. I heard the lock turning; the door swung open and a lane of light ribboned the porch; Saul stood on the threshold with Orrie back of him. Fred and I were there too. I faced the throng:

"I hereby order you to leave these premises. All of you. In other words, beat it. Now do as you damn please, but its on the record that you're here illegally, for future reference. We resent your scuffing up the porch, but if you try coming in the house we'll resent that a lot worse. Back up, Saul. Come on, Fred."

We went in. Saul closed the door and locked it. I looked around. knowing that the joint belonged to McNair, I halfway expected to see some more decorators' delights, but it was rustic. Nice big chairs and seats with cushions and a big heavy wooden table, and a blaze crackling in a wide fireplace at one end. I turned to Fred Durkin:

"You darned liar. You said there was no fire."

He grinned, rubbing his hands in front of it. "I didn't think Mr. Wolfe ought to think we was too comfortable."

"He wouldn't mind. He doesn't like hardship, even for you." I looked around again and spoke to Saul in a lower tone. "Where's what you've got with you?"

He nodded at a door. "In the other room. No light in there."

"You didn't find the box?"

"No sign of it. All cubic inches accounted for."

Since it was Saul, that settled it. I asked him, "Is there another door?"

"One at the back. We've got it propped."

"Okay. You and Fred stay here. Orrie, come with me."

He lumbered over and I led him into the other room. After I closed the door behind us it was good and dark, but there were two dim rectangles for windows, and after a few seconds I made out an outline in a chair. I said to Orrie, "Sing."

He grumbled, "What the hell, I'm too hungry to sing."

"Sing anyway. If one of them happens to glue his ear to a window I want him to hear something. Sing 'Git Along, Little Dogie.'"

"I can't sing in the dark—"

"Damn it, will you sing?"

He cleared his throat and started it up. Orrie had a pretty good voice. I went close to the outline in the chair and said to it:

"I'm Archie Goodwin. You know me."

"Certainly." Gebert's voice sounded purely conversational. "You're the fellow who doesn't like scenes."

"Right. That's why I'm out here when I ought to be in bed. Why are you out here?"

"I drove out to get my umbrella which I left here last fall."

"Oh. You did. Did you find it?"

"No. Someone must have taken it."

"That's too bad. Listen to me a minute. Out on the porch is an army of state police and New York detectives and a Putnam County prosecutor. How would you like to have to tell them about your umbrella?"

I saw the outline of his shoulders move with his shrug. "If it would amuse them. I hardly suppose they know where it is."

"I see. You're fancy free, huh? Not a care in the world. In that case, what are you doing sitting in here alone in the dark? —A little louder, Orrie."

Gebert shrugged again. "Your colleague—the little chap with the big nose—asked me to come in here. He was very courtecus to me when I was trying a window because I had no key."

"so you wanted to be courteous to him. That was darned swell of you. Then it's okay if I let the cops in and tell them we found you trying to break in?"

"I'm really indifferent about it." I couldn't see his smile but I knew he was wearing it. "Really. I wasn't breaking in, I was only trying a window."

I straightened up, disgusted. He wasn't giving me
anything at all to bargain with , and even if it was a
bluff I guessed that he was sardonic enough to go right
through with it. Orrie stopped, and I grunted at him
to carry on. The conditions were bad for negotiation. I
leaned over him again:

"Look here, Gebert. We've got your number—
Nero Wolfe has—but we're willing to give you a
chance. It's midnight. What's wrong with this: I'll let
the cops in and tell them they can look for the red box
all they want to. I happen to know they won't find it.
You are one of my colleagues. Your name's Jerry.
We'll leave my other colleagues here and you and I will
get in my car and go back to New York, and you can
sleep in Wolfe's house—there's a good bed in the room
above mine. The advantage of that is that you'll be
there in the morning to have a talk with Wolfe. That
strikes me as a good program."

I could see him shaking his head. "I live at the
Chesebrough. Thanks for your invitation, but I prefer
to sleep in my own bed."

"I'm asking you, will you come?"

"To Mr. Wolfe's house to sleep? No."

"All right. You're crazy. Surely you've got brains
enough to realize that you're going to have to have a
talk with somebody about your driving sixty miles to
go through a window to get an umbrella. Knowing
Wolfe, and knowing the police, I merely advise you to
talk with him instead of them. I've not trying to
shatter your aplomb, I like it, I think it's attractive,
but I'll be damned if I'm going to stand here and beg
you all night. In a couple of minutes I'll begin to get
impatient."

Gebert shrugged again. "I confess I don't like the
police. I leave here with you incognito. Is that it?"

"That's it."

"Very well. I'll go."

"To Wolfe's for the night?"

"I tell you so."

"Good for you. Don't worry about your car; Saul will take care of it. Your name's Jerry. Act tough and ignorant, like me or any other detective. —Okay, Orrie, choke it. Come on. Come on, Jerry."

I opened the door to the lighted room and they followed me in. I collected Saul and Fred and briefly explained the strategy, and when Saul objected to letting the cops in I agreed with him without an argument. Our trio was supposed to resume operations in the morning, and in the meantime they had to have some shut-eye. It was settled that no one was to be permitted to enter, and excavations by strangers outdoors were barred. They were to send Fred to the village to get grub, and to phone the office, in the morning.

I went to a window and pushed my nose against the glass and saw that the party was still gathered about the steps. At a nod from me Saul unlocked the door and swung it open, and Gebert and I passed through to the porch. In our rear, Saul and Fred and Orrie occupied the doorsill. We clattered to the edge:

"Lieutenant Rowcliff? Oh, there you are. Jerry Martin and I are going back to town. I'm leaving three men here, and they still prefer privacy. They need some sleep and so do you. Just as a favor, I'll tell you straight that Jerry and I haven't got the red box on us, so there's nothing to gnash your teeth about. —Okay, Saul, lock up, and one of you stay awake." The door shut, leaving the porch in the dark again, and I turned. "Come on, Jerry. If anyone jostles you, stick a hatpin in him."

But the instant the door had closed someone had got smart and clicked on a flashlight and aimed it at Gebert's face. I had his elbow to urge him along, but there was a stir in front of us and a growl: "Now you don't need to run." A big guy was standing in front of Gebert and holding the light on him. He growled again. "Look here, Lieutenant, look at this Jerry. Jerry hell. This is that guy that was at Frost's apartment when I was up there this morning with the inspector. His name's Gebert, a friend of Mrs. Frost's."

I snickered. "I don't know you, mister, but you must be cross-eyed. The country air maybe. Come on, Jerry."

No go. Rowcliff and two other dicks and the pair of troopers all barred the way, and Rowcliff sang at me, "Back up, Goodwin. You've heard of Bill Northrup and you know how cross-eyed he is. No mistake, Bill?"

"Not a chance. It's Gebert."

"You don't say. Keep the light on him. How about it, Mr. Gebert? What do you mean by trying to fool Mr. Goodwin and telling him your name's Jerry Martin? Huh?"

I kept my trap shut. Through a bad piece of luck I was getting a kick on the shin, and there was nothing to do but take it. And I had to hand it to Gebert; with that light right in his face and that bunch of gorillas all sticking their chins at him, he smiled as if they were asking him whether he took milk or lemon.

He said, "I wouldn't try to fool Mr. Goodwin. Indeed not. Anyway, how could I? He knows me."

"Oh, he does. Then I can discuss the Jerry Martin idea with him. But you might tell me what you're doing out here at the McNair place. They found you here, huh?"

"Found me?" Gebert looked urbane but a little annoyed. "Of course not. They brought me. At their request I came to show them where I thought McNair might have concealed the red box they are looking for. But no; it wasn't there. Then you arrived. Then Mr. Goodwin arrived. He thought it would be pleasanter if you did not know I had come to help them, and he suggested I should be Mr. Jerry Martin. I saw no reason not to oblige him."

Rowcliff grunted. "But you didn't see fit to mention this place to Inspector Cramer this morning when he asked if you had any idea where the red box might be. Did you?"

Gebert had a cute reply for that too, and for several more questions, but I didn't listen to them with much interest. I was busy taking a trial balance. I shied off because Gebert was being a little too slick. Of course he figured that I would let his story slide because I wanted to save him for Nero Wolfe, but it began to look to me as if he wasn't worth the price. It wasn't an attack of qualms; I would just as soon kick dust in the eyes of the entire Police Department from Commissioner Hombert up in anything that resembled a worthy cause; but it appeared more than doubtful whether Wolfe would be able to squeeze any profit out of Gebert anyhow, and if he couldn't, we would just be giving Cramer another reason to get good and sore without anything to console us for it. I knew I was taking a big risk, for if Gebert had murdered McNair there was a fair chance that they would screw it out of him at headquarters, and there would be our case up the flue; but I wasn't like Wolfe, I was handicapped by not knowing whether Gebert was guilty. While I was making these calculations I was listening with one ear to Gebert smearing it on

Rowcliff, and he did a neat job of it; he had smoothed it down to a point where he and I could have got in a car and driven off without even being fingerprinted.

"See that you're home in the morning," Rowcliff was growling at him. "The inspector may want to see you. If you go out leave word where." He turned to me, and you could have distilled vinegar from his breath. "You're so full of lousy tricks, I'll bet when you're alone you play 'em on yourself. The inspector will let you know what he thinks of this one. I'd hate to tell you what I think of it."

I grinned at him, his face in the dark. "And here I am all ready with another one. I've been standing here listening to Gebert reel it off just to see how slick he is. He could slide on a cheese grater. You'd better take him to headquarters and give him a bed."

"Yeah? What for? You through with him?"

"Naw, I haven't even started. A little before nine o'clock this evening he got here in his car. Not knowing there was anyone here because the lights were out, he tried to pry open a window to get in. When Saul Panzer asked him what he wanted, he said he left his umbrella here last fall and drove out to get it. Maybe it's in your lost and found room at headquarters; you'd better take him there to look and see. Material witness would do it."

Rowcliff grunted. "You were ready with another one all right. When did you think this up?"

"I didn't have to. Fact is stranger than fiction. You shouldn't be always suspecting everybody. If you want me to I'll call them out and you can ask them; they were all three here. I would say that an umbrella that's worth going in a window after is worth asking questions about."

"Uh-huh. And you were calling this guy Jerry and

trying to smuggle him out. Where to? How would you like to come down and look over some umbrellas yourself?"

That disgusted me. I wasn't any too pleased anyhow, letting go of Gebert. I said, "Poop and pooh. Both for you. You sound like a flatfoot catching kids playing wall ball. Maybe I wanted the glory of taking him to headquarters myself. Or maybe I wanted to help him escape from the country by putting him on a subway for Brooklyn, where I believe you live. You've got him, haven't you, with a handle I gave you to hold him by? Poops and poohs for all of youse. It's past my bedtime."

I strode through the cordon, brushing them aside like flies, went to the roadster and got in, backed out through the gate, circling into the road and missing the fender of the troopers' chariot by an inch, and rolled off the ruts and bumps. I was so disgruntled with the complexion of things that I beat my former time between Brewster and 35th Street by two minutes.

Of course I found the house dark and quiet. There was no note from Wolfe on my desk. Upstairs, in my room, whither I carried the glass of milk I had got in the kitchen, the pilot light was a red spot on the wall, showing that Wolfe had turned on his switch so that if anyone disturbed one of his windows or stepped in the hall within eight feet of his door, a gong under my bed would start a hullabaloo that would wake even me. I hit the hay at 2:19.

Chapter 14

I swiveled my chair to face Wolfe. "Oh, yes, I forgot to tell you. This may strike a chord. That lawyer Collinger said that they are proceeding with McNair's remains as instructed in his will. Services are being held at nine o'clock this evening at the Belford Memorial Chapel on 73rd Street, and tomorrow he'll be cremated and the ashes sent to his sister in Scotland. Collinger seems to think that naturally the executor of McNair's estate will attend the services. Will we go in the sedan?"

Wolfe murmured, "Puerile. You are no better than a gadfly. You may represent me at the Belford Memorial Chapel." He shuddered. "Black and white. Dreary and hushed obeisance to the grisly terror. His murderer will be there. Confound it, don't badger me." He resumed with the atlas, doing the double page spread of Arabia.

It was noon Friday. I had had less than six hours' sleep, having held my levee at eight in order to be ready, without skimping breakfast, to report to Wolfe at nine o'clock in the plant rooms. He had asked me first off if I had got the red box, and beyond that had listened with his back as he examined a bench of cattleya seedlings. The news about Gebert appeared to bore him, and he could always carry that off without my being able to tell whether it was a pose or on the level. When I reminded him that Collinger was due at ten to discuss the will and the estate, and asked if there were any special instructions, he merely shook his head without bothering to turn around. I left him and went down to the kitchen and ate a couple more pancakes so as to keep from taking a nap. Fritz was friendly again, forgiving and forgetting that I had jerked Wolfe back from the brink of the Wednesday relapse. He never toted a grudge.

Around 9:30 Fred Durkin phoned from Brewster. After my departure from Glennanne the night before the invaders had soon left, and our trio had had a restful night, but they had barely finished their stag breakfast when dicks and troopers had appeared again, armed with papers. I told Fred to tell Saul to keep an eye on the furniture and other portable objects.

At ten o'clock Henry H. Barber, our lawyer, came, and a little later Collinger. I sat and listened to a lot of guff about probate and surrogate and so forth, and went upstairs and got Wolfe's signature to some papers, and did some typing for them. They were gone before Wolfe came down at eleven. He had arranged the orchids in the vase, rung for beer, tried his pen, looked through the morning mail, made a telephone call to Raymond Plehn, dictated a letter, and then gone to the bookshelves and returned with the atlas; and settled down with it. I had never been able to think of more than one possible advantage to be expected from Wolfe's atlas work: If we ever got an international case we would certainly be on familiar ground, no matter where it took us to.

I went ahead with a lot of entries from Theodore Horstmann's slips into the plant records.

Around a quarter to one Fritz knocked on the door and followed it in with a cablegram in his hand. I opened it and read it:

SCOTLAND NEGATIVE NUGANT GAMUT CARTAGENA NEGATIVE DESTRUCTION RIOTS DANNUM GAMUT

HITCHCOCK

I got out the code book and did some looking, and scribbled in my book. Wolfe stayed in Arabia. I cleared my throat like a lion and his eyes flickered at me.

I told him, "If no news is good news, here's a treat from Hitchcock. He says that in Scotland there are no results yet because the subject refuses to furnish help or information but that efforts are being continued. In Cartagena likewise no results on account of destruction in riots two years ago, and likewise efforts are being continued. I might add on my own hook that Scotland and Cartagena have got it all over 35th Street in one respect anyhow. Gamut. Efforts are being continued."

Wolfe grunted.

Ten minutes later he closed the atlas. "Archie. We need that red box."

"Yes, sir."

"Yes, we do. I phoned Mr. Hitchcock in London again, at the night rate, after you left last evening, and I fear got him out of bed. I learned that Mr. McNair's sister is living on an old family property, a small place near Camfirth, and thought it possible that he had concealed the red box there during one of his trips to Europe. I requested Mr. Hitchcock to have a search made for it, but apparently the sister—from this cable—will not permit it."

He sighed. "I never knew a plaguier case. We have all the knowledge we need, and not a shred of presentable evidence. Unless the red box is found—are we actually going to be forced to send Saul to Scotland or Spain or both? Good heavens! Are we so inept that we must half encircle the globe to demonstrate the motive and the technique of a murder that happened in our own office in front of our eyes? Pfui! I sat for two hours last evening considering the position, and I confess that we have an exceptional combination of luck and adroitness against us; but even so, if we are driven to the extreme of buying steamship tickets across the Atlantic we are beneath contempt."

"Yeah." I grinned at him; if he was getting sore there was hope. "I'm beneath yours and you're beneath mine. At that, it may be one of those cases where nothing but routine will do it. For instance, one of Cramer's hirelings may turn the trick by trailing a sale of potassium cyanide."

"Bah." Wolfe upturned a whole palm; he was next door to a frenzy. "Mr. Cramer does not even know who the murderer is. As for the poison, it was probably bought years ago, possibly not in this country. We have to deal not only with adroitness, but also with forethought."

"So I suspected. You're telling me that you do know who the murderer is. Huh?"

"Archie." He wiggled a finger at me. "I dislike mystification and never practice it for diversion. But I shall load you with no burdens that will strain your powers. You have no gift for guile. Certainly I know who the murderer is, but what good does that do me?

I am in no better boat than Mr. Cramer. By the way, he telephoned last evening a few minutes after you left. In a very ugly mood. He seemed to think we should have told him of the existence of Glennanne instead of leaving him to discover it for himself from an item among Mr. McNair's papers; and he hotly resented Saul's holding it against beleaguerment. I presume he will cool off now that you have made him a gift of Mr. Gebert."

I nodded. "And I presume I would look silly if he squeezed enough sap out of Gebert to make the case jell."

"Never. No fear, Archie. Mr. Gebert is not likely, under any probable pressure, to surrender the only hold on the cliff of existence he has managed to cling to. It would have been useless to bring him here; he has his profit and loss calculated. —Yes, Fritz? Ah, the soufflé chose to ignore the clock? At once, certainly."

He gripped the edge of the desk to push back his chair.

We did not ignore the soufflé.

My lunch was interrupted once, by a phone call from Helen Frost. Ordinarily Wolfe flatly prohibited my disturbing a meal to go to the phone, letting it be handled by Fritz on the kitchen extension, but there were exceptions he permitted. One was a female client. So I went to the office and took it, not with any overflow of gaiety, for all morning I had been thinking that we might get word from her any minute that the deal was off. Up there alone with her mother, there was no telling what she might be talked into. But all she wanted was to ask about Perren Gebert. She said that her mother had phoned the Chesebrough at breakfast time and had learned that Gebert had not been there for the night, and after phoning and fussing all morning, she had finally been informed by the police that Gebert was being detained at headquarters, and they had told her mother something about Gebert being held on information furnished by Mr. Goodwin of Nero Wolfe's office, and what about it?

I told her, "It's all right. We caught him trying to get in a window out at Glennanne, and the cops are asking him what for. Just a natural sensible question. After a while he'll either answer it or he won't, and they'll either turn him loose or keep him. It's all right."

"But they won't . . ." She sounded harassed. "You see, I told you, it's true there are things about him I don't like, but he is an old friend of mother's and mine too. They won't do anything to him, will they? I can't understand what he was doing at Glennanne, trying to get in. He hasn't been there . . . I don't think he ever was there . . . you know he and Uncle Boyd didn't like each other. I don't understand it. But they can't do anything to him just for trying to open a window. Can they?"

"They can and they can't. They can sort of annoy him. That won't hurt him much."

"It's terrible." The shiver was in her voice. "It's terrible! And I thought I was hard-boiled. I guess I am, but . . . anyway, I want you and Mr. Wolfe to go on. Go right on. Only I thought I might ask you—Perren is really mother's oldest friend—if you could go down there and see where he is and what they're doing . . . I know the police are very friendly with you . . ."

"Sure." I made a face at the phone. "Down to headquarters? Surest thing you know. Bless your heart, I'd be glad to. It won't take me long to finish my

lunch, and I'll take it on the jump. Then I'll phone you
and let you know."

"Oh, that's fine. Thank you ever so much. If I'm not
at home mother will be. I . . . I'm going out to buy
some flowers . . ."

"Okay. I'll phone you."

I went back to the dining room and resumed with
my tools and told Wolfe about it. He was provoked, as
always when business intruded itself on a meal. I took
my time eating, on to the coffee and through it,
because I knew if I hurried and didn't chew properly it
would upset Wolfe's digestion. It didn't break his heart
if I was caught out in the field at feeding time and had
to grab what I could get, but if I once started a meal
at that table I had to complete it like a gentleman.
Also, I wasn't champing at the bit for an errand I
didn't fancy.

It was after two when I went to the garage for the
roadster, and there I got another irritation when I
found that the washing and polishing job had been
done by a guy with one eye.

Downtown, on Centre Street, I parked at the
triangle, and went in and took the elevator. I walked
down the upstairs corridor as if I owned it, entered
the anteroom of Cramer's office as cocky as they come,
and told the hulk at the desk:

"Tell the inspector, Goodwin of Nero Wolfe's office."

I stood up for ten minutes, and then was nodded in.
I was hoping somewhat that Cramer would be out and
my dealings would be with Burke, not on account of
my natural timidity, but because I knew it would be
better for everyone concerned if Cramer had a little
more time to cool off before resuming social intercourse with us. But he was there at his desk when I

entered, and to my surprise he didn't get up and take a bite at my ear. He snarled a little:

"So it's you. You walk right in here. Burke made a remark about you this morning. He said that if you ever wanted a rubdown you ought to get Smoky to do it for you. Smoky is the little guy with a bum leg that polishes the brass railings downstairs at the entrance."

I said, "I guess I'll sit down."

"I guess you will. Go ahead. Want my chair?"

"No, thanks."

"What *do* you want?"

I shook my head at him wistfully. "I'll be doggoned, Inspector, if you're not a hard man to please. We do our best to help you find that red box, and you resent it. We catch a dangerous character trying to make an illegal entry, and hand him over to you, and you resent that. If we wrap this case up and present you with it, I suppose you'll charge us as accessories. You may remember that in that Rubber Band affair—"

"Yeah, I know. Past favors have been appreciated. I'm busy. What do you want?"

"Well . . ." I tilted my head back so as to look down on him. "I represent the executor of Mr. McNair's estate. I came to invite Mr. Perren Gebert to attend the funeral services at the Belford Memorial Chapel at nine o'clock this evening. If you would kindly direct me to his room?"

Cramer gave me a nasty look. Then he heaved a deep sigh, reached in his pocket for a cigar, bit off the end and lit it. He puffed at it and got it established in the corner of his mouth. Abruptly he demanded:

"What have you got on Gebert?"

"Nothing. Not even passing a red light. Nothing at all."

"Did you come here to see him? What does Wolfe want you to ask him?"

"Nothing. As Tammany is my judge. Wolfe says he's just clinging to the cliff of existence or something like that and he wouldn't let him in the house."

"Then what the devil do you want with him?"

"Nothing. I'm just keeping my word. I promised somebody I would come down here and ask you how he is and what his future prospects are. So help me, that's on the level."

"Maybe I believe you. Do you want to look at him?"

"Not especially. I would just as soon."

"You can." He pressed a button in a row. "As a matter of fact, I'd like to have you. This case is open and shut, open for the newspapers and shut for me. If you've got any curiosity about anything that you think Gebert might satisfy, go ahead and take your turn. They've been working on him since seven o'clock this morning. Eight hours. They can't even make him mad."

A sergeant with oversize shoulders had entered and was standing there. Cramer told him: "This man's name is Goodwin. Take him down to Room Five and tell Sturgis to let him help if he wants to." He turned to me. "Drop in again before you leave. I may want to ask you something."

"Okay. I'll have something thought up to tell you."

I followed the sergeant out to the corridor and down it to the elevator. We stayed in for a flight below the ground floor, and he led me the length of a dim hall and around a corner, and finally stopped at a door which may have had a figure 5 on it but if so I couldn't see it. He opened the door and we went in and he closed the door again. He crossed to where a guy sat on a chair mopping his neck with a handkerchief, said something to him, and turned and went out again.

It was a medium-sized room, nearly bare. A few plain wooden chairs were along one wall. A bigger one with arms was near the middle of the room, and Perren Gebert was sitting in it, with a light flooding his face from a floor lamp with a big reflector in front of him. Standing closer in front of him was a wiry-looking man in his shirt sleeves with little fox ears and a Yonkers haircut. The guy on the chair that the sergeant had spoken to was in his shirt sleeves too, and so was Gebert. When I got close enough to the light so that Gebert could see me and recognize me, he half started up, and said in a funny hoarse tone:

"Goodwin! Ah, Goodwin—"

The wiry cop reached out and slapped him a good one on the left side of his neck, and then with his other hand on his right ear. Gebert quivered and sank back. "Sit down there, will you?" the cop said plaintively. The other cop, still holding his handkerchief in his hand, got up and walked over to me:

"Goodwin? My name's Sturgis. Who are you from, Buzzy's squad?"

I shook my head. "Private agency. We're on the case and we're supposed to be hot."

"Oh. Private, huh? Well . . . the inspector sent you down. You want a job?"

"Not just this minute. You gentlemen go ahead. I'll listen and see if I can think of something."

I stepped a pace closer to Gebert and looked him over. He was reddened up a good deal and kind of blotchy, but I couldn't see any real marks. He had no necktie on and his shirt was torn on the shoulder and there was dried sweat on him. His eyes were blood-shot from blinking at the strong light and probably

from having them slapped open when he closed them.
I asked him:

"When you said my name just now, did you want to
tell me something?"

He shook his head and made a hoarse grunt. I
turned and told Sturgis: "He can't tell you anything if
he can't talk. Maybe you ought to give him some
water."

Sturgis snorted. "He could talk if he wanted to. We
gave him water when he passed out a couple of hours
ago. There's only one thing in God's world wrong with
him. He's contrary. You want to try him?"

"Later maybe." I crossed to the row of chairs by
the wall and sat down. Sturgis stood and thoughtfully
wiped his neck. The wiry cop leaned forward to get
closer to Gebert's face and asked him in a wounded
tone:

"What did she pay you that money for?"

No response, no movement.

"What did she pay you that money for?"

Again, nothing.

"What did she pay you that money for?"

Gebert shook his head faintly. The cop roared at
him in indignation, "Don't shake your head at me!
Understand? What did she pay you that money for?"

Gebert sat still. The cop hauled off and gave him a
couple more slaps, rocking his head, and then another
pair.

"What did she pay you that money for?"

That went on for a while. It appeared to me
doubtful that any progress was going to be made. I
felt sorry for the poor dumb cops, seeing that they
didn't have brains enough to realize that they were
just gradually putting him to sleep and that in another
three or four hours he wouldn't be worth fooling with.

Of course he would be as good as new in the morning, but they couldn't go on with that for weeks, even if he was a foreigner and couldn't vote. That was the practical viewpoint, and though the ethics of it was none of my business, I admit I had my prejudices. I can bulldog a man myself, if he has it coming to him, but I prefer to do it on his home grounds, and I certainly don't want any help.

Apparently they had abandoned all the side issues which had been tried on him earlier in the day, and were concentrating on a few main points. After twenty minutes or more consumed on what she had paid him the money for, the wiry cop suddenly shifted to another one, what had he been after at Glennanne the night before. Gebert mumbled something to that, and got slapped for it. Then he made no reply to it and got slapped again. The cop was about on the mental level of a woodchuck; he had no variety, no change of pace, no nothing but a pair of palms and they must have been getting tender. He stuck to Glennanne for over half an hour, while I sat and smoked cigarettes and got more and more disgusted, then turned away and crossed to his colleague and muttered wearily:

"Take him a while, I'm going to the can."

Sturgis asked me if I wanted to try, and I declined again with thanks. In fact, I was about ready to leave, but thought I might as well get a brief line on Sturgis' technique. He stuck his handkerchief in his hip pocket, walked over to Gebert and exploded at him:

"What did she pay you that money for?"

I gritted my teeth to keep from throwing a chair at the sap. But he did show some variation; he was more of a pusher than a slapper. The gesture he worked most was to put his paw on Gebert's ear and administer a few short snappy shoves and then put his other paw on the other ear and even it up. Sometimes he took him full face and shoved straight back and then ended with a pat.

The wiry cop had come back and sat down beside me and was telling me how much bran he ate. I had decided I had had my money's worth and was taking a last puff on a cigarette, when the door opened and the sergeant entered—the one who had brought me down. He walked over and looked at Gebert the way a cook looks at a kettle to see if it has started to boil. Sturgis stepped back and pulled out his handkerchief and started to wipe. The sergeant turned to him:

"Orders from the inspector. Fix him up and brush him off and take him to the north door and wait there for me. The inspector wants him out of here in five minutes. Got a cup?"

Sturgis went and opened the door of a cupboard and came back with a white enameled cup. The sergeant poured into it from a bottle and returned the bottle to his pocket. "Let him have that. Can he navigate all right?"

Sturgis said he could. The sergeant turned to me: "Will you go up to the inspector's office, Goodwin? I've got an errand on the main floor."

He went on out and I followed him without saying anything. There was no one there I wanted to exchange telephone numbers with.

I took the elevator back upstairs. I had to wait quite a while in Cramer's anteroom. Apparently he was having a party in there, for three dicks came out, and a little later a captain in uniform, and still later a skinny guy with grey hair whom I recognized for Deputy Commissioner Alloway. Then I was allowed the gangway. Cramer was sitting there looking sour and chewing a cigar that had gone out.

"Sit down, son. You didn't get a chance to show us how downstairs. Huh? And we didn't show you much either. There was a good man working on Gebert for four hours this morning, a good clever man. He couldn't start a crack. So we gave up the cleverness and tried something else."

"Oh, that's it." I grinned at him. "That's what those guys are, something else. It describes them all right. And now you're turning him loose?"

"We are." Cramer frowned. "A lawyer was beginning to heat things up, I suppose hired by Mrs. Frost. He got a habeas corpus a little while ago, and I couldn't see that Gebert was worth fighting for, and anyway, I doubt if we could have held him. Also the French consul started stirring around. Gebert's a French citizen. Of course we're putting a shadow on him, and what good will that do? When a man like that has got knowledge about a crime there ought to be some way of tapping him the way you do a maple tree, and draw it out of him. Huh?"

I nodded. "Sure, that'd be all right. It would be better than . . ." I shrugged. "Never mind. Any news from the boys at Glennanne?"

"No." Cramer clasped his hands behind his head, leaned back into them, chewed his cigar, and scowled at me. "You know, I hate to say this to you. But it's what I think. I wouldn't like to see you get hurt, but it might have been more sensible if we had had you down in Room Five all day instead of that Gebert."

"Me?" I shook my head. "I don't believe it. After all I've done for you."

"Oh, don't kid me. I'm tired, I'm not in a mood for it. I've been thinking. I know how Wolfe works. I don't pretend I could do it, but I know how he does it. I admit he never yet has finished up on the wrong side, but you only have to break an egg once. It's just possible that in this case he has got his feet tangled up. He's working for the Frosts."

"He's working for *a* Frost."

"Sure, and that's funny too. First he said Lew hired him, and then the daughter. I never knew him to shift clients like that before. Has it got anything to do with the fact that the fortune belongs to the daughter, but that it has been controlled by Lew's father for twenty years? And Lew's father, Dudley Frost, is a great one for keeping things to himself. We put it up to him that we're investigating a murder case and asked him to let us check the assets of the estate because there might be a connection that would be helpful. We asked him to cooperate. He told us to go chase ourselves. Frisbie up at the D.A.'s office tried to get at it through court action, but apparently there's no loophole. Now why did Wolfe all of a sudden quit Lew and transfer his affections to the other side of the family?"

"He didn't. It was what you might call a forced sale."

"Yeah? Maybe. I'd like to see Nero Wolfe forced into anything. I noticed it happened right after McNair was croaked. All right; Wolfe had got hold of some kind of positive information. Where did he get it from? From that red box. You see, I'm not trying to play foxy, I'm just telling you. His stunt at Glennanne was a cover. Your play with Gebert was a part of it too. And I warn you and I warn Wolfe: don't think I'm too dumb to find out eventually what was in that red box, because I'm not."

I shook my head sadly. "You're all wet, inspector. Honest to God, you're dripping. If you've quit looking for the red box let us know, and we'll take a shot at it."

"I haven't given it up. I'm making all the motions. I don't say Wolfe is deliberately covering a murderer, he'd have to get more than his feet tangled before he'd be fool enough to do that, but I do say he's withholding valuable evidence that I want. I don't pretend to know why; I don't pretend to know one damn thing about this lousy case. But I do think it's in the Frost family, because for one thing we haven't been able to uncover any other connection of McNair's that offers any line at all. We don't get anything from his sister in Scotland. Nothing in McNair's papers. Nothing from Paris. No trail on the poison. My only definite theory about the Frosts is something I dug up from an old family enemy, some old scandal about Edwin Frost disinheriting his wife because he didn't like her ideas about friendship with a Frenchman, and forcing her to sign away her dower rights by threatening to divorce her. Well, Gebert's a Frenchman, but McNair wasn't, and then what? It looks as if we're licked, huh? Remember what I said Tuesday in Wolfe's office? But Wolfe is absolutely not a damned fool, and he ought to know better than to try to sit on a lid which sooner or later can be pried off. Will you take him a message from me?"

"Sure. Shall I write it down?"

"You won't need to. Tell him this Gebert is going to have a shadow on him from now on until this case is solved. Tell him that if the red box hasn't been found, or something else just as good, one of my best men will sail for France on the *Normandie* next Wednesday. And tell him that I know a few things already, for instance that in the past five years $60,000 of his client's money has been paid to this Gebert, and the Lord knows how much before that."

"Sixty grand?" I raised the brows. "Of Helen Frost's money?"

"Yes. I suppose that's news to you."

"It certainly is. Shucks, that much is gone where we'll never see it. How did she give it to him, nickels and dimes?"

"Don't try to be funny. I'm telling you this to tell Wolfe. Gebert opened a bank account in New York five years ago, and since then he has deposited a thousand dollar check every month, signed by Calida Frost. You know banks well enough to be able to guess how easy it was to dig that up."

"Yeah. Of course, you have influence with the police. May I call your attention to the fact that Calida Frost is not our client?"

"Mother and daughter, what's the difference? The income is the daughter's, but I suppose the mother gets half of it. What's the difference?"

"There might be. For instance, that young lady up in Rhode Island last year that killed her mother. One was dead and the other one alive. That was a slight difference. What was the mother paying Gebert the money for?"

Cramer's eyes narrowed at me. "When you get home, ask Wolfe."

I laughed. "Oh, come, Inspector. Come, come. The trouble with you is you don't see Wolfe much except when he's got the sawdust in the ring and ready to crack the whip. You ought to see him the way I do sometimes. You think he knows everything. I could tell you at least three things he never will know."

Cramer socked his teeth into his cigar. "I think he knows where that red box is, and he's probably got it. I think that in the interest of a client, not to mention his own, he's holding back evidence in a murder case.

And do you know what he expects to do? He expects to wait until May seventh to spring it, the day Helen Frost will be twenty-one. How do you think I like that? How do you think they like it at the D.A.'s office?"

I slapped a yawn. "Excuse it, I only had six hours' sleep. I'll swear I don't know what I can say to convince you. Why don't you run up and have a talk with Wolfe?"

"What for? I can see it. I sit down and explain to him why I think he's a liar. He says 'indeed' and shuts his eyes and opens them again when he gets ready to ring for beer. He ought to start a brewery. Some great men, when they die, leave their brains to a scientific laboratory. Wolfe ought to leave his stomach."

"Okay." I got up. "If you're so sore at him that you even resent his quenching his thirst occasionally every few minutes, I can't expect you to listen to reason. I can only repeat you're all wet. Wolfe himself says that if he had the red box he could finish up the case"—I snapped my fingers—"like that."

"I don't believe it. Give him my messages, will you?"

"Right. Best regards."

"Go to hell."

I didn't let the elevator take me that far, but got off at the main floor. At the triangle I found the roadster and maneuvered it into Centre Street.

Of course Cramer was funny, but I wasn't violently amused. It was no advantage to have him so cockeyed suspicious that he wouldn't even believe a plain statement of fact. The trouble was that he wasn't broad-minded enough to realize that Wolfe and I were inherently as honest as any man should be unless he's a hermit, and that if McNair had in fact given us the red box or told us where it was, our best line would have been to say so, and to declare that its contents were confidential matters which had nothing to do with any murder, and refuse to produce them. Even I could see that, and I wasn't an inspector and never expected to be.

It was after six when I got home. There was a surprise waiting there for me. Wolfe was in the office, leaning back in his chair with his fingers laced at the apex of his frontal buttress; and seated in the dunce's chair, with the remains of a highball in a glass he clutched, was Saul Panzer. They nodded greetings to me and Saul went on talking:

". . . the first drawing is held on Tuesday, three days before the race, and that eliminates everyone whose number isn't drawn for one or another of the entries. The horses. But another drawing is held the next day, Wednesday . . ."

Saul went on with the sweepstakes lesson. I sat down at my desk and looked up the number of the Frost apartment and dialed it. Helen was home, and I told her I had seen Gebert and he had been rather exhausted with all the questions they had asked him, but that they had let him go. She said she knew it; he had telephoned a little while ago and her mother had gone to the Chesebrough to see him. She started to thank me, and I told her she'd better save it for an emergency. That chore finished, I swiveled and listened to Saul. It sounded as if he had more than theoretical knowlege of the sweep. When Wolfe had got enough about it to satisfy him he stopped Saul with a nod and turned to me:

"Saul needs twenty dollars. There is only ten in the drawer."

I nodded. "I'll cash a check in the morning." I pulled out my wallet. Wolfe never carried any money.

I handed four fives to Saul and he folded it carefully and tucked it away.

Wolfe lifted a finger at him: "You understand, of course, that you are not to be seen."

"Yes, sir," Saul turned and departed.

I sat down and made the entry in the expense book. Then I whirled my chair again:

"Saul going back to Glennanne?"

"No." Wolfe sighed. "He has been explaining the machinery of the Irish sweepstakes. If bees handled their affairs like that, no hive would have enough honey to last the winter."

"But a few bees would be rolling in it."

"I suppose so. At Glennanne they have upturned every flagstone on the garden paths and made a general upheaval without result. Has Mr. Cramer found the red box?"

"No. He says you've got it."

"He does. Is he closing the case on that theory?"

"No. He's thinking of sending a man to Europe. Maybe he and Saul could go together."

"Saul will not go—at least, not at once. I have given him another errand. Shortly after you left Fred telephoned and I called them in. The state police have Glennanne in charge. Fred and Orrie I dismissed when they arrived. As for Saul . . . I took a hint from you. You meant it as sarcasm, I adopted it as sound procedure. Instead of searching the globe for the red box, consider, decide first where it is, then send for it. I have sent Saul."

I looked at him. I said grimly, "You're not kidding me. Who came and told you?"

"No one has been here."

"Who telephoned?"

"No one."

"I see. It's just blah. For a minute I thought you really knew—wait, who did you get a letter from, or a telegram or a cable or in short a communication?"

"No one."

"And you sent Saul for the red box?"

"I did."

"When will he be back?"

"I couldn't say. I would guess, tomorrow . . . possibly the day after . . ."

"Uh-huh. Okay, if it's only flummery. I might have known. You get me every time. We don't dare find the red box now anyway; if we did, Cramer would be sure we had it all the time and never speak to us again. He's disgusted and suspicious. They had Gebert down there, slapping him around and squealing and yelling at him. If you're so sure violence is inferior technique, you should have seen that exhibition; it was wonderful. They say it works sometimes, but even if it does, how could you depend on anything you got that way? Not to mention that after you had done it a few times any decent garbage can would be ashamed to have you found in it. But Cramer did give me one little slice of bacon, the Lord knows why: in the past five years Mrs. Edwin Frost has paid Perren Gebert sixty grand. One thousand smackers per month. He won't tell them what for. I don't know if they've asked her or not. Does that fit in with the phenomena you've been having a feeling for?"

Wolfe nodded. "Satisfactorily. Of course I had not known what the amount was."

"Oh. You hadn't. Are you telling me that you knew she is paying him?"

"Not at all. I merely surmised it. Naturally she is paying him; the man has to live or at least he thinks so. Was he bludgeoned into confessing it?"

"No. They screwed it out of his bank."

"I see. Detective work. Mr. Cramer needs a mirror to make sure he has a nose on his face."

"I give in." I compressed my lips and shook my head. "You're the pink of the pinks. You're the without which nothing." I stood up and shook down my pants legs. "I can think of only one improvement that might be made in this place; we could put an electric chair in the front room and do our own burning. I'm going to tell Fritz that I'll dine in the kitchen, because I'll have to be leaving around eight-thirty to represent you at the funeral services."

"That's a pity." He meant it. "Need you actually go?"

"I will go. It'll look better. Somebody around here ought to do something."

Chapter 15

At that hour, 8:50 p.m., parking spaces were few and far between on 73rd Street. I finally found one about half a block east of the address of the Belford Memorial Chapel, and backed into it. I thought there was something familiar about the license number of the car just ahead, and sure enough, after I got out and took a look, I saw that it was Perren Gebert's convertible. It was spic and span, having had a cleaning since its venture into the wilds of Putnam County. I handed it to Gebert for a strong rebound, since he had evidently recovered enough in three hours to put in an appearance at a social function.

I walked to the portal of the chapel and entered, and was in a square anteroom of paneled marble. A middle-aged man in black clothes approached and bowed to me. He appeared to be under the influence of a chronic but aristocratic melancholy. He indicated a door at his right by extending his forearm in that direction with his elbow fastened to his hip, and murmured at me:

"Good evening, sir. The chapel is that way. Or . . ."

"Or what?"

He coughed delicately. "Since the deceased had no family, a few of his intimate friends are gathering in the private parlor . . ."

"Oh. I represent the executor of the estate. I don't know. What do you think?"

"I should think, sir, in that case, perhaps the parlor . . ."

"Okay. Where?"

"This way." He turned to his left, opened a door, and bowed me through.

I stepped into thick soft carpet. The room was elegant, with subdued lights, upholstered divans and chairs, and a smell similar to a high-class barber shop. On a chair over in a corner was Helen Frost, looking pale and concentrated and beautiful in a dark gray dress and a little black hat. Standing protectively in front of her was Llewellyn. Perren Gebert was seated on a divan at the right. Two women, one of whom I recognized as having been at the candy-sampling session, were on chairs across the room. I nodded at the ortho-cousins and they nodded back, and aimed one at Gebert and got his, and picked a chair at the left. There was a murmur coming from where Llewellyn bent over Helen. Gebert's clothes looked neater than his face, with its swollen eyes and its general air of having been exposed to a bad spell of weather.

I sat and considered Wolfe's phrase: dreary and hushed obeisance to the grisly terror. The door opened and Dudley Frost came in. I was closest to the door. He looked around, passing me by without any pretense of recognition, saw the two women and called to them "How do you do?" so loud that they jumped, sent a curt nod in Gebert's direction and crossed toward the corner where the cousins were:

"Ahead of time, by Gad I am! Almost never happens! Helen, my dear, where the deuce is your mother? I phoned three times—good God! I forgot the flowers after all! When I thought of it, it was too late to send them, so I decided to bring them with me—"

"All right, Dad. It's all right. There's plenty of flowers . . ."

Maybe still dreary, but no longer hushed. I wondered how they managed with him during the minute of memorial silence on Armistice Day. I had thought of three possible methods when the door opened again and Mrs. Frost entered. Her brother-in-law came to meet her with ejaculations. She looked pale too, but certainly not as much as Helen, and apparently had on a black evening gown under a black wrap, with a black satin piepan for a hat. There was no sag to her as she more or less disregarded Dudley, nodded at Gebert, greeted the two women, and went across to her daughter and nephew.

I sat and took it in.

Suddenly a newcomer appeared, so silently through some other door that I didn't hear him do it. It was another aristocrat, fatter than the one in the anteroom but just as melancholy. He advanced a few steps and bowed:

"If you will come in now, please."

We all moved. I stood back and let the others go ahead. Lew seemed to be thinking that Helen should have his arm, and she seemed to think not. I followed along behind with the throttle wide open on the decorum.

The chapel was dimly lighted too. Our escort whispered something to Mrs. Frost, and she shook her head and led the way to seats. There were forty or fifty people there on chairs. A glance showed me several faces I had seen before; among others, Collinger the lawyer, and a couple of dicks in the back row. I stepped around to the rear because I saw the door to the anteroom was there. The coffin, dead black with chromium handles, with flowers all around it and on top, was on a platform up front. In a couple of minutes a door at the far end opened and a guy came out and stood by the coffin and peered around at us. He was in the uniform of his profession and he had a wide mouth and a look of comfortable assurance by no means flippant. After a decent amount of peering he began to talk.

For a professional I suppose he was okay. I had had enough long before he was through, because with me a little unction goes a long way. If I had to be slid up to heaven on soft soap, I'd just as soon you'd forget it and let me find my natural level. But I'm speaking only for myself; if you like it I hope you get it.

My seat at the rear permitted me to beat it as soon as I heard the amen. I was the first one out. For having admitted me to the private parlor I offered the aristocrat in the anteroom two bits, which I suppose he took out of noblesse oblige, and sought the sidewalk. Some cur had edged in and parked within three inches of the roadster's rear bumper, and I had to do a lot of squirming to get out without scraping the fender of Gebert's convertible. Then I zoomed to Central Park West and headed downtown.

It was nearly ten-thirty when I got home. A glance in at the office door showed me that Wolfe was in his chair with his eyes closed and an awful grimace on his face, listening to the "Pearls of Wisdom Hour" on the radio. In the kitchen Fritz sat at the little table I ate breakfast on, playing solitaire, with his slippers off and his toes hooked over the rungs of another chair.

As I poured a glass of milk from a bottle I got from the refrigerator, he asked me:

"How was it? Nice funeral?"

I reproached him. "You ought to be ashamed. I guess all Frenchmen are sardonic."

"I am not a French! I'm a Swiss."

"So you say. You read a French newspaper."

I took a first sip from the glass, carried it into the office, got into my chair, and looked at Wolfe. His grimace appeared even more distorted than when I had glanced in on my way by. I let him go on suffering a while, then took pity on him and went to the radio and turned it off and came back to my chair. I sipped at my milk and watched him. By degrees his face relaxed, and finally I saw his eyelids flicker, and then they came open a little. He heaved a sigh that went clear to the bottom.

I said, "All right, you richly deserve it. What does it mean? Not more than twelve steps altogether. As soon as that hooey started, you could get out of your chair and walk fifteen feet to it and back again makes thirty, and you'd be out of your misery. Or if you honestly believe that would be overdoing, you could get one of those remote control things—"

"I wouldn't, Archie." He was in his patient mood. "I really wouldn't. You are perfectly aware that I have enough enterprise to turn off the radio; you have seen me do it; the exercise is good for me. I purposely dial the station which will later develop into the "Pearls of Wisdom," and I deliberately bear it. It's discipline. It fortifies me to put up with ordinary inanities for days. I gladly confess that after listening to the "Pearls of Wisdom" your conversation is an intellectual and esthetic delight. It's the tops." He grimaced. "That's what a Pearl of Wisdom just said that cultured interests are. He said they are the tops." He grimaced again. "Great heavens, I'm thirsty." He jerked himself up and leaned forward to press the button for beer.

But it was a little while before he got it. An instant after he pressed the button the doorbell rang, which meant that Fritz would have to attend to that chore first. Since it was nearly eleven o'clock and no one was expected, my heart began to beat, as it always does when we're on a case with any kick to it and any little surprise turns up. As a matter of fact, I got proof that I had fallen for Wolfe's showmanship again, for I had a sudden conviction that Saul Panzer was going to walk in with the red box under his arm.

Then I heard a voice in the hall that didn't belong to Saul. The door opened and swung around and Fritz stepped back to admit the visitor, and Helen Frost walked in. At the look on her face I hopped up and went over and put a hand on her arm, thinking she was about ready to flop.

She shook her head and I dropped the hand. She walked toward Wolfe's desk and stopped. Wolfe said:

"How do you do, Miss Frost? Sit down." Sharply: "Archie, put her in a chair."

I got her arm again and eased her over and got a chair behind her, and she sank into it. She looked at me and said, "Thank you." She looked at Wolfe: "Something awful has happened. I didn't want to go home and I . . . I came here. I'm afraid. I have been all along, really, but . . . I'm afraid now. Perren is dead. Just now, up on 73rd Street. He died on the sidewalk."

"Indeed. Mr. Gebert." Wolfe wiggled a finger at her. "Breathe, Miss Frost. In any event, you need to breathe. —Archie, get a little brandy."

Chapter 16

Our client shook her head. "I don't want any brandy. I don't think I could swallow." She was querulous and shaky. "I tell you . . . I'm afraid!"

"Yes." Wolfe had sat up and got his eyes open. "I heard you. If you don't pull yourself together, with brandy or without, you'll have hysterics, and that will be no help at all. Do you want some ammonia? Do you want to lie down? Do you want to talk? Can you talk?"

"Yes." She put the fingertips of both hands to her temples and caressed them delicately—her forehead, then the temples again. "I can talk. I won't have hysterics."

"Good for you. You say Mr. Gebert died on the sidewalk on 73rd Street. What killed him?"

"I don't know." She was sitting up straight, with her hands clasped in her lap. "He was getting in his car and he jumped back, and he came running down the sidewalk toward us . . . and he fell, and then Lew told me he was dead—"

"Wait a minute. Please. It will be better to do this neatly. I presume it happened after you left the chapel where the services were held. Did all of you leave together? Your mother and uncle and cousin and Mr. Gebert?"

She nodded. "Yes. Perren offered to drive mother and me home, but I said I would rather walk, and my uncle said he wanted to have a talk with mother, so they were going to take a taxi. We were all going slow along the sidewalk, deciding that—"

I put in, "East? Toward Gebert's car?"

"Yes. I didn't know then . . . I didn't know where his car was, but he left us and my uncle and mother and I stood there while Lew stepped into the street to stop a taxi, and I happened to be looking in the direction Perren had gone, and so was my uncle, and we saw him stop and open the door of his car . . . and then he jumped back and stood a second, and then he yelled and began running toward us . . . but he only got about halfway when he fell down, and he tried to roll . . . he tried . . ."

Wolfe wiggled a finger at her. "Less vividly, Miss Frost. You've lived through it once, don't try to do so again. Just tell us about it; it's history. He fell, he tried to roll, he stopped. People ran to succor him. Did you? Your mother?"

"No. My mother held my arm. My uncle ran to him, and a man that was there, and I called to Lew and he came and ran there too. Then mother told me to stay where I was, and she walked to them, and other people began to come. I stood there, and in about a minute Lew came to me and said they thought Perren was dead and told me to get a taxi and go home and they would stay. The taxi he had stopped was standing there and he put me in it, but after it started I didn't want to go home and I told the driver to come here. I . . . I thought perhaps . . ."

"You couldn't be expected to think. You were in no

condition for it." Wolfe leaned back. "So. You don't know what Mr. Gebert died of."

"No. There was no sound . . . no anything . . ."

"Do you know whether he ate or drank anything at the chapel?"

Her head jerked up. She swallowed. "No, I'm sure he didn't"

"No matter." Wolfe sighed. "That will be learned. You say that after Mr. Gebert jumped back from his car he yelled. Did he yell anything in particular?"

"Yes . . . he did. My mother's name. Like calling for help."

One of Wolfe's brows went up. "I trust he yelled it ardently. Forgive me for permitting myself a playful remark; Mr. Gebert would understand it, were he here. So he yelled 'Calida.' More than once?"

"Yes, several times. If you mean . . . my mother's name . . ."

"I meant nothing really. I was talking nonsense. It appears that, so far as you know, Mr. Gebert may have died of a heart attack or a clot on the brain or acute misanthropy. But I believe you said it made you afraid. What of?"

She looked at him, opened her mouth, and closed it again. She stammered. "That's why . . . that's what . . ." and stopped. Her hands unclasped and fluttered up, and down again. She took another try at it: "I told you . . . I've been afraid . . ."

"Very well." Wolfe showed her a palm. "You needn't do that. I understand. You mean that for some time you have been apprehensive of something malign in the relations of those closest and dearest to you. Naturally the death of Mr. McNair made it worse. Was it because—but forgive me. I am indulging one of my vices at a bad time—bad for you. I would not hesitate to torment you if it served our end, but it is useless now. Nothing more is needed. Did you intend to marry Mr. Gebert?"

"No. I never did."

"Did you have affection for him?"

"No. I told you . . . I didn't really like him."

"Good. Then once the temporary shock is past you can be objective about it. Mr. Gebert had very little to recommend him, either as a sapient being or as a biological specimen. The truth is that his death simplifies our task a little, and I feel no regret and shall pretend to none. Still his murder will be avenged, because we can't help ourselves. I assure you, Miss Frost, I am not trying to mystify you. But since I am not yet ready to tell you everything, I suppose it would be best to tell you nothing, so I'll confine myself, for this evening, to one piece of advice. Of course you have friends—for instance, that Miss Mitchell who attempted loyalty to you on Tuesday morning. Go there, now, without informing anyone, and spend the night. Mr. Goodwin can drive you. Tomorrow—"

"No." She was shaking her head. "I won't do that. What you said . . . about Perren's murder. He was murdered. Wasn't he?"

"Certainly. He died ardently. I repeat that because I like it. If you make a conjecture from it, all the better as preparation for you. I do not advise your spending the night with a friend on account of any danger to yourself, for there is none. In fact, there is no danger left for anyone, except as I embody it. But you must know that if you go home you won't get much sleep. The police will be clamoring for minutiae; they are probably bullying your family at this moment, and it would only be common sense to save yourself from that catechism. Tomorrow morning I could inform you of developments."

She shook her head again. "No." She sounded decisive. "I'll go home. I don't want to run away . . . I just came here . . . and anyhow, mother and Lew and my uncle . . . no. I'll go home. But if you could only tell me . . . please, Mr. Wolfe, please . . . if you could tell me something so I would know . . ."

"I can't. Not now. I promise you, soon. In the meantime—"

The phone rang. I swiveled and got it. Right away I was in a scrap. Some sap with a voice like a foghorn was going to have me put Wolfe on the wire immediately and no fooling, without bothering to tell me who it was that wanted him. I derided him until he boomed at me to hold it. After waiting a minute I heard another voice, one I recognized at once:

"Goodwin? Inspector Cramer. Maybe I don't need Wolfe. I'd hate to disturb him. Is Helen Frost there?"

"Who? Helen Frost?"

"That's what I said."

"Why should she be? Do you think we run a night shift? Wait a minute, I didn't know it was you, I think Mr. Wolfe wants to ask you something." I smothered the transmitter and turned: "Inspector Cramer wants to know if Miss Frost is here."

Wolfe lifted his shoulders half an inch and dropped them. Our client said, "Of course. Tell him yes."

I told the phone, "No, Wolfe can't think of anything you'd be likely to know. But if you mean *Miss* Helen Frost, I just saw her here in a chair."

"Oh. She's there. Some day I'm going to break your neck. I want her up here right away, at her home—no, wait. Keep her. I'll send a man—"

"Don't bother. I'll bring her."

"How soon?"

"Right now. At once. Without delay."

I rang off and whirled my chair to face the client. "He's up at your apartment. I suppose they all are. Do we go? I can still tell him I'm shortsighted and it wasn't you in the chair."

She rose. She faced Wolfe and she was sagging a little, but then she straightened out the spine. "Thank you," she said. "If there really isn't anything . . ."

"I'm sorry, Miss Frost. Nothing now. Perhaps tomorrow. I'll get word to you. Don't resent Mr. Cramer more than you must. He unquestionably means well. Good night."

I got up and bowed her ahead and through the office door, and snared my hat in the hall as I went by.

I had put the roadster in the garage, so we had to walk there for it. She waited for me at the entrance, and after she got in and I turned into Tenth Avenue, I told her:

"You've been getting lefts and rights both, and you're groggy. Lean back and shut your eyes and breathe deep."

She said thank you, but she sat straight and kept her eyes open and didn't say anything all the way to 65th Street. I was thinking that presumably I would make a night of it. Ever since she had busted in on us with the news, I had been kicking myself for having been in such a hell of a hurry to get away from 73rd Street; it had happened right there at Gebert's car, parked in front of mine, not five minutes after I left. That had been luck for you. I could have been right there, closer than anyone else . . .

I didn't get to make a night of it, either. My sojourn at the Frost apartment as Helen's escort was short and sour. She handed me her key to the door to the

entrance hall, and as soon as I got it open there stood
a dick. Another one was in a chair by the mirrors.
Helen and I started to go on by, but got blocked. The
dick told us:

"Please wait here a minute? Both of you."

He disappeared into the living room, and pretty
soon that door opened again and Cramer entered. He
looked preoccupied and unfriendly.

"Good evening, Miss Frost. Come with me, please."

"Is my mother here? My cousin—"

"They're all here. —All right, Goodwin, much
obliged. Pleasant dreams."

I grinned at him. "I'm not sleepy. I can stick
around without interfering—"

"You can also beat it without interfering. I'll watch
you do that."

I could tell by his tone there was no use; he would
merely have gone on being adamant. I ignored him. I
bowed to our client:

"Good night, Miss Frost."

I turned to the dick: "Look sharp, my man, open
the door."

He didn't move. I reached for the knob and swung
it wide open and went on out, leaving it that way. I'll
bet by gum he closed it.

C h a p t e r 17

The next morning, Saturday, there was no early indication that the detective business of Nero Wolfe had any burden heavier than a feather on either its mind or its conscience. I had my figure laved and clothed before eight o'clock, rather expecting a pre-breakfast summons to some sort of action from the head of the firm, but I might as well have snoozed my full 510 minutes. The house phone stayed silent. As usual, Fritz took a tray of orange juice, crackers and chocolate to Wolfe's room at the appointed moment, and there was no indication that I was scheduled for anything more enterprising than slitting open the envelopes of the morning mail and helping Fritz empty the wastebasket.

At nine o'clock, when I was informed by the hum of the elevator that Wolfe was ascending for his two hours with Horstmann in the plant rooms, I was seated at the little table in the kitchen, doing the right thing by a pile of toast and four eggs cooked in black butter and sherry under a cover on a slow fire, and absorbing the accounts in the morning papers of the sensational death of Perren Gebert. It was a new one on me. The idea was that when he started to enter his car he had bumped his head against a sauce dish full of poison which had been perched on a piece of tape stuck to the cloth of the top above the driver's seat, and the poison had spilled on him, most of it going down the back of his neck. The poison wasn't named. I decided to finish with my second cup of coffee before going to the shelves in the office for a book on toxicology to glance over the possibilities. There couldn't be more than two or three that would furnish results as sudden and complete as that, applied externally.

A little after nine o'clock a phone call came from Saul Panzer. He asked for Wolfe and I put him through to the plant rooms; and then, to my disgust but not my surprise, Wolfe shooed me off the line. I stretched out my legs and looked at the tips of my shoes and told myself that the day would come when I would walk into that office carrying a murderer in a suitcase, and Nero Wolfe would pay dearly for a peek. Soon after that, Cramer phoned. He was also put through to Wolfe, and this time I kept my line and scribbled it in my notebook, but it was a waste of paper and talent. Cramer sounded tired and bitter, as if he needed three drinks and a good long nap. The gist of his growlings was that they were on the rampage at the District Attorney's office and about ready to take drastic action. Wolfe murmured sympathetically that he hoped they would do nothing that would interfere with Cramer's progress on the case, and Cramer told Wolfe where to go. Kid stuff.

I got out a book on toxicology, and I suppose to an ignorant onlooker I would have appeared to be a studious fellow buried in research, but as a matter of fact I was a caged tiger. I wanted to get in a lick somewhere, so much that it made my stomach ache. I wanted to all the more, because I had scored a couple of muffs on the case, once when I had failed to bring Gebert away from that gang of gorillas up at Glennanne, and once when I had beat it from 73rd Street three minutes before Perren Gebert got his right there on the spot.

It was the humor I was in that made me not any too hospitable when, around ten o'clock, Fritz brought me the card of a visitor and I saw it was Mathias R. Frisbie. I told Fritz to show him in. I had heard of this Frisbie, an Assistant District Attorney, but had never seen him. I observed, when he entered, that I hadn't missed much. He was the window-dummy type—high collar, clothes pressed very nice, and embalmed stiff and cold. The only thing you could tell from his eyes was that his self-esteem almost hurt him.

He told me he wanted to see Nero Wolfe. I told him that Mr. Wolfe would be engaged, as always in the morning, until eleven o'clock. He said it was urgent and important business and he required to see him at once. I grinned at him:

"Wait here a minute."

I moseyed up three flights of stairs to the plant rooms and found Wolfe with Theodore, experimenting with a new method of pollenizing for hybrid seeds. He nodded to admit I was there.

I said, "The drastic action is downstairs. Name of Frisbie. The guy that handled the Clara Fox larceny for Muir, remember? He wishes you to drop everything immediately and hurry down."

Wolfe didn't speak. I waited half a minute and then asked pleasantly, "Shall I tell him you're stricken dumb?"

Wolfe grunted. He said without turning, "And you were glad to see him. Even an Assistant District Attorney, and even that one. Don't deny it. It gave you an excuse to pester me. Very well, you've pestered me. Go."

"No message?"

"None. Go."

I ambled back downstairs. I thought Frisbie might like to have a few moments to himself, so I stopped in the kitchen for a little chat with Fritz regarding the prospects for lunch and other interesting topics. When I wandered into the office Frisbie was sitting down, frowning, with his elbows on the arms of his chair and his fingertips all meeting each other, properly matched.

I said, "Oh, yes. Mr. Frisbie. Since you say you must talk with Mr. Wolfe himself, can I get you a book or something? The morning paper? He will be down at eleven."

Frisbie's fingertips parted. He demanded, "He's here, isn't he?"

"Certainly. He's never anywhere else."

"Then—I won't wait an hour. I was warned to expect this. I won't tolerate it."

I shrugged. "Okay. I'll make it as easy as I can for you. Do you want to look at the morning paper while you're not tolerating it?"

He stood up. "Look here. This is insufferable. Time and time again this man Wolfe has had the effrontery to obstruct the operations of our office. Mr. Skinner sent me here—"

"I'll bet he did. He wouldn't come again himself, after his last experience—"

"He sent me, and I certainly don't intend to sit here until eleven o'clock. Owing to an excess of leniency with which Wolfe has too often been treated by certain officials, he apparently regards himself as above the law. No one can flout the processes of justice—no one!" The high color had got higher. "Boyden McNair was murdered three days ago right in this office, and there is every reason to believe that Wolfe knows more about it than he has told. He should have been brought to see the District Attorney at once—but no, he has not even been properly questioned! Now another man has been killed, and again there is good reason to believe that Wolfe has withheld information which might have prevented it. I have made a great concession to him by coming here at all, and I want to see him at once. At once!"

I nodded. "Sure, I know you want to see him, but keep your shirt on. Let's make it a hypothetical question. If I say you'll have to wait until eleven o'clock, then what?"

He glared. "I won't wait. I'll go to my office and I'll have him served. And I'll see that his license is revoked! He thinks his friend Morley can save him, but he can't get away with this kind of crooked underhanded—"

I smacked him one. I probably wouldn't have, except for the bad humor I was in anyway. It was by no means a wallop, merely a pat with the palm at the side of his puss, but it tilted him a little. He went back a step and began to tremble, and stood there with his arms at his sides and his fists doubled up.

I said, "They're no good hanging there at your knees. Put 'em up and I'll slap you again."

He was too mad to pronounce properly. He sputtered, "You'll re—regret this. You'll—"

I said, "Shut up and get out of here before you make me mad. You talk of revoking licenses! I know what's eating you, you've got delusions of grandeur, and you've been trying to hog a grandstand play ever since they gave you a desk and a chair down there. I know all about you. I know why Skinner sent you, he wanted to give you a chance to make a monkey of yourself, and you didn't even have gump enough to know it. The next time you shoot off your mouth about Nero Wolfe being crooked and underhanded I won't slap you in private, I'll do it with an audience. Git!"

In a way I suppose it was all right, and of course it was the only thing to do under the circumstances, but there was no deep satisfaction in it. He turned and walked out, and after I had heard the front door close behind him I went and sat down at my desk and yawned and scratched my head and kicked over the wastebasket. It had been a fleeting pleasure to smack him and read him out, but now that it was over there was an inclination inside of me to feel righteous, and that made me glum and in a worse temper than before. I hate to feel righteous, because it makes me uncomfortable and I want to kick something.

I picked up the wastebasket and returned the litter to it piece by piece. I took out the plant records and opened them and put them back again, went to the front room and looked out of the window onto 35th Street and came back, answered a phone call from Ferguson's Market which I relayed to Fritz, and finally got myself propped on my coccyx again with the book on toxicology. I was still fighting with that when Wolfe came down from the plant rooms at eleven o'clock.

He progressed to his desk and sat down, and went through his usual motions with the pen, the mail, the vase of orchids, the button to subpoena beer. Fritz came with the tray, and Wolfe opened and poured and drank and wiped his lips. Then he leaned back and sighed. He was relaxing after his strenuous activities among the flower pots.

I said, "Frisbie got obnoxious and I touched him on the cheek with my hand. He is going to revoke your license and serve you with different kinds of papers and maybe throw you into a vat of lye."

"Indeed." Wolfe opened his eyes at me. "Was he going to revoke the license before you hit him or afterward?"

"Before. Afterward he didn't talk much."

Wolfe shuddered. "I trust your discretion, Archie, but sometimes I feel that I am trusting the discretion of an avalanche. Was there no recourse but to batter him?"

"I didn't batter him. I didn't even tap him. It was just a gesture of annoyance. I'm in an ugly mood."

"I know you are. I don't blame you. This case has been tedious and disagreeable from the beginning. Something seems to have happened to Saul. We have a job ahead of us. It will end, I think, as disagreeably as it began, but we shall do it in style if we can, and with finality—ah! There, I hope, is Saul now."

The doorbell had rung. But again, as on the evening before, it wasn't Saul. This time it was Inspector Cramer.

Fritz ushered him in and he lumbered across. He looked as if he was about due for dry dock, with puffs under his eyes, his graying hair straggly, and his shoulders not as erect and military as an inspector's ought to be. Wolfe greeted him:

"Good morning, sir. Sit down. Will you have some beer?"

He took the dunce's chair, indulged in a deep breath, took a cigar from his pocket, scowled at it and put it back again. He took another breath and told both of us:

"When I get into such shape that I don't want a

cigar I'm in a hell of a fix." He looked at me. "What did you do to Frisbie, anyway?"

"Not a thing. Nothing that I remember."

"Well, he does. I think you're done for. I think he's going to plaster a charge of treason on you."

I grinned. "That hadn't occurred to me. I guess that's what it was, treason. What do they do, hang me?"

Cramer shrugged. "I don't know and I don't care. What happens to you is the least of my worries. God, I wish I felt like lighting a cigar." He took one from his pocket again, looked it over, and this time kept it in his hand. He passed me up. "Excuse me, Wolfe, I guess I didn't mention I don't want any beer. I suppose you think I came here to start a fracas."

Wolfe murmured, "Well, didn't you?"

"I did not. I came to have a reasonable talk. Can I ask you a couple of straight questions and get a couple of straight replies?"

"You can try. Give me a sample."

"Okay. If we searched this place would we find McNair's red box?"

"No."

"Have you ever seen it or do you know where it is?"

"No. To both."

"Did McNair tell you anything here Wednesday before he died that gave you any line on motive for these murders?"

"You have heard every word Mr. McNair said in this office; Archie read it to you from his notes."

"Yeah. I know. Have you received information as to motive from any other source?"

"Now, really." Wolfe wiggled a finger. "That question is preposterous. Certainly I have. Haven't I been on the case four days?"

"Who from?"

"Well, for one, from you."

Cramer stared. He stuck his cigar in his mouth and put his teeth into it without realizing he was doing it. He threw up his hands and dropped them.

"The trouble with you, Wolfe," he declared, "is that you can't forget for one little moment how terribly smart you are. Hell, I know it. Do you think I ever waste my time making calls like this on Del Pritchard or Sandy Mollew? When did I tell you what?"

Wolfe shook his head. "No, Mr. Cramer. Now—as the children say—now you're getting warm. And I'm not quite ready. Suppose we take turns at this; I have my curiosities, too. The story in the morning paper was incomplete. What sort of contraption was it that spilled the poison on Mr. Gebert?"

Cramer grunted. "You want to know?"

"I am curious, and we might as well pass the time."

"Oh, we might." The inspector removed his cigar and looked at its end with surprise at finding it unlit, touched a match to it, and puffed. "It was like this. Take a piece of ordinary adhesive tape an inch wide and ten inches long. Paste the ends of the tape to the cloth of the top of Gebert's car, above the driver's seat, about five inches apart, so that the tape swings loose like a hammock. Take an ordinary beetleware sauce dish, like they sell in the five and ten, and set it in that little hammock, and you'll have to balance it carefully, because a slight jar will upset it. Before you set the dish in the hammock, pour into it a couple of ounces of nitrobenzene—or, if you'd rather, you can call it essence of mirbane, or imitation oil of bitter almonds, because it's all the same thing. Also pour in with it an ounce or so of plain water, so that the nitrobenzene will settle to the bottom and the layer of water on top

will keep the oil from evaporating and making a smell.
If you will make the experiment of getting into a car
the way a man ordinarily does, you will find that your
eyes are naturally directed toward the seat and the
floor, and there isn't one chance in a thousand that you
would see anything pasted to the roof, especially at
night, and furthermore you will find that your head
will go in within an inch of the roof and you're sure to
bump the sauce dish. And even if you don't, it will fall
and spill on you the first hole you hit or the first corner
you turn. How do you like that for a practical joke?"

Wolfe nodded. "From the pragmatic standpoint,
close to perfect. Simple, effective, and cheap. If you
had had the poison in your possession for some time,
as provision against an emergency, your entire outlay
would not be more than fifteen cents—tape, an ounce
of water, and sauce dish. From the newspaper account
I suspected the nitrobenzene. It would do that."

Cramer nodded emphatically. "I'll say it would.
Last year a worker in a dye factory spilled a couple of
ounces on his pants, not directly on his skin, and he
was dead in an hour. The man I had tailing Gebert
handled him when he ran up to him after he fell, and
got a little on his hands and some strong fumes, and
he's in a hospital now with a blue face and purple lips
and purple fingernails. The doctor says he'll pull
through. Lew Frost got a little of it too, but not bad.
Gebert must have turned his head when he felt it
spilling and smelled it, because he got a little on his
face and maybe even a couple of drops in his eyes. You
should have seen him an hour after it happened."

"I think not." Wolfe was pouring beer. "For me to
look at him could have done him no good, and certainly
me none." He drank, and felt in his pocket for a
handkerchief and had none, and I got him one from the

drawer. He leaned back and looked sympathetically at the inspector. "I trust, Mr. Cramer, that the routine progresses satisfactorily."

"Smart again. Huh?" Cramer puffed. "I'll call the turn again in a minute. But I'll try to satisfy you. The routine progresses exactly as it should, but it don't get anywhere. That ought to make you smack your lips. You tipped me off Wednesday to stick to the Frost family—all right, any of them could have done it. If it was either of the young ones they did it together, because they went together to the chapel. They would have had barely enough time to do the taping and pouring, because they got there only a minute or two after Gebert did. It could have been done in two minutes; I've tested it. The uncle and the mother went separately, and either of them would have had plenty of time. They've accounted for it, of course, but not in a way you can check it up to the minute. On opportunity none of them is absolutely out."

The inspector puffed some more. "One thing, you might think we could find some passerby who saw someone making motions with the top of that car, but it could have been done sitting inside with the door closed and wouldn't have attracted much attention, and it was night. We've had no luck on that so far. We found the empty bottles in the car, in the dashboard compartment—ordinary two-ounce vials, stocked by every drug store, no labels. Of course there were no fingerprints on them or on the sauce dish, and as for finding out where they came from, you might as well try to trace a red-headed paper match. We're checking up on sources of nitrobenzene, but I agree with you that whoever is handling this business isn't leaving a trail like that.

"I'll tell you." Cramer puffed again. "I don't think

we can do it. We can keep on trying, but I don't believe we can. There's too much luck and dirty cleverness against us. It'll be months before I get in my car again without looking up at the top. We've got to get at it through motive, or I swear I'm beginning to believe we won't get it at all. I know that's what you've wanted too, that's why you said the red box would do it. But where the hell is it? If we can't find it we'll have to get at the motive without it. So far it's a blank, not only with the Frosts, but with everyone else we've investigated. Granted that Dudley Frost is short as trustee of the estate, which he may or may not be, what good does it do him to croak McNair and Gebert? With Lew and the girl, there's not even a hair of a motive. With Mrs. Frost, we know she's been paying Gebert a lot of jack for a long time. She says she was paying off an old debt, and he's dead and he wouldn't tell us anyhow. It was probably blackmail for something that happened years ago, but what was it that happened, and why did she have to kill him right now, and where did McNair fit in? McNair was the first to go."

Cramer reached to knock ashes into the tray, sat back in his chair, and grunted. "There," he said bitterly. "There's one or two questions for you. I'm back to where I was last Tuesday, when I came here and told you I was licked, only there's been two more people killed. Didn't I tell you this one was yours? It's not my type. Down at the D.A.'s office an hour ago they wanted to put a ring in your nose, and what I told Frisbie would have fried an egg. You're the worst thorn in the flesh I know of, but you are also half as smart as you think you are, and that puts you head and shoulders above everybody since Julius Caesar. Do you know why I've changed my tune since yesterday? Because Gebert's been killed and you're still keeping your client. If you had run out on the case this morning, I would have been ready and eager to put three rings in your nose. But now I believe you. I don't think you've the red box—"

The interruption was Fritz—his knock on the office door, his entry, his approach within two paces of Wolfe's desk, his ceremonial bow:

"Mr. Morgan to see you, sir."

Wolfe nodded and the creases of his cheeks unfolded a little; I hadn't seen that since I had jerked him back from the relapse. He murmured, "It's all right, Fritz, we have no secrets from Mr. Cramer. Send him in."

"Yes, sir."

Fritz departed, and Saul Panzer entered. I put the eye on him. He looked a little crestfallen, but not exactly downhearted; and under his arm he carried a parcel wrapped in brown paper, about the size of a cigar box. He stepped across to Wolfe's desk.

Wolfe's brows were up. "Well?"

Saul nodded. "Yes, sir."

"Contents in order?"

"Yes, sir. As you said. What made me late—"

"Never mind. You are here. Satisfactory. Archie, please put that package in the safe. That's all for the present, Saul. Come back at two o'clock."

I took the package and went and opened the safe and chucked it in. It felt solid but didn't weigh much. Saul departed.

Wolfe leaned back in his chair and half closed his eyes. "So," he murmured. He heaved a deep sigh. "Mr. Cramer. I remarked a while ago that we might as well pass the time. We have done so. That is always a triumph, to evade boredom." He glanced at the clock.

"Now we can talk business. It is past noon, and we lunch here at one. Can you have the Frost family here, all of them, at two o'clock? If you will do that, I'll finish this case for you. It will take an hour, perhaps."

Cramer rubbed his chin. He did it with the hand that held his cigar, and ashes fell on his pants, but he didn't notice it. He was gazing at Wolfe. Finally he said:

"An hour. Huh?"

Wolfe nodded. "Possibly more. I think not."

Cramer gazed. "Oh. You think not." He jerked forward in his chair. "What was in that package Goodwin just put in the safe?"

"Something that belongs to me. —Now wait!" Wolfe wiggled a finger. "Confound it, why should you explode? I invite you here to observe the solution of the murders of Molly Lauck and Mr. McNair and Mr. Gebert. I shall not discuss it, and I won't have you yelling at me. Were I so minded I could invite, instead of you, representatives of the newspapers, or Mr. Morley of the District Attorney's office. Almost anyone. Sir, you are churlish. Would you quarrel with good fortune? Two o'clock, and all the Frosts must be here. Well, sir?"

Cramer stood up. "I'll be damned." He glanced at the safe. "That's the red box. Huh? Tell me that."

Wolfe shook his head. "Two o'clock."

"All right. But look here. Sometimes you get pretty fancy. By God, you'd better have it."

"I shall, at two o'clock."

The inspector looked at the safe again, shook his head, stuck his cigar between his teeth, and beat it.

Chapter 18

The Frost tribe arrived all at the same time, a little after two, for a good reason: they were escorted by Inspector Cramer and Purley Stebbins of the Homicide Squad. Purley rode with Helen and her mother in a dark blue town car which I suppose belonged to Helen, and Cramer brought the two men in his own bus. Lunch was over and I was looking out of the front window when they drove up, and I stood and watched them alight, and then went to the hall to let them in. My instructions were to take them directly to the office.

I was as nervous as a congressman on election day. I had been made acquainted with the high spots on Wolfe's program. It was all well and good for him to get up these tricky charades as far as he himself was concerned, because he didn't have any nerves, and he was too conceited to suffer any painful apprehension of failure, but I was made of different stuff and I didn't like the feeling it gave me. True, he had stated just before we went in to lunch that we had a hazardous and disagreeable task before us, but he didn't seriously mean it; he was merely calling my attention to the fact that he was preparing to put over a whizz.

I admitted the visitors, helped get hats and top-coats disposed of in the hall, and led them to the office. Wolfe, seated behind his desk, nodded around at them. I had already arranged chairs, and now allotted them: Helen the closest to Wolfe, with Cramer at her left and Llewellyn next to Cramer; Uncle Dudley not far from me, so I could reach him and gag him if necessary, and Mrs. Frost the other side of Dudley, in the big leather chair which was usually beside the big globe. None of them looked very festive. Lew looked as if he had the pop-eye and his face had a gray tinge, I suppose from the nitrobenzene he had got too close to. Mrs. Frost wasn't doing any sagging, but looked pale in black clothes. Helen, in a dark brown suit with a hat to match, twisted her fingers together as soon as she sat down and put her eyes on Wolfe, and stayed that way. Dudley looked at everybody and squirmed. Wolfe had murmured to the inspector:

"Your man, Mr. Cramer. If he would wait in the kitchen?"

Cramer grunted. "He's all right. He won't bite anybody."

Wolfe shook his head. "We won't need him. The kitchen would be better for him."

Cramer looked as if he'd like to argue, but called it off with a shrug. He turned: "Go on out to the kitchen, Stebbins. I'll yell if I want you."

Purley, with a sour glance at me, turned and went. Wolfe waited until the door had closed behind him before he spoke, looking around at them:

"And here we are. Though I am aware that you came at Mr. Cramer's invitation, nevertheless I thank you for coming. It was desirable to have you all here, though nothing will be expected of you—"

Dudley Frost blurted, "We came because we had

to! You know that! What else could we do, with the attitude the police are taking?"

"Mr. Frost. Please—"

"There's no please to it! I just want to say, it's a good thing nothing will be expected of us, because you won't get it! In view of the ridiculous attitude of the police, we refuse to submit to any further questioning unless we have a lawyer present. I've told Inspector Cramer that! I, personally, decline to say a word! Not a word!"

Wolfe wiggled a finger at him. "On the chance that you mean that, Mr. Frost, I promise not to press you; and we now have another good reason for admitting no lawyers. I was saying: nothing will be expected of you save to listen to an explanation. There will be no questioning. I prefer to do the talking myself, and I have plenty to say. —By the way, Archie, I may as well have that thing handy."

That was the cue for the first high spot. For me it wasn't a speaking part, but I had the business. I arose and went to the safe and got out Saul's package and put it on the desk in front of Wolfe; but the wrapping paper had been removed before lunch. What I put there was an old red leather box, faded and scuffed and scarred, about ten inches long and four wide and two deep. On one side were the backbones of two gilt hinges for the lid, and on the other a small gilt escutcheon with a keyhole. Wolfe barely glanced at it, and pushed it to one side. I sat down again and picked up my notebook.

There was some stirring, but no comments. They all stared at the box, except Helen Frost; she stuck to Wolfe. Cramer was looking wary and thoughtful, with his eyes glued on the box.

Wolfe spoke with sudden sharpness: "Archie. We

can dispense with notes. Most of the words will be mine, and I shall not forget them. Please take your gun and keep it in your hand. If it appears to be needed, use it. We don't want anyone squirting nitrobenzene around here—that will do, Mr. Frost! I say stop it! I remind you that a woman and two men have been murdered! Stay in your chair!"

Dudley Frost actually subsided. It may have been partly on account of my automatic which I had got from the drawer and now held in my hand resting on my knee. The sight of a loaded gun out in the open always has an effect on a guy, no matter who he is. I observed that Cramer had shoved his chair back a few inches and was looking even warier than before, with a scowl on his brow.

Wolfe said, "This, of course, is melodrama. All murder is melodrama, because the real tragedy is not death but the condition which induces it. However." He leaned back in his chair and aimed his half-closed eyes at our client. "I wish to address myself, Miss Frost, primarily to you. Partly through professional vanity. I wish to demonstrate to you that engaging the services of a good detective means much more than hiring someone to pry up floorboards and dig up flower beds trying to find a red box. I wish to show you that before I ever saw this box or its contents, I knew the central facts of this case; I knew who had killed Mr. McNair, and why. I am going to shock you, but I can't help that."

He signed. "I shall be brief. First of all, I shall no longer call you Miss Frost, but Miss McNair. Your name is Glenna McNair, and you were born on April 2nd, 1915."

I got a glimpse of the others from the corner of my eye, enough to see Helen sitting rigid and Lew starting from his chair and Dudley staring with his mouth open, but my chief interest was Mrs. Frost. She looked paler than she had when she came in, but she didn't bat an eye. Of course the display of the red box had prepared her for it. She spoke, cutting through a couple of male ejaculations, cool and curt:

"Mr. Wolfe. I think my brother-in-law is right. This sort of nonsense makes it a case for lawyers."

Wolfe matched her tone: "I think not, Mrs. Frost. If so, there will be plenty of time for them. For the present, you will stay in that chair until the nonsense is finished."

Helen Frost said in a dry even tone, "But then Uncle Boyd was my father. He was my father. All the time. How? Tell me how?" Lew was out of his chair, with a hand on her shoulder, staring at his Aunt Callie. Dudley was making sounds.

Wolfe said, "Please. Sit down, Mr. Frost. Yes, Miss McNair, he was your father all the time. Mrs. Frost thinks that I did not learn that until this red box was found, but she is wrong. I was definitely convinced of it on Thursday morning, when you told me that in the event of your death before reaching twenty-one all of Edwin Frost's fortune would go to his brother and nephew. When I considered that, in combination with other points that had presented themselves, the picture was complete. Of course, the first thing that brought this possibility to my mind was the fact of Mr. McNair's unaccountable desire to have you wear diamonds. What special virtue did a diamond have on you—since he seemed not otherwise fond of them? Could it be this, that the diamond is the birthstone for April? I noted that possibility."

Llewellyn muttered, "Good God. I said—I told McNair once—"

"Please, Mr. Frost. Another little point: Mr. Mc-Nair told me Wednesday evening that his wife died, but not that his daughter did. He said he 'lost' his daughter. That of course is a common euphemism for death, but why had he not employed it for his wife also? A man may either be direct or euphemistic, but not often both in the same sentence. He said his parents died. Twice he said his wife died. But not his daughter; he said he lost her."

Glenna McNair's lips were moving. She muttered, "But how? How? How did he lose me . . ."

"Yes, Miss McNair. Patience. There were various other little points, things you told me about your father and yourself; I don't need to repeat them to you. Your dream about the orange, for instance. A subconscious memory dream? It must have been. I have told you enough, I hope, to show you that I did not need the red box to tell me who you are and who killed Mr. McNair and Mr. Gebert and why. Anyway, I shan't further coddle my vanity at your expense. You want to know how. That is simple. I'll give you the main facts— Mrs. Frost! Sit down!"

I don't know whether Wolfe regarded my automatic mostly as stage property or not, but I didn't. Mrs. Edwin Frost had stood up, and she had a fair-sized black leather handbag she was clutching. I'll admit it was unlikely she would be lugging an atomizer loaded with nitrobenzene into Wolfe's office, to have it found if she was searched, but that wasn't a thing to take a chance on. I thought I'd better butt in for the sake of an understanding. I did so:

"I ought to tell you, Mrs. Frost, if you don't like this gun pointed at you, give me that bag or lay it on the floor."

She ignored me, looking at Wolfe. She said with

calm indignation, "I can't be compelled to listen to this rubbish." I saw a little flash back in her eyes from the fire inside. "I am going. Helen! Come."

She moved toward the door. I moved after her. Cramer was on his feet and got in front of her before I did. He blocked her way but didn't touch her. "Wait, Mrs. Frost. Just a minute." He looked at Wolfe. "What have you got? I'm not playing this blind."

"I've got enough, Mr. Cramer." Wolfe was crisp. "I'm not a fool. Take that bag from her and keep her in here or you'll eternally regret it."

Cramer didn't hesitate more than half a second. That's one thing I've always liked about him, he never fiddle-faddles much. He put a hand on her shoulder. She stepped back, away from it, and stiffened. He snapped, "Give me the bag and sit down. That's no great hardship. You'll have all the chance for a come-back you want."

He reached for it and took it. I noticed that at that juncture she didn't appeal to her masculine relatives; I don't imagine she was very strong on appeals. She wasn't doing any quivering, either. She gave Cramer the straight hard eye:

"You keep me here by force. Do you?"

"Well . . ." Cramer shrugged. "We think you'll stay for a while. Just till we get through."

She walked back and sat down. Glenna McNair sent her one swift glance, and then looked back at Wolfe. The men weren't looking at her.

Wolfe said testily, "These interruptions will help no one. Certainly not you, Mrs. Frost; nothing can help you now." He looked at our client. "You want to know how. In 1916 Mrs. Frost went with her baby daughter Helen, then only a year old, to the east coast of Spain. There, a year later, her daughter died. Under the terms of her deceased husband's will, Helen's death meant that the entire fortune went to Dudley and Llewellyn Frost. Mrs. Frost did not like that, and she made a plan. It was wartime, and the confusion all over Europe made it possible to carry it out. Her old friend Boyden McNair had a baby daughter almost the same age as Helen, just a month apart, and his wife was dead and he was penniless, with no means of making a livelihood. Mrs. Frost bought his daughter from him, explaining that the child would be better off that way anyhow. Inquiry is now being made in Cartagena regarding a manipulation of the record of deaths in the year 1917. The idea was, of course, to spread the report that Glenna McNair died and Helen Frost lived.

"Immediately Mrs. Frost took you, as Helen Frost, to Egypt, where there was little risk of your being seen by some traveler who had known you as a baby in Paris. When the war ended even Egypt was too hazardous, and she went on to the Far East. Not until you were nine years old did she chance your appearance in this part of the world, and even then she avoided France. You came to this continent from the west."

Wolfe stirred in his chair, and gave his eyes a new target. "I suppose it would be more polite, Mrs. Frost, from this point on, to address myself to you. I am going to speak of the two unavoidable difficulties your plan encountered—one from the very beginning. That was your young friend Perren Gebert. He knew all about it because he was there, and you had to pay for his silence. You even took him to Egypt with you, which was a wise precaution even if you didn't like to have him around. As long as you paid him he represented no serious danger, because he was a man who knew how to hold his tongue. Then a cloud sailed into your sky, about ten years ago, when Boyden McNair, who had made a success in London and regained his self-respect, came to New York. He wanted to be near the daughter he had lost, and I have no doubt that he made a nuisance of himself. He kept to the essentials of the bargain he had made with you in 1917, because he was a scrupulous man, but he made annoying little pecks at you. He insisted on his right to make himself a good friend of his daughter. I presume that it was around this time that you acquired, probably on a trip to Europe, certain chemicals which you began to fear might some day be needed."

Wolfe wiggled a finger at her. She sat straight and motionless, her eyes level at him, the lips of her proud mouth perhaps a little tighter than ordinary. He went on, "And sure enough, the need arose. It was a double emergency. Mr. Gebert conceived the idea of marrying the heiress before she came of age, and insisted on the help of your influence and authority. What was worse, Mr. McNair began to get his scruples mixed up. He did not tell me the precise nature of the demands he made, but I believe I can guess them. He wanted to buy his daughter back again. Didn't he? He had made even a greater success in New York than in London, and so had plenty of money. True, he was still bound by the agreement he had made with you in 1917, but I suspect he had succeeded in persuading himself that there was a higher obligation, both to his paternal emotions and to Glenna herself. No doubt he was outraged by Mr. Gebert's impudent aspiration to marry Glenna and by your seeming acquiescence.

"You were certainly up against it, I can see that. After all your ingenuity and devotion and vigilance, and twenty years of control of a handsome income.

With Mr. Gebert insisting on having her for a wife, and Mr. McNair demanding her for a daughter, and both of them threatening you daily with exposure, the surprising thing is that you found time for the deliberate cunning you employed. It is easy to see why you took Mr. McNair first. If you had killed Gebert, McNair would have known the truth of it no matter what your precautions, and would have acted at once. So your first effort was the poisoned candy for McNair, with the poison in the Jordan almonds, which you knew he was fond of. He escaped that; it killed an innocent young woman instead. He knew of course what it meant. Here I permit myself another surmise: my guess is that Mr. McNair, being a sentimental man, decided to reclaim his daughter on her real twenty-first birthday, April second. But knowing your resourcefulness, and fearing that you might somehow get him before then, he made certain arrangements in his will and in an interview with me. The latter, alas, was not completed; your second attempt, the imitation aspirin tablets, intervened. And just in the nick of time! Just when he was on the verge—Miss McNair! I beg you . . ."

Glenna McNair disregarded him. I suppose she didn't hear him. She was on her feet, turned away from him, facing the woman with the straight back and proud mouth whom for so many years she had called mother. She took three steps toward her. Cramer was up too, beside her; and Lew Frost was there with a hand on her arm. With a convulsive movement she shook his hand off without looking at him; she was staring at Mrs. Frost. A little quiver ran over her, then she stood still and said in a half-choked voice:

"He was my father, and you killed him. You killed

my father. Oh!" The quiver again, and she stopped for it. "You . . . you *woman!*"

Llewellyn sputtered at Wolfe, "This is enough for her—good God, you shouldn't have let her be here—I'll take her home—"

Wolfe said curtly, "She has no home. None this side of Scotland. Miss McNair, I beg you. Sit down. You and I are doing a job. Aren't we? Let's finish it. Let's do it right, for your father's sake. Come."

She quivered once more, shook off Lew's hand again, and then turned and got to her chair and sat down. She looked at Wolfe: "All right. I don't want anybody to touch me. But it's all over, isn't it?"

Wolfe shook his head. "Not quite. We'll go on to the end." He straightened out a finger to aim it at Mrs. Frost. "You, madam, have a little more to hear. Having got rid of Mr. McNair, you may even have had the idea that you could stop there. But that was bad calculation, unworthy of you, for naturally Mr. Gebert knew what had happened and began at once to put pressure on you. He was even foolhardy about it, for that was his humor; he told Mr. Goodwin that you had murdered Mr. McNair. He presumed, I suppose, that Mr. Goodwin did not know French, and did not know that *calida*, your name, is a Latin word meaning 'ardently.' No doubt he meant merely to startle you. He did indeed startle you, with such success that you killed him the next day. I have not yet congratulated you on the technique of that effort, but I assure you—"

"Please!" It was Mrs. Frost. We all looked at her. She had her chin up, her eyes at Wolfe, and didn't seem ready to do any quivering. "Need I listen to your . . . need I listen to that?" Her head pivoted for the eyes to aim at Cramer. "You are a police inspector. Do you realize what this man is saying to me? Are you responsible for it? Are you . . . am I charged with anything?"

Cramer said in a heavy official tone, "It looks like you're apt to be. Frankly, you'll stay right here until I have a chance to look over some evidence. I can tell you now, formally, don't say anything you don't want used against you."

"I have no intention of saying anything." She stopped, and I saw that her teeth had a hold on her lower lip. But her voice was still good when she went on, "There is nothing to say to such a fable. In fact, I . . ." She stopped again. Her head pivoted again, for Wolfe. "If there is evidence for such a story about my daughter, it is forged. Haven't I a right to see it?"

Wolfe's eyes were slits. He murmured, "You spoke of a lawyer. I believe a lawyer has a legal method for such a request. I see no occasion for that delay." He put his hand on the red box. "I see no reason why—"

Cramer was on his feet again, and at the desk. He was brisk and he meant business: "This has gone far enough. I want that box. I'll take a look at it myself—"

It was Cramer I was afraid of at that point. Maybe if I had let Wolfe alone he could have managed him, but my nerves were on edge, and I knew if the inspector once got his paws on that box it would be a mess, and I knew damned well he couldn't take it away from me. I bounced up and got it. I pulled it from under Wolfe's hand and held it in my own. Cramer growled and stared at me, and I returned the stare but I don't growl. Wolfe snapped:

"That box is my property. I am responsible for it and shall continue to be so until it is legally taken from my possession. I see no reason why Mrs. Frost should not look at it, to save delay. I have as much at stake as

you, Mr. Cramer. Hand it to her, Archie. It is unlocked."

I crossed to her and put it in her extended hand,
black-gloved. I didn't sit down again because Cramer
didn't, and I stayed five feet closer to Mrs. Frost than
he was. Everybody looked at her, even Glenna Mc-
Nair. She put the box on her lap with the keyhole
toward her, and opened the lid part way; no one could
see in but her; she was deliberate, and I couldn't see a
sign of a tremble in her fingers or anywhere else. She
looked in the box and put her hand in, but didn't take
anything out. She left her hand inside, with the lid
resting on it, and gazed at Wolfe, and I saw that her
teeth were on her lip again.

Wolfe said, leaning a little toward her, "Don't
suspect a trick, Mrs. Frost. There is no forgery in the
contents of that box; it is genuine. I know, and you
know, that all I have said here today is the truth. In
any event, you have lost all chance at the Frost
fortune; that much is certain. It is also certain that the
fraud you have practiced for nineteen years can be
proved with the help of Mr. McNair's sister and
corroboration from Cartagena, and will be made public; and of course the money goes to your nephew and
brother-in-law. Whether you will be convicted of the
three murders you committed, frankly, I cannot be
sure. It will doubtless be a bitterly fought trial. There
will be evidence against you, but not absolutely conclusive, and of course you are an extremely attractive
woman, just middle-aged, and you will have ample
opportunity for smirking at the judge and jury, weep-
ing at the proper intervals for arousing their compas-
sion; and unquestionably you will know how to dress
the part—ah, Archie!"

She did it as quick as lightning. Her left hand had

been holding the lid of the box partly open, and her right hand, inside, had been moving a little—not fumbling, just efficiently moving; I doubt if anyone but me noticed it. I'll never forget the way she handled her face. Her teeth stayed fastened to her lip, but aside from that there was no sign of the desperate and fatal thing she was doing. Then, like a flash, her hand came out of the box and went to her mouth with the bottle, and her head went back so far that I could see her white throat when she swallowed.

Cramer jumped for her, and I didn't move to block him because I knew she could be depended on to get it down. As he jumped he let out a yell:

"Stebbins! Stebbins!"

I submit that as proof that Cramer had a right to be an inspector, because he was a born executive. As I understand it, a born executive is a guy who, when anything difficult or unexpected happens, yells for somebody to come and help him.

Chapter 19

Inspector Cramer said, "I'd like to have it in the form of a signed statement." He chewed at his cigar. "It's the wildest damned stuff I ever heard of. Do you mean to say that was all you had to go on?"

It was five minutes past six, and Wolfe had just come down from the plant rooms. The Frosts and Glenna McNair had long been gone. Calida Frost was gone too. The fuss was over. The chain was on the front door to make it easier for Fritz to keep reporters out. Two windows were wide open and had been for over two hours, but the smell of bitter almonds, from some that had spilled on the floor, was still in the air and seemed to be there to stay.

Wolfe, nodding, poured beer. "That was all, sir. As for signing a statement, I prefer not to. In fact, I refuse. Your noisy indignation this afternoon was outrageous; furthermore, it was silly. I resented it then; I still do."

He drank. Cramer grunted. Wolfe went on, "God knows where Mr. McNair hid his confounded box. It appeared to me more than likely that it would never be found; and if it wasn't it seemed fairly certain that the proof of Mrs. Frost's guilt would at best be tedious and arduous, and at worst impossible. She had had all the luck and might go on having it. So I sent Saul Panzer to a craftsman to get a box constructed of red leather and made to appear old and worn. It was fairly certain that none of the Frosts had ever seen Mr. McNair's box, so there was little danger of its authenticity being challenged. I calculated that the psychological effect on Mrs. Frost would be appreciable."

"Yeah. You're a great calculator." Cramer chewed his cigar some more. "You took a big chance, and you kindly let me take it with you without explaining it beforehand, but I admit it was a good trick. That's not the main point. The point is that you bought a bottle of oil of bitter almonds and put it in the box and handed it to her. That's the farthest north, even for you. And I was here when it happened. I don't dare put it on the record like that. I'm an inspector, and I don't dare."

"As you please, sir." Wolfe's shoulders lifted a quarter of an inch and fell again. "It was unfortunate that the outcome was fatal. I did it to impress her. I was thunderstruck, and helpless, when she—er—abused it. I used the poisonous oil instead of a substitute because I thought she might uncork the bottle, and the odor . . . That too was for the psychological effect—"

"Like hell it was. It was for exactly what she used it for. What are you trying to do, kid me?"

"No, not really. But you began speaking of a signed statement, and I don't like that. I like to be frank. You know perfectly well I wouldn't sign a statement." Wolfe wiggled a finger at him. "The fact is, you're an ingrate. You wanted the case solved and the criminal punished, didn't you? It is solved. The law is an envious monster, and you represent it. You can't tolerate a decent and swift conclusion to a skirmish between an individual and what you call society, as long as you have it in your power to turn it into a ghastly and prolonged struggle; the victim must squirm like a worm in your fingers, not for ten minutes, but for ten months. Pfui! I don't like the law. It was not I, but a great philosopher, who said that the law is an ass."

"Well, don't take it out on me. I'm not the law, I'm just a cop. Where did you buy the oil of bitter almonds?"

"Indeed." Wolfe's eyes narrowed. "Do you mean to ask me that?"

Cramer looked uncomfortable. But he stuck to it: "I ask it."

"You do. Very well, sir. I know, of course, that the sale of that stuff is illegal. The law again! A chemist who is a friend of mine accommodated me. If you are petty enough to attempt to find out who he is, and to take steps to punish him for his infraction of the law, I shall leave this country and go to live in Egypt, where I own a house. If I do that, one out of ten of your murder cases will go unsolved, and I hope to heaven you suffer for it."

Cramer removed his cigar, looked at Wolfe, and slowly shook his head from side to side. Finally he said, "I'm all right, I'm sitting pretty. I won't snoop on your friend. I'll be ready to retire in another ten years. What worries me is this, what's the police force going to do, say a hundred years from now, when you're dead? They'll have a hell of a time." He went on hastily, "Now don't get sore. I know a jack from a deuce. There's another thing I wanted to ask you. You know I've got a room down at headquarters where we keep some curiosities—hatchets and guns and so on that have been used at one time or another. How's chances to take that red box and add it to the collection? I'd really like to have it. You won't need it any more."

"I couldn't say." Wolfe leaned forward to pour more beer. "You'll have to ask Mr. Goodwin. I presented it to him."

Cramer turned to me. "How about it, Goodwin? Okay?"

"Nope." I shook my head and grinned at him. "Sorry, Inspector. I'm going to hang onto it. It's just what I needed to keep postage stamps in."

I'm still using it. But Cramer got one for his collection too, for about a week later McNair's own box was found on the family property in Scotland, behind a stone in the chimney. It had enough dope in it for three juries, but by that time Calida Frost was already buried.

Chapter 20

Wolfe frowned, looking from Llewellyn Frost to his father and back again. "Where is she?" he demanded.

It was Monday noon. The Frosts had telephoned that morning to ask for an interview. Lew was in the dunce's chair; his father was on one at his left, with a taboret at his elbow and on it a couple of glasses and the bottle of Old Corcoran. Wolfe had just finished a second bottle of beer and was leaning back comfortably. I had my notebook out.

Llewellyn flushed a little. "She's out at Glennanne. She says she phoned you Saturday evening to ask if she could go out there. She . . . she doesn't want to see any Frosts. She wouldn't talk to me. I know she's had an awful time of it, but my God, she can't go on forever without any human intercourse . . . we want you to go out there and talk to her. You can make it in less than two hours."

"Mr. Frost." Wolfe wiggled a finger at him. "You will please stop that. That I should ride for two hours—for you to entertain the notion at all is unpardonable, and to suggest it seriously to me is brazen impudence. Your success with that idiotic letter you brought me a week ago today has gone to your head. I don't wonder at Miss McNair's wanting a temporary vacation from the Frost family. Give her another day or two to accustom herself to the notion that you do not all deserve extermination. After all, when you do get to talk with her again you will possess two newly acquired advantages: you will not be an ortho-cousin, and you will be worth more than a million dollars. At least, I suppose you will. Your father can tell you about that."

Dudley Frost put down the whiskey glass, took a delicate sip of water with a carefulness which indicated that an overdose of ten drops of that fluid might be dangerous, and cleared his throat. "I've already told him," he declared bluntly. "That woman, my sister-in-law, God rest her soul, has been aggravating me about that for nearly twenty years—well, she won't any more. In a way she was no better than a fool. She should have known that if I handled my brother's estate there would sooner or later be nothing left of it. I knew it; that's why I didn't handle it. I turned it over in 1918 to a lawyer named Cabot—gave him a power of attorney—I can't stand him, never could, he's bald-headed and skinny and he plays gold all day Sunday. Do you know him? He's got a wart on the side of his neck. He gave me a quarterly report last week from a certified public accountant, showing that the estate has increased to date twenty-two percent above its original value, so I guess my son will get his million. And I will, too. We'll see how long I can hang onto it—I've got my own ideas about that. But one thing I wanted to speak to you about—in fact, that's why I came here with Lew this morning—it seems to me that's the natural place for your fee to come from, the million I'm getting. If it wasn't for you

I wouldn't have it. Of course I can't give you a check now, because it will take time—"

"Mr. Frost! Please! Miss McNair is my client—"

But Dudley Frost was under way. "Nonsense! That's tommyrot. I've thought all along my son ought to pay you; I didn't know I'd be able to. Helen . . . that is . . . damn it, I say Helen! She won't have anything, unless she'll take part of ours—"

"Mr. Frost, I insist! Mr. McNair left private instructions with his sister regarding his estate. Doubtless—"

"McNair, that booby? Why should she take money from him? Because you say he was her father? Maybe. I have my doubts on these would-be discoveries about parentage. Maybe. Anyhow, that won't be anything like a million. She may have a million, in case she marries my son, and I hope she will because I'm damned fond of her. But they might as well keep all of theirs, because they'll need it, whereas I won't need mine, since there isn't much chance that I'll be able to hang onto it very long whether I pay you or not. Not that ten thousands dollars is a very big slice out of a million— unless it's more than ten thousand on account of the new developments since I had my last talk with you about it. Anyway, I don't want to hear any more talk about Helen being your client—it's nonsense and I won't listen to it. You can send me your bill and if it isn't preposterous I'll see that it's paid. —No, I tell you there's no use talking! The fact is, you ought to regard it as I do, a damned lucky thing that I got the notion of turning the management of the estate over to Cabot—"

I shut the notebook and tossed it on my desk, and leaned my head on my hand and shut my eyes and tried to relax. As I said before, that case was just one damned client after another.

Not for publication
Confidential Memo
From Rex Stout
September 15 1949

DESCRIPTION OF NERO WOLFE

Height 5 ft. 11 in. Weight 272 lbs. Age 56.
Mass of dark brown hair, very little greying, is not
parted but sweeps off to the right because he brushes
with his right hand. Dark brown eyes are average in
size, but look smaller because they are mostly half
closed. They always are aimed straight at the person
he is talking to. Forehead is high. Head and face
are big but do not seem so in proportion to the whole.
Ears rather small. Nose long and narrow, slightly
aquiline. Mouth mobile and extremely variable; lips
when pursed are full and thick, but in tense moments
they are thin and their line is long. Cheeks full but
not pudgy; the high point of the cheekbone can be seen
from straight front. Complexion varies from some
floridity after meals to an ivory pallor late at night
when he has spent six hard hours working on someone.
He breathes smoothly and without sound except when he
is eating; then he takes in and lets out great gusts of
air. His massive shoulders never slump; when he stands
up at all he stands straight. He shaves every day. He
has a small brown mole just above his right jawbone,
halfway between the chin and the ear.

DESCRIPTION OF ARCHIE GOODWIN

Height 6 feet. Weight 180 lbs. Age 32. Hair is
light rather than dark, but just barely decided not to
be red; he gets it cut every two weeks, rather short,
and brushes it straight back, but it keeps standing up.
He shaves four times a week and grasps at every excuse
to make it only three times. His features are all regular, well-modeled and well-proportioned, except the
nose. He escapes the curse of being the movie actor
type only through the nose. It is not a true pug and
is by no means a deformity, but it is a little short
and the ridge is broad, and the tip has continued on
its own, beyond the cartilage, giving the impression
of startling and quite independent initiative. The eyes
are grey, and are inquisitive and quick to move. He is
muscular both in appearance and in movement, and upright
in posture, but his shoulders stoop a little in unconscious
reaction to Wolfe's repeated criticism that he is too
self-assertive.

DESCRIPTION OF WOLFE'S OFFICE

The old brownstone on West 35th Street is a double-
width house. Entering at the front door, which is seven
steps up from the sidewalk, you are facing the length of

a wide carpeted hall. At the right is an enormous coat
rack, eight feet wide, then the stairs, and beyond the
stairs the door to the dining room. There were originally two rooms on that side of the hall, but Wolfe had
the partition removed and turned it into a dining room
forty feet long, with a table large enough for six (but
extensible) square in the middle. It (and all other
rooms) are carpeted; Wolfe hates bare floors. At the
far end of the big hall is the kitchen. At the left of the
big hall are two doors; the first one is to what Archie calls
the front room, and the second is to the office. The front
room is used chiefly as an anteroom; Nero and Archie do
no living there. It is rather small, and the furniture
is a random mixture without any special character.

The office is large and nearly square. In the far
corner to the left (as you enter from the hall) a small
rectangle has been walled off to make a place for a
john and a washbowl — to save steps for Wolfe. The door
leading to it faces you, and around the corner, along its
other wall, is a wide and well-cushioned couch.

SKETCH OF OFFICE

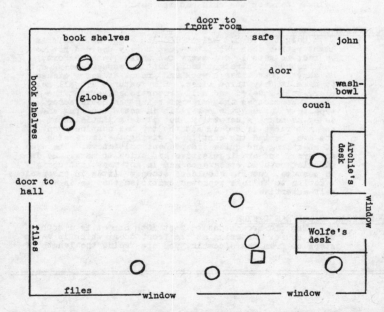

In furnishings the room has no apparent unity
but it has plenty of character. Wolfe permits nothing
to be in it that he doesn't enjoy looking at, and that
has been the only criterion for admission. The globe
is three feet in diameter. Wolfe's chair was made by
Meyer of cardato. His desk is of cherry, which of
course clashes with the cardato, but Wolfe likes it.
The couch is upholstered in bright yellow material
which has to go to the cleaners every three months.
The carpet was woven in Montenegro in the early nine-
teenth century and has been extensively patched. The
only wall decorations are three pictures: a Manet, a
copy of a Corregio, and a genuine Leonardo sketch. The
chairs are all shapes, colors, materials, and sizes.
The total effect makes you blink with bewilderment at
the first visit, but if you had Archie's job and lived
there you would probably learn to like it.

Rex Stout

REX STOUT, the creator of Nero Wolfe, was born in Noblesville, Indiana, in 1886, the sixth of nine children of John and Lucetta Todhunter Stout, both Quakers. Shortly after his birth, the family moved to Wakarusa, Kansas. He was educated in a country school, but by the age of nine he was recognized throughout the state as a prodigy in arithmetic. Mr. Stout briefly attended the University of Kansas, but left to enlist in the Navy, and spent the next two years as a warrant officer on board President Theodore Roosevelt's yacht. When he left the Navy in 1908, Rex Stout began to write free-lance articles and worked as a sightseeing guide and as an itinerant bookkeeper. Later he devised and implemented a school banking system which was installed in four hundred cities and towns throughout the country. In 1927 Mr. Stout retired from the world of finance and, with the proceeds of his banking scheme, left for Paris to write serious fiction. He wrote three novels that received favorable reviews before turning to detective fiction. His first Nero Wolfe novel, *Fer-de-Lance*, appeared in 1934. It was followed by many others, among them *Too Many Cooks, The Silent Speaker, If Death Ever Slept, The Doorbell Rang* and *Please Pass the Guilt*, which established Nero Wolfe as a leading character on a par with Erle Stanley Gardner's famous protagonist, Perry Mason. During World War II, Rex Stout waged a personal campaign against Nazism as chairman of the War Writers' Board, master of ceremonies of the radio program "Speaking of Liberty," a member of several national committees. After the war he turned his attention to mobilizing public opinion against the wartime use of thermonuclear devices, was an active leader in the Authors' Guild, and resumed writing his Nero Wolfe novels. Rex Stout died in 1975 at the age of eighty-eight. A month before his death, he published his seventy-second Nero Wolfe mystery, *A Family Affair*. Ten years later, a seventy-third Nero Wolfe mystery was discovered and published in *Death Times Three*.